Bai Hua's Poetry in English

Translations and Critical Essays

柏桦诗歌
英译精选

杨安文◎编著

华东师范大学出版社
·上海·

华东师范大学出版社六点分社　策划

目　录

绪论　柏桦诗歌及其在海外的译介与接受 ·············· 1

第一部分　柏桦诗歌译者及英译文本精选

第一章　霍布恩(Brian Holton)译诗精选 ·············· 11
一、译者简介及翻译述评 ·············· 11
二、译诗精选12首 ·············· 14
  1. 在清朝 ·············· 14
    In the Qing Dynasty
  2. 秋天的武器 ·············· 18
    Autumn's Weapons
  3. 献给曼杰斯塔姆 ·············· 20
    To Mandelstam
  4. 琼斯敦 ·············· 24
    Jonestown
  5. 踏青 ·············· 28
    Spring Jaunt
  6. 1966年夏天 ·············· 30

Summer 1966
7. 苏州记事一年　　　　　　　　　32
　　　The Suzhou Year

8. 小城故事　　　　　　　　　　　40
　　　Small Town Tale

9. 乡村，1977　　　　　　　　　　42
　　　Village，1977

10. 假儿歌　　　　　　　　　　　　44
　　　Mock Nursery Rhyme

11. 生活的幻觉　　　　　　　　　　46
　　　The Illusion of Life

12. 思由猪起　　　　　　　　　　　48
　　　Thoughts Arising from the Pig

第二章　戴迈河（Michael Day）译诗精选　　50
一、译者简介及翻译述评　　　　　　50
二、译诗精选10首　　　　　　　　　54

13. 表达　　　　　　　　　　　　　54
　　　An Expression

14. 震颤　　　　　　　　　　　　　60
　　　A Quiver

15. 下午　　　　　　　　　　　　　66
　　　Afternoon

16. 或别的东西　　　　　　　　　　68
　　　Or Something Else

17. 琼斯敦　　　　　　　　　　　　72
　　　Jonestown

18. 美人　　　　　　　　　　　　　74
　　　A Beauty

19. 夏天,呵,夏天 78
    Summer, Ahh, Summer

20. 现实 82
    Reality

21. 纪念朱湘 84
    In Memory of Zhu Xiang

22. 生活 86
    Life

第三章　西敏(Simon Patton)译诗精选 88
一、译者简介及翻译述评 88
二、译诗精选 8 首 90

23. 悬崖 90
    Precipice

24. 奈何天 94
    Heaven Watches on

25. 恨 96
    Hate

26. 鱼 98
    Fish

27. 望气的人 100
    Cloud Diviner

28. 麦子:纪念海子 102
    Wheat in Memory of Haizi

29. 现实 106
    Reality

30. 广陵散 108
    Ancient Tune

第四章　陶忘机（John Balcom）译诗精选 110
一、译者简介及翻译述评 110
二、译诗精选 2 首 112
31. 夏天还很远 112
32. 望气的人 113

第五章　约翰·卡雷（John Cayley）译诗精选 114
一、译者简介及翻译述评 114
二、译诗精选 3 首 116
33. 往事 116
    Things past
34. 幸福 120
    Happiness
35. 夏日读诗人传记 124
    Reading the Poet's Life One Summer

第六章　顾爱玲（Eleanor Goodman）译诗精选 128
一、译者简介及翻译述评 128
二、译诗精选 10 首 130
36. 在清朝 130
    In the Qing Dynasty
37. 现实 134
    Reality
38. 怒风下 136
    Under an Angry Wind
39. 猪头与张爱玲对话 138
    A Pig's Head or In Conversation with Eileen Chang
40. 衰老经（一） 140
    The Scripture of Aging (I)

41. 衰老经(二) —————————— *142*
    The Scripture of aging (II)

42. 演春与种梨 —————————— *144*
    Performing Spring and Planting Pears

43. 忆江南：给张枣 —————————— *148*
    Remembering Jiangnan：for Zhang Zao

44. 学习 —————————— *150*
    Studying

45. 望气的人 —————————— *152*
    The Aura-Seer

第七章　罗辉译诗精选 —————————— *154*
一、译者简介及翻译述评 —————————— *154*
二、译诗精选 9 首 —————————— *156*

46. 夏天还很远 —————————— *156*
    Summer is still far away

47. 往事 —————————— *158*
    Reminiscence

48. 未来 —————————— *162*
    The Future

49. 嘉陵江畔 —————————— *164*
    By the Jialing River

50. 我的锁骨菩萨如今在哪里呀？ —————————— *166*
    Where is My Clavicle Goddess Now?

51. 窗户的生活 —————————— *168*
    Life at the Window

52. 推云 —————————— *170*
    Pushing Clouds

53. 共听蚊睫落地声 —————————— *174*

We hear the sound of mosquito lashes landing
　54. 学问人生 ———————————— *178*
　　　　Life Learning

第八章　得一忘二（范静晔）译诗精选 ———— *182*
　一、译者简介及翻译述评 ———————— *182*
　二、译诗精选12首 ———————————— *184*
　　55. 未来 —————————————— *184*
　　　　The Future
　　56. 悬崖 —————————————— *186*
　　　　A Precipice
　　57. 骑手 —————————————— *188*
　　　　The Rider
　　58. 家居 —————————————— *190*
　　　　Home Life
　　59. 对酒 —————————————— *192*
　　　　Before Wine
　　60. 晚霞里 ————————————— *194*
　　　　Afterglow
　　61. 登双照楼 ————————————— *196*
　　　　Ascending the Double-Shine Tower
　　62. 向南方呼吸…… ——————————— *198*
　　　　Breathe in the South...
　　63. 胖 ——————————————— *200*
　　　　Plump
　　64. 一种相遇 ————————————— *202*
　　　　A Way of Crossing Paths
　　65. 江南来信 ————————————— *204*
　　　　Letter from Jiangnan

66. 夏日读杜拉斯 ——————————————— *206*
  Reading Duras in Summertime

第九章　李赋康/孔慧怡译诗精选 ——————— *208*
 一、译者简介及翻译述评 ————————— *208*
 二、译诗精选 4 首 ——————————— *210*
  67. 秋天的武器 ————————————— *210*
    Autumn's Weapon
  68. 夏天还很远 ————————————— *211*
    Summer is Still Far Away
  69. 1966 年夏天 ————————————— *212*
    The Summer of 1966
  70. 麦子：纪念海子 ———————————— *213*
    Wheat -in memory of Hai Zi

第十章　李赋康/阿米莉娅·戴尔（Amelia Dale）译诗精选
  ——————————————————— *215*
 一、译者简介及翻译述评 ————————— *215*
 二、译诗精选 2 首 ——————————— *217*
  71. 望气的人 —————————————— *217*
    The Air Alchemist
  72. 一切黑 ——————————————— *218*
    Dark Matter

第十一章　李赋康译诗精选 ————————— *220*
 一、译者简介及翻译述评 ————————— *220*
 二、译诗精选 12 首 —————————— *224*
  73. 饮酒人 ——————————————— *224*
    The Drinker

74. 谁 —————————————— *226*
　　Who Is It

75. 当你老了 ————————— *230*
　　When You Are Old

76. 若风的人尽醉归 —————— *232*
　　The Wind Man Returns Drunken

77. 丛书欲入门 ——————— *234*
　　A Primer on Craze for Book Series

78. 呼吸 —————————— *236*
　　Breathing

79. 致林克 ————————— *238*
　　For Lin Ke

80. 年轻 —————————— *240*
　　Being Young

81. 人生如梦 ———————— *242*
　　Life Is Like a Dream

82. 错过 —————————— *246*
　　Gone Missing

83. 易经 —————————— *248*
　　Code of Changes

84. 侏儒的话 ———————— *250*
　　Words from a Dwarf

第十二章　少况（王伟庆）译诗精选 ———————— *252*
一、译者简介及翻译述评 ———————— *252*
二、译诗精选 8 首 ———————— *256*

85. 消失 —————————— *256*
　　Vanishing

86. 致老木 ————————— *258*

For Lao Mu

87. 胡兰成再说 *262*
　　Hu Lancheng Says Again

88. 缅甸 *264*
　　Burma

89. 这是…… *268*
　　This is

90. 登双照楼 *270*
　　Ascending the Double-enlightenment Tower

91. 阿维尼翁 *272*
　　Avignon

92. 踏青 *274*
　　Spring Outing

第十三章　姜山译诗精选 276
一、译者简介及翻译述评 276
二、译诗精选 7 首 280

93. 重写悬崖 *280*
　　A Re-write of the Cliff

94. 消失 *284*
　　Disappearing

95. 还有什么比现实主义老得更快？ *288*
　　There's Anything Aging Faster than Realism?

96. 最后 *290*
　　At Last

97. 相遇 *292*
　　Encounter

98. 当你老了 *296*
　　When You Are Old

99. 死亡不喜欢唐突　　　　　　　　　　　300
　　　　Never liking to be abrupt

第十四章　菲奥娜·施-罗琳(Fiona Sze-Lorrain)译诗精选　　　　302

　一、译者简介及翻译述评　　　　302
　二、译诗精选10首　　　　305
　　100. 海的夏天　　　　305
　　101. 在清朝　　　　306
　　102. 李后主　　　　307
　　103. 献给曼杰斯塔姆　　　　307
　　104. 教育　　　　308
　　105. 以桦皮为衣的人　　　　308
　　106. 山水手记　　　　309
　　107. 风在说　　　　314
　　108. 人物速记　　　　316
　　109. 西藏书:无常(二)　　　　318

第二部分　柏桦诗歌翻译研究举隅

个案研究一:《在清朝》的"西行漫记"
　　——以《在清朝》的英文文本分析为中心　　　　321
个案研究二:从比较文学变异学视角看霍布恩英译柏桦诗歌
　　　　356
个案研究三:柏桦诗歌《夏天还很远》中英文本对照分析
　　　　375
个案研究四:英语世界里的望气者
　　——柏桦诗歌《望气的人》中英文本对照分析　　　　401

个案研究五：柏桦诗歌英译译者风格评析 ——————— 427
个案研究六：柏桦诗歌中外译者合作翻译案例述评
———————— 432

后记 ———— 443

绪论　柏桦诗歌及其在海外①的译介与接受

党的二十大报告指出，要增强文化自信，传承中华优秀传统文化，不断提升国家文化软实力和中华文化影响力；要增强中华文明传播力影响力，深化文明交流互鉴，推动中华文化更好走向世界。中华文化和中国文学"走出去"已成为新时代的迫切要求。诗歌历来是文学的重镇。根植于中国博大精深之传统文化的中国当代诗歌，既折射了中国社会的发展和时代的变迁，也反映了当代诗人富有时代特色的精神面貌、思想情感和艺术追求。诗人们不断进行着汉语语言试验，不断尝试语言本体的解放和边界的突破，展现出中国当代诗歌在语言、文学和文化等领域独特的风貌和价值。在中外文学交流与互鉴的历史进程中，中国当代诗歌的海外译介也成为一种必然，并逐步显示其重要性和迫切性。

柏桦是我国当代著名诗人、西南交通大学人文学院教授、博士研究生导师，在诗歌创作之外主要从事诗歌批评及诗歌理论、海外汉学研究。他成名于20世纪80年代，是中国当代诗歌史上一位极为重要的诗人，无论从国内诗坛的地位和影响还是从海外译介的角度来看，柏桦都颇具代表性和特殊性。国内诗人对柏桦的评价普遍很高。早期柏桦被北岛称为"中国最优秀的抒情诗人"，张枣认为柏桦"无疑是80年代'后朦胧诗'最杰出的诗人"，钟

---

① 笔者将考察范围确定为"海外"，原应仅指中国以外的国家和地区，包括柏桦诗歌译介所至的英语世界国家(美国、英国、澳大利亚、加拿大等)，以及非英语国家(法国、德国、荷兰、俄国、阿根廷、墨西哥、日本、韩国等)。需要特别说明的是，虽然香港、澳门和台湾不属于海外，但由于其历史、政治和文化因素，这三个地区在中国当代诗歌的对外译介上起到了重要的桥梁作用，所以笔者将其纳入考察范围。

鸣曾将柏桦与黄翔、北岛并列,称三人为"三只共和国的颧骨",翟永明说柏桦是自己最佩服的两个诗人之一,凌越称柏桦"被普遍认为是朦胧诗之后最为优秀的抒情诗人",蒋蓝称柏桦为"当代汉语诗歌中最为优秀的诗人之一"。国内文学批评界对柏桦的评论和评价总体不多,且较为多元。敬文东认为柏桦是1980年代以来一位非常重要的诗人,但却是"极其特殊的一位,在正统和主流的文学批评界也是几近被人遗忘的一位"。他的话某种程度上道出了柏桦的"特殊性",柏桦不谙诗坛交际,不"入圈入流",向来以"独行侠"的姿态独立、"自我"地写作。同时,柏桦后来诗歌的"逸乐"书写、"史记"书写在许多评论者和读者看来可谓"先锋"和"前卫",其"互文、杂糅、拼贴"的写作方式以及"截句"式的写作也十足新潮、"另类"。再者,柏桦写作中大量征引中外作家(如张爱玲、纳博科夫、芥川龙之介等)所展现出来的独特感受和"另类"观点,具有"异质性"的审美冲击,与大众读者的审美情趣时有差异。这些"先锋"特征使得批评家们利用现有的批评话语和范式均无法很好地应对柏桦的诗歌文本,产生了诸如批评家陈超所说的"我们不知道怎么写你"的现象。但是,不得不说,现有的中国当代诗歌史对柏桦的介绍和书写显得远远不够。可以说,正是以柏桦为代表的一批中国当代诗人"视诗歌如生命",专注于当代诗歌写作技艺的精进、语言的创新、对诗歌艺术和美学的不懈追求,才使得中国当代诗歌不断向前发展。抒情诗人柏桦已经深入人心,"逸乐"诗人柏桦近期诗歌语言的创新性、诗歌话语的独创性和诗歌美学的"自成高格",也终将显现出其巨大的诗学价值。

早期的抒情诗人柏桦被普遍认为是最优秀的、最具代表性的"后朦胧"诗人,除北岛、杨炼、多多、顾城、舒婷、海子等几位知名朦胧诗人以外,他是最早被较多地译介到海外的当代诗人。自1997年起,柏桦曾中止写诗15年,在2008年复出之后,则表现为一个"逸乐"诗人、学者诗人,大量的诗歌创作和大量的著作出版使得柏桦在国内的影响力继续提升,不过其诗歌在海外的译介虽仍在继续,却不如当年,尽管柏桦有强烈的对外译介意识和行动。柏桦诗歌在新时期的译介状况非常具有代表性,能够折射出中国当代诗歌海外译介的总体面貌。柏桦迄今已创作诗歌近万首,已发表或出版诗歌约1500首。早期创作的百余首诗歌已全部在国内发表,其中绝大部分都已被译介到海外,且不少诗歌有不同语种的多个译本,可以说已经在一定程度上经典化。柏桦近期诗歌创作量巨大,在国内发表或出版的多,译介到国外的偏少。截至 2023 年底,柏桦诗歌被翻译成英语、法语、德语、西班牙语、俄语、荷兰语、韩语、日语等 8 种外文,译介至美国、英国、法国、德国等 15 个国家以及中国香港、澳门和台湾,总共被翻译为外文的诗歌有 320 首,其中翻译为英语的为 236 首;已出版的柏桦个人外文诗集 2 部,聚焦柏桦的诗人合集 2 部,在外文刊物或诗集中发表的译诗共 32 首,在海外网络杂志或知名诗歌网站发表的译诗 10 首,在国内译者和柏桦的自媒体平台发布的英译诗歌有 120 余首。此外,柏桦还在中国香港和台湾出版著作 6 部,其中诗集 5 部,回忆录 1 部。相对于柏桦已在中国大陆出版 24 本个人诗集、已在刊物或诗集发表诗歌 122 次(每次发表数量不等的多首诗歌,总共约 1500 首)而言,柏桦诗歌在海外的译介规模还不大、范围还不广。

正如荷兰汉学家柯雷所言,在经典化的过程中,"外语人"是跟着"母语人"走的,对于国内诗人和诗歌的评价,国外的评论与研究首先得基于国内的批评话语和理论导向。海外对柏桦的评价虽不算多,但已见诸文字的评价总体较高。哈佛大学的王德威认为,"柏桦的诗歌是中国当代最好的诗歌之一,精妙并扣人心弦";德国汉学家顾彬说,"作为日常生活的诗人,柏桦像宋朝的大诗人一样,到处可以找到诗歌",他是里尔克那种"诚实写作的典范";美国诗人、评论家约翰·蔡瑟(John Zeiser)将柏桦视为"当代中国诗坛的中心人物";新加坡文学评论者扎法尔·安朱姆(Zafar Anjum)将柏桦描述为"20 世纪 80 年代中国最杰出的后朦胧诗人之一"。评论家李陀高度评价柏桦诗歌及其自传体回忆录《左边:毛泽东时代的抒情诗人》,认为该书"实际上是一本文学史",是首部了不起的"私修"文学史。在中国台湾,对柏桦已有的评价也极高。诗人、诗评家黄梁称柏桦是"大陆民间诗界公认的第三代诗歌重镇",认为"柏桦情韵深远风格鲜明的汉诗名篇精神气象从容,开辟一代诗风",称柏桦诗歌的"风度型仪将与岁月共酿而永怀芬芳"。诗人、评论家杨小滨认为柏桦早期诗歌"极大地开辟了汉语诗的表现力"。历史学家李孝悌高度评价柏桦的"史记"系列作品的历史文本价值。尽管如此,可以说目前海外读者所接触和了解的柏桦仅仅是柏桦诗歌和诗学的一小部分。随着柏桦诗歌海外译介、传播与接受的不断深入,柏桦诗歌的整体面貌和价值当会逐步清晰、完整地呈现在海外读者面前。

柏桦诗歌译介呈现出的诸多特点对中国当代诗歌对外译介具有一定启示意义。第一,除了早期几位知名的朦胧诗人,柏桦是自上世纪80年代以来最早译介到国外并得到关注的当代诗人之一。究其原因,除了柏桦自身80年代后期到90年代在国内诗坛的声名与影响以外,还与外语出身的柏桦所具有的很强的中西交流互鉴意识有密切关系。柏桦在1985年自己创办的地下诗刊《日日新》中就刊发了自己的2首诗的英译本(柏桦自译)。1989年,柏桦主导译者李赋康翻译了其首本英文个人诗集和首本"后朦胧"诗歌选集。两本英译诗集虽未出版,却直接促成柏桦诗歌于1991年在澳大利亚刊物发表,于1992年在香港知名译学杂志《译丛》(Renditions)发表。该杂志于当年推出一期"后朦胧诗"专辑,将柏桦和另外8位"后朦胧"诗人及其诗歌首次大规模译介到英语世界,使得"后朦胧诗"(Post-misty Poetry)的概念和提法在海外汉学界和诗歌界广为使用。可见,成功的对外译介首先基于诗人自身较强的对外译介和交流意识。第二,早期柏桦诗歌在荷兰、德国、法国等欧洲国家译介和发表较早,在英语国家则稍晚,这与当时旅欧知名诗人北岛和张枣的大力引荐密切相关。尤其是北岛及其主导的海外文学杂志《今天》及"今天"基金会,对推动包括柏桦在内的优秀诗人走向世界起到了极为重要的作用。我们发现,旅居海外的华语诗人的作品的译介数量和质量均远高于国内诗人,这表明他们具有自身的独特优势。因此,与海外知名华语诗人合作或由他们参与译介,无疑是国内诗人对外译介的一条有效通道。通过他们,国内诗人可以更便捷地了解和接触到国外汉学家及优秀译者、国外出版机构及市场需求,可以更有效地组织开展译介活动。第三,柏桦诗歌译介涉及的译者较多,但专注于柏桦诗歌翻译且与其配合默契的译者并不多。据已公开发表(包括网络发表)的柏桦译诗来看,目前翻译柏桦诗歌的中外译者共有28位。外国译者有19位,且大多数为国外优秀的汉学家或诗人译者,但比较集中翻译柏桦的只有菲奥娜、尚德兰、戴迈河3位译者,而且他们同时还翻译了其他多位当代中国诗人。3位译者与柏桦虽相熟,但还说不上彼此深入了解,更称不上气质相近、性情相投,所以还不能像杜博妮译北岛、霍布恩译杨炼、柯夏智译西川、罗辉译郑单衣那样默契投合,其译本自然也无法达到与原诗完美融合的境界。柏桦目前在海外发表或出版的译诗总体反响平平,没有带来犹如原诗给国内读者带来的那种冲击和感受,这至少可以部分归因于翻译问题。就笔者个人的阅读感受而言,许多译诗还没有很好地体现出柏桦诗歌中独特的声音和气质,没能展示其独特的语言风格和诗学创新。因此,笔者认为,国内包括柏桦在内的诗人们需要耐心寻觅一位自己的"缘分中人",一位适合翻译自己且投缘的译者。否则,译诗缺乏原诗内在特质、无法再现原诗独特风格、毫无诗意和灵性,这样的译诗又何谈延续原诗生命?第四,就翻译主体而言,柏桦诗歌翻译大部分是由外国汉学家译者或诗人译者独立完成,中外译者合作翻译的情况不多。然而,外国译者独立翻译完成的译本或多或少反映出译者对原诗的理解存在障碍。就汉语诗歌翻译而言,以译入语为母语的外国译者原本就不多,要想寻得一位中文语言能力强、翻译技艺高超同时还能配合默契的理想译者更是难上加难。所以,即使外国译者值得依靠,中国当代诗歌的对外译介也不能完全指望他们,国内译者必须承担其应有的责任。笔者并不赞同由国内译者单独翻译,认为基于彼此信任、理解和良性沟通的中外译者合作翻译是理想的翻译模式。在这种模式中,中国译者初译,重在把关诗歌文本的准确理解,包括文本中"声音"的感知和风格的体会,外国译者再予修改润色,着重把握语言的诗性表达,诗意、"声音"的有效转换以及原诗风格的再现,原作者则以开放、宽容的心态,给予译者充分的信任和"创造性叛逆"的空间,也许这样才能创造出优秀的诗歌翻译文本。第五,柏桦诗歌对外译介在利用网络媒介方面做得还远远不够。这也是绝大部分当代中国诗人存在的问题。他们并非没有利用网络进行诗歌写作和传播,而是没有依托和利用以英语(或其他外语)为语言媒介的网络平台,无法与外国读者和诗人进行直接的网络互动交流,在英(外)文诗歌网站或自媒体网络平台发表译诗也非常少。然而,纸质刊物的读者受众和影响传播是有限的。在网络信息时代,没有抓住网络读者是极大的损失。中国当代诗歌若要想更好地为海外读者所了解和接受,就必须努力克服外语障碍,利用好网络媒介加强交流、扩大影响。比如,诗人西川就建有自己个人的英文博客网站,及时发布自己的创作动态和诗歌译文,这必然有利于其诗歌更好地走向世界。

柏桦诗歌在海外的接受现状亦可对中国当代诗歌的译介和研究提供参考和启思。首先,就翻译文本的选择来看,外国译者选择翻译的诗歌文本与柏桦推荐翻译的诗歌文本之间存在不小差异,这既反映了西方读者(译者)独立的审美判断,也反映出他们别样的、独特的审美趣味。因此,从对外译介的角度来说,译者(或编者)在做翻译选本的时候,不能完全站在自身的审美角度,还要适度考虑目的国读者的审美需求和期待视野。其次,从海外学者对柏桦诗歌的研究现状来看,他们普遍紧密结合中国的社会、政治和文化语境,关注诗歌所反映的历史和社会现实,总体呈现出对柏桦诗歌作过度的意识形态解读的倾向,体现出西方读者典型的意识形态偏见和"他者"想象。同时值得注意的是,他们也注重文本细读,强调诗歌研究必须深入诗歌文本,不能重"语境"轻文本,不能忽视诗歌本体(诗歌的语言、内容、形式、声音等)研究。这一点特别值得国内诗歌研究者学习借鉴。此外,目前国外对柏桦的研究较多聚焦于柏桦诗歌写作与中国古典诗歌和诗学传统之间的关系,以及柏桦诗歌的历史书写等,这值得国内学者关注。总体而言,正如法国华裔学者徐爽所总结的,中国当代诗歌在海外的译介与接受呈现出两大特点,一是与国家的社会政治背景紧密联系,从译介诗歌的选本到读者、评论者的批评话语都体现出对意识形态的关注,常常夸大了诗歌的意识形态意义,却因此掩盖了诗歌自身的诗学价值;二是偏爱"古典"和"异国",这符合西方读者的"古典中国"想象,而这种"他者"想象又决定了西方读者的古典审美趣味和猎奇心态。这一点在柏桦诗歌的翻译选本上体现得尤其明显,许多有多个语种、多个译本的诗都是柏桦古风、古韵浓郁的诗。中国当代诗歌在西方世界接受的过程中,遭遇意识形态偏见不可避免,中国诗人需要以更加优秀的诗歌文本来予以消解。然而,西方读者对"古典"和"异国"的偏好却值得我们重视,这正是宇文所安所说的世界诗歌不能丢失的所谓"民族性"或"本土性"的体现。

此外,通过对柏桦诗歌多译本对比研究、翻译变异研究以及中外译者所采取的翻译策略、方法的对比研究,可以发现不同译者的翻译风格差异明显,对原文的理解各有不同,在对原诗的形式、内容、情感、节奏和意境的传递上各有高下。中国译者对原诗文本的理解、音乐性的感知与转换表现出明显优势,外国译者在语言表达的准确性和结构的有效转换上具有优势。但在笔者看来,真正实现了诗意的有效转换,传递了原诗丰富的艺术内涵和诗人独特而丰满的思想情感的译文则仅仅来自少数具有"创造性"特质的翻译,如霍布恩的译文。霍布恩从译入语文学与文化接受的角度对原文进行了改写和再创作,通过创造性的翻译尝试解决柏桦诗歌中看似不可译的语言文化转换难题,正是这种变异——翻译中的"创造性叛逆"——造就了译入语读者能够接受的译文,让原作在异国文学中获得新生。美国阐释学理论家赫施区分了"含义"(Significance)和"意义"(Meaning)两个概念,从此视角看,诗歌文本自身具有其语言符号所固化的内在"含义",但其"意义"是在历史时空中与读者共同生成的,具有历史性和开放性。所以,译者既有"忠实"于原诗文本的责任,亦有创造性阐释和转换的巨大空间。无论是诗人、译者,还是评论者、读者,都不应该以自己个人对诗歌的理解和阐释为标准去评判他人,而应该以开放的心态看待诗歌阐释和翻译。诗歌翻译批评固然重要,但需要的不是狭隘的批评,而是包容开放的、有真知灼见的、建设性的批评。

  近年来,柏桦笔耕不辍,诗歌创作成果丰硕,在国内获得多个诗歌奖项。2014年,柏桦以长篇叙事诗史《史记:1950—1976》获得首届"新诗"奖(该奖由《新诗》杂志授予)。2015年,柏桦再次以其16首近期诗作组成的《柏桦诗集》获得了第四届"红岩文学奖"中国诗歌奖。2016年,柏桦以诗集《为你消得万古愁:柏桦诗集2009—2012》荣获广东《羊城晚报》2016年"花地文学榜"年度诗歌大奖,《羊城晚报》2016年4月11日以一整版的篇幅予以专题报道。同在该月,柏桦还获得了第14届"华语文学传媒盛典"之"年度诗人"提名。2018年8月,柏桦获得第九届四川文学奖,获奖作品为《惟有旧日子带给我们幸福:柏桦诗选集》。四川文学奖是代表四川省省内最高荣誉的文学奖,由四川省作家协会主办。2019年12月,柏桦以《惟有旧日子带给我们幸福:柏桦诗选集》获得首届东吴文学奖诗歌奖。该奖是由中国作家协会中华文学基金会、中共苏州市吴中区委宣传部联合设立的文学奖项。

综上可见,无论是早期还是近期的柏桦诗歌在国内均广受好评,在海外诗歌翻译圈(包括诗人翻译家)、汉学家中也享有较高的知名度和接受度。然而,总体来看,国内外学者对中国当代诗歌的译介与研究仍十分有限,现有研究多为新诗在英语世界总体译介情况的综述,而且大多是对译介概貌的粗线条梳理和总体评述,对海外学界关于中国当代诗歌研究的关注较少,从诗歌文本细读及不同译本比较入手的诗歌翻译研究也不多。笔者期望,以柏桦诗歌在海外的译介与接受这一个案研究,管窥中国当代诗歌在海外译介与接受的总体状况和特征,推进中国当代诗歌在海外的译介研究,从而促进中国当代诗歌与世界的交流与对话,增进海外文学界、诗歌界、汉学界对中国当代诗歌发展的了解。中国当代诗歌巨大的诗学价值,文化、社会和历史价值都不容置疑,其丰富性、多样性和独特性还不为大多数外国读者所了解,其在海外的译介与研究还远远不够,还需要更多中外诗歌研究者和译介者共同努力,以推动中国当代诗歌更好地走向世界。

杨安文
2023 年 6 月于西南交通大学

第一部分
柏桦诗歌译者及英译文本精选

第一章 霍布恩(Brian Holton)译诗精选

一、译者简介及翻译述评

　　柏桦诗歌英译者霍布恩是知名的海外汉学家、翻译家。他1949年出生于苏格兰边区小镇加拉希尔斯,中学时期接受传统的苏格兰式教育,系统学习了拉丁语、希腊语、法语和英语,1975年获爱丁堡大学汉学研究专业硕士学位,1976年至1978年在杜伦大学继续从事汉学研究。其后霍布恩在爱丁堡大学(1985—1988,1989—1991)、宁波大学(1989)、杜伦大学(1992—1997)、纽卡斯尔大学(1993—1999)以及香港理工大学(2000—2009)从事汉语、中国古典文学和现代文学、汉英翻译教学及研究工作。从其工作经历可见,他两度在中国大学任教,在香港理工大学任教长达十年。他与中国的渊源同样见于其婚姻,其前妻郭莹是一名中国作家,著有环球行纪实作品《相识西风》以及首部外国人群体在中国的纪实作品《老外侃中国》。霍布恩为国内外学者所熟知是因其系首位《水浒传》苏格兰语译者和诗人杨炼的英语翻译。他于1981年将《水浒传》译为苏格兰语,于1992年开始与杨炼合作,翻译出版其诗歌。他酷爱文学翻译,坚持将中国文学尤其是中国当代诗歌翻译为英语和苏格兰语,其译作得到海外汉学界及中国诗人们的认可,他本人则被认为是英国当代最为出色的文学翻译家之一。由霍布恩领衔翻译、杨炼编选的中国当代新诗选《玉梯:中国当代诗歌》(*Jade Ladder: Contemporary*

Chinese Poetry),自2012年由英国著名的血斧出版社(Bloodaxe Books)出版以来广受好评。

霍布恩翻译的柏桦诗歌共12首,其中7首是柏桦早期代表诗作,载于《玉梯:中国当代诗歌》,另外5首全部为柏桦2008年复笔后创作的诗歌,发表在《人民文学》在海外推出的英文版《路灯》(*Pathlight*)2013年夏季号上。这12首诗均非霍布恩选出,是由编辑选出交其翻译。而霍布恩在整个翻译过程中,没有与原诗作者取得任何联系,全凭自己对诗歌文本的理解,独立完成翻译。在香港中文大学翻译研究中心第四届《译丛》文学翻译杰出讲座中,霍布恩指出:

> 译者实际上同时扮演解读者(interpretive personas)、幽灵作家(ghost writers)和创作者(composers)多重角色,介于原作者与既定读者之间。译者往往会对原作品有所取舍及加工,文学翻译可理解为一种再创造的行为,这亦可归类为译者的自我选择——选择用何种方式在何种程度上以何种文字效果解读作品。①

可见,霍布恩强调译者主体性,强调译者享有对翻译文本的"自主权"和"决策权"。这样的翻译观也就决定了在他的译本中,文学翻译的"创造性叛逆"或"变异"是必然的。在本书所编选的柏桦诗歌中,《献给曼杰斯塔姆》《在清朝》等诗有包括霍布恩译本在内的多个译本。通过多译本对比可以发现,霍布恩的译本更具创造性,更注重原诗情感和意境的传递,较好地实现了原诗诗意的转换。当然,由于内容和形式难以两全,其译诗在注重译文准确性和语言流畅度的同时,自然也难以还原原诗语言精炼简洁的风格。

谈到霍布恩对自己诗歌的翻译,柏桦总是不吝赞美之辞,认为其创造性的翻译转换使得译诗甚至超过了原诗。从霍布恩前妻郭莹的部分纪实文章

---

① 引自香港中文大学中国文化研究所网页:http://cloud.itsc.cuhk.edu.hk/enewsasp/app/article-details.aspx/C1E4F4D98C9C63CC3DC8E4B115B1A894/。

中可以了解到,霍布恩虽非诗人,却有着诗人般的浪漫和艺术气质,这使其译诗既有学者式的严谨,又有诗人般的唯美。如今已年过七旬的他仍活跃在诗歌翻译界,为各类诗歌翻译工作坊和实训班提供辅导培训,续写着自己挚爱的诗歌翻译人生。

二、译诗精选 12 首

1. 在清朝

在清朝①

在清朝
安闲和理想越来越深
牛羊无事,百姓下棋
科举也大公无私
货币两地不同
有时还用谷物兑换
茶叶、丝、瓷器

在清朝
山水画臻于完美
纸张泛滥,风筝遍地
灯笼得了要领
一座座庙宇向南
财富似乎过分

在清朝
诗人不事营生、爱面子
饮酒落花、风和日丽
池塘的水很肥
二只鸭子迎风游泳
风马牛不相及

---

① 选自《望气的人》,台北:唐山出版社,1999 年,第 44—45 页。

In the Qing Dynasty[①]

in the Qing Dynasty
idleness and the ideal went deeper and deeper
cows and ships were at peace, the people played chess
and imperial exams were just and fair
currencies were different in different places
sometimes even grain as exchanged for
tea leaves, silk, porcelain

in the Qing Dynasty
landscape painting had attained perfection
papers were overflowing, kites everywhere
lanterns were well-proportioned
temple after temple faced south
there seemed an excess of wealth and fortune

in the Qing Dynasty
poets cared nothing for a living, only for reputation
drank wine as petals fell, the wind gentle and the sun warm
even the pond-water as fertile
ducks swam in pairs before the wind
—just so horses in heat do not couple with cattle[②]

---

① Translated by Brian Holton, W. N. Herbert & Lee Man-Kay. In W. N. Herbert & Yang Lian. *Jade Ladder: Contemporary Chinese Poetry*. Northumberland: Bloodaxe Books Ltd., 2012, pp. 109—110.

② This line references Zuo Zhuan, 4th year of Duke Xi. See Legge's translation, *Tso Chuan, Duke Hsi in The Chinese Classics*. One metaphoric interpretation of this line is "Even if my herds wander far away, they'll never come into contact with yours", i. e. why do you make war on me when we are so far apart we can do no harm to each other.

在清朝

一个人梦见一个人

夜读太史公、清晨扫地

而朝廷增设军机处

每年选拔长指甲的官吏

在清朝

多胡须和无胡须的人

严于身教、不苟言谈

农村人不愿认字

孩子们敬老

母亲屈从于儿子

在清朝

用款税激励人民

办水利、办学校、办祠堂

编印书籍、整理地方志

建筑弄得古色古香

在清朝

哲学如雨,科学不能适应

有一个人朝三暮四

无端端地着急

愤怒成为他毕生的事业

他于1840年死去

1986年10月

in the Qing Dynasty

someone dreamed about someone

reading the Grand Historian in the night①, sweeping the floor at dawn

and the Court established the Council of State

every year promoted long-nailed mandarins

in the Qing Dynasty

men both bewhiskered and clean-shaven

were strict on teaching by example, solemn in speech and manners

country folk were reluctant to learn their letters

children respected their elders

mothers ceded power to their sons

in the Qing Dynasty

with taxes and with dues the people were heartened

irrigation works were built, schools managed, ancestral halls maintained

books were printed, local gazetteers assembled

habitations decked out in the antique style

in the Qing Dynasty

philosophy poured down like rain, science couldn't keep up

someone was playing six and two threes②

gratuitously anxious

rage became his life-long career

until, in 1840, he died

---

① The Grand Historian is Sima Qian (ca. 145 or 135 BC—86 BC), author of the *Historical Records*.
② Literally "3 in the morning and 4 at night"—a quotation from the Zhuangzi story about the monkeys dissatisfied with their 3 nuts in the morning and 4 nuts at night, who were pacified with the offer of 4 in the morning and 3 at night.

2. 秋天的武器

秋天的武器①

斗争走向极端
口号走向极端
吃石头的刺刀走向极端
我听到空气的坠落

这完全适合于你
在古代的秋天
一个人因此而死亡
吞下厌烦
吞下纸老虎
而人民的嘴不朝向耳朵

今天我要重新开始
研究各种牺牲
漫天要价的光芒
尖锐的革命的骨头

在此时,在成都
所有的人迎面走来
把汽车给我
把极端给我
把暴力和广场给我

1986年秋

---

① 选自《望气的人》,台北:唐山出版社,1999年,第47—48页。

Autumn's Weapons[①]

struggle moves to extremes

slogans move to extremes

the stone-eating bayonet moves to extremes

I hear the degeneration of the air

this suits you perfectly

in ancient autumns

a man would die for this

swallowing ennui

swallowing paper tigers

the voice of the people never in the ear

today I want to start again

investigate each kind of sacrifice

the radiance of charging extortionate prices

sharp revolutionary bones

at this time, in Chengdu

everybody's in my face

giving me cars

giving me extremes

giving me violence and the market

Autumn 1986

---

① Translated by Brian Holton, W. N. Herbert & Lee Man-Kay. In W. N. Herbert & Yang Lian. *Jade Ladder: Contemporary Chinese Poetry*. Northumberland: Bloodaxe Books Ltd., 2012, pp. 110—111.

3. 献给曼杰斯塔姆

献给曼杰斯塔姆[①]

那个生活在神经里的人
害怕什么呢?
害怕赤身裸体的纯洁?
不!害怕声音
那甩掉了思想的声音

我梦想中的诗人
穿过太重的北方
穿过瘦弱的幻觉的童年
你难免来到人间

今天,我承担你怪僻的一天
今天,我承担你天真的一天
今天,我突出你的悲剧

沉默在指明
诗篇在心跳、在怜惜
无辜的舌头染上语言
这也是我记忆中的某一天

牛已经停止耕耘
镰刀已放弃亡命
风正屏住呼吸

[①] 选自《望气的人》,台北:唐山出版社,1999年,第61—62页。

To Mandelstam[①]

He who lived on his nerves
what did he fear?
did he fear the pure state of nudity?
No: he feared the voice
the voice that threw away thought

the poet in my dream
passed through a north too heavy
passed through a childhood thin, feeble, hallucinatory
inevitably you came to the mortal world

today is the day I shoulder your eccentricity
today, the day I shoulder your naiveté
today I shout out your tragedy

silence makes clear
poetry's heart beats, poetry shows mercy,
a guiltless tongue infects language
and this too is one day in my memory

the oxen have stopped the plough
the sickle has given up running for its life
the autumn wind is holding its breath—

---

① Translated by Brian Holton, W. N. Herbert & Lee Man-Kay. In W. N. Herbert & Yang Lian. *Jade Ladder: Contemporary Chinese Poetry*. Northumberland: Bloodaxe Books Ltd., 2012, pp. 111—112.

啊,寒冷,你在加紧运送冬天

焦急的莫斯科
你握紧了动人的肺腑
迎着漫天雪花、翘首以待
啊,你看,他来了
我们诗人中最可泣的亡魂!
他正朝我走来

我开始属于这儿
我开始钻进你的形体
我开始代替你残酷的天堂
我,一个外来的长不大的孩子
对于这一切
路边的群众只能更孤单

1987.11

Cold, you've pushed Moscow's anxiety

on to the bringing in of winter
you've got a grip on bowels, hearts and wordless throats
you face a skyful of snow, craning your neck, expectant—
look, he's coming
of all our poets the most exasperating ghost!
he's heading toward me

I've begun to belong here
I've begun to squeeze myself into your shape
I've begun to take the place of your brutal heaven
I, this child from outside ho can never grow up
faced with all this—
the masses on the roadside—can only be more alone

November 1987

4. 琼斯敦①

琼斯敦②

孩子们可以开始了
这革命的一夜
来世的一夜
人民圣殿的一夜
摇撼的风暴的中心
已厌倦了那些不死者
正急着把我们带向那边

幻想中的敌人
穿梭般地袭击我们
我们的公社如同斯大林格勒
空中充满纳粹的气味

热血旋涡的一刻到了
感情在冲破
指头在戳入
胶水广泛地投向阶级
妄想的耐心与反动作斗争

从春季到秋季
性急与失望四处蔓延
示威的牙齿啃着难捱的时日

---

① 1978年11月18日,914名美国公民在圭亚那热带丛林集体自杀,"琼斯敦"是自杀的地点。这个地点以美国当时宗教性组织"人民圣殿"的领导者吉姆·琼斯敦命名。
② 选自《望气的人》,台北:唐山出版社,1999年,第65—67页。

Jonestown[①]

children, you may begin
this one night of revolution
one night of the life to come
one night of the People's Temple
the shaking eye of the storm
weary of those invincible
desperate to bring us there

the enemies in our hallucinations
shower us with attacks
our commune the same as Stalingrad
the air heavy with the smell of Nazis

the time of the hot-blooded vortexis come
emotions breaking through
fingertips stabbing
glue unconditionally surrenders to class
the patience of vain hope struggles with reaction

from spring to autumn
impatience and disappointment spreading everywhere
marching teeth gnaw at an unbearable time

---

① Translated by Brian Holton & Lee Man-Kay. In W. N. Herbert & Yang Lian. *Jade Ladder: Contemporary Chinese Poetry*. Northumberland: Bloodaxe Books Ltd., 2012, pp. 112—113.

男孩们胸中的军火渴望爆炸
孤僻的禁忌撕咬着眼泪
看那残食的群众已经发动

一个女孩在演习自杀
她因疯狂而趋于激烈的秀发
多么亲切地披在无助的肩上
那是十七岁的标志
唯一的标志

而我们精神上初恋的象征
我们那白得炫目的父亲
幸福的子弹击中他的太阳穴
他天真的亡灵仍在倾注：
信仰治疗、宗教武士道
秀丽的政变的躯体

如山的尸首已停止排演
空前的寂静高声宣誓：
度过危机
操练思想
纯洁牺牲

面对这集中肉体背叛的白夜
这人性中最后的白夜
我知道这也是我痛苦的丰收夜

1987年12月

the ammunition in boys' chests longs to explode
eccentric taboos worry at tears
watch the left-over masses already launched

a girl is rehearsing suicide
her lovely hair tending to intensity because she's crazy
hanging so kindly on her helpless shoulders
the mark of her seventeen years
the one and only mark

but the token of first love in our spirit
our dazzlingly white father
the bullets of bliss bang into his temples
his naïve dead soul still pouring forth:
a faith-healing, bushido religion
his body beautiful in its coup d'État

the mountains of corpses are no longer rehearsing
the unprecedented silence swears oaths aloud:
GET THROUGH THE CRISS
DRILL THE MIND
PURE SACRIFICE

confronting this White Night gathers in the betrayal of the flesh
this last White Night of humanity
I know this is the night for me to harvest my pain too.

December 1987

5. 踏　青

踏青①

红墙里的人儿想回家
青蛙躺在白杨树下
是哪一种花在坚持着柔情
迎春花,哦,不,一朵无名的花

我看到女孩用小手投掷皮球
我看到素食者手握一把细沙
老年即命令,断肠即天涯
处处花园开满大地
处处怜惜倾洒

而我惟一的俊友啊
惟一的春天的舞蹈家
我想,我想
我想分享你明净的前额

1989 年 3 月 7 日

---

①　选自《望气的人》,台北:唐山出版社,1999 年,第 87 页。

Spring Jaunt[①]

the character inside the red walls wants to go home
the frog lying prone under the poplar trees
is which flower, insisting on tendresse?
Jasmine? oh, no—a flower that is nameless

I see a girl throwing a leather ball from her little hand
I see a vegetarian holding a fistful of fine sand
old age is a command, heartbreak the ends of the earth
everywhere gardens of flowers cover the land
everywhere tender pity is pouring forth

yet, my one and only dear companion and friend
my one and only dance at springtime's end
I want, I want
I want to share my joy in your brow, so cool, so radiant

7 March 1989

---

① In W. N. Herbert & Yang Lian. *Jade Ladder: Contemporary Chinese Poetry*. Northumberland: Bloodaxe Books Ltd., 2012, p. 113.

6. 1966年夏天

1966年夏天①

成长啊,随风成长
仅仅三天,三天!

一颗心红了
祖国正临街吹响

吹啊,吹,早来的青春
吹绿爱情,也吹绿大地的思想

瞧,政治多么美
夏天穿上了军装

生活啊!欢乐啊!
那最后一枚像章
那自由与怀乡之歌
哦,不!那十岁的无瑕的天堂

1989年12月26日

---

① 选自《望气的人》,台北:唐山出版社,1999年,第104页。

Summer 1966[①]

to grow up, oh, to grow up
only three days, three days!

a heart turned red
a motherland trumpeting on the streets

blow, oh, blow, oh youth come early
blow green love, blow the whole world's thoughts green too

see how lovely politics is
army uniforms worn in summer

oh, life! oh, joy!
that very last badge
that song of homesickness and freedom
oh, no, that ten-year-old's flawless heaven

26 December 1989

---

① In W. N. Herbert & Yang Lian. *Jade Ladder: Contemporary Chinese Poetry*. Northumberland: Bloodaxe Books Ltd., 2012, p. 114.

7. 苏州记事一年

苏州记事一年①

正月初一,岁朝
农民晨起看水
开门,放爆竹三声

继续晨,幼辈叩头
邻里贺年
农民忙于自己

初五,财神的生日
农民应接不暇
采购布匹

十五,悬灶灯于厨下
连续五夜
挂起树火,大张灯市
山水,人物不见天日
妇女为祛病过三座石桥
民众击乐,鼓励节日

二月初八,大帝过江,和尚吃肉
前三后四风雨必至
有人称龙头,有人吞土
农家因天气而成熟
有利无利但看"二月十二"

---

① 选自《山水手记》,重庆:重庆大学出版社,2011年,第122—125页。

The Suzhou Year[①]

First Lunar Month, *first day*: the Rising of the Year
farmers wake at dawn to watch the water
open the doors, set off firecrackers tree times
carrying in the morning, the younger generations kowtow
the neighbourhood offers New Year greetings
farmers are busy with their own affairs

fifth day: birthday of the God of Wealth
farmers greet visitors one after the other
buy cloth

fifteenth day: hang stove lanterns beneath the kitchen cabinet
for five successive nights
hang up tree-lanterns, set out a grand lantern market
in the countryside, crowds blot out the sun
women cross three stone bridges to drive away disease
the public beat drums and gongs, bring the festival to life

Second Month eighth day: the Great King crosses the river, monks eat meat
in the holiday week, storms will come
some people are named as deacons, some swallow dirt
farming families will get ready with this weather
for good or bad luck, look at Second Month twentieth day

---

① Translated by Brian Holton, W. N. Herbert & Lee Man-Kay. In W. N. Herbert & Yang Lian. *Jade Ladder: Contemporary Chinese Poetry*. Northumberland: Bloodaxe Books Ltd., 2012, pp. 114—116.

三月初三,蚂蚁搬米上山
农妇洗发、清目
又吃油煎食品

清明,小麦拔节,踏青游春
深蓝、浅绿插入水中
妇女结伴同行
以祈青春长存

四月初一,闲人扛大锣、茶箱
老爷从属西军夜
红衣班扮刽子手
(演员出自肉店、水果店、豆腐店)

立夏见三新:樱桃、青梅、元麦
中医这天勿用
蚕豆也等待尝新

四月十四日,轧神仙
吕纯阳过此
无需回避
他的影子在群众中济世

五月五,端午出自蒲剑
也出自夏至的替身
儿童写王字于前额
身披虎皮,手握蒜头
而城隍是大老爷

Third Month third day: ants move rice-grains uphill
farm wives wash their hair, clear their vision
and eat deep-fried food

Qingming Festival: wheat straw cut, early Spring picnics
shafts of deep blue and light green in the water
women go in groups
to gray for everlasting youth

Fourth Month first day: loafers shoulder big gongs and tea chests
in *The Night the Squire Joined the Western Army*
the russet-clad cast play headsmen
(the actors are butchers, greengrocers, bean curd sellers)

Summer Solstice: three new things are seen—cherry, green plum, barley
on this day, no need for doctors
broad beans are waiting to come into season

Fourth Month fourteenth day: befriend immortals
Master Lu the Progenitor passes by
no need to hide from him
his shadow falling on the crowd saves the world

Fifth Month fifth day: Dragon Boat Festival comes with swords of rushes
comes out of the stand-in for Summer Solstice
kids write *KING* in stripes upon their foreheads
drape themselves in tiger skins, grab garlic
while the city god is Boss of Bosses

六月六,寺院晒经
各户晒书籍、图画、衣被
黄狗洗澡、打滚
老人或下棋、或听书、或无事
小孩吃茶于七家
面貌动荡不宁

立秋之日,以西瓜供献
也制巧果、蝶形油炸
以期颐养天年

八月十五,中秋
柿饼、月饼于月下
蔬菜吃完了
摆上鲤鱼
得下签者不予参加

九月九,郊外登高
望云、望树、望鸟
小贩漫游山下

十一月,日短夜长,市场发达
财主收租、收账、剥皮
而冬至大如年
农民重视

冬至,全家吃夜饭
豆芽如意,青菜安乐
年糕、汤团、圆之意

Sixth Month sixth day: monasteries and temples sun the scriptures
every household airs books, paintings, clothes and blankets
stray dogs roll on their backs in puddles
old folk play chess, listen to the storyteller or do nothing
children take tea in seven homes
surfaces seem to shimmer and break up

Autumn Equinox: offer watermelons
make fritters and butterfly-cakes
for a hundred heaven-sent years

Eight Month fifteenth day: Mid-Autumn Festival
dried persimmons, moon cakes under the moon
when the greens are eaten
serve up the carp
jinxes are not allowed to join in

Ninth Month ninth day: visit the heights outside town
watch clouds, watch trees, watch birds
hawkers will roam the foot of the hill

Eleventh Month: short days and long nights, markets prosper
the rich collect their rents, call in debts, add salt to our wounds
and Winter Solstice is as big as the New Year
farmers respect this day

Winter Solstice: the family share New Year's Eve dinner
bean sprouts for all you desire, cabbage for happiness
sticky rice cake and sweet rice balls mean union and unity

儿子不得外出
嫁女不利亲人
南瓜放出门外过夜

十二月过年,送灶
灯具多自制
热热闹闹、繁文缛节

除夕,又是鸡鸭鱼肉
提灯笼要钱者
来往不绝,直到天明

除夕之末,男孩怀旧
果子即压岁,即吉利
老鼠即女孩的敌人
唯大人不老,放爆竹三声

1989年12月

sons are not allowed to leave town
married daughters bring bad luck to their own families
leave pumpkins outside the door all night

Twelfth Month: bring the year in, see the Kitchen God off
many hand-made lanterns and lamps
the bustle, the buzz and the genteel excuse me

New Year's Eve: more chicken and duck and fish and pork
beggars with lanterns after luck-pennies
endless coming and going, up till dawn

End of New Year's Eve: boys talk of absent friends
with melon seeds comes a new year and good luck
mice are young girls' enemies
only the great don't grow old: set off firecrackers three times

8. 小城故事

小城故事①

"旅馆走廊之拙劣模仿。
宁静与死亡之拙劣模仿。"
夜之风尘被送货卡车震醒

他俩开始争吵并必然撞见
户外那株从不死亡的白杨

灯下他仍是一个年轻老人
正在他糖尿病屁股上打针

于是她努力从鼻孔喷烟气
若两管戳过来的弯弯象牙

2012年10月5日

---

① 选自《革命要诗和学问——柏桦诗选:2012—2013》,成都:四川文艺出版社,2016年,第36页。

Small Town Tale[①]

"A shoddy excuse for a hotel corridor.
A shoddy excuse for calm and death."
Startled awake by delivery vans from night's travel-weariness

both begin to bicker, and inevitably encounter
the undying poplars outside the door

in lamplight he's an old man still young
in the process of injecting his diabeticarse

she blows the smoke hard through her nose
two elephant tusks curve upward and away

---

① *Pathlight: New Chinese Writing* (Summer), 2013: 133.

9. 乡村,1977

乡村,1977①

鸡贩卖蛋,锡匠补锅,磨刀人还在;
除了疾病,连生气也是祖传的吗?

缠绕的、消磨的、梯田图案的,1977;
猪肝贵,牛肺贱,简书记欢喜的都在。

一种属于驯服的家庭幸福气氛,清晨
刚从邮局后院的肉丝面里飘出;晚间

读报乎?巴县平静,龙凤公社平静,
不睡、不睡,神秘代数宜于深夜学习。

然而黑巷尽头,右边,春灯一盏,
那安详的睡者(来自民国)死了半年。

2012年10月28日

---

① 选自《革命要诗和学问——柏桦诗选》,台北:秀威资讯科技股份有限公司,2015年,第72页。

Village, 1977[①]

The poultryman sells eggs, the tinker mends pots, the knife grinder still here;
apart from illness, is anger passed down through the generation too?

Tangled, tiresome, paddy-terraced 1997;
pig's liver was dear, ox lungs cheap, but there was everything to make Secretary Jian happy.

That contented atmosphere of a cowed household, early morning
The aroma of pork noodles drifting from behind the Post Office.

This evening, will we read the paper? Ba County at peace, Longfeng Commune likewise.
I'm not sleeping, not sleeping. That mysterious algebra can be studied at night.

However, at the end of the dark alley, on the right, one red lantern:
that serene sleeper (from the old Republic) has been dead for six months now

---

① *Pathlight*: *New Chinese Writing* (Summer), 2013: 133.

10. 假儿歌

假儿歌①

脸,是蟹壳脸
奶,是口袋奶
鼓,是拨浪鼓
幔,是金帐幔

红,是寂寞红
春,是玉堂春
秋,是汉宫秋
鱼,是黄花鱼

味,是上海味
玲,是张爱玲

附录一:
狠好,周瘦鹃
静好,胡兰成

附录二:
早行,齐韵叟
晚来,华铁眉

2013年1月8日

---

① 选自《革命要诗和学问——柏桦诗选:2012—2013》,成都:四川文艺出版社,2016年,第107页。

Mock Nursery Rhyme[①]

face	is a crab-shell face
milk	is a bag of milk
drum	is a rattle drum
drape	is a golden drape
red	is *Lady In Red*
spring	is *Might As Well Be Spring*
autumn	is *When Autumn Leaves Start to Fall*
fish	is *Like A Sturgeon Touched For The Very First Time*
taste	is the taste of Shanghai
clang	is Eileen Chang

APPENDIX 1

merciless good	is Air Rested Kailed
unmoving good	is Tray Tor Eggs Siled

APPENDIX 2

early off	is Old Master Rhymester
late back	is Wah! Iron Eyebrows

---

① *Pathlight: New Chinese Writing* (Summer), 2013: 134.

11. 生活的幻觉

生活的幻觉①

单是活着就是桩大事,几乎是个壮举……
——张爱玲

什么人的生活是奇特的呢?
仆人的生活?姚合②的生活?
很可能是路易第九的生活
在花园橡树下他断案真好。

那行礼如仪的日本考古学家
他的人生出自身体的遗传么?
真好,他恰是一个小气的人,
准时、细心,无迟到的家风。

可惜,树死若风灭。一百年!
你吓了一跳,惊叫道:"看
真好,潮湿温暖的不是马槽
是我那老年健在的阴囊。"

昨天在兴福寺,你刚剪了头,
还发现了另一条多余的回廊
真好,你刚从它的幽深里走出
就看见我们在门边的树下等你。

2012 年 10 月 25 日

---

① 选自《革命要诗和学问——柏桦诗选:2012—2013》,成都:四川文艺出版社,2016 年,第 50—51 页。
② 姚合(约 779—846),陕州峡石(今河南陕南县)人。唐元和进士,授武功主簿。官秘书少监。世称姚武功,其诗派也称"武功体"。所作诗篇多写个人日常生活与自然景色,喜为五律,刻意求工,颇似贾岛,故"姚贾"并称。

The Illusion of Life[①]

Merely staying alive is big affair; a heroic achievement, almost.
—Eileen Chang

Whose life is strangest?
A servant's life? The poet Yao He's life?[②]
Probably the life of Louis IX was,
who, under the oak in the garden, dispensed justice very well.

That punctilious Japanese archaeologist,
did his life grow of his body's inheritance?
How nice, he happens to be narrow-minded,
punctual, meticulous, with no learned habit of being late.

How sad—the tree died like a flame extinguished. A hundred years!
Startled, you cried in alarm: Look!
How nice, it isn't the horse trough that's moist and warm,
but my hale and hearty old scrotum.

Yesterday at Fortune Revival Temple. You'd had your hair cut,
and found yet another of its superfluous cloisters.
How nice, as you came from its silent depths you saw us
waiting for you under the trees by the gate.

---

① *Pathlight: New Chinese Writing* (Summer), 2013: 135.
② Author's note: Yao He (779—864) was a poet and scholar-official of the Tang dynasty. He liked to write about everyday life and natural settings. Five-character poems were his specialty. His style resembled that of another poet, Jia Dao, to such an extent that contemporaries referred to them as "Yao-Jia".

12. 思由猪起

思由猪起①

梅花一树猪蹄熟。
——破山海明

猪脚爪（汉人的最爱）也叫猪蹄。
羊蹄马蹄牛蹄呢，但我们从不说
猫蹄、狗蹄。是的"鱼和马铃薯
不行啊！"腰肝肠舌耳心甚至脑，
行。牛肺鸡冠鸟头，也行。快看，
我们在火锅里吞滚烫的猪脑花呢。

猪油失传。炼猪油者已无人问津。
（我突然翻到箴言第二十四章：
好人可摔跤七次，恶人一次为祸）
"蛇吃女人奶，蚂蚁挤蚜虫的奶"
我们嚼牛头马面多年，但不喝奶。

东方棕榈树如故，食如故。独缺
猪油。而石榴。电力。女性男人。
你问起三色堇，就是问思想——
那梨当然白了当它的黄皮被剥掉。
那汉人的"美丽生活"重睹须惊。

2012年08月12日

---

① 选自《革命要诗和学问——柏桦诗选：2012—2013》，成都：四川文艺出版社，2016年，第4—5页。

Thoughts Arising from the Pig[①]

A treeful of plum blossom, and the pig's trotters ready
Zen Master Splendor-Maris, of Brokenhill (1597—1666)

Pig's feet (Chinese people love'em best) are also known as trotters.
There's sheep shank horse hock shin of beef, but we don't say,
cat trotters, dog trotters. Yes, indeed, "fish and chips
won't do!" Loin liver intestine tongue ear heart even brain
will do nicely. Ox lungs cockscombs bird's heads will do too. Quick,
see us gulp scalding pig's brain from the hotpot.

Lard is a lost art. Lard refiners are no longer wanted.
(I happen upon Proverbs 24. xvi: "For a just man falleth
seven times and riseth up again, but the wicked
shall fall into mischief.") We've been munching on
ox head horse face for years, but don't drink milk.

In the East palm trees are what they always were, and so is food.
All that's lacking is lard. And pomegrantates, Electricity. Female men.
You ask the wild pansy, you're asking about thought—
of course the pear whitens when its yellow skin is peeled.
Another look at the "beautiful life" of the Chinese would cause alarm.

---

① *Pathlight: New Chinese Writing* (Summer), 2013: 136.

第二章　戴迈河（Michael Day）译诗精选

一、译者简介及翻译述评

　　加拿大汉学家、诗歌翻译家戴迈河是较早英译柏桦诗歌的外国译者。他于20世纪90年代中期翻译了柏桦的22首诗歌①，并且撰文对诗人及其诗歌风格进行介绍，同时对其部分诗歌进行解读。戴迈河出生在加拿大温哥华，于1981—1985年、1991—1994年在温哥华的不列颠哥伦比亚大学完成本科和硕士研究生教育，专业是中国语言文学。在就读本科的1982—1984年，戴迈河通过中加文化交换项目先后在山东大学和南京大学各交换学习一年，其间接触到并喜欢上了中国当代诗歌。

　　本科毕业之后，戴迈河1986—1992年居于中国，其间辗转于多个城市：1986—1987年在广东湛江一个培训中心做英语教师，1987—1988年在北京外文局新世界出版社做编辑和翻译，1989—1990年在西安外国语大学教大学英语和英美文学，1990—1991年在香港一家英文杂志做助理

---

①　戴迈河翻译柏桦的22首诗歌是：《表达》《震颤》《春天》《悬崖》《下午》《夏天还很远》《谁》《或别的东西》《琼斯敦》《美人》《往事》《夏天，啊，夏天》《十夜十夜》《生活》《现实》《纪念朱湘》《家人》《老诗人》《衰老经》《未来》《生活颂》《棉花之歌》。

编辑和翻译。在中国工作期间,尤其是1987—1988年在外文局做翻译期间,戴迈河开始翻译中国当代诗歌。而真正专注于中国当代诗歌的翻译与研究则是在他开始攻读硕士的1991年。他硕士论文研究的对象是四川地下诗人与诗歌,与此相应,在读研期间,他做了大量的诗歌翻译工作。1994年,戴迈河获得不列颠哥伦比亚大学中国现代文学硕士学位。其后,他很快开始在该校继续攻读中国现代文学的博士学位,方向同样是中国当代诗歌研究。1994年至1997年,戴迈河又翻译了17位中国当代诗人的诗歌,至此他已累计翻译了数百首中国当代诗歌。然而在1997年,因博士论文选题困惑,戴迈河暂停了博士学业。2002年,在伦敦大学亚非学院教授贺麦晓(Michel Hockx)的帮助下,戴迈河被录取为荷兰莱顿大学的博士生,导师是中国当代诗歌研究学者柯雷。2005年,戴迈河获得莱顿大学汉学博士学位,博士论文题目为《中国的第二诗界:四川先锋诗人,1982—1992》。硕士毕业后至2005年,戴迈河在攻读博士的同时,还游走于加拿大、德国、英国、捷克等国的多个学校,从事英语、汉语以及中国现代诗歌课程教学工作。

2006年,戴迈河随妻子到美国生活,在加州圣地亚哥的美国国立大学(National University)任教,一手创办了该校的汉语本科专业。近年来,戴迈河一直从事中国当代文学尤其是当代诗歌的翻译和研究工作。前文已提及,他于2003年在德国海德堡大学与荷兰莱顿大学合作创建的汉学研究数字档案馆莱顿分馆(DACHS)建立了中国当代诗歌专区,并一直为其提供文稿素材和资源。2007年以来,戴迈河翻译并发表了陈东东、韩东、黄怒波等多位诗人的诗歌作品。他还与知名诗歌研究专家、北京大学教授洪子诚合作,翻译了洪子诚的名作《中国当代文学史》,该译本作为由香港城市大学教授张隆溪和哥廷根大学教授施耐德(Axel Schneider)共同主编的"博睿中国人文研究"(Brill's Humanities in China Library)的第一卷,于2007年由荷兰博睿学术出版社(Brill Academic Publisher)出版,受到海外学界的普遍关注和认可。

戴迈河的教育经历、学术背景以及个人对诗歌的兴趣爱好对于外国的中国当代诗歌译介者来说是十分罕见的。他热爱中国文学文化,酷爱中国当代诗歌,自20世纪80年代开始接触中国当代诗歌,深入民间诗歌(地下诗歌)第一线,同诗人们保持着密切交往,长时间跟踪中国当代诗歌的发展,可以说,他一直处于中国当代诗歌的现场。毫无疑问,在外国译者中,他是最熟悉、最了解中国当代诗歌的人之一。同时,戴迈河本科、硕士和博士专业都是汉语和中国现代文学,硕士、博士的研究方向都是中国当代诗歌,在中国语言文学专业接受了长期正规而系统的教育,汉语语言文字和文学功底扎实,具备了一位汉学家必备的语言文化基础和素养,加之他中文口语非常流利,除普通话外还会讲不少方言,以及作为诗人和诗歌研究者,他的诗歌理解力和感受力也十分细腻敏锐,因此他才成为当今少见的中国当代诗歌优秀译介者和研究者。

戴迈河自20世纪80年代末就开始了中国当代诗歌的翻译与研究,他于1993年完成的硕士论文《中国的另一诗界:三位四川地下诗人》(*China's Other World of Poetry: Three Underground Poets from Sichuan*)和2005年完成的博士论文《中国的第二诗界:四川先锋诗人,1982—1992》(*China's Second World of Poetry: The Sichuan Avant-Garde, 1982—1992*)均以四川先锋诗人为研究对象。在其博士论文的多个章节中,戴迈河都曾写到柏桦,涉及几个民间诗歌流派和诗歌民刊,论及柏桦的多首诗歌。他将自己的两篇学位论文以及20世纪90年代以来翻译的数位中国当代诗人①的数百首诗歌英译文本分享在自己的个人网页上,供读者免费获取。

戴迈河对中国当代诗歌近30年的翻译和研究经历令其在海外汉学界

---

① 包括柏桦、陈东东、韩东、黑大春、李亚伟、吕德安、陆忆敏、欧阳江河、唐晓渡、唐亚平、万夏、王小妮、王寅、西川、于坚、翟永明、郑敏、周伦佑等。

以及国内外诗歌界颇具影响,他将翻译和研究成果免费共享的义举更得到学界和广大读者的钦佩和欢迎。毫无疑问,戴迈河在互联网上的资源分享,为广大诗歌爱好者和研究者尤其是海外读者了解和研究中国当代诗歌提供了通畅、便捷的渠道,这无疑有利于促进中国当代诗歌在海外的影响与传播。

二、译诗精选 10 首

13. 表　达

表达①

我要表达一种情绪
一种白色的情绪
这情绪不会说话
你也不能感到它的存在
但它存在
来自另一个星球
只为了今天这个夜晚
才来到这个陌生的世界

它凄凉而美丽
拖着一条长长的影子
可就是找不到另一个可以交谈的影子

你如果说它像一块石头
冰冷而沉默
我就告诉你它是一朵花
这花的气味在夜空下潜行
只有当你死亡之时
才进入你意识的平原

音乐无法呈现这种情绪

---

①　选自《表达》，桂林：漓江出版社，1988 年，第 1—4 页。

An Expression[①]

I want to express a mood

a white sentiment

This mood can't speak for itself

Neither can you feel its presence

But it exists

It comes from another celestial body

Only for this day, this night

does it come into this strange world

It's desolate yet beautiful

dragging a long shadow

but it can't find another shadow to speak with

If you say it's like a stone

cold and silent

I'll tell you it's a flower

The scent of this flower moves stealthily under the night sky

Only when you die

does it enter your plain of awareness

Music is incapable of carrying this mood

---

① Translated by Michael Day in 1995. Bai Hua: A Chinese Lyricist [OL] // Digital Archive for Chinese Studies (DACHS) [2021.11.20]. https://projects.zo.uni-heidelberg.de/archive2/DACHS_Leiden/poetry/MD/Bai_Hua_trans.pdf.

舞蹈也不能抒发它的形体
你无法知道它的头发有多少
也不知道它为什么要梳成这样的发式

你爱她,她不爱你
你的爱是从去年春天的傍晚开始的
为何不是今年冬日的黎明?

我要表达一种细胞运动的情绪
我要思考它们为什么反叛自己
给自己带来莫名的激动和怒气

我知道这种情绪很难表达
比如夜,为什么在这时降临?
我和她为什么在这时相爱?
你为什么在这时死去?

我知道鲜血的流淌是无声的
虽然悲壮
也无法溶化这铺满钢铁的大地

水流动发出一种声音
树断裂发出一种声音
蛇缠住青蛙发出一种声音
这声音预示着什么?
是准备传达一种情绪呢?
还是表达一种内含的哲理?

还有那些哭声

Dance can't express its form
You can not know the number of its hairs
and don't know why it is combed in this style

You love her, she doesn't love you
Your love began last year on the eve of spring
Why not this year at the dawn of winter?

I want to express a mood of the motion of cells
I want to ponder why they rebel against themselves
bringing to themselves odd stirrings and rage

I know that this mood is hard to express
like the night, why does it fall at this moment?
Why do she and I fall in love at this time?

Why do you die now?
I know that the flow of blood is soundless
Though tragic
this iron-paved earth will not be melted by it

The flow of water makes sound
The crackle of a tree makes sound
A snake wound around a frog makes sound
This sound presages what?
Does it mean to pass on a particular mood?
or express a philosophy contained within it?

or is it those sounds of crying

那些不可言喻的哭声

中国的儿女在古城下哭泣过

基督忠实的儿女在耶路撒冷哭泣过

千千万万的人在广岛死去了

日本人曾哭泣过

那些殉难者,那些怯懦者也哭泣过

可这一切都很难被理解

一种白色的情绪

一种无法表达的情绪

就在今夜

已经来到这个世界

在我们视觉之外

在我们中枢神经里

静静地笼罩着整个宇宙

它不会死,也不会离开我们

在我们心里延续着,延续着……

不能平息,不能感知

因为我们不想死去

(1981年10月)

Those inexpressible wails
The sons and daughters of China have wept beneath the ancient walls
The true children of Christ have wept in Jerusalem
Tens of thousands have died at Hiroshima
the Japanese have wept
Those who died for a just cause, and the timid have also wept
But all of this is hard to understand

A white mood
an inexpressible sentiment
on this night
has already come into this world
beyond our vision
within our central nerve
it silently shrouds the entire universe
it won't die, neither will it leave us
in our hearts it goes on and on...
It can't be calmed, can't be sensed and known
because we don't want to die

14. 震　颤

震颤①

漆黑的深夜在这里安眠
一切都不会发生
整个房间只有水波在钢琴上如歌低述
你面对不动的空门
会心慌、会害怕、会突然丧失信心
会敏捷地跳开
蜷入房间的一角
一分钟内闪过上千次阴暗的念头

少女在走廊尽头洗着雪白的肌肤
向你喃喃倾诉
孤寂是诗人的皇后
那个声音困扰着你
影子已在窗上晃动
花园寂寞的芬芳
吹入你羸瘦的胸中
你会突然揭开窗帘
愉快地偷看一眼
外面辽阔繁衍的灯火

火焰还在徐徐降落
这里没有一丝风
那个声音渐渐消失

---

① 选自《表达》,桂林:漓江出版社,1988年,第14—16页。

A Quiver[①]

The black night sleeps soundly here
Nothing can happen
In this entire room only the waves upon the piano speak softly like a song

When you face an empty, motionless doorway
you'll be alarmed, frightened, you'll suddenly lose confidence
you'll jump nimbly aside
curling up in a corner of the room
within a minute a thousand dark thoughts flash by

At the end of the corridor a young girl washes her snow-white skin
murmuring she pours out her heart to you
loneliness is the poet's empress
the sound perplexes him
shadows are already swaying in the window

The lonesome scents of the flower garden
blowing into your thin breast
you will suddenly open the curtains
and happily take a peek
at the vast increase of lights outside

The flames are still slowly falling
not a trace of wind here
the sound gradually disappears

[①] Translated by Michael Day in 1995. Bai Hua: A Chinese Lyricist [OL] // Digital Archive for Chinese Studies (DACHS) [2021. 11. 20]. https://projects.zo.uni-heidelberg.de/archive2/DACHS_Leiden/poetry/MD/Bai_Hua_trans.pdf.

你会突然想到东京乐团

此刻正在繁华地演奏

想到亚历山大城浩瀚的夏夜

滚烫的海水侵蚀古代的炮楼

金黄头发的罗马少女

站立悬崖岸边

聆听密林深处老虎的怒吼

依然安详地微笑

等待你的歌声,你的痛哭

你明年冬夜用手枪杀死一只野兽

你每夜要花一半的时间来冥想

你无法想象有这么多成群的意念

像蜂群在你头脑中涌荡

华尔兹、雪亮的灯光、丰盈的皮肤

一个向你转过头来的陌生人

一具优美僵直的尸体

即将迫近的火车、乌云和浪潮

你会受不住

会突然沉重地倒在沙发上

扣着心口喘气、愤怒、悒郁或忘却

死去一个夜晚

好久才复活

那个声音又向你走来

很近,几乎贴上你的脸

她的呼吸和气味进入你的身体

整个儿把你围住

今夜你无论如何得死去

you will suddenly think of the Tokyo philharmonic
at this moment it is busily performing
you think of Alexandria's vast summer nights
the boiling seawater erodes the blockhouses of antiquity
a golden-haired maiden of Rome
has arrived on the teetering coast
listening closely to the angry roar of the tiger in the depths of the thick forest
she still smiles serenely
waiting for your song, your bitter wail
on a winter night next year you will kill a wild beast with a pistol

Each evening you spend half the night in meditation
you can't imagine how large the flocking throngs of thoughts are
waltzes, snow-bright lamp lights
like a swarm of bees roiling in your head, the full-figure of white skin
the stranger who's turned his head toward you
an elegant rigid corpse
trains, black clouds and waves bearing down on you
you won't be able to bear it
you'll suddenly drop heavily on the couch
clutching at your chest you'll gasp, rage, worry or forget
you'll die for a night
After a long while you'll revive
the sound comes toward you again
very near, almost brushing up onto your face
it's breath and odor enter your body
surrounding you entirely
no matter what, you must die tonight

因为她明天就要来临
黎明已传来了她遥远的海边情歌

(1982年8月)

because she will be coming tomorrow

the dawn already passed on her distant seaside love-song

15. 下　午

下午①

焦虑的寂静已经感到
在一本打开的散文里
在一首余音绕梁的歌里
是的,我注意到了
还有更重要的一点
某个人走进又走出

入睡前你一直在沉思
徒劳的镜子凝视着什么
即将切开的水果
或棕色的浅梦

下午你睡得很稳
脾气也成了酒
是的,我注意到了这一切
包括窗帘有一点美丽
你的梦在过渡

这是最好的时间
但要小心
因为危险是不说话的
它像一件事情
像某个人的影子很轻柔
它走进又走出

1985 年春

---

① 　选自《表达》,桂林:漓江出版社,1988 年,第 58—59 页。

Afternoon[1]

An anxious silence
you can already feel
in the open pages of a piece of prose
in the sounds of a song curling along the beams
yes, I've taken note
but there's one more important point
someone who walked in and walked out

Before sleeping you're lost in thought
what is that useless mirror staring at
the apple that is about to be sliced open
or a shallow brown dream

You sleep soundly in the afternoon
and your disposition turns to alcohol
yes, I've observed it, all of this
including the shade of beauty in the curtain
your dreams are fording the river

This is the best time
but be careful, even though you're at ease
because danger won't speak
it's like a thing, an event
soft and gentle as someone's shadow
going in and out

---

[1] Translated by Michael Day in 1995. Bai Hua: A Chinese Lyricist [OL] // Digital Archive for Chinese Studies (DACHS) [2021.11.20]. https://projects.zo.uni-heidelberg.de/archive2/DACHS_Leiden/poetry/MD/Bai_Hua_trans.pdf.

16. 或别的东西

或别的东西①

钉子在漆黑的边缘突破

欲飞的瞳孔及门

暗示一次方向的冲动

可以是一个巨大的毛孔

一束倒立的头发

一块典雅的皮肤

或温暖的打字机的声音

也可以是一柄镶边小刀

一片精致的烈火

一枝勃起的茶花

或危险的初夏的堕落

娇小的玫瑰与乌云进入同一呼吸

延伸到月光下的凉台

和树梢的契机

沉着地注视

无垠的心跳的走廊

正等待

亲吻、拥抱、掐死

雪白的潜伏的小手

以及风中送来的抖颤的苹果

被害死的影子

---

① 选自《表达》,桂林:漓江出版社,1988年,第12—13页。

Or Something Else[①]

The nail suddenly breaks through at the edge of blackness
longing to fly, the pupil of the eye and the door
signal an impulse in some way
it might be a huge pore
a tuft of hairs standing on end
a piece of fine skin
or the warm sound of a typewriter
it might also be the blade edge of an inlaid dagger
a delicate raging flame
a suddenly vigorous sprig of camellia
or the dangerous degeneration of early summer

The delicate rose and the black cloud enter into the same breath
stretch to the moonlit balcony
and the juncture of the tree top
the unbounded corridors of your heartbeat
waiting for
kisses, hugs, to be strangled
a small, concealed snow-white hand
and the trembling apple delivered on the wind

The murdered shadow

---

① Translated by Michael Day in 1995. Bai Hua: A Chinese Lyricist [OL] // Digital Archive for Chinese Studies (DACHS) [2021.11.20]. https://projects.zo.uni-heidelberg.de/archive2/DACHS_Leiden/poetry/MD/Bai_Hua_trans.pdf.

变成阴郁的袖口
贴紧你
充满珍贵的死亡的麝香
化为红色的嘴唇
粘着你
青苔的气氛使你的鼻子眩晕,下坠

此刻你用肃穆切开子夜
用膝盖粉碎回忆
你所有热烈的信心与胆怯
化为烟雾
水波
季节
或老虎

(1984年5月)

becomes a gloomy sleeve-cuff

it sticks close to you

full of death's precious musk

it transforms into red lips

and adheres to you

the mossy atmosphere makes your nose dizzy，makes it droop

At this moment you slice open the night with solemnity

with your kneecap smash in memory

all of your enthusiastic confidence and timidity

turns to vapor

a wave

a season

or tiger

17. 琼斯敦①

Jonestown②

The children can start

this night of revolution

night of the next life

night of the People's Temple

The rocking center of the storm

has already tired of those yet to die

and is anxious to carry us off in that direction

The enemy of our hallucinations

makes repeated assaults on us

our commune is like Stalingrad

the sky is full of a Nazi smell

The vortex of hot blood's moment has arrived

emotions are breaking through

fingers are being jabbed in

glue is thrown across all the classes

the patience of vain hopes does battle with reaction

Through spring until fall

sexual anxiety and disappointment spreads everywhere

---

① 译者对该诗的翻译在该诗出版前,所据原文应该是诗人直接提供的。前文已出现中文原诗,此处省略。

② Translated by Michael Day in 1995. Bai Hua: A Chinese Lyricist [OL] // Digital Archive for Chinese Studies (DACHS) [2021.11.20]. https://projects.zo.uni-heidelberg.de/archive2/DACHS_Leiden/poetry/MD/Bai_Hua_trans.pdf.

bared teeth gnaw on unapproachable times
the yen for munitions in boy's chests explodes
the taboo on eccentricity rips and bites back our tears
See! the ravenous mob is already incensed

A girl is practicing suicide
due to her madness, her beautiful hair tending to get sharper and sharper
laid so tenderly across her helpless shoulders
it is a sign of her being seventeen
the only sign

And our spirits' symbol of first-love
that dazzling white father of ours
happy bullets score direct hits on his temples
his naive specter gushes still:
faith cures,"bushido"
the beautiful body of a coup d'etat

The mountain of corpses has already stopped the rehearsals
a loud voice in an unheard-of silence swears an oath:
pass through crisis
drill your thoughts
make a sincere sacrifice

Confronted by this white night, the concentrated betrayal of flesh
this last white night of humanity
I know that this is also my night of a painful bumper harvest

18. 美 人

美人①

我听见孤独的鱼
燃红恭敬的街道
是否有武装上膛的声音
当然还有马群踏弯空气

必须向我致敬,美的行刑队
死亡已整队完毕
开始从深山涌进城里

而一些颜色
一些伪装的沉重与神圣
从我们肉体中碎身

衰老的雷管定时于夜半的腹部
孩子们在食物中寻找颓废
年青人由于形象走向斗争

此时谁在吹
谁就是火
谁就是开花的痉挛的脉搏

我指甲上的幽魂,攀登的器官

---

① 选自《望气的人》,台北:唐山出版社,1999 年,第 63—64 页。译者对该诗的翻译在该诗出版前,所据原文应该是诗人直接提供的。

A Beauty①

I hear a solitary fish blaze red
a respectable street
the sound of bullets entering the firing chambers?
of course there's also a herd of horses trampling a curve into the air

The parade to the execution of beauty, you must salute me
death has already put a stop to the lot of you
and from deep in the hills is beginning to surge into the city

And from out of our flesh, some hues
some feigned seriousness and holiness
overwhelming our bodies

A faulty detonator is set in the belly of midnight
children search for decadence amidst edible things
as a matter of form young people step up to struggle

Whoever blows now
that person is fire
that person is convulsing the pulse of a blooming flower

These climbing organs, the ghosts on my fingernails

---

① Translated by Michael Day in 1995. Bai Hua: A Chinese Lyricist [OL] // Digital Archive for Chinese Studies (DACHS) [2021. 11. 20]. https://projects.zo.uni-heidelberg.de/archive2/DACHS_Leiden/poetry/MD/Bai_Hua_trans.pdf.

在酒中成长
雨不停地敲响我们的脑壳

啊,挑剔的气候,心之森林
推动着检阅着泪水
时光的泥塑造我们的骨头

整整一个秋天,美人
我目睹了你
你驱赶了、淹死了
我们清洁的上升的热血

1987年11月

grow in alcohol

the rain knocks incessantly on our skulls

Hey! forest of the heart, the nitpicking weather

pushes up-close and reviews our tears

the clay of the times makes our bones

Throughout one entire autumn, Beauty

I bore witness

you drove out

our clean, rising hot blood

and sunk it under

19. 夏天,呵,夏天

夏天,呵,夏天①

这夏天,它的血加快了速度
这下午,病人们怀抱石头
命令在反复,麻痹在反复
这热啊,热,真受不了!

这里站立夏天的她
宣誓吧,腼腆的她
喘不过气来呀
左翼太热,如无头之热

这里上演冰冻之诗,放荡之诗
街道变软、变难
她装上知识的白牙
这光、这白、这继续的白

她曾代表沉默的人民
她曾裸露一只乳房
她曾试图灭亡

再看看这躯体,这晕倒的娇躯
躺在翠黄的树叶间
孤单单地被免掉

---

① 选自《望气的人》,台北:唐山出版社,1999 年,第 70—71 页。译者对该诗的翻译在该诗出版前,所据原文应该是诗人直接提供的。

Summer. Ahh, Summer[①]

The summer, its blood has increased speed
this afternoon, patients cherish stones
the orders are repeated, and the repeated paralysis
This heat! Too hot. Can't take it!

Here stands this summertime she
swearing an oath, the shy she
I can't breathe, can't breathe
It's too hot in the left wing, a mindless kind of heat

Here unconventional poems, icy poems are performed
the street becomes soft, difficult
she puts in the white teeth of knowledge
the brilliance, the white, continuous white

Once she represented a silent people
exposed one breast
attempted dying

Take another look at her body, this swooning delicate body
lying among brittle yellow leaves
dispensed with, all on its own

---

① Translated by Michael Day in 1995. Bai Hua: A Chinese Lyricist [OL] // Digital Archive for Chinese Studies (DACHS) [2021. 11. 20]. https://projects.zo.uni-heidelberg.de/archive2/DACHS_Leiden/poetry/MD/Bai_Hua_trans.pdf.

再看看,她向公园开枪
向自己开枪,向笑开枪

再看看,她把花分给大家
谁要就给谁
再看看,荒凉的球场,空旷的学校
再看看,夏天,呵,夏天

(1988年)

Look again, she's opening fire on the park
firing on herself, on laughter

Look again, she's passing out flowers to everyone
whoever wants them gets them

Look again, a deserted playing field, the wide campus
and look at it again. Summer. Ahh, summer

20. 现　实

现实[1]

这是温和,不是温和的修辞学
这是厌烦,厌烦本身

呵,前途、阅读、转身
一切都是慢的

长夜里,收割并非出自必要
长夜里,速度应该省掉

而冬天也可能正是春天
而鲁迅也可能正是林语堂

(1990年12月11日)

---

[1] 选自《望气的人》,台北:唐山出版社,1999年,第124页。译者对该诗的翻译在该诗出版前,所据原文应该是诗人直接提供的。

Reality①

This is gentle, not the rhetoric of gentleness
this is disgust, disgust itself

Hey! Reading, your prospects, the body's turn
all of it is slow

In the long night, reaping isn't done out of necessity
in the long night, speed should be omitted

And winter is probably spring
and Lu Xun probably Lin Yu-tang②

---

① Translated by Michael Day in 1995. Bai Hua: A Chinese Lyricist [OL] // Digital Archive for Chinese Studies (DACHS) [2021.11.20]. https://projects.zo.uni-heidelberg.de/archive2/DACHS_Leiden/poetry/MD/Bai_Hua_trans.pdf.

② Lu Xun(鲁迅) and Lin Yu-tang(林语堂) were writers who flourished prior to 1937 and Japan's invasion of China. Lu is held up as the supreme example of a "serious" writer, while Lin was considered to be his opposite number.

21. 纪念朱湘

纪念朱湘①

这是我一眼就注意的形象
秋风中谵狂的形象
但在一本书中是那么安详

内秀的孤独的饮酒人
不可理喻的敏感的就义者
临死前又饮下一大杯
投身江水进入必然的长眠

我知道,你从小演习烈士的仪表
你的青春曾在流浪里受尽流浪
但你的歌只能属于天堂

唉,为什么这榜样到死才出众
才让我们忙着纪念
忙着说话,忙着通信
忙着这一切,直到1989年

(1989年11月)

---

① 选自《望气的人》,台北:唐山出版社,1999年,第105页。译者对该诗的翻译在该诗出版前,所据原文应该是诗人直接提供的。

In Memory of Zhu Xiang[①]

I noticed your form at a glance
a figure raving in the autumn wind
but so serene in a book

A solitary seemingly unintelligent drinker
a martyr of fathomless sensitivity
before dying he drinks another large cup
bows his body down and enters into that long, inevitable sleep

I know, since you were a child you've practiced the martyr's bearing
your green spring had its fill of roving through gossip
but your songs can only belong to heaven

Ach, why did this exemplar only come to light at death
and then leave us busy memorializing
busy talking, corresponding
busy with all that, up until 1989

---

① Translated by Michael Day in 1995. Bai Hua: A Chinese Lyricist [OL] // Digital Archive for Chinese Studies (DACHS) [2021.11.20]. https://projects.zo.uni-heidelberg.de/archive2/DACHS_Leiden/poetry/MD/Bai_Hua_trans.pdf. Zhu Xiang was one of China's better modern poets prior to 1949.

22. 生 活

生活①

生活,你多么宽广,像道路
带着政权的气味赶往远方

远方,各族人民在歌唱
大嘴唇、尖声音,加上蓝天和广场

广场呀,生长着漫长而颓唐的农业
饕餮或饥饿在四季里彷徨

一切皆遥远,一切皆无关
热情的自身,死的自身,生活的自身

像一个小孤儿独坐大地
像缺乏营养的云,像啊……

像生活,干脆就剥竹、毁稻、杀猪
像生活,干脆就在睡眠中,在睡眠中清账

1990年9月30日

---

① 选自《望气的人》,台北:唐山出版社,1999年,第121页。译者对该诗的翻译在该诗出版前,所据原文应该是诗人直接提供的。

Life[①]

Life, you're so broad, like a road
carrying the smell of political power rushing on to a place far-off

The far-off place, where the people of all nationalities sing
about a blue sky and a square on the top of big lips and high-pitched voices

The square, where endless and dejected farmers are reared
over the four seasons, voracity or starvation loiter

Everything is far off, nothing is of any importance
life itself, death itself, enthusiasm of itself

Like a little orphaned son sitting alone on the earth
like an undernourished cloud, like oh...

Like life, just stripping bamboo, destroying rice, killing pigs
like living, only in your sleep, squaring accounts in your sleep

---

① 选自吉狄马加、海岸主编:《中国当代诗歌前浪》,西宁:青海人民出版社,2009 年,第 37 页。

第三章　西敏（Simon Patton）译诗精选

一、译者简介及翻译述评

在柏桦诗歌的英文译者中，西敏的背景与霍布恩相似。西敏是澳大利亚文学翻译家、诗评家。他在墨尔本大学取得汉学博士学位，主攻中国当代文学。多年来，他一直从事中国文学尤其是当代诗歌的自由翻译和编辑工作，同时在澳洲部分高校兼职教授汉语。西敏翻译较多的诗人是于坚和伊沙。他翻译并在《今日中国文学》上发表了于坚的长诗《小镇》，与陶乃侃合作翻译了伊沙诗选《饿死诗人》(*Starve the Poet*，英国血斧出版社，2008年)。自2002年以来，他同于坚合作为"诗歌国际"网站①编辑中国板块的诗文，为该网站贡献了许多中国当代诗人诗作的原创翻译，其中包括柏桦诗歌的翻译。该网站"诗人"栏目收入了柏桦，以中英双语对照的形式发表了由西敏翻译的 8 首诗歌②，即《奈何天》《恨》《鱼》《悬崖》《麦子：纪念海子》《现实》《广陵散》《望气的人》，同时提供了西敏撰写的诗人简介和译者对部分翻译诗歌的解读。2009 年，诗人吉狄马加和海岸主编出版了中英双语诗

---

① "诗歌国际"(Poetry International)网站由荷兰国际诗歌基金会于 2002 年创办。鹿特丹国际诗歌节(Poetry International Festival in Rotterdam)是该基金会主办的最重要活动，自 1970 年开始，至 2019 年已整整举办了 50 届。该网站主要提供基金会在世界各地组织的一年一度的国际诗歌节及其他活动的相关信息。同时，作为综合性的国际诗歌网站，该网站还设"诗人""诗歌""论文""访谈"等栏目，收集了来自世界各地著名现代诗人的数千首诗歌，以及诗歌论文、诗人访谈文章等。

② 网络发表的网址为：https://www.poetryinternational.org/pi/poet/11546/Bai-Hua。

歌选集《中国当代诗歌前浪》,收入了柏桦的《生活》(Life)和《悬崖》(Precipice)两诗,其中《悬崖》一诗由西敏翻译。

从本书所收录的柏桦诗歌英译本对比情况来看,西敏的翻译风格与霍布恩比较相似。西敏在翻译《望气的人》时,采取了更胜于霍布恩的充分翻译方式,用词最多,在内容的有效转换以及语言的准确性方面是几个译本中最好的。陈吉荣在《论中国文学的跨语言真实性——以 Simon Patton 的中国文学翻译识解为例》一文中,从审美真实论、身份真实论和语言真实论三个方面论述了西敏的翻译真实论,指出其性质在于认知性体验,即真实体验原文,真实体验翻译,真实体验语言。西敏认为,翻译绝非仅是"技术性"工作,它必须是"具有自我真实性的艺术活动"。对于一个待译的文本,西敏首先是作为读者去文本中获得自己真实的艺术审美感受,去接近原文本的艺术内涵,然后用自己真实感受的语言进行转换表达。翻译过程中,西敏遇到自己无法理解的地方,一定会设法向原作者询问细节以求获得真实的认知体验。他不会容忍不求甚解的字对字翻译。西敏在"诗歌国际"网站柏桦诗歌专栏中提道,"柏桦不希望我们太快读懂他的诗,不允许他的诗被轻易解读",所以在读他的诗时,"一开始,会被一个意象或引用困住,继续下去,会对诗歌的走向有所理解,接着再次被困住,然后又回到开头寻找新的线索"。他说,读者应能从《麦子:纪念海子》《恨》等诗的译文中听到尖叫声,"我不得不连踢带打地把它们翻译成英文,与它们的文化和诗意的抵抗进行寸步不让的斗争。就像'望气的人'一样,柏桦利用中国的诗歌文化来登高,创造一个制高点,从这个制高点可以看到在语言的迷雾中显现的黄金、几何和宫殿"。[①] 可见,西敏在竭力用自己的体验和方式,将柏桦诗歌中的美学带给英语读者。

[①] 陈吉荣:《论中国文学的跨语言真实性——以 Simon Patton 的中国文学翻译识解为例》,载《天津外国语大学学报》,2011 年第 18 卷第 3 期。

二、译诗精选 8 首

23. 悬　崖

悬崖①

一个城市有一个人
两个城市有一个向度
寂静的外套无声地等待

陌生的旅行
羞怯而无端端的前进
去报答一种气候
克制正杀害时间

夜里别上阁楼
一个地址有一次死亡
那依稀的白颈项
正转过头来

此时你制造一首诗
就等于制造一艘沉船
一棵黑树
或一片雨天的堤岸

忍耐变得莫测
过度的谜语

---

① 选自《望气的人》,台北:唐山出版社,1999 年,第 20—21 页。

Precipice[①]

In one city there is one man?

In two cities there is one orientation?

The lonely overcoat waits in silence?

A strange journey?

A bashful yet gratuitous advance?

To requite one kind of weather?

Restraint is murdering time?

Don't go up to the attic at night?

An address has one death of its own?

That indistinct white neck?

Will turn around and face you?

At this moment you are making a poem?

Which amounts to making a sunken ship?

A black tree?

Or a rain-shrouded embankment?

Endurance becomes unfathomable?

Excessive riddles?

[①] 选自吉狄马加、海岸主编:《中国当代诗歌前浪》,西宁:青海人民出版社,2009 年,第 38—39 页。

无法解开的貂蝉的耳朵
意志无缘无故地离开

器官突然枯萎
李贺痛哭
唐代的手再不回来

1984年秋

Ears of the enigmatic Diao Chan[①]

For no good reason, determination departs?

Organs shrivel all at once

Li He[②] weeps bitterly?

Those Tang-dynasty hands will never return

---

① Dian Chan, a legendary Chinese beauty, lived during the eastern Han Dynasty (25—220).

② Li He (791—817) was a brilliant songwriter and poet from the Tang Dynasty.

24. 奈何天

奈何天①

黄昏来了
我的祖国也干了
窗外一排队伍
门前五株柳树

我枯坐窗下
看有人在街上吃豆
有人在对面打土
有人无端端地站立
望着对面的山坡

天将息了
地主快要死了
由他去吧
红军正在赶路

1985 年

---

① 选自《望气的人》,台北:唐山出版社,1999 年,第 35 页。

Heaven Watches on[①]

Twilight falls
My homeland dries out
A line of soldiers pass outside my home
Five willow trees stand before the gate

I sit bored by a window
Watching a man in the street eat beans
Someone opposite is ramming the earth
Someone stands around for no reason
Gazing at the hills opposite

The day is about to go out
Landlords will soon be killed
Let them do as they please
The Reds are on their way

---

① Translated by Patton Simon in 2008. Poetry International Archives [2021.11.20]. https://www.poetryinternational.org/pi/poet/11546/Bai-Hua.

25. 恨

恨①

这恨的气味是肥肉的气味
也是两排肋骨的气味
它源于意识形态的平胸
也源于阶级的毛多症

我碰见了她,这个全身长恨的人
她穿着惨淡的政治武装
一脸变性术的世界观
三年来除了磕头就神经涣散

这非人的魂魄疯了吗?
这沉湎于斗争的红色娘子军
看她正起义,从肉体直到喘气
直到牙齿浸满盲目的毒汁

一个只为恨而活着的人
一个烈火烧肺的可怜人
她已来到我们中间
她开始了对人类的深仇大恨

1987 年

---

① 选自《望气的人》,台北:唐山出版社,1999 年,第 68 页。

Hate[①]

This hate has the smell of fatty meat
And the smell of ribs
It springs from ideology's flat chest
And from the excess hair of class

I have met her, this woman who hates with every cell
She wears a bleak political uniform
Her face filled with a sex-changed world view
Her nerves slack after three years of kow-towing

Has she gone mad, this inhuman soul?
Watch how this Red woman soldier who wallows in struggle
Is starting an uprising, from her flesh to her breathing
To the blind venom that drips from her teeth

A woman who lives only to hate
A pathetic woman whose lungs burn
She is here in amongst us already
And her war on us has begun

---

① Translated by Patton Simon in 2008. Poetry International Archives [2021. 11. 20]. https://www.poetryinternational.org/pi/poet/11546/Bai-Hua.

26. 鱼

鱼①

难以理解的鱼不会歌唱
从寂静游进寂静

需要东西、需要说话
但却盲目地看着一块石头

忍受的力量太精确
衰老催它走上仁慈的道路

它是什么？一个种族的形象
或一个无声的投入的动作

埋怨的脸向阴影
死亡的沉默向错误

出生为了说明一件事的比喻
那源于暧昧的痛苦的咽喉

1985 年秋

---

① 选自《往事》,石家庄:河北教育出版社,2022 年,第 42 页。

Fish[①]

The bewildering fish does not know how to sing
From silence on to silence it swims

Needs it has, and the need to speak
Instead, blind and blank, it stares at a rock

To endure is a power so precise in it
Physical decline hurries it along the road of kindness

What can it be? An image of a people
Or the act of a soundless absorption?

The face of Blame is turned towards Shadow
The reticence of Death is turned towards Error

A metaphor born to explain some fact:
The throat an ambiguous pain gives rise to

---

① Translated by Patton Simon in 2008. Poetry International Archives [2021.11.20]. https://www.poetryinternational.org/pi/poet/11546/Bai-Hua.

27. 望气的人

望气的人①

望气的人行色匆匆
登高眺远
眼中沉沉的暮霭
长出黄金、几何与宫殿

穷巷西风突变
一个英雄正动身去千里之外
望气的人看到了
他激动的草鞋和布衫

更远的山谷浑然
零落的钟声依稀可闻
两个儿童打扫着亭台
望气的人坐对空寂的傍晚

吉祥之云宽大
一个干枯的导师沉默
独自在吐火、炼丹
望气的人看穿了石头里的图案

乡间的日子风调雨顺
菜田一畦,流水一涧
这边青翠未改
望气的人已走上了另一座山巅

1986年暮春

---

① 选自《望气的人》,台北:唐山出版社,1999年,第41—42页。

Cloud Diviner[①]

The Cloud Diviner is in a hurry to depart
He climbs a height and gazes down from afar
Gold, geometry, and palaces grow
In the heavy evening mist in his eyes

The west wind abruptly changes course in a slum lane
A hero is about to set out on a thousand-mile journey
The Cloud Diviner has spied
The excitement in his straw sandals and his cloth shirt

Remoter mountain valleys coalesce in the distance
At odd intervals the faint sound of bells is heard
Two boys sweep the pavilion's terrace
The Cloud Diviner sits facing the solitary dusk

Auspicious clouds are magnanimous
A wizened spiritual guide sits in silence
Alone, he breathes fire and makes pills of immortality
The Cloud Diviner sees through to the patterns inside stones

Days pass in the country with timely winds and rain
Vegetables grow in the fields, and water flows in the creeks
While the verdant freshness is still changed here
The Cloud Diviner has already reached the next hilltop

---

① Translated by Patton Simon in 2008. Poetry International Archives [2021.11.20]. https://www.poetryinternational.org/pi/poet/11546/Bai-Hua.

28. 麦子:纪念海子

麦子:纪念海子①

为有牺牲多壮志,
敢叫日月换新天。
——毛泽东

麦子,我面对你
我垂下疼痛的双手
麦子,我左胸的一枚像章
我请求你停止疯长!

麦子!麦子!麦子!
北方就要因此而流血
看吧,从安徽直到我手里
直到祖国的中心
一粒精神正飞速传递

是谁发出绝食的命令
麦子!麦子!麦子!
一滴泪打在饥饿的头顶
你率领绝食进入第168个小时

麦子,我们的麦子
啊,麦子,大地的麦子!
长空星辰照耀

---

① 选自《望气的人》,台北:唐山出版社,1999年,第106—107页。

Wheat in Memory of Haizi[①]

Bitter sacrifice strengthens bold resolve
Which dares to make sun and moon shine in new skies.
—Mao Zedong

Wheat, as I stand here before you
I let my aching hands hang down by my sides
Wheat, with my Mao badge pinned over my heart
I ask you to desist from your mad growth!

Wheat! Wheat! Wheat!
There will be bloodshed in the North account of this
See for yourself: from Anhui province to my hands
And then all the way to China's core
A grain of spirit is transmitted at lightning speed

Who gave the order to begin the hunger strike?
Wheat! Wheat! Wheat!
A tear falls and strikes the crown of Starvation's head
You lead the hunger strike into its 168th hour

Wheat. Our wheat
Ah, wheat, wheat of Mother Earth
In the vast sky stars shine brightly

[①] Translated by Patton Simon in 2008. Poetry International Archives [2021. 11. 20]. https://www.poetryinternational.org/pi/poet/11546/Bai-Hua.

南方在肉体中哭泣

请宣告吧!麦子,下一步,下一步!
下一步就是牺牲
下一步不是宴席

1989年冬

The South weeps within bodies of flesh

Please announce the next move, wheat! The next move!
The next move can only be Sacrifice
The next move can never be Feast

29. 现 实

现实①

这是温和,不是温和的修辞学
这是厌烦,厌烦本身

呵,前途、阅读、转身
一切都是慢的

长夜里,收割并非出自必要
长夜里,速度应该省掉

而冬天也可能正是春天
而鲁迅也可能正是林语堂

(1990年12月11日)

---

① 选自《望气的人》,台北:唐山出版社,1999年,第124页。

Reality[①]

This is gentleness, not the rhetoric of gentleness
This is tedium, the sheer fact of tedium

Ah! Prospects, readings, about-faces
All of these things are so slow

Through long nights, the harvesting is not done out of necessity
Through long nights, the speed should be left out

And winter could just as well be summer
And Lu Xun could just as well be Lin Yutang

---

① Translated by Patton Simon in 2008. Poetry International Archives [2021.11.20]. https://www.poetryinternational.org/pi/poet/11546/Bai-Hua.

30. 广陵散

广陵散①

一

一个青年向深渊滑去
接着又一个青年……

幸福就快报废了
一个男孩写下一行诗

唉,一行诗,只有一行诗
二十四桥明月夜

二

冬天的江南
令你思想散漫,抓不住主题

肴肉、个园、上海人
热气腾腾的导游者

照相吧,照相吧
他冻红的脸在笑

1993 年 2 月

---

① 选自《望气的人》,台北:唐山出版社,1999 年,第 134 页。

Ancient Tune[①]

I

One youth slides off towards the abyss
And is followed by another...

Happiness will soon be obsolete
A boy writes down a line of poetry

One line, alas, just one single line:
"Above the Bridge of Twenty Four the moon dispels the night"

II

Winter, South of the River
You cannot focus your thoughts or find a theme

Yaorou pork leg, the Ge Garden, Shanghai folk
The tour guide is hot with enthusiasm

Photo, please. A photo
His frozen red face smiles

---

① Translated by Patton Simon in 2008. Poetry International Archives [2021. 11. 20]. https://www.poetryinternational.org/pi/poet/11546/Bai-Hua.

第四章 陶忘机(John Balcom)译诗精选

一、译者简介及翻译述评

2011年,美国汉学家、翻译家陶忘机翻译了两首柏桦诗歌代表作《夏天还很远》和《望气的人》,两诗被收入当年在美国出版的中英双语诗歌选集《推开窗:当代中国诗歌》(*Push Open the Window: Contemporary Poetry from China*)。

陶忘机本、硕、博均为中文专业,研究兴趣是中国现当代诗歌和小说、比较文学和翻译学。他曾在中国台湾、中国内地及香港工作和生活多年(其妻子是中国台湾人),辗转多地后他最终回到自己的母校美国明德学院担任教授,主要教授文学翻译课程。他曾担任美国文学翻译家协会主席,第一届莎尔茨堡全球文学翻译研讨会联合主席。工作之余贯穿其一生的志业是中国文学的译介事业,他先后翻译了中国台湾和大陆当代诸多作家的作品,并获得过许多重要的翻译和图书奖项。同时,他还在欧美及亚洲许多国家做文学翻译讲座,并举办翻译工作坊。

陶忘机选译的两首诗均为柏桦早期的经典诗歌。《望气的人》有6个英译本,译者分别为李赋康、西敏、陶忘机、菲奥娜、顾爱玲以及李赋康/阿米莉娅·戴尔(两人合译了另一版本)。《夏天还很远》有5个英译本,译者分别为李赋康/孔慧怡、戴迈河、陶忘机、菲奥娜和罗辉。从各英译本的对比情况来看,陶忘机的翻译风格与西敏和霍布恩较为相近。在文本语言风格和外在形式方面,陶忘机译本比霍布恩和西敏译本更接近原诗,比如《望气的人》一诗,陶译本的词数明显比西敏译本少,总体呈现出原诗语言精练、节奏明快的特点。在内容的完整性和语言的准确度方面,陶译本似乎要略逊于西敏译本。在翻译《望气的人》时,西敏采取了更胜于霍布恩的充分翻译方式,用词最多,在内容的有效转换以及语言的准确性方面是6个译者中最好的。此外,在陶忘机译本中,有少数地方反映出其对原诗文本的理解存在问题,比如在《夏天还很远》的译文中,其对诗中隐身人物的角色把握不到位,导致添加出来的人物主角显得有些混乱。有关这两首诗歌的多译本对比分析详见本书第二部分的个案研究三和个案研究四。

二、译诗精选 2 首①

31. 夏天还很远

夏天还很远②

一日逝去又一日
某种东西暗中接近你
坐一坐,走一走
看树叶落了
看小雨下了
看一个人沿街而过
夏天还很远

真快呀,一出生就消失
所有的善在十月的夜晚进来
太美,全不察觉
巨大的宁静如你干净的布鞋
在床边,往事依稀、温婉
如一只旧盒子
一个褪色的书签
夏天还很远

偶然遇见,可能想不起
外面有一点冷
左手也疲倦

---

① 因涉及版权问题,此处无法一一呈现译文,仅注明译文出处,以便读者查阅。
② 选自《望气的人》,台北:唐山出版社,1999 年,第 22—23 页。

暗地里一直往左边

偏僻又深入

那唯一痴痴的挂念

夏天还很远

再不了,动辄发脾气,动辄热爱

拾起从前的坏习惯

灰心年复一年

小竹楼、白衬衫

你是不是正当年?

难得下一次决心

夏天还很远

1984 年冬

Summer Is Still Very Far Away[①]

32. 望气的人[②]

The Seer[③]

[①] In Qingping Wang (ed.), *Push Open the Window*: *Contemporary Poetry from China* (C). Washington: Copper Canyon Press. 2011. pp. 57—59.
[②] 前文已出现中文原诗,此处省略。
[③] In Qingping Wang (ed.), *Push Open the Window*: *Contemporary Poetry from China* (C). Washington: Copper Canyon Press. 2011. pp. 58—61.

第五章 约翰·卡雷（John Cayley）译诗精选

一、译者简介及翻译述评

约翰·卡雷是加拿大籍诗人、翻译家，布朗大学教授。在 2007 年入职布朗大学之前，他曾在英国多所大学任教，并担任伦敦大学皇家霍洛威学院英语系荣誉副研究员，曾在美国加州大学圣地亚哥分校任教或指导研究工作。约翰·卡雷于 1996 年在伦敦议程出版社（Agenda Editions）出版了诗集《墨竹》（*Ink Bamboo*），其中包括诗歌、翻译和改编作品，之后主要从事数字媒体创作，并于 2001 年获得了电子文学组织的首届诗歌奖。最近他主要研究可编程媒体中的环境诗学。

1994 年，由赵毅衡和约翰·卡雷编选的《今天》文学杂志双年选集第一集（*Under-sky Underground: Chinese Writing Today I*）在英国伦敦出版，其中收入了柏桦诗歌 3 首：《往事》（Things Past）、《幸福》（Happiness）和《夏日读诗人传记》（Reading the Poet's Life One Summer）；译者即是约翰·卡雷。

这三首译诗同时还发布在纸托邦（Paper Republic）英文网站上。这是一家致力于推广华语文学英译作品的网站，2007 年由定居中国的美国人艾瑞克·阿布汉森（Eric Abrahamsen）创建。作为一名优秀的中国文学译者，出于对中国文学的喜爱，艾瑞克矢志不渝地投入中国文学在英语世界的译介工作，他要做的是"发现最好的华语新作品，并向英文读者推荐"①。为此,除了努力发现优秀的当代华语作品,他还努力为译者创建信息分享、翻译交流与翻译培训的平台,推动优秀译者发现优秀作品,同时帮助译者产出高质量的译品。2010年,纸托邦曾与《中国文学》杂志合作创办译介中国文学的英文季刊《路灯》(*Pathlight*)。2015年,纸托邦推出"纸托邦短读计划",持续推荐当代华语作家的短篇作品。2016年,纸托邦在英国注册为非营利组织,它的目标是"让更多人加入翻译、出版并阅读华语作品"②。经过十余年的不懈坚持,纸托邦已成为一个中国文学出版推介平台、一个英语世界了解中国文学的窗口,在国内外文学出版界、文学翻译界和海外汉学家中具有广泛影响。

约翰·卡雷翻译的这三首诗均是诗人柏桦1988年至1989年间在南京农业大学任教期间创作的诗歌,这一阶段属于诗人诗歌创作的"往事"期,《往事》也是这一阶段的代表作。对比该诗约翰·卡雷译本和罗辉译本(两位译者采用的原诗版本略有不同),可以感受到约翰·卡雷译本更传情,较好地传递了原诗中所蕴含的复杂而丰富的情感,罗辉的译本更达意,更准确,语言精练,情感表达较为内敛。从对照原诗和译诗的角度来看,可以说约翰·卡雷对部分语词的翻译并不准确,如将"无知的疲乏"译为"stupefied exhaustion",将"本地普通话"译为"'received pronunciation' out of town",将"中午的清风"译为"the cool breeze of middle age"。但是,如果抛开原文,仅读译诗,我们能感受到约翰·卡雷译本颇有诗意,饶有韵味,一些背离原文的"创造性叛逆"似乎给译诗带来了别样的意蕴。

---

① 参见纸托邦网站的介绍页面:https://paper-republic.org/guanyu。
② 同上。

二、译诗精选 3 首

33. 往事

往事①

这些无辜的使者
她们平凡地穿着夏天的衣服
坐在这里,我的身旁
向我微笑
向我微露老年的害羞的乳房

那曾经多么热烈的旅途
那无知的疲乏
都停在这陌生的一刻
这善意的,令人哭泣的一刻

老年,如此多的鞠躬
本地普通话(是否必要呢?)
温柔的色情的假牙
一腔烈火

我已集中精力看到了
中午的清风
它吹拂相遇的眼神
这伤感

---

① 选自《望气的人》,台北:唐山出版社,1999 年,第 72—73 页。译者对该诗的翻译在该诗出版前,所据原文应该是诗人直接提供的。

Things past[①]

These innocent messengers
wearing their usual summer dresses
sitting down here, beside me
smiling
giving me a glimpse of their ageing withered dugs

those journeys of such great excitement
and stupefied exhaustion
they come to a halt in this strange moment
this well-meaning, tear-jerking moment

old age, so much bowing and scraping
'received pronunciation' out of town (is it really necessary?)
false teeth—soft, obscene—
the burning throat

already I've pulled myself together, strained to see
the cool breeze of middle age
sweep away the expression in meeting eyes
the sentimentality

---

① *Under-sky Underground*, *Chinese Writing Today*, Number 1, 1994. London: The Well-sweep Press. p. 73.

这坦开的仁慈

这纯属旧时代的风流韵事

啊,这些无辜的使者

她们频频走动

悄悄叩门

满怀恋爱和敬仰

来到我经历太少的人生

1988年10月

thecandour and compassion

those dissolute, romantic affairs living purely in the past

ah, these innocent messengers

endlessly bustling about

furtively knocking

bursting with love and respect

visiting our lives which have known too little

34. 幸　福

幸福①

请重视这些孤儿
这些尖锐的不长胡子的孤儿
他们沿街走来
一边吃肉、刺耳
一边敬祝宏伟的灵魂

不死的决心单纯而急躁
仿佛要让世界咽下这掬热泪
或者我们必须一致
加入这行列
这孤儿的赤卫队
怀病、残缺、两眼生辉

呵,他们也歌唱
为聆听的风景
为沉默的谦逊的美
可谁会羞愧?
谁会挺身而出?
这嗫嚅的营养不良的歌声?

不。孤儿,对于拯救
我们将从何说起

---

① 选自《望气的人》,台北:唐山出版社,1999年,第90—91页。译者对该诗的翻译在该诗出版前,所据原文应该是诗人直接提供的。

Happiness[①]

consider these orphans

sharp but beardless

walking down the street

praising the great spirit, while they

gnaw at their gristle, harshly grinding

deathless determination, pure but impetuous

as if they'd have the whole world swallow back hot tears

or must we all together

join the ranks

of Red Army orphans

sickly, crippled, eyes spilling brightness

ah yes, and they sing

sing for the landscape which listens respectfully

and for silent, modest loveliness,

but who feels any shame?

who dares raise their head

above this halting music of malnutrition?

No. Orphans, how can we

speak of salvation

---

① *Under-sky Underground*, *Chinese Writing Today*, Number 1, 1994. London: The Wellsweep Press. p. 74.

这并非是一个事实
但他们却强迫地梦到这些

还有苦水,还有呼声
还有春风拍打树林
孤儿们更孤独
我们更多毁容的激情?

1989年3月

this is certainly not a matter of fact
they have simply forced themselves to dream it up

there is still the taste of bitterness, still the call
still the spring breeze striking the trees
the orphans are ever more lonely
we feel still more self-effacing desperation

35. 夏日读诗人传记

夏日读诗人传记①

这哲学令我羞愧
他期望太高
两次打算放弃
不!两次打算去死
漫长的三个月是他沉沦的三个月
我漫长的痛苦跟随他
从北京直到重庆

整整三个月,云游的小孤儿
暗中要成为大诗人
他的童年已经结束
他已经十六岁
他反复说
"要么为自己牺牲自己
要么为别人而活着。"
这哲学令我羞愧

他表达的速度太快了
我无法跟上这意义
短暂的夏日翻过第89页
瞧,他孤单的颈子开始发炎
在意义中,也在激情中发炎

---

① 选自《望气的人》,台北:唐山出版社,1999年,第95—96页。译者对该诗的翻译在该诗出版前,所据原文应该是诗人直接提供的。

Reading the Poet's Life One Summer[①]

This philosophy makes me uncomfortable.
His expectations were too great.
Twice he thought of giving up.
But, no? Twice he thought of death.
Three endless months were, for him, three months of falling.
My endless suffering followed him
down from Beijing to Chongqing.

Three full months, a little orphan, cloud-wandering
hoping to grow up to be a "great poet".
His childhood already at an end,
he'd reached the age of sixteen.
Over and over he repeated,
"Either sacrifice yourself to yourself
or live for others".
This philosophy makes me uncomfortable.

He expressed himself too hurriedly.
I could not keep up with the sense.
One short summer's day, turning the 89th page—
Look, his neck, alone, becomes inflamed
inflamed with significance, with passion

---

① *Under-sky Underground*, *Chinese Writing Today*, Number 1, 1994. London: The Wellsweep Press. pp. 75—76.

并在继续下去
这哲学令我羞愧

再瞧,他的身子
多敏感,多难看
太小了,太瘦了
嘴角太平凡了
只有狡黠的眼神肯定了他的力量
但这是不幸的力量
这哲学令我羞愧

其中还有一些绝望的细节
无人问津的两三个细节
梦游的两三个细节
竖着指头的两三个细节
由于一句话而自杀的一个细节
那是十八岁的一个细节
这唯一的哲学令我羞愧

1989年冬

and he continues downwards.
This philosophy makes me uncomfortable.

Look again, his body,
so sensitive, so ugly
too small, too thin
the corners of his mouth, too plain
but the cunning in his eyes confirms his strength,
albeit the strength of misfortune.
This philosophy makes me uncomfortable.

Besides these, there are some other hopeless details,
one or two details that no one bother to ask about,
one or two details still sleepwalking,
one or two details still raising a finger,
the small detail of suicide over a single word.
That was a small detail of his eighteenth year.
This unique philosophy makes me uncomfortable.

第六章　顾爱玲（Eleanor Goodman）译诗精选

一、译者简介及翻译述评

2013年至2014年，美国青年诗人、翻译家、哈佛大学费正清中国研究中心研究员顾爱玲翻译了10首柏桦诗歌，发表于美国出版的《新华夏集：当代中国诗选》(*New Cathay*: *Contemporary Chinese Poetry*)和中国出版的《飞地》(*Enclave*)杂志。

如果说陶忘机可代表酷爱中国文学、热衷中国文学翻译的美国老一代汉学家的话，1979年出生的顾爱玲则可视为美国年轻一代汉学家的代表。顾爱玲从小学习汉语，大学辅修中文，从波士顿大学创意写作专业硕士毕业后，开始从事中国诗歌的翻译工作。她是哈佛大学费正清中国研究中心研究员，翻译了王小妮、臧棣等中国当代诗人的诗集，同时还翻译了一本中国当代打工诗选。她的译作《有什么在我心里一过：王小妮诗选》（美国西风出版社，2014年）获得2013年度美国笔会基金资助，并荣获2015年美国文学翻译协会"卢西恩·斯泰克"奖。与其前辈陶忘机不同的是，顾爱玲在翻译之余还自己创作诗歌，出版了个人诗集《九龙岛》。同样值得注意的是，顾爱玲在北京和上海都生活过，2013年她获得富布莱特基金资助到北京大学做访学研究两年，其后也经常来中国参加各种诗歌交流活动和翻译坊活动。如其所说："对我而言，翻译中国诗歌是乐趣，也是一种义务。"① 出于对中文

---

① 陈佩珍：《顾爱玲：从诗歌出发走向中国故事》，载《文汇报》，2017年12月27日第11版。

和中国诗歌的热爱，她走上了诗歌翻译之路，努力使自己能成为中美之间诗歌交流与互动的桥梁。

顾爱玲最初只翻译中国古诗，是在中国旅美诗人王敖的鼓励下开始接触中国当代诗歌的。中国当代诗歌不像古诗那样很容易找到注解，其理解障碍使得她在译诗之初无法独立完成翻译，便与王敖合译。在一次接受采访时，顾爱玲谈到了她与王敖合作翻译的有关情形："我们经常见面，他帮我了解一首诗，我把它译成英文。我们合作了三年，后来我才慢慢有自信，自己一个人翻译。"[1]顾爱玲与王敖合作翻译了柏桦诗3首（《在清朝》《现实》《怒风下》），2013年发表于美国出版的《新华夏集：当代中国诗选》。从顾爱玲所译的《在清朝》和《望气的人》来看，其翻译风格与新加坡诗人译者菲奥娜（详见第十四章）有些接近，译本在语言风格上偏于简洁，用词数偏少，在形式上较为接近原诗。总体来看，顾爱玲的译本比较忠实于原文，译文中规中矩，但少数地方在翻译选词的准确性上有所欠缺，也有部分地方似乎过于拘泥于字词对译，创造性的转换并不太多。

---

[1] 陈佩珍:《顾爱玲：从诗歌出发走向中国故事》，前揭。

二、译诗精选 10 首

36. 在清朝

在清朝①

在清朝
安闲和理想越来越深
牛羊无事,百姓下棋
科举也大公无私
货币两地不同
有时还用谷物兑换
茶叶、丝、瓷器

在清朝
山水画臻于完美
纸张泛滥,风筝遍地
灯笼得了要领
一座座庙宇向南
财富似乎过分

在清朝
诗人不事营生、爱面子
饮酒落花、风和日丽
池塘的水很肥
二只鸭子迎风游泳
风马牛不相及

---

① 选自《望气的人》,台北:唐山出版社,1999 年,第 44—45 页。

In the Qing Dynasty[①]

In the Qing Dynasty
lightheartedness and idealism grew deeper
cows and sheep were idle, people played chess
the imperial examination was impartial
every place had its own currency
grain could be used to barter
for tea leaves, silk, porcelain

In the Qing Dynasty
landscape painting neared perfection
paper was abundant, kites flew everywhere
lanterns understood the essentials
temple after temple faced south
the wealth seemed excessive

In the Qing Dynasty
poets didn't work for a living, concerned with reputation
drinking under falling petals, in warm sunny weather
the lakes brimmed with water
two ducks swam against the wind
everything was at odds

In the Qing Dynasty
one man dreamt of another

---

① Translated by Eleanor Goodman & Ao Wang. In Ming Di (ed.), 2013. *New Cathay: Contemporary Chinese Poetry* (C). North Adams: Tupelo Press. pp. 21—22.

在清朝
一个人梦见一个人
夜读太史公、清晨扫地
而朝廷增设军机处
每年选拔长指甲的官吏

在清朝
多胡须和无胡须的人
严于身教、不苟言谈
农村人不愿认字
孩子们敬老
母亲屈从于儿子

在清朝
用款税激励人民
办水利、办学校、办祠堂
编印书籍、整理地方志
建筑弄得古色古香

在清朝
哲学如雨,科学不能适应
有一个人朝三暮四
无端端地着急
愤怒成为他毕生的事业
他于1840年死去

1986年10月

read The Grand History at night, swept at dawn
the court created a Military Office
each year selecting officials with long fingernails

In the Qing Dynasty
men with and without beards
taught by example instead of with words
farmers didn't want to learn to read
the young respected the old
mothers submitted to their sons

In the Qing Dynasty
taxes inspired the people
and built irrigation works, schools, temples
books were printed, gazetteers collected
the architecture was designed to look antique

In the Qing Dynasty
philosophy fell like rain, science couldn't adapt
one man changed his mind night and day
always unreasonably anxious
resentment became his lifelong vocation
until his death in 1842.
(1986)

37. 现 实

现实①

这是温和,不是温和的修辞学
这是厌烦,厌烦本身

呵,前途、阅读、转身
一切都是慢的

长夜里,收割并非出自必要
长夜里,速度应该省掉

而冬天也可能正是春天
而鲁迅也可能正是林语堂

(1990年12月11日)

---

① 选自《望气的人》,台北:唐山出版社,1999年,第124页。

Reality[①]

This is gentleness, not the rhetoric of gentleness
this is aggravation, aggravation itself

Ah, prospects for the future, reading, turning around
everything is slow

on long nights, the harvest doesn't come from need
on long nights, one should give up on speed

and winter perhaps is spring
and Lu Xun perhaps is Lin Yutang

(1990)

---

① Translated by Eleanor Goodman & Ao Wang. In Ming Di (ed.), 2013. *New Cathay: Contemporary Chinese Poetry* (C). North Adams: Tupelo Press. p. 23.

38. 怒风下

怒风下①

是紫风吗?想得美。是怒风
狗胖起叫,双耳遭风割,
它想吃你肚子里那个橱柜。

正好我就吐了那体内的集体
右边厚嘴上夹紧二寸热烟
靠着妻背阅读,舒舒服服地。

日子就这么一天天过呗……
谁说的?(童话)安徒生?
偏偏那手风琴又怪喝了起来。

2012年5月22日

---

① 选自《为你消得万古愁:柏桦诗集 2009—2012》,太原:北岳文艺出版社,2015 年,第 213 页。译者对该诗的翻译在该诗出版前,所据原文应该是诗人直接提供的。

Under an Angry Wind[①]

Was it a purple wind? What pretty thinking. It was an angry wind
the dog grew fat and barked, his ears sliced by the wind,
he wanted to eat that cupboard in your belly.

I'd just vomited collectivism from my body
gripping two inches of hot cigarette in the right side of my thick mouth
leaning on my wife's back reading, totally at ease.

So the days go by one by one...
Who says? (Fairy tales) Anderson?
It's just that that accordion has started its strange shouting again.

(2012)

---

① Translated by Eleanor Goodman & Ao Wang. In Ming Di (ed.), 2013. *New Cathay: Contemporary Chinese Poetry* (C). North Adams: Tupelo Press. p. 24.

39. 猪头与张爱玲对话

猪头与张爱玲对话①

猪头从滚水中冒出。
张爱玲说：
它毛发蓬松，
像个洗了澡的小孩子。
而我却说：
它是老还小的佛陀呢
只是眼睛更小些。
"猪头割下来,嘴里给它衔着
自己的小尾巴。"
张爱玲很困惑。
为什么它会这样呢？
哦,原来那猪头也可以衔着梨
苹果、蕃茄或香蕉……
——我想。

2011年5月2日

---

① 选自《飞地》,深圳:海天出版社,2014年,第8辑,第128页。

A Pig's Head or In Conversation with Eileen Chang[①]

A pig's head emerged from boiling water,

Eileen Chang said:

Its hair is all fluffy,

like a child who's just bathed.

But I said:

It's a youthful old Buddha

except its eyes are smaller.

"The pig's head was cut off, and its mouth holds its own little tail."

Eileen Chang was puzzled:

Why would it turn out that way?

Ah, in fact a pig's mouth can also hold pears

apples, tomatoes, or bananas…

—I suppose.

---

① *Enclave* (8), 2014: 128.

40. 衰老经(一)

衰老经(一)①

疲倦还疲倦得不够
人在过冬

一所房间外面
铁路黯淡的灯火,在远方

远方,远方人呕吐掉青春
并有趣地拿着绳子

啊,我得感谢你们
我认识了时光

但冬天并非替代短暂的夏日
但整整三周我陷在集体里

1991年4月

---

① 选自《飞地》,深圳:海天出版社,2014年,第8辑,第129页。

The Scripture of Aging (I)[①]

Weary but not weary enough
man passes the winter

outside the house
faint lamps by the railroad tracks, far away

far away, far away a man vomits up his youth
amusingly, holding a rope

Ah, I have to thank you all
I've known the passage of time

yet winter won't replace the transient summer
yet for three whole weeks I've been absorbed in the collective

---

① *Enclave* (8), 2014: 129.

41. 衰老经(二)

衰老经(二)①

20年后,远方人还有趣地拿着一根绳子吗?
而窥视人却最爱那卷成8字形的精美细绳。

读:冻僵的鳜鱼、沾湿的银燕
听:"我火烫嗓音中那些鸟啼。"

看:诗人携痛步入,添一种成分(魔法)
"孔雀狭窄的前额是一条带羽冠的蛇。"

脸——黎明,头发——暗夜;雨天绿树。
补充一句:为睡得安稳,晚饭宜于少吃。

2012年5月

---

① 选自《飞地》,深圳:海天出版社,2014年,第8辑,第129页。

The Scripture of aging (II)[1]

Twenty years later, are there still faraway men who hold a rope amused?
The voyeur's favorite is a delicate fine rope rolled into a figure 8.

Read: frozen mandarin fish, damp silver swallows
Listen: "the cawing in my burnt voice."

Look: the poet carries pain to come in, adds another element (sorcery)
"A peacock's narrow forehead is a snake with a plume."

Face—dawn, hair—night; the rainy day green trees.
One more thing: to sleep peacefully, best to eat a light dinner.

---

[1] *Enclave* (8), 2014: 129.

42. 演春与种梨

演春与种梨①

一

日暮,灯火初上
二人在园里谈论春色
一片黑暗,淙淙水响
呵,几点星光
生活开始了……

暮春,我们聚首的日子
家有春椅、春桌、春酒
呵,纸,纸,纸啊
你沦入写作
并暂时忘记了……

二

足寒伤神,园庭荒
他的晚年急于种梨

种梨、种梨
陌生的、温润的梨呀

光阴的梨、流逝的梨

---

① 选自《飞地》,深圳:海天出版社,2014年,第8辑,第131—132页。

Performing Spring and Planting Pears[1]

I

Nightfall, the lights are coming on
two people in the garden talk of spring's colors
all dark, gurgling water
oh, traces of starlight
life begins...

In late spring, the day we met
the house had spring chairs, spring tables, spring wine
oh, paper, paper, paper
you were subsumed in writing
momentarily forgotten...

II

The distress of chilled feet, the garden desolate
he in his old age anxiously plants pears

planting pears, planting pears
unfamiliar pears, warm and supple

pears of time, fleeting pears

---

[1] *Enclave* (8), 2014: 131—132.

来到他悲剧的正面像

梨的命运是美丽的
他的注视是腼腆的

但如果生活中没有梨
如果梨的青春会老死

如果、如果……
那他就没有依傍,就不能歌唱

1990年9月30日

come to his tragic face

the pears' fate is beautiful
his gaze is bashful

but if life had had no pears
if the pears' youth had died of old age

if, if...
he'd have nothing to depend on, no way to sing

43. 忆江南:给张枣

忆江南:给张枣①

江风引雨,春偎楼头,暗点检
这是我病酒后的第二日

我的俊友,来,让我们再玩一会儿
那失传的小弓和掩韵

之后,便忘了吧
今年春事寂寂,晚来燕三两只

"我欲归去,我欲归去。"

不要起身告别,我的俊友
这深奥的学问需要我们一生来学习

就把那马儿系于垂柳边缘
就把那镜中的生涯说说

是的,我还记得你——
昨夜灯下甜饮的样子,富丽而悠长

"我欲归去,我欲归去。"

不!请听,我正回忆到这一节:
另一位隔江人在黎明的雨声中梳洗……

2010年5月4日

---

① 选自《飞地》,深圳:海天出版社,2014年,第8辑,第132页。

Remembering Jiangnan: for Zhang Zao

The river wind brings rain, spring leans on the buildings, secretly examining itself
this is the second day of my wine-sickness

My handsome friend, come, let's have fun again for a while
that little bow and rhyming games lost forever

and after, let's forget everything
This year the spring affairs are quiet, in the evening a few swallows come

"I long to go back, I long to go back."

Don't get up to leave, my handsome friend
these teachings take a lifetime to learn

Just tie your horse at the edge of the weeping willow
Just say something about your life in the mirror

Yes, I still remember you—
the way you drank sweetly in the lamplight, gallant, lingering

"I long to go back, I long to go back."

No! Listen, I just remembered something:
another man on the opposite shore washing himself in the morning rain

44. 学 习

学习①

我的俊友,我中学时代的友人
贫穷使你轻盈

那寂静的木螺丝厂呢
休息……在燕子的翅膀下

神派去一个妙人
又派来一个虐待我的人

以及,笨重的人……
这些人知道,1894 就有了注水猪肉

那失败者呢?他们读书
最失败者呢?他们看电视

而她却在母亲的教育下
成长为一名有洁癖的小农学家

唉,历史学!义和团?
德国兵用机枪扫射穿红裤子的中国妇女

2010 年 9 月 23 日

---

① 选自《为你消得万古愁:柏桦诗集 2009—2012》,太原:北岳文艺出版社,2015 年,第 50—51 页。

Studying[①]

My handsome friend, my middle school friend,
poverty made you lithe

That silent wood screw factory
resting... under a swallow's wing

A god sent away a wonderful man
and sent back a man to abuse me

along with clumsy men...
These men knew, in 1894 there was already water-injected pork

And the losers? They read books
The worst losers? They watch TV

But she from her mother's education
grew up to be a little agronomist obsessed with cleanliness

Ah, the study of history! The Boxer Rebellion?
German soldiers strafed red-trousered Chinese women with machine
guns

---

① *Enclave* (8), 2014: 133.

45. 望气的人①

The Aura-Seer②

The aura-seer hurries
surveying from great heights
The dense evening mist in his eye
grows gold, geometry, and palaces

In the poor quarter, the west wind suddenly changes
a hero sets off on a thousand li journey
The aura-seer watches
his hastening grass sandals and tunic

Farther valleys smudge together
the faint scattered sound of bells
Two children sweep the pavilion terraces
The aura-seer sits in the empty still twilight

Auspicious clouds spread
the silent wizened master
sits alone, spitting fire, performing alchemy
The aura-seer sees patterns in the stones

In the village, the wind and rain are mild

---

① 前文已出现中文原诗,此处省略。
② *Enclave* (8), 2014: 133—134.

a vegetable patch, a flowing brook—
here the bright green hasn't changed
The aura-seer has already left for another summit

第七章　罗辉译诗精选

一、译者简介及翻译述评

　　罗辉,文学文化研究学者,诗歌译者,本科毕业于武汉大学,硕士毕业于美国印第安纳大学伯明顿分校,博士毕业于加拿大多伦多大学,现任职于新西兰惠灵顿维多利亚大学语言与文化学院,教授中国现代文学、汉语和翻译课程。他曾于2010年至2014年担任惠灵顿维多利亚大学孔子学院首任院长,目前任新西兰文学翻译中心的联合主任。罗辉的研究兴趣包括中国文学、电影和视觉研究,翻译研究,接受研究,比较文学和世界文学等。他的研究论文涉及中国电影、诗歌、志怪传说、犯罪小说和文化软实力问题。在他的博士论文中,他深入研究了蒲松龄的《聊斋志异》,还曾为英国广播公司(BBC)录制中国志怪传说,他的创造性非虚构作品被收录在亚洲/新西兰选集《黎明时分》(2021)中。

　　罗辉是一位文学翻译家,对中国现代诗歌尤其感兴趣。他的翻译作品曾多次发表在北美和亚洲的文学杂志和选集上。他翻译的《郑单衣诗集:夏天的翅膀(1984—1997)》(*Wings of Summer: Selected Poems of Zheng Danyi 1984-1997*)于2003年由香港第六指出版社(Sixth Finger Press)出版,在香港、伦敦、多伦多三地同时发行。该英译诗集一经推出就博得国内外诗人和评论者的广泛好评,受到读者的欢迎(该书在海内外热销),诗人郑单衣也因此名扬海内外。"中文文学界冠之以'新生代重要诗人'之名,批评家更将他与文学雄狮——狄兰·托马斯、赖内·马利亚·里尔克相提并论。在最近的'香港国际文学节'中，郑单衣被媒体作为焦点人物进行报道，影响巨大的《南华早报》甚至动用了整版报道。"①著名诗人、翻译家郑敏在其评论文章《读郑单衣诗集〈夏天的翅膀〉有感》中，高度评价了罗辉的翻译，认为其译文"极为传神，自然，冥冥中有一种引导读者深入诗人难以言传的诗情和意境的魅力"，"如此的意会神通，交映成辉的翻译之途，实在令人惊讶"。②

　　成功的译本通常出自原作者和译者的默契与投合。在好的翻译中，你会看到一首诗的两种形态（原诗和译诗）是如此的和谐统一，这背后便是译者与原作者的气质相投。罗辉翻译郑单衣正是这样的成功案例。这犹如本雅明在《译者的任务》中所描述的那样，一个文本一旦诞生就在呼唤译者的出现，此为原文本在寻找"来世"（afterlife）的过程，自然需要缘分。缘分不可强求，这给诗人和译者的启示是，双方是否彼此了解、性情投合对能否产出优质的译作十分重要。

　　罗辉对诗人柏桦高度赞赏，认为他是"一位中国当代诗歌读者和研究者必须面对的诗人"。罗辉翻译柏桦的诗歌不多，本书收录了9首，既有柏桦早期的经典诗歌，如《夏天还很远》《往事》《未来》，也有诗人新近创作的诗，如《窗户的生活》《共听蚊睫落地声——致 Jan Wagner》《学问人生》。柏桦对于罗辉的诗歌翻译极为认可，认为他是能运用精练、地道的语言将原诗的意蕴原汁原味地传递给目标语读者的优秀译者。

　　柏桦的诗歌具有很强的互文性，但罗辉认为不应该将其视为诗歌翻译的障碍。他认为译诗的过程中某些意象的损失是难以避免的，但在这一过程中也会出现"意外之喜"，而诗歌的翻译就像音乐的演奏，可以有不同的风格，译者依据乐谱，用不同的声音谱写诗意的篇章。在罗辉看来，诗歌翻译更应关注那份打动人的"诗意"，回归诗歌的本质。

（杜晨溪、杨安文　撰）

---

　　① 引自汤姆·斯蒂芬斯（Thom Stephens）2003 年在加拿大多伦多《安尼克斯集锦报》（The Annex Gleaner）发表的评论文章《郑单衣诗歌重放异彩》，全文参见 https://www.douban.com/group/topic/20139935/。

　　② 全文参见 https://www.douban.com/group/topic/10809488/。

二、译诗精选 9 首

46. 夏天还很远①

Summer is still far away

—to father

A day passes, another
Something sneaks up to you in the dark
Sit a while, walk a little
See the leaves fall
the rain drizzle
See that man walking past, in the street
Summer is still far away

So swiftly, vanished as soon as born
all the kindness an October evening can hold
Beyond beautiful, imperceptible
A vast calmness like your clean cotton shoes
Beside your bed, the past lingers, tenderly
like an old wooden box
a faded bookmark
Summer is still far away

Chance encounter, vague reminiscence
A hint of chill outside
The tired left hand reaches

---

① 前文已出现中文原诗,此处省略。

in secret, further left

to somewhere deep and far off

to a single-minded longing

Summer is still far away

No more—the quick temper, and quicker passion

Gather up these bad habits of old

Feel disappointment year after year

The bamboo hut, the white shirt—

were you not in the prime of your life?

Time to finally make up your mind

Summer is still far away

Winter, 1984

47. 往　事

往事①

这些无辜的使者
她们平凡地穿着夏天的衣服
坐在这里,我的身旁
向我微笑
向我微露老年的害羞的乳房

从重庆到南京
那曾经多么热烈的旅途
那无知的疲乏
都停在这陌生的一刻
这善意的,令人哭泣的一刻

老年,如此多的鞠躬
如此温柔的色情的假牙
她的暗火,她的烈火
她的本地普通话(是否必要呢?)
她的钢琴还要弹吗?

我已集中精力看到了
中午的清风
它吹拂相遇的眼神
这伤感,这坦开的仁慈
这纯属旧时代的风流韵事

---

① 此版本是诗人的最新修改版,与前文所引的版本有所不同。

Reminiscence

These innocent messengers
wearing ordinary summer clothes
sitting here by my side
smiling to me
giving me glimpses of their shy old breasts

From Chongqing to Nanjing
that once ardent journey
that reckless fatigue
pause in this moment so strange
this moment of kindness, and heartbreak

Old age, too many courtesies
tender, erotic dentures
bosom full of fire
her local accented Mandarin (perhaps unnecessary?)
her piano, still playing?

I focus my energy and see
a midday breeze
blowing across these knowing glances
this melancholy, this naked mercy
this amorous affair of an older time

啊,这些无辜的使者
她们频频走动,悄悄叩门
满怀恋爱和敬仰
快乐和恐惧
来到我经历太少的人生

1988年10月

Oh, innocent messengers

they shuttle back and forth

softly knocking

bearing love and reverence

happiness and fear

arriving, too soon, in my unschooled life

October 1988

48. 未 来

未来①

这漂泊人应该回去
寂寞已伤了他的身子

有幸的肝沉湎于鱼与骄傲
不幸的青春加上正哭的酒精

愤怒还需要更大吗?
骂人还骂得不够

鸟、兽、花、木,春、夏、秋、冬
俱震惊于他是一个小疯子

红更红,白更白
黄上加黄,他是他未来的尸体

1990年12月

---

① 选自《山水手记》,重庆:重庆大学出版社,2011年,第136页。

The Future

The wanderer must return
Loneliness has damaged his health

The unfortunate liver indulged in fish and pride
Unfortunate youth combined with weeping alcohol

Oh, need anger be any larger?
Curses are not enough

Bird, beast, flower, wood; spring, summer, autumn, winter
Are all surprised that he is a little madman

Redder than red, whiter than white
Yellow upon yellow, he is the corpse of his future

December 1990

49. 嘉陵江畔

嘉陵江畔①

不要怕,这只是一面镜子
面对遥远的往昔——

那天,滚烫的梯坎望不到尽头
你锻炼、奔跑……
在江边,正午,或黄昏
无眠不休的喜悦呢!
你总闻到一股怒气冲冲的味道
磅礴不绝,又难以形容

有人从巨石边飞跃入水
有人于江中追逐着驳船

而我却在那里
见到了一位淹死的青年
他面部苍白、肿胀
身上没有毛
看上去让人感到羞耻
如一具女人的尸体

从此,我失去了性别
从此,我看每个人都像死人

2010年7月25日

---

① 选自《山水手记》,重庆:重庆大学出版社,2011年,第188页。

By the Jialing River

Don't panic—this is only a mirror
facing a distant past—

The day the stone steps stretched in sweltering heat
you were exercising, running…
by the river, at noon, or dusk
in sleepless joy!
You smelled an endless torrent
of anger, but had no words for it

Some dived in from a boulder
Some chased the barge in the waves

But there I saw
a drowned youth
his face pale, swollen
his body hairless
It brought shame on the witness
like the corpse of a woman

To this day I am neither man nor woman
Now, in every living being I see the dead

July 25, 2010

50. 我的锁骨菩萨如今在哪里呀?

我的锁骨菩萨如今在哪里呀?①

日光灯的镇流声让我留意到她
北京的夏天正发生在静静的南国……
我的锁骨菩萨,真来到雪白的教室。

合上书,我开始想……亲爱的——
生命,也许不是生命,那是什么?
一种韵律性的影响,我多想得到……

(是的,《小宇宙》也曾试探过我②
一个下午,但我总是静不下来,
要么马痒磨树、要么虎食狗醉)

南国的晚课,白得很短暂,别咳嗽
我闻到了她头发和皮肤上的清凉油……
那透出灯光的小森林在窗外急切地等着

凉鞋! 理所当然来自北京的夏天——
课桌下那双即将步出教室的骨骼呀
三十七年后,她才会让我发疯!

2015年3月6日

---

① 选自《我们的人生:柏桦诗文自选集1981—2021》,成都:西南交通大学出版社,2021年,第246页。
② 《小宇宙》指匈牙利音乐家巴托克的钢琴练习曲集。

Where is My Clavicle Goddess Now?

The humming of fluorescent ballast gave me notice
A Beijing summer was unfolding, quietly in the South
My Clavicle Goddess landed, right in this immaculate classroom

Closing my book, I began to think... Dearest—
Life may not be life as we know it... then what is it?
A rhythmic aftermath... how I desire that

(In fact *Mikrokosmos* once tested me
a whole afternoon, but I couldn't keep still, one minute
horse-itchy-against-tree, another minute tiger-drunk-on-dogs)

Evening class in South Country, quick flash of white, but don't cough
I smell mint and camphor on her hair and skin...
Outside the window, a little forest in dappled light grows impatient

Sandals! The surest sign of summer in Beijing—
That pair of delicate bones, under the desk, will soon leave this room
It will be another thirty-seven years before I go crazy, for her!

March 6, 2015

51. 窗户的生活

窗户的生活

日落时分,光线好奇
透过鲜宅长窗的玻璃
在格子纤维桌布上闪耀
小纸箱里什么东西不见了?
一本解剖学书籍(我们才刚看完)
几颗彩色玻璃珠子……

这是我最初的窗户生活
一个小学生做完作业
他抬起头来看见了什么?
天快要黑了……

那这首诗快要结束了吗?
关于窗户(延绵不绝)的生活——
它的白天和黑夜的故事……
它的过去、现在和未来……
知多少?我不知道。但有一点,
亲爱的,我可以肯定:

如果真的有天堂,那就是
当光穿过我们老年的窗户时
就等你咔嗒一声按动快门!
记住,在花前,但不在月下

2023年4月19日

Life at the Window

The light felt curious at dusk
peering through the tall window of the friend's house
flickering on a checked tablecloth.
What went missing in the cardboard box?
A book on anatomy (that we'd just read)
A few colored marbles…

This is how I started my life at the window
A school kid having just finished homework
What did he see when he raised his head?
The sky turning dark…

Is it going to end, this poem
about (never-ending) life at the window—
its daytime and nighttime stories…
its past, present and future…
What do we know? I don't know. But one thing
my dear, I know for certain:

If there really is heaven, it's when light passes
through the window of our old age
you click the shutter. Remember—
flowers, yes, but no moon

April 19, 2023

52. 推 云

推云

纪念马高明(1958—2022)

白云一片去悠悠
——张若虚《春江花月夜》

死后,就是以后
而你还太年轻,还不是云……
——多多《耳朵上别着十支铅笔》

我们曾经年轻的握手
握紧过我们年轻的潮湿
记得吗,高明兄,人生多么神奇
这事发生在北碚
后来,我们重逢于北京
你致命的喉结又多出来
一股和平里的酒味
哪一次酒后?你在床上翻筋斗
在紧绷绷的卫生间
亲吻了一个妇女

好快,你的诵诗声
被制作成了木纹唱片
木与命有何关系?除了床和棺材
今天,我不想再谈
那杀了你一生的啤酒

Pushing Clouds

A lone white cloud, drifting away
—Zhang Ruoxu

Death is next
But you are still too young, too cloudless
—Duo Duo

Our once youthful handshake
held the moisture of youth.
Remember, Gao Ming, life, how miraculous!
We met in Beipei.
When we met again in Beijing
your Adam's apple had acquired the lethal flavour
of too many drinks in Heping Lane…
After a drink (which one?), you somersaulted in bed
and kissed a woman
stiffly, in the bathroom.

You read your poetry, your voice
quickly turning into LPs.
What has wood to do with doom? Bed with coffin?
Today, I do not want to talk about beer
your lifelong murderer.

我只想打听山中花岗石的价格
问问古刹里的养鹅人
他们是不是假僧?
我要种一棵树
完成末日最后一件事

从此,人放弃远眺
会让人感到平静吗?
河北平原始终一望无际,
却没有人关心,一路走好
死者的双眼已盖上两分币
从此他将不会转世为爬虫
也不会转世为牛、猪、蛇、蚕
某种病毒或可怕的蛆
人的希望啊!买风卖雨多好
他的职业是推云①

2017年5月14日

---

① 见芮虎翻译的君特·格拉斯诗集《万物归一》,成都:天地出版社,2017年,第110页。

I want to ask about the price of granite in these hills,
ask if the goose keepers in the old temples
are really monks in disguise.
I want to plant a tree
and finish my to-do list.

If one gives up the view from hereon
will one find peace?
The Northern plains stretch far into the distance
but no one bothers to look. Go well!
The eyes of the dead now covered with two-cent coins,
he will no longer reincarnate into a worm,
an ox, a pig, a snake, a flea,
some virus or menacing maggot.
Such is the human aspiration! How nice to deal in wind and rain,
to push clouds, his new profession.

May 14, 2017

53. 共听蚊睫落地声

共听蚊睫落地声
——致 Jan Wagner[①]

Jan,五十岁后,你还会
喜欢 Charles Simic 吗?
让我们回到 1997 年 9 月
柏林,一个下午,我们
边走边谈,"云是一条线索"——
我见证了云天下,你作为一名
德国大学生诗人的脚步

一个诗人是怎样成长的?
在你的祖国(统一不久)
你给我留下了这样的形象:
"一张白纸,没有负担,
好写最新最美的文字,
好画最新最美的图画。"
毛泽东的话也适合于你

Jan,你是值得期待的……
多年后,我们不谈新西兰
那就让我们来谈谈蚊子
"这狮身人面像的微小躯体"

---

① Jan Wagner(扬·瓦格纳,1971—),德国当今最有影响力的诗人之一,翻译家,文学评论家。曾获得无数文学奖项,其中两项要在此特别指出:一是 2017 年北京大学中坤国际诗歌奖,二是 2017 年格奥尔格·毕希纳奖。

We hear the sound of mosquito lashes landing

—to Jan Wagner

Jan, after 50, will you still love
Charles Simic?
Let us return to September
1997, our afternoon in Berlin
walking and talking, "the cloud was the clue"—
Under all that, I witnessed the footsteps
of a German student poet

How does a poet become a poet?
In your vaterland (newly reunified)
you gave this impression:
"A blank sheet, unencumbered,
to write the newest and finest words
to paint the newest and finest pictures"
Mao's words also applied to you

And you were the one to watch, Jan...
Now, we no longer talk about New Zealand
Let us then talk about the mosquito
"This tiny body of a sphinx"

它的睫毛(唐朝诗人写过)
落地的声音,你听到了吗?
隔墙有耳,我已经听到……

2023年1月1日

The sound of its lashes (as a Tang poet once wrote)
landing. Have you heard it?
The walls have ears, I've heard...

January 1, 2023

54. 学问人生

学问人生

我们所有人最终不过是一具尸体而已。①
——托卡尔丘克《糜骨之壤》

学问的事何必劳烦
它是人一生的事
人一生何其短暂
它是分秒之间的事

"重与细论文"何时休
答辩从来没有尽头
朝闻道,夕死可矣
每个人都是最后一人

借书还书,借钱还钱
但书依旧是同一本书
而钱不是同一张钱了
人还是同一个人吗?

一个人年轻时的贫穷
岂能等同老年的贫穷
诗穷而后工暂不谈论
穷尸、富尸皆是尸

---

① [波兰]奥尔加·托卡尔丘克:《糜骨之壤》,何娟、孙伟峰译,杭州:浙江文艺出版社,2021年,第7页。

Life Learning

We are all but corpses in the end.
—Olga Tokarczuk

Why worry about learning
Learning is lifelong
How long is lifelong
A matter of seconds

Discourse on *discours*
Defence on *différance*
Enlightened at dawn, dead by dusk
Every person is the last person

Borrowed and returned
Are books the same books
Money, the same money
A person, the same person?

How could poverty in youth
compare to poverty in old age?
Let's not even talk about poverty
and poetry—opus, corpus, corpses

在你生前,在你死后
等着吧,我关注的青春杰作
它在哪里呀?在吾国
唯有"空山不见人"

在法国"绝对的空,
又未免太简单了"
那就再次回到中国吧
多少风流,多少苦

长恨歌罢,长别离
而她永远和她十岁的
回忆同龄,而我觉得
我比我的幻象活得更久

2023年8月11日

Before birth, after death—
that stroke of genius I've been waiting for—
Where is it? In my own country:
"empty mountain, without a person"

In France: *néant absolu*
There's nothing to it!
Then return, once more, to China—
How many hearts captured, how many broken

Everlasting sorrow, everlasting
farewells. She'll be forever young
like childhood memories, and I
I shall outlive my ghost

August 11, 2023

第八章　得一忘二（范静哗）译诗精选

一、译者简介及翻译述评

　　得一忘二，本名范静哗，男，1965年生于苏北农村，本科毕业于北京师范大学外语系，硕士和博士毕业于新加坡国立大学英文系，曾在中国东南大学任教十余年，现任教于新加坡南洋理工大学新加坡华文教研中心。他兼具诗人与诗歌译者双重身份，在中文与英文诗歌创作及翻译领域均有建树。范静哗在中国、新加坡及美国等地的杂志与文选中发表了许多诗作，并多次获邀参加国际诗歌节。他的研究主要聚焦于当代英语诗歌、诗歌与视觉艺术的关系以及文化研究。在写作风格上，范静哗受到中国元白诗歌传统及美国自白派诗歌个人化表达的影响。他的译作有《梦歌77首》（约翰·贝里曼诗集）、《露易丝·格丽克诗集》、《期期之言》、《消失的岛屿：希尼自选诗集》等；诗歌作品有《口技师——赠柏桦》《习惯了一种一贯》《若无近处应有远方，或反之——赠游俊豪》等；学术论文有《漫谈珀迪诗的技术》《当沉默变成了最宏亮的言说形式——皮林茨基的创作》等。

　　范静哗热衷于翻译自白派诗人格丽克的作品，并极力向读者们推荐。他认为格丽克的文学创作并不拘泥于冷战时期的政治化风格，而是着重探讨个人政治与身份认同，凸显了女性在寻找自我声音过程中的挣扎与探索。她的审美观源自对日常生活的深刻审美体验，于平凡小事中提炼出诗意，特别聚焦于女性在日常生活里的感悟。在翻译格丽克诗歌时，范静哗深感其作品具有浓厚的心理学色彩,细腻而深入,不仅触及社会心理层面,更是涉及个人心理层面。因此,他认为只有在翻译时融入情感,深入挖掘格丽克的心理世界,才能更准确地传达出诗歌的深层意境。

在诗歌翻译过程中,范静哗特别重视情感要素与艺术技巧对于诗歌的重要作用。他会首先深入分析作者的写作特色,通过将这些特点与其他类似风格的作家进行对比归类,以选择最为合适的翻译技巧和策略。在此基础上,对于某些特定内容,他更是提出了自己独特的翻译见解,追求个性化的翻译表达,即在保持灵活自由的基础上,融入情感逻辑、技巧上的相互呼应、语境的内在统一、张力的平衡以及深邃的启发性元素。

范静哗还认为译者应该在诗歌翻译中精确再现原诗的诗意形态与灵感,包括对原语和译入语的语境、文本的视觉性和阅读感知度的考量。他特别指出,由于英语和汉语在总体审美取向上存在差异,其语言的微妙之处难以精确转换,因此译者应该选择恰当的诗歌结构,并运用相应的翻译技巧,以增强诗歌的表现力。同时,译者还需关注语境在时间、空间和性别权力等维度上的不同表现,并适当融入意象、情感以及生活智慧的传达等,来丰富诗歌的阅读体验。采用这样的方法,译者不仅能克服语言转换的难题,还能保留诗歌的原有意蕴与美学价值。无疑,译者的文学修养和对翻译语境的洞察力是影响翻译品质的关键因素。

据笔者统计,范静哗翻译了柏桦诗歌 12 首。2006 年英译了柏桦诗歌 3 首(《未来》《悬崖》《骑手》),发表于《诗歌月刊》(*Poetry Monthly*)2006 年 02 期(第 33—34 页);2018 年翻译柏桦诗歌 5 首,其中 2 首(《家居》《对酒》)发表于《诗天空》(*Poetry Sky*)2018 年夏季版,另外 3 首(《夏日读杜拉斯》《胖》《一种相遇》)未见发表;2019 年翻译柏桦诗歌 4 首,其中 1 首(《晚霞里》)发表于《诗天空》2019 年夏季版,另 3 首(《江南来信》《登双照楼》《向南方呼吸……——兼赠诗人杜力》)未见发表。范静哗作为用中英双语创作的诗人,其译诗完全是出自对所爱之诗的一种内在冲动,如其对笔者所言,他"不会为发表而译,完全是想译而刚好有时间",可见,他对柏桦诗歌的翻译恰恰是其认可柏桦诗歌的外在体现。

(文敬懿、杨安文　撰)

二、译诗精选 12 首

55. 未　来

未来①

> 天涯半是伤春客,漂泊烦他青眼看。
> ——袁枚《随园诗话》

这漂泊物应该回去
寂寞已伤了他的身子

不幸的肝沉涵于鱼与骄傲
不幸的青春加上正哭的酒精

啊,愤怒还需要更大吗?
骂人还骂得不够

鸟、兽、花、木,春、夏、秋、冬
俱惊异于他是一个体育迷!

红更红,白更白
黄上加黄,他是他未来的尸体

1990 年 12 月

---

① 选自《我们的人生:柏桦诗文自选集(1981—2021)》,成都:西南交通大学出版社,2021 年,第 72 页。该版本为诗人最新修改版本,与前文版本有所不同。

The Future

The ends of the earth are half-filled with people vexed by spring,
Wanderers cannot withstand the warm gaze from a fellow traveler.
—Yuan Mei, *Harmony Garden*

This drifter should go back,
For loneliness has already taken a toll on his body.

The ill-fated liver indulges in fish and pride,
Star-crossed youthhood is combined with weeping alcohol.

Oh, does anger need to grow stronger?
Has revilement not found its end yet?

Birds, beasts, flowers, trees, spring, summer, autumn, winter,
All are astonished that he is a sports enthusiast.

Red becomes even redder, white even whiter,
And yellow upon yellow. He is the corpse of his own future.

December, 1990

56. 悬 崖①

A Precipice

One city has one soul,
Two cities afford a dimension,
A quiet overcoat waits soundlessly.

The journey to the unknown
Timidly pushes on without any reason,
To repay a climate,
While continence is murdering time.

Do not ascend to the attic at night;
Every address is marked with a death.
The indistinct white neck
Is turning its head.

If you have made a poem at this moment,
You are making a shipwreck,
A black tree,
Or a dike in heavy rains.

Endurance becomes unfathomable,
An overstretched riddle,
The not-unravelable ear of a Diaochan coronet,
Volition vanishes without a ghost of warning.

---

① 前文已出现中文原诗,此处省略。

Organs wither suddenly and collapse;

Li Ho rode his donkey and wailed.

The hands from the Tang Dynasty will never come back.

Autumn, 1984

Translator's Note: In this poem, my interpretation is that the term "Diaochan"(貂蝉) refers to the Diaochan coronet, which was the headwear worn by male officials during the Qin and Han dynasties. Originally modeled after the fur caps worn by the Xiongnu people for equestrian activities, it later became the exclusive headwear for court attendants to the emperor. The character Diaochan in the novel *Romance of the Three Kingdoms* is believed to be named after this headwear. Diaochan is one of the Four Great Beauties of ancient China, and it is said that she had very small ears, prompting the invention of earrings to conceal her imperfection and devise a more favorable appearance.①

---

① "译按:此诗中的'貂蝉',按我的理解,第一层是貂蝉冠,秦汉时的男性官员的冠服,原为对胡冠的仿效,用于骑射,后来成为皇帝臣侍的专用冠服,小说《三国演义》中的貂蝉也从此名。貂蝉,中国古代四大美女之一,据说她耳朵很小,因此她发明了耳坠,遮掩缺陷,取得更好的效果。"

57. 骑　手

骑手①

冲过初春的寒意
一匹马在暮色中奔驰
一匹马来自冬天的俄罗斯

春风释怀,落木开道
一曲音乐响彻大地
冲锋的骑手是一位英俊少女

七十二小时,已经七十二小时
她激情的加速度
仍以死亡的加速度前进

是什么呼声叩击着中国的原野
是什么呼声像闪电从两边退去
啊,那是发自耳边的沙沙的爱情

命运也测不出这伟大的谜底
太远了,一匹马的命运
太远了,一个孩子的命运

1989年春

---

① 选自《往事》,石家庄:河北教育出版社,2012年,第112—113页。

The Rider

Piercing through the early spring chill,
A horse gallops in the dusk,
A horse from wintry Russia.

The breeze lightens, broken twigs clear the way,
And a song echoes over the vast land.
The rider leading the charge is a handsome girl.

Seventy-two hours, for seventy-two hours already,
Her accelerated speed of passion
Is still accelerating at the pace of the dash toward death.

What is the call that raps on the land of China?
What is it that flashes by and retreats like lightning?
Oh, that is love swishing by the ears.

Even destiny cannot fathom the formidable answer to the enigma;
It is just too distant—the destiny of a horse,
It is just too distant—the destiny of a child.

Spring, 1989

58. 家　居

家居①

人之一生：春、夏、秋、冬
很快，你发现了新的喜乐：
女红、饮食、财务及管理。

子曰："仁者静。"
你就在静中洒扫庭除并亲操这份生活。
"其德性举止，乃非常人。"

家务是安详的，余闲也有情：
白日，我们在湖面荡舟，
逸园和洗钵池最让人流连；
夜里，我们在凉亭里私语，
直到雾重月斜，
直到寒意轻袭了我们的身子。

曾记得多少数不清的良辰，
你长饮，说话，若燕语呢喃，
而我不胜酒力，常以茶代酒。
有时，我们又玩别的游戏，
譬如读诗或抄写：
"人闲桂花落，夜静春山空。"

这一切不为别的，只为闻风相悦，
只为唯美，只为消得这水绘的永夜。

---

①　选自《水绘仙侣》2023年修订版。

Home Life

A human life spans: spring, summer, autumn, and winter.
Pretty soon, you had found new delights:
Needlework, cooking, bookkeeping and husbandry.

Confucius saith: Quiet is the benevolent.
Quietly, you swept and sprinkled the yard and handled this living.
"Her virtues and demeanor prove her extraordinary."

Household chores were measured, our spare time affectionate.
In daytime, we rowed on the lake, and lingered
Long in the Garden of Leisure and around the Brush-Washing Pond.
At night, we spoke intimately in a pavilion
Till the moon slanted down into the thickening fog,
And chilliness seeped into our bodies.

For countless good nights as I can now recall,
You drank long, chattering like chirping and cooing,
While I, not up to wine, sated myself with tea instead.
Sometimes we enjoyed other forms of fun,
Like reading or copying poems:
"A man at leisure sees sweet olive flowers fall,
And spring mountains are empty as night grows still."

This has no other purpose but for our rejoicing over the breeze, purely
Aesthetic, for the enjoyment of this eternal night painted with water.

59. 对 酒

对酒①

操琴者在梦游中摸水,醒来;
而鱼嘴已老了,在哭。

破晓的古铜听见
一个身体,又一个身体。

磨光的金属天空有何不妥?
转眼,消息正好:

浓荫下,光阴里
那卤味不错,恰外遇酒肥人肥诗肥。

2012 年 8 月 12 日

---

① 选自《革命要诗与学问》,成都:四川文艺出版社,2015 年,第 3 页。

Before Wine

The zither-player touches water and wakes up from his sleepwalk;
And the fish's lips have grown old, crying.

The bronze of daybreak
Overhears a body, and another.

A sky of polished metal. Anything wrong with it?
In a blink, a welcome message comes:

The tree shade, where time flashes by, canopies
Delicious braised meat. Wine there is fat, so are people and poetry.

August 12, 2012

60. 晚霞里

晚霞里①

这君士坦丁堡的晚霞……里加晚霞……
就这样变成了身体的幸福,他看哭了
那逃亡者目光挑剔,诗生活何其短暂
他最后注意到的东西,将会最先消失?②

晚霞里,他遇见了往生四十年的父亲
刚刚与他在晚霞邮政总局擦肩而过——
好怪,这事怎么发生在昨晚梦中的柔佛③?
(无论记住或忘却,都令人感到高兴)

这君士坦丁堡的晚霞……里加晚霞……
就这样变成了身体的幸福,他看哭了
另一个年轻的纳博科夫像他年轻的母亲
只用指关节打人,从来不用整个拳头。

2017年2月11日于新加坡

---

① 选自《夏天还很远:柏桦抒情诗集 1981—2019》,太原:北岳文艺出版社,2020 年,第 275 页。
② 典出《圣经》。
③ 柔佛(马来文:Johor;英文:Johore),地名,马来西亚十三个州之一,位于亚洲大陆的最南端。

Afterglow

This afterglow over Constantinople... over Riga...
Turns into bliss in his body. He gazes until he cries.
A fugitive's eyes are particular, and poetic life is always
Short. What strikes his eyes last disappears first?

By afterglow he sees his forty-year-dead father,
Rubbing shoulders in front of General PO Afterglow—
How strange this should happen in last night's dream
Of Johor? (Forgotten or remembered, this is a delight.)

This afterglow over Constantinople... over Riga...
Turns into bliss in his body. He gazes until he cries.
Young Nabokov is another, who punches like his mother
When young, with knuckles instead of her fist.

Feb. 11, 2017, Singapore

61. 登双照楼

登双照楼①

1944年,日本细雪若春,
为何?为何梅花惊艳!
是那含羞的病人愈发谦逊,
忆起了杭州的一天?
烟雨里,你在探春
——小姑姑鬟影落春澜。

剧痛,年轻;剧痛,温柔;
在名古屋,风惜残红,雨培新绿,
又是一番江南天气……
瓷器窑变,国运乱变……
光景颠倒,人命关天!
"志士无一物,欲使天下一。"

多年后,双照楼上,他说
竹篮打水,日复一日
诗的风姿也是空的风姿

2013年5月23日

---

① 选自《夏天还很远:柏桦抒情诗集 1981—2019》,太原:北岳文艺出版社,2020年,第142页。

Ascending the Double-Shine Tower

In 1944's Japan, fine snow has a vernal season in it,
Any reasons? Why the plum blossoms so awesome?
Is it for a coy patient who goes ever more self-effaced,
When recalling the day in Hangzhou?
You probe how spring the spring can be in the misty rain
—A maiden's hair-knot casts its shadow on the spring ebb.

Acute is the pain of youth, acuter the pain of tenderness;
In Nagoya, winds feel for lingering petals, rains nourish greening buds,
Another version of the weather over Southern Yangtze area...
China corrupts in china kilns, the country destines to chaos,
All the sights subverted, lives subjected to heaven's way!
"Ambitious men have nothing but the ambition to unite the nations."

Many a year later, on the Double-Shine Tower, he remarks:
It's drawing water with a bamboo basket, day in and day out,
The grace of poetry reflects the grace of emptiness.

May 23, 2013

62. 向南方呼吸……

向南方呼吸……①
——兼赠诗人杜力

向南方呼吸……
因为文学与诗是女性的
（她们有怨）

再向南方呼吸……
厨师则属于精致男人
（他们害羞）

马嘶山稍暖，人语店初明
那是姚合，在送杜立归蜀。

正南？不。快回头，星期天！
我们向西南方呼吸……

2013 年 2 月 23 日

---

① 选自《革命要诗与学问》，成都：四川文艺出版社，2015 年，第 125 页。

Breathe in the South...

–For Du Li a Poet

Breathe the south, breathe in...
Because literature and poetry are feminine
(They brood over their grievances)

Breathe in the south more...
Because cooks are born for exquisite men
(They are unassertive)

"The mountain warms up as horses neigh,
The inn brightens among human voices."
That was Yao He, seeing Du Li off back to Sichuan.

Due south? Hell no! Turn round quick, Sunday!
Let's breathe in the southwest...

Feb. 23, 2013

Translator's Note: Yao He (779? –855?) was a mid-Tang poet. The quoted lines are from his poem titled "Seeing Du Li off back to Shu". The historical kingdom of Shu was based on the Chengdu Plain in Sichuan in the southwest China.

63. 胖

胖①

是豆腐让他胖了？不。是夏日的丝瓜、苦瓜、冬瓜、南瓜。
在去买菜的路上,他笑着说:连迷途的风也长胖了。

当我站住,多么静,我看见飞鹤留下的青影,胖胖的;
可我的心,我的心,我的心呀！它没有胖。

雨睡去。安拉。"伊斯坦布尔是火的圆顶"好胖哩！
朝向麦加,"我的名字叫红",红即胖

2012年6月3日

---

① 选自《为你消得万古愁:柏桦诗选 2009—2012》,太原:北岳文艺出版社,2015年,第217页。

Plump

He gets fleshy because of tofu? No. Because of summer melons:
Silky and towel-like, cooling and bitter, white and wintry, or pumpkin from the south.
On his way to the grocery, he smiles: even the straying wind gets fleshy.

When I stand still, as I am, I see the fleshy indigo shadows
Cranes left behind from their disappeared flight;
But my heart, this heart of mine, this heart in me, does not get fleshy.

The rain falls into sleep. Allah. "Istanbul as the dome of fire" is plump,
As fleshy as it can be! It looks toward Mecca.
"My name is red", and red is plump

June 3, 2012

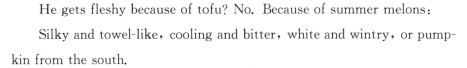

64. 一种相遇

一种相遇①

一亿年后,你总算等到了一个人,我
(又被谁指使),要来歌唱你无人识得的一生。

活着的时候,你总感觉自己年轻,死是别人的事情
可能吗,我,一个新安江的农民,会像谢灵运那样被斩首?

惊回头,安静下来,翻开书,我们一块来读博尔赫斯:
"今年夏天,我将五十岁了,死亡消磨着我,永不停息。"

或者,唉,怎么说呢,"……但愿我生来就已死去"。

因为风不仅仅在寻找树,它也在寻找弄堂与铁桥……
寻找银马上的骑手;风过耳,那死神一眼就把他从风马中选出。

2014年2月8日

---

① 选自《惟有旧日子带给我们幸福:柏桦诗选集》,南京:江苏凤凰文艺出版社,2017年,第181页。

A Way of Crossing Paths

You'll finally meet, ten billion years later, the one you'd been waiting for, and I shall

Come to sing, not knowing at whose command, the unrecognized life of yours.

When alive, you used to think you were so young that death mattered only to others.

Who could imagine a peasant by Hsin-an River beheaded like Master Hsieh, the Duke of Kangle?

Startled and silenced, I opened a book and now we'd read some Borges:

"This summer, I'll turn fifty, and death will come to wear me down, incessantly."

Or, but how could I put into words, "... I wish I were dead upon birth".

Because the wind prowls not only for trees but alleys and iron bridges as well...

And it also hunts down the rider on a silver horse;

The wind whirs by, and Death instantly spots him in the flurry of wind horses.

Feb. 8, 2014

65. 江南来信

江南来信

春风总是十里,秋雨只有一灯
看杜牧登楼的人却偏偏来自德国①

吃饭也是种玩耍解闷哩,热即苦
老信即发烫!我一碰它就喘气

为防止开春后蛆变苍蝇,冬天
我到上海乡下粪缸边用筷子夹蛆②

唉,游仙人何必非补晴天缺陷呢
跑步党应该再升一级!跑步教。

2016 年 7 月 30 日

---

① 指德国汉学家顾彬,他青年时代曾在大学研究杜牧,并写出了有关杜牧的博士论文。
② 第三节来源:从微博读到的复旦大学英语系教授陆谷孙(1940—2016)的一篇回忆文章《身在丝绒樊笼,心有精神家园》(陆谷孙口述,金雯整理)。其中一个情节让我十分吃惊:"大冷天跑到江湾乡间的粪缸旁边,用筷子夹蛆,这是为了防止开春后蛆变苍蝇。"

Letter from Jiangnan

Breeze always winds into the ten-mile spring,
Rain soaks only the depth of one lantern.
The one who watches Du Mu climbing a tower
Might well be a man from Germany. ①

Eating can be a good game to kill boredom,
The heat becomes bitterness,
The old letter burns! I touch, and it gasps.

To preclude flies swarming in Shanghai spring,
I was sent to the suburban countryside
And given a pair of chopsticks to pick maggots
Out of the winter fecal vats. ②

Alas, visitors to the immortals, do you really need
To make up the discontent of a clear day?
A gang of runners should upgrade to a congregation.

---

① A man from Germany refers to Germany sinologist Wolfgang Kubin, whose doctoral dissertation focused on the Tang Dynasty poet Du Mu (803—852).
② The third stanza has its source from a memoir of the Great Cultural Revolution by Chinese lexicographer, Professor Lu Gusun (1940—2016) from Fudan University: "In chilling winter day, we went to fecal vats in the countryside of Jiangwan, using chopsticks to pick up maggots, and this was to prevent the maggots from becoming flies in the spring."

66.夏日读杜拉斯

夏日读杜拉斯①

"玛格丽特在厨房缝衣服
天花板上吊着一个灯泡"

书是黎明,日记是黑夜
她越特别,其实越普通

怎么还是无用?但有时
一杯茶而非酒就会革命

"浴缸是具白色的小棺材"
自由童年则是贫穷童年

有人强大到自杀
有人卑贱至傲慢
有人忧伤如阶级

人平庸,人写作,人耻辱
夏天,生活的幻觉,令你害怕?

2013年6月25日

---

① 选自《惟有旧日子带给我们幸福:柏桦诗选集》,南京:江苏凤凰文艺出版社,2017年,第168页。

Reading Duras in Summertime

"Marguerite is sewing in the kitchen,
A bulb hangs down from the ceiling."

A book is dawn, a diary is night;
She is special, therefore she becomes ordinary.

How come it is still useless? Chances are
A cup of tea, rather than wine, brings about a revolution.

"A bathtub is a compact white coffin";
A childhood in freedom is a childhood in poverty.

Some become strong enough to commit suicide,
Some become mean enough to grow insolent,
Some grow sorrowful like being tagged in classes.

People are mediocre, they write, they are disgraced.
In summertime, life is illusionary. Is it scaring?

June 25, 2016

第九章　李赋康/孔慧怡译诗精选

一、译者简介及翻译述评

李赋康简介见第十一章。

孔慧怡(Eva Hung),香港知名翻译研究学者,作家,翻译家,香港大学一级荣誉文学士、哲学硕士,伦敦大学哲学博士。1986年加入香港中文大学,曾长期担任香港中文大学翻译研究中心主任,兼任国际知名刊物《译丛》主编,长达20年。她的代表作有:《翻译·文学·文化》(1999年,北京大学出版社),《重写翻译史》(2005年,香港中文大学出版社),《不带感伤的回忆》(2017年,牛津大学出版社,荣获香港中文文学双年奖),《寻找声音》(2020年,牛津大学出版社,荣获香港书奖)。她还编著了《名师各法谈翻译》(1993年)、《亚洲翻译传统与现代动向》(2000年)等学术论文集。

孔慧怡是一位多产的翻译家,仅在《译丛》杂志就发表过翻译作品50余部,翻译"《译丛》丛书"1部、"《译丛》文库"10部,对中国文学的海外译介与传播贡献巨大。她译介较多的是女性作家的文学作品,如王安忆的《小城之恋》《荒山之恋》,张爱玲的《海上花列传》(合译)。她在接受穆雷访谈时提道,"自己是被非主流、非正统的东西吸引","女性和女作家的作品一直被边缘化","香港作为一个文化边界地区,作家和作品也被边缘化,所以我的生活体验,就让我对正统的主流以外的东西特别有认同感"。她还翻译过许多当代诗歌,包括顾城、舒婷、冰心等诗人的诗歌。在其主编的《译丛》杂志第

37期(1992年),她特别推出了"后朦胧诗歌"特辑。关于诗歌翻译,她早在1991年发表于《外国语》的《谈中诗英译与翻译批评》和1997年发表于《外国语》的《译诗应否用韵的几点考虑》两篇文章中鲜明地表达了自己的观点:中国古典诗歌英译不必受格律等形式的限制,应当更为注重诗之内涵、意境和文学效果在目标语语境的有效传递。所以她更倾向"散体"译诗,主张以目的国当下的文化场域与文学规范为汉诗翻译的旨归,译诗应该符合目标语读者当下的阅读习惯。

(杨安文、刘九毓　撰)

二、译诗精选 4 首

67. 秋天的武器①

Autumn's Weapon②

Struggles go to extremes

Slogans go to extremes

Stone-eating bayonets also go to extremes

I hear air falling

It becomes you perfectly

In an ancient autumn

A man died of it

Swallowing disgust

Swallowing paper tigers

Yet people's mouths

Didn't speak into his ear

Today I'm starting afresh

Studying the variety of sacrifices

High-priced brightness

sharp revolutionary bones

At this time, in Chengdu

People all come towards me

---

① 前文已出现中文原诗,此处省略。
② Translated by Li Fukang with Eva Hung. *Renditions* 37, 1992: 107.

Handing me carts

Handing me extremes

Handing me violence and the Square

1986

68. 夏天还很远①

Summer is Still Far Away②

A day goes, a day comes

Silently something approaches you

Sit a while, walk a while

Look at the falling leaves

Look at the drizzling rain

Look at a man walking down the street

Summer is still far away

So far! Vanished at birth

All goodness enters this October night

Too beautiful, quite unnoticed

A gigantic quietude like your clean cloth shoes

Beside the bed, vague memories of the past, warm

Like an old box

A faded bookmark

Summer is still far away

---

① 前文已出现中文原诗,此处省略。
② Translated by Li Fukang with Eva Hung. *Renditions* 37, 1992: 106.

A chance encounter, perhaps bringing no recognition

A little chilly outside

The left hand is tired

In the darkness heading left

Where hidden deep within

Is that one incurable yearning

Summer is still far away

No, no longer quick to anger, nor quick to love

Picking up old bad habits

Year after year you lose heart

Your bamboo hut, your white shirt

But are you still the same?

Decisiveness is rare

Summer is still far away

69. 1966 年夏天①

The Summer of 1966②

Grow, oh, grow up with the wind

In three days, a mere three days

A heart reddened

The motherland blowing strong over the street

---

① 前文已出现中文原诗,此处省略。
② Translated by Li Fukang with Eva Hung. *Renditions* 37, 1992: 102.

Blow, oh blow, precocious youth

Blow love green, blow the thought of the land green

Look, how beautiful politics is

The summer has put on an army uniform

Ah, live, ah, rejoice

That last Chairman Mao badge

That song of freedom and home

Oh, no! that perfect paradise aged ten

December 1989

70. 麦子:纪念海子①

Wheat—in memory of Hai Zi②

"Bitter sacrifice strengthens bold resolve

Which dares to make sun and moon dance in the new skies"

—Mao Zedong, Shaoshan Revisited"

Wheat, I turn to face you

I drop my painful hands

Wheat, a badge pinned on my left breast

---

① 前文已出现中文原诗,此处省略。
② Translated by Li Fukang with Eva Hung. *Renditions* 37, 1992: 101.

I beseech you, stop this mad growth

Wheat! Wheat! Wheat!
The north will bleed for you
Look, from Anhui to my hands and then
To the heart of our motherland
A grain of spirit travels speedily

Who gave the order for the hunger strike!
Wheat! Wheat! Wheat!
A teardrop falls on a starving head
You have led the hunger strike into the 168th hour

Wheat, our wheat
Oh, wheat, the wheat of our broad land!
Stars shine in the far sky
The south weeps in its flesh

Please announce Wheat, the next step, the next step!
It will be a sacrifice
It will not be a banquet!

December 1989

第十章 李赋康/阿米莉娅·戴尔（Amelia Dale）译诗精选

一、译者简介及翻译述评

李赋康简介见第十一章。

阿米莉娅·戴尔，文学学者、诗人、译者，现任教于澳大利亚国立大学英语系。她于悉尼大学获得文学博士学位，曾任职于南京大学、上海对外经贸大学以及悉尼大学。其研究聚焦于18世纪和浪漫主义时期的文学和文化，特别关注书史、性别与文学体裁以及身体史。同时，她身兼编辑职务，担任文学杂志《香登》（*The Shandean*）①以及诗歌杂志《兔子》（*Rabbit*）②的访谈编辑。

作为一名诗人，阿米莉娅·戴尔曾在2017年举行的"华东师范大学澳大利亚文学论坛"中谈及其诗歌理念："诗歌或者说任何一种文学，都需要前期的阅读和积累，并且敢于创新，不拘泥于一些基本的艺术形式，敢于在前人的基础上创造自己的文学理念。"她认为写诗的一个核心前提是完全不关注诗本身的所谓价值。她创造了成为诗之前只是一种东西的文字，这个东西从来不想成为诗，但当我们称其为诗时，它成为了诗或者获得了诗的特

---

① 《香登》是一本专门研究劳伦斯·斯特恩（Laurence Sterne，1713—1768）生平、作品和时代的学术杂志。该杂志创刊于1989年，由国际劳伦斯·斯特恩基金会出版。
② 《兔子》是一本非虚构诗歌期刊，2011年创刊，总部位于澳大利亚墨尔本。该期刊发表包括诗歌、诗评、诗学论文、诗人访谈以及诗人的视觉艺术等与诗歌相关的所有内容。

点。作为一名诗歌译者,阿米莉娅·戴尔在"第六届中国酒城·泸州老窖文化艺术周'诗歌的创作与翻译'国际翻译论坛"中提及其译诗理念:"讨论翻译就是讨论文学在跨民族和跨语言传统中的转换,可以说翻译是在试图将一部文学作品重置于另一种语言之中,而且是在不同文化、不同时空之中。翻译是一门复杂的艺术,所以当我们翻译一首诗并且翻译得很好的时候,就可以认为这是在另外一种语言当中的创造。"换言之,她的译诗理念偏向于"创造性"重构。她尝试跳出诗歌的语言外壳,将其置于新的语言和文化环境中进行创造,保留其原有的艺术价值和情感深度,重塑原作的精神与意义。其译诗理念强调翻译过程中的创新和再创造,将翻译视为一种跨文化的艺术实践。

2018年,李赋康应诗人、诗歌翻译家海岸的邀约翻译两首柏桦诗歌,他选择了《望气的人》(1986年)和《一切黑》(2018年)两首诗,意在体现柏桦诗歌前后风格的变化。李赋康初译之后,阿米莉娅·戴尔进行了润色修改,形成译文终稿,发表于包慧怡和海岸主编的诗集《归巢与启程:中澳当代诗选(中国卷,汉英对照)》(青海人民出版社,2018年)。有关两位译者合作翻译这两首诗的讨论可详见本书第二部分的个案研究六。

(唐鹏程、杨安文 撰)

二、译诗精选 2 首

71. 望气的人①

The Air Alchemist②

The air alchemist's in a hurry walking
High, looks far out
Of evening mist his eyes
Grow gold geometry and palaces

West wind abruptly took
Thousands of miles beyond a hero
The air alchemist saw
His straw sandals and shirt agitate

Further: valley in harmony
Shattered tolls vaguely heard
Two boys sweep the terrace
The air alchemist sat in lonely lateness

Auspicious clouds, vast
Dry-boned master, silent
Solitary work on alchemical fire
The air alchemist saw patterns inside stone

Country life goes on just fine
A field of vegetables, a stream of water
While this side is still green
The air alchemist is atop another mountain

---

① 前文已出现中文原诗,此处省略。
② 选自《归巢与启程:中澳当代诗选(中国卷,汉英对照)》,西宁:青海人民出版社,2018 年,第 205—206 页。

72. 一切黑

一切黑①

飞奔的黑空气里
我听到它的喘气
敛翅伪装的黑瓢虫
打完麻药,准备
做一个开颅手术。

藏而不露黑中黑
黑夜黑发黑衣裤
哪种人？所有人！
常常他们想要的
并非他们所需的。

卷上珠帘总不如
嘴唇黑,喉咙黑
口水浪波非眼波
闪电风暴在滚动！

2018年4月27日

---

① 选自《归巢与启程:中澳当代诗选(中国卷,汉英对照)》,西宁:青海人民出版社,2018年,第207页。

Dark Matter[①]

Galloping black air flying
Gasping air hear
A dark ladybird, wing-folded
Etherized, prepared
For its craniotomy

Hide hoods darkly visible:
Black night on black hair on brief's black
What of them? All of them!
What they do are not is want
They ask for or wish for often

Pare pearl curtain unroll, unveil
Dark lips larynx dark throat through
Alluring waves of saliva desire but eyes
Rolling storm flash rolling break!

---

① 选自《归巢与启程:中澳当代诗选(中国卷,汉英对照)》,西宁:青海人民出版社,2018年,第207页。

第十一章　李赋康译诗精选

一、译者简介及翻译述评

李赋康(Li Fukang)是柏桦诗歌最早的译者。李赋康 1963 年生于四川宜宾,本名李富康,曾以"康夫"为另一笔名。1984 年,他本科毕业于四川大学外国语学院英语语言文学专业。1984 年至 1986 年,他在山东大学现代美国文学研究所攻读美国文学硕士学位,与当代华裔美籍作家哈金(金雪飞)是同学。1988 年至 1991 年,他在北京外国语大学英语学院攻读英美文学硕士学位,师从王佐良、钱青、吴冰等知名学者。李赋康热爱文学,1982 年开始写诗,在北外学习期间,结识了诗人柏桦,并在其鼓励下开始了后朦胧诗的译介工作。1989 年,他完成了包含 57 首诗歌的柏桦诗集的翻译,取名为"The Sky-watcher: Selected Poems of Bai Hua"(《望气的人:柏桦诗歌选集》)。同年 10 月,在柏桦的策划组织下,李赋康翻译了《后朦胧诗选》,该诗集收录了柏桦、张枣、海子、西川、欧阳江河、陈东东、陆忆敏、韩东、于坚 9 位诗人的 90 首诗作。1991 年至 1993 年,他还翻译了韩东的《他们诗选》中的 60 首诗,以及诗人郑单衣的 10 首诗。李赋康翻译的 3 本诗集均未正式出版,其中部分译诗在文学期刊发表:《望气的人:柏桦诗歌选集》中的 9 首诗经英国牛津大学汉学家闵福德润色后发表于澳大利亚文学杂志《我所写》(1991 年第 7 卷第 1 期),《后朦胧诗选》中的 36 首经香港中文大学翻译研究所所长孔慧怡润色后发表于《译丛》杂志(1992 年 37 期),郑单衣诗 2

首发表于诗人严力主编的中文诗歌杂志《一行》,译者名署"康夫"。其后,李赋康因忙于工作未再继续译诗。他先后在外交部北美大洋洲司、外交学院、首都经贸大学等单位从事翻译及外语教学等工作,曾兼职担任以色列第一大报《国土报》(Ha'aretz)北京代表处首席代表。1996年起下海经商,创办传科数据集团,20余年来企业规模不断壮大,经营良好。李赋康的公司主要与国外医疗机构和企业合作,这使本为英语科班出身的他英语语言能力得以保持甚至不断加强。

李赋康自1994年以来虽未继续进行中国当代诗歌的译介工作,但他钟爱文学,心中的诗歌情结始终勃郁待发。他与包括柏桦在内的许多诗人一直保持着联系。2010年3月,李赋康以笔名"康夫"与柏桦合作创设"张枣诗歌奖"。之后他断断续续有些诗歌创作,也应诗人朋友之托零星做些诗歌翻译。直到2018年,他的"诗歌之火"重新点燃,遂开始重新写诗和译诗。从其新浪博客可看到他2018年至2019年以来的成果:创作诗歌68首,翻译诗歌164首,其中,翻译柏桦诗歌94首,其中5首为复译柏桦早期诗歌,89首是新译柏桦复出后的作品,其余翻译的是俞心樵、周瑟瑟等人的诗作,以及部分古典诗词的翻译和英语诗歌的汉译。此番复出,李赋康重点在于翻译柏桦诗歌,计划陆续翻译出版柏桦2至3本英文诗集。如前文所述,李赋康重拾诗歌翻译志业,完全是出于对诗歌的热爱和对柏桦诗歌的高度认可。笔者采访李赋康时,他坦言:译诗一不能挣钱,二耗费时间,三无权威评判标准,译得是好是坏、能否为外国读者所接受很难说清楚,所以很难坚持下来。他选择继续翻译柏桦诗歌,是因为真心觉得柏桦的诗好,文本深厚,有思想、有内容、有味儿、有诗意,值得译;同时柏桦诗歌结构怪异,与古今中外互文,寓意深刻,极为难译,正因为这样,他才想挑战一般译者不敢译或译不好的柏桦诗歌文本。李赋康为人直率、干练、自信,在诗歌翻译上效率极高,通常是译前对原诗反复诵读、品味,思考如何进行有效的转换(即其所称的腹译),待思考成熟后便是一稿成文,基本不作修改。他的英文词汇量很大,自己估计约有两万,因此翻译过程中较少用到词典。据笔者观察,一般的非英语母语译者很难具备这样的英语语言能力。李赋康的诗歌翻译注重传递原诗的意境、韵味，强调对原诗结构、节奏韵律的有效转换，看重译诗在英语语境中是否具有诗意、在英语读者看来是否是诗。因此，李赋康推崇发挥译者主体性，翻译时不拘泥于原诗的结构和字面表达，大胆地进行创造性的翻译转换。据其翻译思想和风格，李赋康亦可归于"诗人译诗"的译者类型。

比较本书中柏桦诗歌英译各译本，就保留原诗的外在形式、节奏韵律以及对原诗文本的准确理解而言，中国译者李赋康明显占据上风，这得益于他的母语优势，同时也因其对文学及诗歌的热爱，他对原诗文本的理解准确而深入，对原诗音乐性的感知十分到位。这些优势使得他的译本能够准确地传递原诗的文本意义，特别是能够较好地还原原诗的"形美"，呈现原诗的韵律与音乐美感。毫无疑问，在这一点上李赋康是几位译者中做得最好的。然而，也正是因为他极力模拟原诗的韵律与乐感，译文意义的准确性受到了一定影响，有时甚至译文语言的基本规范也有所牺牲（当然从某种角度讲，作为诗歌语言，打破常规似乎是诗人惯常的做法）。此外，李赋康早期译诗的英语语言表达的准确性尤其是用词的精确度不够，语法规范意识不够强。在句法结构上，译诗中语法意义完整的句子用得少，许多诗行都采用了名词加分词构成的独立主格结构，且无规律，显得有些凌乱、不够严谨。这可能是因为译者追求还原原诗精练、简洁的语言风格，从而牺牲了句法规范。自2018年以来，李赋康再译柏桦诗歌，译诗在语言层面、原诗结构的有效转换以及原诗"声音"（尤其是节奏）的再现等方面，都有质的飞跃。

李赋康认为，译诗应当文体先行，文体是魂，对原文本的文体把握错了，方向就错了，就不能处理好语调（tone）、结构（structure）、文本肌理（texture）、词语颗粒度（granularity）四个要素。他总结道，柏桦诗歌的翻译应当先"声"，后"象"，再"意"，所以必须强化节奏；译诗时，译者不可面面俱到，应该首取原文本独特优异之秉性，或声音，或意象，或意义，然后在译文中突出呈现；好的诗歌翻译不是词的对应，而是诗意有效转换,要突破原文,有所创造。可见,李赋康延续了早期注重传递原诗节奏、韵律和意境的翻译风格,同时进一步强调译诗的有效性,即译诗语言在英语语境中是否具有诗意、在英语读者读来是否是诗。

二、译诗精选 12 首

73. 饮酒人

饮酒人①

房间里一片酒的空气
饮酒人面貌掷地有声

他就要绞死自己了
正昂起白玉般的颈子

酒杯里发出血液的歌唱啊
酒杯里荡着自由的亡灵

是谁在唱,在看灯?
是谁在一夜千金散尽?

发凉的小手,发凉的小手
还来不来得及拯救呢?

"处在黎明的头颅
陷在半夜的身子"
饮酒人反复念着这两句

1989 年 2 月

---

① 选自《山水手记》,重庆:重庆大学出版社,2011 年,第 91 页。

The Drinker

In the room the fumes of alcohol
The drinker looks metallic.

He's going to hang himself,
His silvery neck stretched high.

Inside the bottle his blood is singing,
The dead soul of liberty quivering.

Who is he, drinking and looking into the night?
Who is he, spending thousands overnight?

Little hand, little frozen hand,
Could you come in time to rescue him?

"The head abandoned at dawn"
"The body fallen at midnight"–
The drinker mutters over and over again

February 1989

74. 谁

谁

一

一些我们永不可知的名字
在我们身外消失……

这冥想中的某一个
落叶和阳光洒在他身后
那不是你,也不是我

在一次陌生的相遇中
我仿佛碰过你的手指?

握手、交谈、激动
何足道哉,我们已忘了
犹如睡眠与日复日的工作

日、夜显得局促
我想它们也是不够的
有这么多的表情变着……

二

你讲话
你低语一本书的名字
可这书不认得你

Who Is It

1

There're some names, never known to us
That disappear outside us...

There's someone, a mental image
That lets fall off his back leaves and sunshine
It's not you, nor me

A chance encounter
A vague touch of your finger?

Handshake, chat, excitement
All is trivial, and lost in our memory
Like sleep and routine work

Daytime and night time, equally meagre
To me they're not enough
With so many versions of face changing...

2

You talk
You say the name of a book in murmur
but the book does not know you

你哭嚷
为一件怒事或一件惨事
可这事不认得你

你穿的衣服也不认得你
衣柜不认得忧伤的气候

在窗台,书桌,栏杆……
在一些未知的地方……

一些我们永不可知的名字
在我们身外消失……

1985 年

You cry

angered or saddened

but the incident does not know you

The dress you wear does not know you either

the way the wardrobe knowing not the sad weather

On the windowsill, on the desk, and on the railings...

In places unknown...

There're some names, never known to us

That disappear outside us...

1985

75. 当你老了

当你老了①

往昔的桉树,尿槽,我初中时代的木床,
我不止一次写到;1971年隆冬的精液呀
真的,体内奔腾着多少埋名勃发的深河!

后来,一切都太慢了,生与死,这一对
神秘的珍宝(惠特曼或许破解了它)可
孩子们对它已失去了耐心,请原谅他们。

当你老了,你对我谈起塞内加尔,那里
过街人无论男女,总有一种童年的快乐
而垂死人终将明白,只有不死才是危险。

2014年2月8日

---

① 选自《惟有旧日子带给我们幸福:柏桦诗选集》,南京:江苏凤凰文艺出版社,2017年,第181页。

When You Are Old

Eucalyptus, urine trench, and the wood bed of my middle school
of which I've written more than once, the semen in 1971 midwinter
and of the sprouting river deeply buried in the body!

What follow are slow, so slow that, with life and death, a pair of
magic gems (Walter Whitman might know), the children
have lost patience, and pardon them please

When old, you would chat with me about Senegal, where
People cross the street, man or woman, with a bliss of childhood
The dying man will eventually see that being undead is a risk.

Feb. 8, 2014

76. 若风的人尽醉归

若风的人尽醉归①

一

有何便宜可拣,葡萄架下,秋千空荡荡;
风,塔科夫斯基式的,拜伦式的……
电影里,总会有这儿一股,那儿一股……

在南朝,但绝不会在日本和朝鲜
人尚轻凉,若风;人不爱体制,若风。

二

淘米溲溲,蒸饭浮浮,煎肉熏熏
我有咸菜一瓮,过冬,过冬……

昨天,你用箭去射母猪、射小猪
我能送你什么呢,除了一把花椒

瘦羊头重,瘦马毛长;美人硕大
有双下巴;你不管不顾,不醉不归。

2012 年 7 月 21 日

---

① 选自《夏天还很远:柏桦抒情诗集 1981—2019》,太原:北岳文艺出版社,2020 年,第 116 页。

The Wind Man Returns Drunken

1

No bargains are there, under the grape trellis, but an idle swing.
A wind, a Tarkovskyist wind, a Byronesque wind...
Always in the movies, a gust here, and a gust there...

In the South Dynasty, but never in Japan or North Korea
He who likes being alone is wind-like, and he who dislikes
being grouped is wind-like.

2

Rice rinsing, rice steaming, and meat smoking
Pickles in a jar, I winter at home, at home

The other day, you shot a mother pig with one arrow, then a baby pig with another
What else can I contribute? Except for a handful of pepper

A thin goat has a heavy head, a thin mare having long hair, and a chubby beauty
Having a double chin. You let them all go, returning drunken and drunken.

July 21, 2012

77. 丛书欲入门

丛书欲入门
——再赠臧棣

丛书欲入门？就让我们从此开头——
世间事，随物婉转，到女性结束，
可风吹来的不是麦子是海子的哭。

世间事，也有些神秘得令人心悸，
辟邪，狗舌；辟邪，蚂蚁的眼睛。
清秀人清闲呢，谁说的，我在想……
忘却吧！过分简朴其实是一种恨。
庄子爱上刻意呢，白乐天乐于感伤；

常言道兵刀可避，但老年不可避。
江南红，北国白，俞平伯[1]哭过后，
"我们飞向俄罗斯，那儿有奶奶"[2]

2015年5月15日

---

[1] 俞平伯（1900—1990），现代诗人、作家、红楼梦学家。
[2] 这句台词出自俄罗斯老电影《美国女儿》。

A Primer on Craze for Book Series
—A Second Poem for Zang Di

A primer on craze for book series? Let's begin from the beginning—
Things on the planet, up and down, all end up with women,
Though what wind brought over is not wheat but the weep of Hai Zi.

Things on the planet, can also be astonishingly mysterious—
Exorcising, by dog's tongue; Exorcising, with ant's eyes.
Smart is the handsome man to keep his hands off things, as it is said…
Let it be! Excessive simplicity can actually be a hatred.
Zhuang Zi can be trivial, and Bai Juyi can be sad;

As the saying goes, ageing is not avoidable though war is.
While the South reddens, the North is white. After crying of Yu Pingbo,
"We'll be flying to Russia, to see Granny there"

May 15, 2015

78. 呼　吸

呼吸

年轻时我们在规则中大肆尖叫
今天，我们在规则中学习呼吸
这多么难啊，请别吵了！
来，让我们从头开始练习——
一二三，一二三，一二三……

记住生命中最重要的是呼吸，
请集中一生的注意力于呼吸
来，让我们从头开始练习——

"而最主要的，你知道是什么吗？
要有轻盈的呼吸……
你听，我是怎么呼吸的——
对吗，是这样的吗？"①

这呼吸究竟出自怎样的神奇？
来，让我们从头开始练习——

1993年2月

---

① 第三节出自蒲宁短篇小说《轻盈的气息》的一段对话。

Breathing

Young, we screamed against the rules
Now, we are learning to breathe with them
Tough it could be, silence please!
Come on, let's practice from zero—
One two three, one two three, one two three

Remember that breath is vital to life
Please focus all your life on breathing
Come on, let's practice from zero—

"But the main thing, you know what the main thing is
Light breathing! And I've got it...
Just you listen how I can sigh—
It's true, I've got it, don't I?"[①]

What's the magic that produces breath?
Come on, let's practice from zero—

(Tr. Li Fukang, based on the version by Chen Zihong)

Feb. 1993

---

① Quoted lines are from "Light Breath", a short story by Ivan Bunin.

79. 致林克

致林克①

在成都,花园悠闲但很难古老
我们用鸡汁锅贴与花生米下酒
不是面包,更不是洋葱、土豆。
橘子的气味真是好闻呀,透来
一股童年的暮色,镜子——冬意
纸箱打开,怎么会有饼干味道?

香的总是年轻的,我见过多少
崭新的酸奶青年迎风跑过严寒
……香的也是老的,我见过多少
翻译家直喝到年高德劭的尽头

安身处已给淡泊之人准备停当②
可谁说孩子们就一定喜欢童话
神秘的钥匙只为开门吗?请听:
灯光并不只为了照亮,也为了消失

2014年10月20日

---

① 选自《惟有旧日子带给我们幸福:柏桦诗选集》,南京:江苏凤凰文艺出版社,2017年,第216页。
② 见林克翻译的《特拉克尔全集》之《林边的角落》,重庆:重庆大学出版社,2014年,第48页。

For Lin Ke[①]

In Chengdu, a garden can be carefree but can hardly be ancient
We drink over chicken sauce fried dumplings and peanuts
Not over bread, nor over onions or potatoes
The orange smells so good, dropping
A twilight of childhood, and a mirror—the winter feel
The carton open, smelling of biscuits, how come?

What smells good is young, and I've seen many
brand-new yogurt young men running against wind in biting cold
—What smells good is also old, and I've seen many
translators drinking to the close of their respectful old age

A residence is ready for the simple man to settle down
But nobody can be sure that children like fairy tales
Is the mysterious key for unlocking only? Look:
Light is not for lighting only, it is also for vanishing

Oct. 20, 2014

---

① Lin Ke, professor of German language and literature at China Chengdu-based Southwest Jiaotong University where the poet works as professor of Chinese literature. Lin is also a famous translator of major German language poets, including Georg Trakl, Rainer Maria Rilke, Johann Christian Friedrich Hölderlin, and Novalis.

80. 年　轻

年轻

年轻的痛带着一种斑斓的成分
年轻的苦又总是高人一等
年轻,觉得别人看上去老自己不老
年轻,觉得别人都会死自己不死

电话震惊,他从一本肉感小书抬头
什么东西隔着眼皮一跳的距离闪过——
没有事情小到可以从他指缝间溜走

惊风,还是风惊？一千零一夜,
还是永远零一天？年轻的生活常在
我们该如何将年轻与年轻人分开？

2019 年 4 月 28 日

Being Young

Young pain was a colored ingredient
Young suffering was a superiority
Young, you saw everyone old except you
Young, you saw everyone fading except you

A phone call startles him out of a sensual pictorial
There goes something at a flash of eyelid twitches—
Nothing is trivial enough to slip through his fingers

Wind surprise or surprise wind? One thousand and one nights or
Eternity plus one more day? Being young means young being
How could we split a young man from a man young?

April 28, 2019

81. 人生如梦

人生如梦
——因读陈东飚翻译博尔赫斯《最后的对话》而作

我是十岁的我,我是一百岁的我,
我唯独不是此刻的我;不用说
"每一个人在他生命中的每一刻,
都是他曾是的和他将是的一切。"

每一只蚊子都是独一无二的吗?
是的,"蚊子的宝贵与独一无二
并不逊色于莎士比亚"(博尔赫斯)。
那也是宇宙密码中的一只蚊子呀。

加尔文在日内瓦很美,顾彬①兄
加尔文在爱丁堡很美,斯帕克②
加尔文在南方美吗?道法自然——
诗,自然发生;灵,随意而吹……

诗人,说白了就是记忆之人
回到源头,惠特曼就是清晨亚当。
我梦见了我,梦者梦见了梦
唯心主义者梦见了人生如梦

---

① 顾彬(Wolfgang Kubin,1945—),诗人,德国汉学家。
② 斯帕克(Muriel Spark,1918—2006),苏格兰小说家。

Life Is Like a Dream

I'm the one me at ten, the one me at centenary
I'm me at all moments except now; needless to say
"Everyone at every moment of his lifetime
Is all he was and all he will be."

Is every mosquito unique perse?
Yes,"A mosquito has its value and uniqueness
That's no less than William Shakespeare". (J. L. Borges)
It's also the mosquito decoded in the universe.

Calvinism is beautiful in Geneva, Wolfgang Kubin
Calvinism is beautiful in Edinburg, Muriel Spark
Calvinism is beautiful in South America? Tao's after the nature—
Poetry, produces itself in itself; Inspiration, is windblown with wind—

A poet, is a person of memories perse
Back to the origin, Walt Whitman is the morning Adam
I dream of me, and the dreamer dreams of a dream
An idealist dreams of life as a dream

所有职业真不如生活这个职业
生活没有希望,又何来绝望——
终其一生,你在庐山寻找庐山
而在庐山你却找不到庐山。

2019年6月19日

All professions are but life, the one and only profession
If there's no hope in life, where's hope abandoned—
Throughout your life, you look for Mt. Lushan at Mt. Lushan
And eventually you miss out on Mt. Lushan at Mt. Lushan

June 19, 2019

82. 错　过

错过

年轻时我曾经喜欢在黄昏的小市闲逛……
观看琳琅夺目的店铺，人消失在人群里……
我的人生，常常就这样，与人间擦肩而过——

年轻时我也是写信狂，一夜写二十多封信……
日月颠倒，信来信去……，但有一封信，
我读到它时，三十七年零八天已经过去了——
它的体温还在？呼吸还在？那澳洲人还在？！

今年元旦，哀歌作古经年，邮局消失如报纸
"另一封信打开是空的，是空的，你熟睡如橘……"

2015年1月24日

Gone Missing

When young I loved hanging out in the evening marts...

Watching the glittering stores, watching the one disappear in the crowd...

That's my life, ever and always, that's gone missing out human—

When young I was also crazy about writing letters, twenty a night...

Writing to and being written to, day in day out...

With one letter, however, reaching me thirty-seven years and eight days delayed—

Its temperature still there? Its breath still there? Its writer there, still in Australia?!

On this New Year's Day, the elegy's gone for years, and so is the post office like a piece of newspaper

"Another letter is opened, empty and blank, and you're deep in sleep as an orange..."

Jan. 24, 2015

83. 易　经

易经

身体在世为了什么?
为了三十岁的摧残,
为了六十岁的保健。
到九十岁还没成熟?
只是忘了空气之哭①,
忘了着急必将出丑。

怕痛,就忍了过来。
怕黑,就有种兴奋。
怕死比死更骇人吗?
五十步不等于百步。

我们一生,又一生
在那个保密的国家,
年轻人是阴郁的人,
老人是笑扯扯的人。

2018年6月26日

---

① 何谓"空气之哭"?参见莎士比亚《李尔王》:"当我们嗅到尘世的第一缕空气时,我们都号啕大哭。"

Code of Changes

What's the body alive for?
For being tortured at thirty,
For being exercised at sixty.
Immature even when ninety?
Nothing is forgotten but the cries of air,
Nothing is forgotten but haste and stagger.

For fear of pain, we are enduring.
For fear of dark, we get excited.
Is fear of death more fearful than death?
Fifty steps are not one hundred steps.

We live one life, after another
In that code-protected country,
The young are gloomy and gray,
The old love giggles and gurgles.

June 26, 2018

84. 侏儒的话

侏儒的话

写小诗的人才知道尸体只需小墓穴。
写大诗的人真懂得人体应配大地球?

没良心,有神经;不信神,信神经
这是某大阪来的唯物论者的可爱处。

"鸟儿活在此刻,人活在过去和未来"
沐浴、吃粥、谈话,这说的悉达多?

一期一会①,一刀一拜②,一扇一舞③……
朱舜水④之后,日本有一种宁波之美!
可你说白居易之后日本就有了苏州之美。

而我能否再找到风的老师呀,在仙台
——大海,未完成……白鹤,待续飞……

2015年12月9日

---

① 日本茶道用语,"一期"表示人的一生,"一会"则意味着只有一次相会。
② 日本古人雕刻佛像,刻一刀拜一拜,或刻一刀拜三拜,后引申为小心谨慎的意思。
③ 是说来自日本的折扇之美,舞之美。
④ 我在《一点墨》之《302、日本人的怀念》里说过:"远的不说(如白居易之于平安朝),就说近的,日本人对两位中国浙江人永志难忘:一是明末清初的亡命客宁波余姚人朱舜水,二是常怀无名大志的民国亡命客绍兴嵊县人胡兰成。"

Words from a Dwarf

It's a writer of small poetry that knows a small tomb good enough for a corpse

It's a writer of great poetry that knows the great earth right fit for the human body?

Where conscience absent, the nerve comes in place; when God is not there for belief, the nerve will be the replacement

That's what makes him welcome a materialist from Osaka

"Birds live for this moment, humans live in the past and future"

Bathing, eating porridge, chatting-does it allude to Siddhartha?

Tea party and departing, Buddha carving and praying, dancing with fans

Japan had a Ningbo style of beauty after Zhu Sunshui

And the Suzhou style of beauty thanks to Bai Juyi, you added

But can I relocate the mentor of the wind at Sendai

There's the sea, unfinished, and the white crane, in flight connection

December 9, 2015

第十二章 少况（王伟庆）译诗精选

一、译者简介及翻译述评

少况，本名王伟庆，诗人、翻译家，1964年生于上海，1982年考入北京外国语大学英语系，1989年获得该校英美文学硕士学位，入职该校外国文学研究所，现供职于一家国际企业，居住在南京。20世纪90年代，少况翻译了英美诗歌和后现代主义小说家巴塞尔姆的《白雪公主》以及布朗蒂甘的《在西瓜糖里》，他是国内最早介绍美国后现代主义小说和诗歌的翻译家之一。他出版了诗集《次要的雪》和译诗集《新九叶·译诗集》（多人合译），其诗歌作品和翻译作品还发表在《中国作家》《雨花》《扬子江诗刊》《诗歌月刊》《世界文学》《江南诗》《香港文学》《一行》等刊物上。

其中《新九叶·译诗集》由包括少况等10位曾求学于北京外国语大学的诗人翻译家合作而成。"九叶诗派"是20世纪中国的一个现代诗流派，因1981年出版诗集《九叶集》而得名，也被称为"中国新诗派"。他们在诗歌中追求将人生与时代现实及艺术紧密结合，"不让艺术逃避现实，也不让现实扼死艺术"；他们大胆地借鉴西方现代诗歌，同时大胆地加以创新，使中国新诗中的现代主义诗歌逐步走向成熟。以"九叶"之名，姚风、李笠、金重、高兴、少况、树才、黄康益、骆家、姜山、李金佳等十位诗人翻译家组成了"新九叶"。"新九叶"诗人的显著特征是他们都是"喝唐诗的母乳和西方现代诗的'洋奶'"而生，而且都"亦诗亦译"，既是诗歌创作者,也是诗歌翻译者。如今,这十位诗人译者继承20世纪40年代西南联大诗人群的传统,译介自己最爱的外国诗人诗作,"以诗人的独特语境,读解诗人的精神世界",向读者呈现了涵盖7个语种、13位世界著名诗人的经典之作《新九叶·译诗集》。

作为"新九叶"诗人,外语出身的少况是外国文学的爱好者,更是译介者。他是美国当代著名诗人约翰·阿什贝利(John Ashbery,1927—2017)诗歌的知名译者。阿什贝利是美国诗坛最具影响力的诗人之一,曾获国家图书奖和普利策奖,是后现代诗歌代表人物。他的诗风格新奇,"挑战读者抛弃对目的、主题、诗风的一切既往认识,反映语言之局限、意识之不居变动"。超现实主义和先锋派艺术在其"梦境式的语言意识流"中展现,其作品鲜明地体现了20世纪上半叶现代主义兴起后西方诗歌的重大转变。毫无疑问,少况的诗歌创作深受阿什贝利的影响。在其《次要的雪》诗集分享会上,少况称自己的写作为"非经验写作",他认为写诗就是好玩儿,"诗歌不是表示什么,而是存在","非经验的东西要靠想象力,哪怕只是生活里常见的东西,你也要把它置于想象力中"。他提到自己的写作没有结构,没有结果:"诗歌对我来说是一种开放性的东西,我可能甚至会拒绝结构,有的时候写东西我就故意删掉,删掉特别明显的结构。"可见,少况的诗学观里有阿什贝利的身影,有后现代主义思潮的深刻影响。

少况翻译的柏桦诗歌主要是柏桦新近修改的部分诗作,有《消失》《致老木》《胡兰成再说》《缅甸》《这是……》《登双照楼》《阿维尼翁》《踏青》8首。从译文总体来看,少况的译诗用词精致准确,表达简洁精练,语言纯净清新,无论在形式还是内容上都对原文极为忠实。例如《消失》第三诗节:

原文:

  活着让人停不下来

  禅定就反其道而行之

  生生谓易,物物相克

  读知性诗就读臧棣

译文：

　　Living keeps one restless

　　Zen meditation takes the other way

　　life changes life, things restrict things

　　For intellectual poetry, read Zang Di

译者将"生生谓易,物物相克"译为"life changes life, things restrict things",形式上再现了原文的简洁对仗,内容上精准地传递了原文的内涵。再如《登双照楼》第二诗节以及全诗最后三行：

原文：

　　剧痛,年轻;剧痛,温柔;

　　在名古屋,风惜残红,雨培新绿,

　　又是一番江南天气……

译文：

　　Acute pain, being young; acute pain, being tender;

　　In Nagoya, **wind cherished fallen red, while rain nourished budding green**,

　　Once more a Southern China weather...

原文：

　　多年后,双照楼上,他说

　　竹篮打水,日复一日

　　诗的风姿也是空的风姿

译文：

　　Many years later, on the Double-enlightenment Tower, he said

　　Drawing water with a bamboo basket, one day after another,

　　The charm of poetry is also the charm of being empty.

译者采用直译的方式,完成了"风惜残红,雨培新绿"一句的经典迻译,译文"wind cherished fallen red, while rain nourished budding green"不但再现了原文的工整对仗,更通过精准的选词,将原文诗句的节奏韵律在译文中创造性地呈现出来:两个分句首尾单词"wind""red"和"rain""green"押韵,动词"cherish""nourish"形音对应,两句诗的音步数亦相同,实为神来之译。同样,该诗最后三行的翻译也展现了译者对原诗节奏韵律的完美再现。

(杨安文、吴佳怡 撰)

二、译诗精选 8 首

85. 消　失

消失

到来是为了遇见
遇见是为了离开
——引子

触碰,五月之夜,
轻摸他的肩膀,这好致命——
二十岁大放光明的夏天!
我首次爱上陌生的自己。

老年,闲谈有什么好?
一句,复一句……
没钱好,散步多,
与儿女们相安无事……

活着让人停不下来
禅定就反其道而行之
生生谓易,物物相克
读知性诗就读臧棣

酒后的南方山岭起伏……
不懂也是懂的一部分
夜色的本质是什么?
让一切生命消失。

2020 年 11 月 21 日

Vanishing

We come to meet
We meet to depart
—An Introduction

Touch, night of May
caressing his shoulders, how fatal it is—
The splendid summer of being 20!
For the first time I had a crush on my strange other.

Old age, what's good of idle talking?
One sentence after another...
Good to have no money and walk a lot
At peace with one's own children...

Living keeps one restless
Zen meditation takes the other way
life changes life, things restrict things
For intellectual poetry, read Zang Di

After drinking, the mountains in the south undulate
Incomprehension is part of comprehension
What is the essence of night?
To make all the lives vanish

Nov. 21, 2020

86. 致老木

致老木①

> 我是老木。
> 我于2016年回了中国。
> 近期,我周末来一趟成都。
> ——老木致柏桦短信

卡夫卡说过这句话吗?
"我们可与上帝交谈,
却不可谈论上帝。"

狂人,随走随哭的人?
上坡下坡,去了巴黎,
又去瑞典,他到底是谁?

五查经《耶利米书》:
"你也必默默无声,
刀剑必追赶你"——

"危险变得比保险更可靠"
这还有可能反过来吗?
我好像患了幽闭症。

---

① 老木(1963—2020),本名刘卫国,1980年代初北大四才子之一,另三位是西川、海子、骆一禾。

For Lao Mu

I'm Lao Mu.
I came back to China in 2016.
I will pay a visit to Chengdu some weekend soon.
—Messages to Bai Hua from Lao Mu

Did Kafka say this?
"We can talk with God,
But we can't talk about God."

A mad man? A man who wept as he went,
up and down the hill, went to Paris,
And then to Sweden, who on earth was he?

I finally found this In Jeremiah:
"You too will be silenced;
The sword will pursue you"—

"Danger becomes more reliable than insurance"
Could it be the other way around?
I seem to become claustrophobic.

萍乡,老木永恒的家乡
鸽子在白杨树上筑巢?
这地上有酱油,不是血。

2018年4月4日

Pingxiang, the eternal hometown of Lao Mu
Do doves build their nests in the poplars?
There is soy sauce on the ground, not blood.

April 4, 2018

87. 胡兰成再说

胡兰成再说

我们总是离路很近,
走上去,路活了;
我们总是离风很近,
迎上去,风来了。

我们总是在空山
听到声音,不可应答;
我们总是在深夜
听到声音,不可应答。

你说梅归隐,马如龙,
书是姿不是法;
你说花是思的风韵,
文章是永恒肉身。

你说贱人习艺,
而桃之夭夭只是个兴;
你说衣食艰难,
但周礼为世界开风景。

2013 年 2 月 22 日

Hu Lancheng Says Again

We are always so close to the road,
walking on it and it comes alive
We are always so close to the wind,
facing it and it approaches

We always hear voices in the empty mountains,
unable to respond
We always hear voices in the dead of nights,
unable to respond

You say plum blossoms return to seclusion and horses race like dragons;
Calligraphy is rather a posture than a technique
You say flowers are charm of thoughts;
writings are immortal flesh

You say mean people learn craftsmanship,
taking blooming peach flowers as inspiration
you say in hard times,
the Rites of Zhou presents the world a new landscape

Feb. 22, 2013

88. 缅　甸

缅甸

聂鲁达吗,是的,旅人聂鲁达
让我留心到了1927年缅甸的气味
"那似乎是宝塔上的苔藓,
是香料和粪便,花粉,火药……"

年轻的叶芝在伦敦自言自语:
我爱上了这世上最美的女人,
想想吧,她给我的生活带来了
一种缅甸皿型钟的声响……

缅甸闪耀着裸身搬运工。① 还有
中国、日本、越南、印尼、新加坡……
还有从一座纪念碑的碑文(一首诗)
华莱士·史蒂文斯发现更多的搬运工。

缅甸的英国警察呢,写作之外
"我认为最大的快乐就是
将刺刀捅进佛教徒的躯体。"②
刹那间,奥威尔,人得以永生③——

---

① 参见华莱士·史蒂文斯的诗《一座纪念碑的碑文》,马永波译。
② 见乔治·奥威尔《猎象记》,载《我为什么写作》,南京:南京大学出版社,2008年,第117页。
③ 唐代临济宗开山人义玄禅师说:"欲得如法见解,但莫受人惑。向里向外,逢着便杀:逢佛杀佛,逢祖杀祖,逢罗汉杀罗汉,逢父母杀父母,逢亲眷杀亲眷,始得解脱,不与物拘,透脱自在。"

Burma

Neruda? Yes, the traveler Neruda
Draws my attention to the smell of Burma in 1927.
"That seems to be the mosses on the pagodas,
the perfumes and excrements, the pollen, the gunpowder..."

The young Yeats said to himself in London:
I fall in love with the most beautiful woman in this world,
To think about it, she brought into my life
a sound as if a Burmese gong...

Burma shining with naked porters. And also
China, Japan, Vietnam, Indonesia, Singapore...
And from the inscription on a monument (a poem)
Wallace Stevens discovered more porters.

What about British police in Burma? Besides writing,
"I thought that the greatest joy in the world would be
To drive a bayonet into a Buddhist priest's guts."
For an instant, Orwell, one becomes immortal—

后记:新华社2016年11月22日电:这几天,缅甸人抬着家里养的猪,一窝蜂向中国境内逃难。这几天,向里向外,逢着便杀:逢佛杀佛,逢祖杀祖,逢罗汉杀罗汉,逢父母杀父母,逢亲眷杀亲眷……

2020年11月30日

Postscript: November 22, 2016. According to Xinhua News Agency, recently, Myanmarese refugees carried their home pigs and swarmed to China border. Recently, inward and outward, killing when meeting; killing a Buddha when meeting a Buddha, killing ancestors when meeting ancestors, killing arhats when meeting arhats, killing parents when meeting parents, killing relatives when meeting relatives...

89. 这是……

这是……

这是你的世界,一个小世界。
这是你的事情,天大的事情。

这是一双黑布鞋,令人害怕。
这是一双黑棉鞋,令人害怕。

这是空鞋子,让我想到死人子。
这是空园子,让我想到风信子。

这是柏林未遇之大变局?
这是遍地土耳其肉夹馍①!

这是生活,也是电影。
这是照片,也是死亡。②

这是……
这是……

2020年12月6日

---

① 土耳其肉夹馍(Doener),风靡德国柏林的一种街头快餐食品。
② 生活是电影,照片是死亡,苏珊·桑塔格的一个观点。

This is

This is your world, a small world.
This is your business, a big business.

This is a pair of black cloth shoes, scary.
This is a pair of black cotton shoes, scary.

This shoe is empty, reminding me of dead man.
This garden is empty, reminding me of hyacinth.

Is this the great unprecedented change of Berlin?
This is the ubiquitous doner kebab of Turkey!

This is life, and also a movie.
This is a photograph, and also death.

This is...
This is...

Dec. 6, 2020

90.登双照楼

登双照楼①

1944年,日本细雪若春,
为何? 为何梅花惊艳!
是那含羞的病人愈发谦逊,
忆起了杭州的一天?
烟雨里,你在探春
——小姑姑鬟影落春澜。

剧痛,年轻;剧痛,温柔;
在名古屋,风惜残红,雨培新绿,
又是一番江南天气……

瓷器窑变,国运乱变……
光景颠倒,人命关天!
"志士无一物,欲使天下一。"
多年后,双照楼上,他说
竹篮打水,日复一日
诗的风姿也是空的风姿

2013年5月23日

---

① 选自《夏天还很远:柏桦抒情诗集 1981—2019》,太原:北岳文艺出版社,2020年,第142页。

Ascending the Double-enlightenment Tower

1944, the fine snow of Japan was like spring,
Why? Why plum blossoms so stunning?
Was it because that shy patient became more unassuming,
Remembering one day in Hangzhou?
You were visiting spring in the misty rain,
—The hair-knot of little aunt casting shadows on spring waves.

Acute pain, being young; acute pain, being tender;
In Nagoya, wind cherished fallen red, while rain nourished budding green,
Once more a Southern China weather…

China kiln in transmutation, a nation in amputation…
The time was overturned, but life was precious!
"Patriots don't have one thing, yet desire to make the world one!"
Many years later, on the Double-enlightenment Tower, he said
Drawing water with a bamboo basket, one day after another,
The charm of poetry is also the charm of being empty.

May 23, 2013

91. 阿维尼翁

阿维尼翁①

没有生活就没有故事和细节
阿维尼翁,关于南方的极限
关于灰长袍、抒情的老太婆……
"到这里以后,我就得掉头。"②

阴雨绵绵的阿维尼翁啊,我
足不出户,我在火炉旁读书:
"人们开始以怀疑的目光看
罗讷河了。……看门人擦着
嘴巴,拿着一串钥匙走来了。"

阿维尼翁,是回忆美化了你?
还是你的气息像钟声般传来?
阿维尼翁,是风景还是命运!
让我想想,应该是它的发音——
在冬天明亮而强烈的阳光下。

2019 年 11 月 20 日

---

① 选自《我们的人生:柏桦诗文自选集(1981—2021)》,成都:西南交通大学出版社,2021 年,第 387—388 页。

② 诗中引文见亨利·詹姆斯(Henry James,1843—1916)的游记书《漫游法兰西》(*A Little Tour in France*)。

Avignon

Without life there will be no stories nor details
Avignon, about the southern extremity,
about the gray robe, the old woman expressing herself...
"after which I was to turn round and proceed back."

Oh Avignon soaked in the rain, I
stayed indoors and read by fireside:
"and people had begun to look askance at
the Rhone... the guardian, who arrived
with a bunch of keys, wiping his mouth."

Avignon, was the memory that embellished you?
Or your smell that came like a bell?
Avignon, more fate than scenery!
Let me think, must be its pronunciation
In the bright, strong sunlight of the winter

Nov. 20, 2019

92. 踏 青

踏青

踏青人不愿意回家
青蛙蹲坐在梧桐树下
那不能生育的骡子呢
四脚不停地绕圈拉磨
它是怎样来到世上的?

我看到老师投掷皮球
我看到抒情人手握细沙
素食者磨着两个核桃
孩子们牵起风筝奔跑
老年从来就是命令
断肠当场就是天涯

"1858年4月21日。
美好的一天。在花园
和井边,与农妇们做爱。
我好像着魔了一样。"
是的,托尔斯泰,这一天
好美。读你的日记……

还有更美的事吗?
道德的纯洁性来自
那农民雪白的牙齿。
而踏青,瞬间成为了
我们神奇的往昔。

1989年3月7日

Spring Outing

Spring outing people are reluctant to go home
Frogs squat in the shade of a plane tree
How about that sterile mule that keeps
Circling and dragging the stone mill
What has brought it into this world?

I see teachers throwing the ball
I see the expressive one holding sands
The vegetarian grinding two walnuts
Children running by with kites
Old age has always been an order
The heart breaking spot is the end of the world

"April 21, 1858.
A beautiful day. In the garden
And by the well, making love with peasant wives.
It seems that I was possessed."
Yes, Tolstoy, what a beautiful
Day! Reading your diary...

Are there more beautiful things?
The moral purity comes
From the white teeth of peasants.
And spring outing instantly becomes
Our miraculous past.

March 7, 1989

第十三章　姜山译诗精选

一、译者简介及翻译述评

姜山,1971年出生,现居上海、悉尼。他1994年毕业于北京外国语大学,1999年毕业于美国印第安纳大学商学院,大学毕业后一直从事金融相关职业,曾就职于华尔街投行。作为一名文学爱好者,姜山在大学时代开始写诗,但其真正的诗歌创作却是在2008年之后,金融危机让他重新开始写诗。他在诗歌创作之余也从事诗歌翻译,翻译英语、法语作品,出版有《危兰》《给歌》《从雨果到夏尔——法语诗里的现代性》《新九叶·译诗集》《爱不可能——普鲁斯特诗选》等。

谈及对诗歌的理解,姜山认为,诗歌在任何时代都应该是属于少数人的。但是,诗歌的艺术形式又不能限制得太窄,不能说写在纸上的一行行文字是诗,别的形式就不是诗。他认为用影像也可以拍出诗来,或者用声音也可以制造诗。而就他个人而言,写诗完全是个人的东西,诗来源于生活。他创作的诗歌,更多的是自己的生活体会和感受。他认为写诗大概是两方面,一方面是跟别人的一种交流,另外一方面是自我的一种慰藉。他对优秀诗人的解读犹如他在"中国诗歌网"的名家专访中所提及的:"从一扇小门进去,带你走进大房子的诗人,可能是一个好的诗人。用切身的感受,而不是想象的感受,从一个角度带你去认识世界。这种认识不同于科学,通过科学去认识世界,会让你有一种满足感和成就感。而诗歌带来的那种发现,可能更多的是一种慰藉。"

谈及诗歌的译介,他在2020年《后疫情时代的诗歌译介与交流》中指出:"诗和译,作为一种认知、表达、慰藉,我会借之尝试寻找与我们的历史相似的历史中的诗人们,阅读他们,把他们的经验变成我的经验一部分。这包括真实的历史,比如上一次全球化解体、修复、再生,也包括想象的历史,比如小说《一九八四》所描述的世界。(需要指出的是,真实和想象的界限业已模糊。)这种交流与传播,则可能是'比特币主义'的:分布式、点对点、加密、不可篡改……"对于姜山而言,阅读、翻译和创作是共生的,他曾说:"对我来说翻译可能意味着深入的阅读,从阅读到翻译的路很长,但是开始了翻译才能把这些内容变成自己的东西。"

姜山翻译的柏桦诗歌是柏桦新近创作或修改的作品,有《重写悬崖》《消失》《还有什么比现实主义老得更快?》《最后》《相遇》《当你老了》《死亡不喜欢唐突》7首。不难发现,他所译之诗多围绕现实主义,探讨时间、生命、死亡、城市、变迁、自我意识、孤独、爱与分离等主题。总体而言,译者倾向于异化翻译策略,多采用直译方法,力求将原诗所含的本土意象及隐喻进行直接呈现。例如,将《消失》中的"土地革命"直接译为"land reform",将《当你老了》中的"梆硬的木床"译为"bone-hard hardboard dorm bed",此类直译的处理方式在某种程度上给目标语读者带来诗歌的"陌生化"效果。

然而,在诗歌句架结构和诗句断行方面上,译者却时有创造性的调整。如《还有什么比现实主义老得更快?》第一诗节前三行:

原文:

> 西欧教人生活,东欧教人死亡
> 亚洲我不谈,非洲我不谈……
> 拉丁美洲很魔幻,谈了也白谈

译文:

> West Europe teaches how to live; East Europe
> Preaches how to die. I do not talk about Asia
> Nor Africa. Latin America is magic

Making any discussion meaningless.

此处,译者将原诗的三行调整为四行,不同于原文的断句,这大概是为了让译文在形式上如原诗一般整齐。再如《死亡不喜欢唐突》第一诗节前两行:

原文:
    死亡不喜欢唐突
    喜欢逐渐适应生活

译文:
    Never liking to be abrupt Death
    Prefers gradual acclimation

通常而言,在译文中"Death"这个句子主语宜放在第二诗行的开头,或者至少放在第一诗行的开头。但译者却将其放在了第一诗行的末尾,显得异常"唐突",正如译者所言,这样的调整在某种程度上切合了该诗的"唐突"主题。

此外,译者在译诗中比较注重韵律的呈现。例如,《消失》中的"题记":

原文:
    有一句童谣就是这么唱的
    不睡觉,夜老虎把你吃掉

译文:
    As one ditty goes, stay up
    And the Night Tiger'll eat you up

显然,译者通过调整断句,呈现"stay up"与"eat you up"押尾韵的诗歌效果。再如《当你老了》第一诗节第四至七诗行:

原文：

> 那1970年隆冬的精液
> 我体内奔腾过的多少勃发的深河！
> 唯有十四岁的黑夜知道
> 委屈的永恒的不为人知的黑夜呀！

译文：

> The semen in the dead of winter of 1970
> Such streams flowing furiously deep from my **body**
> Known only to the nights of a fourteen-year old **boy**!
> Such obscure, under-appreciated, eternal nights!

译者在译文中增译出"boy"，在准确传达原诗内涵的同时，通过"boy"与上一诗行的"body"押上尾韵，令译诗更具诗意。

此外还值得一提的是，由于译者姜山亦从事法语翻译，他在翻译《最后》时将原文中的"这就是生活"处理为了"c'est la vie"，这种法式的处理也是他的鲜明特点之一。再如《最后》一诗的最后两行：

原文：

> 一天，1942，越南西贡拍来了电报
> "通过小哥哥的死发现了永恒"，最后！

译文：

> One day in 1942, a telegram came from Saigon, Vietnam
> "Eternity came across the death du Petit Frère", at last!

"小哥哥"被译为法文"du Petit Frère"（小哥哥）。当然，此处不单是译者对法文的情结，更是为了提示读者，原诗引用的这句话取自法国作家玛格丽特·杜拉斯的知名小说《情人》（*L'Amant*），小说原话为"Comme plus tard l'éternité **du petit frère** *à* travers la mort."（就像后来通过**小哥哥**的死发现永恒一样）。

（唐鹏程、杨安文　撰）

二、译诗精选 7 首

93. 重写悬崖

重写悬崖

一个城市有一个人
两个城市有一个向度
三个城市、四个城市……
一时多少城市
陌生的旅行渴望着
去报答一种气候
克制正杀害时间

夜里别上阁楼
一个地址有一次死亡
那危险藏在哪里？
藏在鲜宅吗？
还是藏在西师？
那依稀的白颈项
将转过头来

此时你制造一首诗
就等于制造一艘沉船
一棵黑树
一片雨天的堤岸
一件空了的衣服
甚至一首四手联弹的
匈牙利狂想曲

A Re-write of the Cliff

One person, one city

Two cities, one dimension

Three cities, four...

How many cities all at once

An unfamiliar journey craves

For reciprocating a certain climate

Restrains are only killing the time

Avoid the attics at night

One death, one address

Wherein then hides the danger?

In the House of Xians?

Or, in the Southwestern Normal College?

That waxen neck in the mist

Is turning back

Now if you weave a poem

You are to fabricate a sunken ship

A dark tree

A riverbank in a rainy day

A piece of clothing emptied of its wearers

Even Hungarian Rhapsodies

Played by four hands

忍耐变得莫测
过度的谜语……
无法解开的貂蝉的耳朵
意志无缘无故地离开
须要一别四十年吗
那结果终于出现了
她的骨灰归于尘土

2023 年 11 月 21 日

Forbearance is turning unpredictable
A riddling excess...
Indecipherable ears of an ancient courtesan-spy
The willpower resigns for no reason
Necessary for a separation to last forty years
Till the full consequences shows
To dust finally turn her ashes?

23 November 2023

94. 消　失

消失

有一句童谣就是这么唱的
不睡觉，夜老虎把你吃掉
——题记

第一次触碰，五月之夜
轻摸他的肩膀，这好致命——
二十岁大放光明的夏天！
我首次爱上了陌生的自己
你爱上了你自己的反面

现在，你停止了触碰
我们开始谈吐，一来一回
说个不停、走个不停……
你平静之后的回忆怎么
仍显得急，并一直朝前

因为从小你已经知道
一直朝前是生命的本能
但下面这点你就不知道了：
我们到来是为了遇见
我们遇见是为了离开

酒后的南方山岭起伏
"横看成岭侧成峰"

Disappearing

As one ditty goes, stay up
And the Night Tiger'll eat you up
—Epigraph

The first touch, on the evening of May
On his shoulder, is near fatal—
The summer of the 20th year shines so!
I fell in love with myself as a stranger
As did you with you opposite yourself

Now, you've stopped touching
And we start talking, back and forth
Walking along, on and on...
Why the haste in remembering
After the calm falls, and always forward

For you know from very young
Always forward is the instinct of living
While you never realize
We come so we meet
We meet so we part ways

The southern hills wave after a drink
"A range viewed in face and peaks from the side"

不懂也是懂的一部分
那夜色的本质是什么?
让一切生命消失

2020 年 11 月 21 日
2024 年 1 月 2 日

Incomprehension's part of comprehension
Is it the essence of the night
To disappear all in a life?

January 2, 2024

95. 还有什么比现实主义老得更快？

还有什么比现实主义老得更快？

西欧教人生活,东欧教人死亡
亚洲我不谈,非洲我不谈……
拉丁美洲很魔幻,谈了也白谈
人的生命其实多么的简单
人生来就要在短暂的一生里劳作
还有什么比现实主义老得更快？

有个苏州人来预言:螺蛳三年
疫情三年,摸爬滚打又三年
而他说隔绝也是一件好事
这不,纳博科夫就曾经说过:
"隔绝意味着自由和发现。"
还有什么比现实主义老得更快？

暴风雨！暴风雨！暴风雨！
是莎士比亚？还是土地革命？
古今中外不说也罢,要说就说
那桌子的长抽屉,很难拉开！
这是穷人家庭的一个标志——
还有什么比现实主义老得更快？

2022年3月30日

There's Anything Aging Faster than Realism?

West Europe teaches how to live; East Europe
Preaches how to die. I do not talk about Asia
Nor Africa. Latin America is magic
Making any discussion meaningless.
In truth one's life is so simple
Nothing but toiling from end to end.
There's anything aging faster than Realism?

Someone at Suzhou predicts: mandala in snail shell
For three years, pandemic three years, keep hustling
For three more years. Quarantine
Says he, can well be a good thing.
Is it that Nabokov once said
"Isolation means liberty and discovery"?
There's anything aging faster than Realism?

Tempest! Tempest! Tempest!
Is it Shakespeare? Or the land reform again?
Forget about home and abroad, now and then,
If there's one thing worth mentioning
It is damn hard to draw out the drawer of that desk
A chronical ill for poor households—
There's anything aging faster than Realism?

30 March 2022

96. 最　后

最后

那从我身边走过的人不久将死去
一个两个三个,百个千个万个……
人不会错过尘土,人错过的是人
我错过的不是人世,错过的是你

铁笑后有竹笑,我们有苦恼人的笑,
悲伤吗?我们笑起来的声音响极了。
是的,人的眼泪有一种愉悦之情,
这就是生活,无论黑人、白人、黄人……

一天,1976,在重庆巴县龙凤公社
猪发出隆冬热腾腾的咕噜声,最后!
一天,1942,越南西贡拍来了电报
"通过小哥哥的死发现了永恒",最后!

2012年10月15日

At Last

Those who pass by me will soon pass away
One, two, three and counting, hundreds, thousands, tens of thousands...
One never misses the dust, one misses only one another
It is not this life that I waste, it is you that I do.

Bamboo laughter after iron laughter, it is bitter laughter that we have,
Out of sorrow? It's real loud when we laugh.
Yes, there's an air of joyfulness in one's tears,
C'est la vie, be it for the black, a white or a brown-skinned ones.

One day in 1976, atLongfeng Commune, Ba County, Chongqing City
Pigs were steaming bubbling in the dead of winter, at last!
One day in 1942, a telegram came from Saigon, Vietnam
"Eternity came across the death du Petit Frère", at last!

15 October 2012

97. 相　遇

相遇

活着时你总感觉自己年轻
并将永远年轻下去……
老或死都是别人的事情
这是真的吗？终于有一天
年轻的你，作为还未成名的诗人
满怀远大的抱负
在你的家乡——夜郎
像谢灵运那样被斩首了
生命戛然结束，有何不幸可言

五百三十六年后
你又转世来到这个国家
又碰巧成为了一个诗人
这次有人说你碰到了好运
即便"你只是索引中的一个词"
但你总算等到了一个人——
我（又被谁指使？）
要来歌唱你同样无人识得的一生
小诗人，我的兄弟，听，

那次暮春课堂午间休息
刚上小学的你，趴着的头动了
动了要罚站，你总逃不脱
那次风不仅仅在寻找树、
山峰、平原、河流……

Encounter

While alive you always feel young
And forever young...
To age or to die, that is other people's concern
Is this true? There comes a day
A young version of you, a poet of little renown
Full of great expectations, is
Decapitated, in the fashion of Xie Lingyun
In your hometown – Yelang
A suddenly-truncated life, what woe is there to be found?

Five hundred and thirty-six years later
You reincarnates in this country
As a poet by chance, again
This time around people say
That you have the good fortune
Albeit "you remain a mere entry in the index"
Of encountering someone–
I (under whose arrangement is this then?)
Who sings about your life no one knows of
As a lesser poet, my brother, listen

During a noontime class recess in that late spring
You, who just start school, are given a time-out
For fidgeting while ordered to nap
With head down, you cannot escape
From this wind, it seeks out not only trees
Hills, plains, rivers...

也在寻找弄堂和桥梁……
寻找那匹白马上的骑手……
风过耳——死神煞白
一眼就把你从煞白中选出

当时,你还来不及发抖!
我说过吗,每个人的童年
都应该有个地方可以透气
你的地方在哪里呀,来,
让我们抬起头,张开口呼吸……
很快你就安静下来翻开书
用中文朗读博尔赫斯——
"今年夏天我将五十岁了,
死亡消磨着我,永不停息。"

唉,这一次,怎么说呢?
大劫前蚕有四眠小劫……
你不得不学那文王小心翼翼
你不得不在某本书中发现自己
易经？还是佛经？
圣经？还是可兰经？
韵律中的万类变化莫测……
你其实永远不知道你是谁
但我知道我将与你相遇

2014年2月8日

But also alleys, bridges…
As well as the rider of that white horse…
The wind blows by—Death so pale
Picks you out right away from the paleness

In that moment, you have no time to shudder!
Have I not said that everyone
Needs breathing room during childhood?
Where's your room? Come on
Chin up, mouth open, let's breathe…
Soon you are quiet again and open a book
Start reading Borges in Chinese, aloud—
"This summer I will be fifty years old.
Death is using me up, relentlessly."

Alas, this time, how to put it?
A silkworm sleeps through four smallkalpas before one great kalpa…
You have to learn treading with caution
Following the footsteps of Sage-King Ji Chang
You have to identify yourself in a certain book
The Yi-Ching? The Sutras?
The Bible? Or, the Quran?
All the tens of thousands of unpredictable rhyming mutations…
You never find out who you are in fact
Meanwhile I always know you and I meet at last

8 February 2014

98. 当你老了

当你老了

一

那往昔的十五中学
我初中时代梆硬的木床
我不止一次写到……
那1970年隆冬的精液
我体内奔腾过的多少勃发的深河!
唯有十四岁的黑夜知道
委屈的永恒的不为人知的黑夜呀!

后来,生与死,隐姓埋名
这是一对神秘的珍宝
(世上很少有人知道)
惠特曼或许已经破解了它
可孩子们对它却失去了耐心
觉得一切都太慢了
人生,请原谅他们吧

二

风乍起! 吹得辽远——
达喀尔汽车拉力赛结束了
在冬日最后的晚宴上
那德国车手刚接受了大家
有礼貌地依次告别

When You Are Old

1.

The past No. 15 Middle School
The bone-hard hardboard dorm bed of my junior-high years
That I revisit repeatedly by way of writing...
The semen in the dead of winter of 1970
Such streams flowing furiously deep from my body
Known only to the nights of a fourteen-year old boy!
Such obscure, under-appreciated, eternal nights!

Then, life and death, that anonymous
Mysterious pair of treasures
(Known to so few on earth)
Walter Whitman might have had it decoded
For which the youngsters have lost patience
Nothing is fast enough for them
Life, forgive them for this, please

2.

The wind rises. So immense so far-reaching—
The finish line of the Dakar Rally
The last feast of the winter season
The German racer has just received
The courteous farewells paid by the folks one by one

有个中国承包商突然站起来
流下了安静的眼泪

现在,当你老了
你又对我谈起塞内加尔
人们还会为你当时的哭泣感到尴尬吗?
那里的人一年四季无论男女
都有一种童年的快乐……
而怕死人难道终将不明白
只有不死才是危险的?

2014年2月8日

A Chinese contractor rises unexpectedly
Shedding tears in the quietness

Now, when you are old
You recount Senegal to me once more
Anyone still embarrassed by your crying then?
Men and women there all year around
Are blessed with a mirth found only in childhood…
Is it ignorance the fear for the dead
Of the dangers of being alive?

8 February 2014

99. 死亡不喜欢唐突

死亡不喜欢唐突

死亡不喜欢唐突
喜欢逐渐适应生活
所以不经过三十年
你怎么可能想起这个人?

三十年,她生活在别处
但你感觉她已经死了
三十年,你心绪平静
因为你从来不为她难过

日月之行,星汉灿烂
现在,刚刚,她真的死了
她的"前我、远我、无我"
开始进入浩瀚的裂变……

在哪里?但不会在这里
三十年、三百年、三千年……
她下一次死亡,谁知道
会在第几个三十年之后?

2024年7月2日

Never liking to be abrupt

Never liking to be abrupt Death
Prefers gradual acclimation
So how will you recall this person
Not until thirty years'll have passed?

For thirty years elsewhere she lives
Though you do sense her absence
You live in a thirty-year inner peace
Never for her caught up in sadness

Time flies, constellations constantly bright
Now, just now, she dies a real death
All of her "before me, beside me, without me"
Start merging into an immense fission

Where? Anywhere but here
For thirty years, 300 years, 3000...
Next death of hers'll come, who can divine
After which another thirty-years?

2 July 2024

第十四章　菲奥娜·施-罗琳
（Fiona Sze-Lorrain）译诗精选

一、译者简介及翻译述评

　　柏桦诗歌的英译者中，翻译其诗歌数量多且在刊物或诗集正式发表最多的是菲奥娜·施-罗琳。菲奥娜是一名青年诗人、文学翻译家、古筝演奏家。她1980年在新加坡出生，父母是华裔知识分子。她从小接受了良好的教育，学习了古筝、钢琴、书法、戏剧、电影、文学等多种艺术，本科毕业于美国哥伦比亚大学，硕士学位在纽约大学获得，博士学位在法国索邦大学（巴黎第四大学）获得。菲奥娜的教育背景和成长历程多是围绕着音乐和艺术。作为一名古筝演奏家，她九岁时就在新加坡的维多利亚音乐厅进行了首演，其演出之行后来扩展到世界各地。她还为时尚艺术杂志、网络平台撰写时尚新闻、音乐和艺术批评、戏剧评论等。从其个人网站①的首页布局和栏目设置可见，菲奥娜是从音乐、艺术起家，逐步过渡、发展到以诗歌创作和诗歌翻译为主要事业。目前，菲奥娜定居巴黎，从事自由写作和翻译，尤其是中国当代诗歌翻译。菲奥娜能够用英文、法文和中文三种语言进行文学艺术创作和翻译。自幼受到的艺术熏陶和系统的艺术学习使得菲奥娜具有敏锐的艺术洞察力，早年的留学生涯锻造了她坚韧、勤奋、特立独行的性格，出生

---

　　①　菲奥娜个人网站网址为：http://www.fionasze.com/。网站首页封面标题是"古筝·诗歌"，其下所列内容及链接也首先是其古筝表演的内容。网站导航条首先列出的是"音乐"，然后是"写作"和其他栏目。可见，菲奥娜自我认定的身份首先是音乐艺术家、古筝演奏家。

在新加坡、求学于美国、欧洲的她在多元文化的浸润下成长。菲奥娜于2007年与高行健合著《剪影/阴影:高行健的电影艺术》(法国轮廓出版社),2010年出版了首部个人诗集《浇月亮》(美国马瑞克出版社),获得了2011年埃里克·霍弗图书奖(Eric Hoffer Book Award)提名。2016年,其个人诗集《毁灭的优雅》(美国普林斯顿大学出版社)被列入"普林斯顿当代诗人"系列,同时荣获美国《图书馆杂志》2015年度十大最佳诗集之一,并入围了2016年《洛杉矶时报》图书大奖。2020年,菲奥娜的第四部诗集《复数的雨》(*Rain in Plural*)由普林斯顿大学出版社出版,该诗集入围2021年德里克·沃尔科特诗歌奖(Derek Walcott Poetry Prize)。迄今,菲奥娜已著有5部英文诗集(其中一部为中英双语诗集,由台湾诗人零雨翻译)。从2011年开始,菲奥娜翻译出版了13部中国当代诗人的诗集①。她还翻译了已故诗人张枣的诗集《镜中》和海子的诗集《麦子熟了》,两部诗集尚未正式出版。

  菲奥娜是一位极其勤奋、多产的诗歌译者,十年的时间就翻译了15部中国当代诗人的个人诗集,另外还将两部法文诗集译为英文出版。作为华裔,菲奥娜的中文读写能力较强,听说能力次之。其母语不是英语,但其英语语言能力已完全达到母语水平,因此她的诗歌创作语言基本是英语,诗歌翻译也多从中文译为英文,或从法文译为英文。多语优势为其诗歌翻译奠定了很好的基础,其作为诗人的艺术气质和对诗歌的敏锐感悟力,为其产出优秀的诗歌翻译作品带来了可能。菲奥娜工作严谨、认真,在翻译阐释原诗的过程中遇到任何理解障碍,她都会立刻与诗人联系,寻求帮助,译稿出来后也会发给诗人征求意见。翻译诗集出版后,她会努力参与诗集推广,如推动评论家为诗集写书评等。菲奥娜对诗歌翻译有着自己独特的思考,认为翻译是一种艺术、一种精神探索,能胜任诗歌翻译的前提是熟练地掌握原语,能够在原语诗学空间而非语言空间进行思考,所以她并不赞同合作翻译模式,认为同不精通目标语的原作诗人或与不懂原语的英语国家诗人合作

---

① 这13部诗集为:宇向的《低调》(2011年),蓝蓝的《你不在这里》(2012年),柏桦的《风在说》(2012年),宇向的《我几乎看到滚滚尘埃》(2012年),蓝蓝的《钉子》(2013年),蓝蓝的《身体里的峡谷》(2014年),零雨的《无形之眼》(2015年)以及《种在夏天的一棵树》(2015年),阿芒的《女战车》(2016年),伊路的《海中的山峰》(2016年),宇向的《沿着》(2017年),叶丽隽的《我的山国》(2019年),余秀华的诗歌散文集《月光落在左手上》(2021年)。

都是不妥的。她主张诗歌译者应该是既精通原语又精通目标语,同时也深谙诗歌奥秘的人——当然,最好是诗人。而原作诗人同诗人译者之间应该心有灵犀,息息相通,彼此欣赏。菲奥娜视自己的诗歌翻译为艺术创造,坚持独立完成诗作翻译,也不愿翻译别人已经译过的作品。从其翻译思想来看,菲奥娜属于"诗人译诗",注重译者主体性和翻译的创造性转换,但从其《风在说》(*Wind Says*,柏桦汉英双语诗集)的翻译文本观察,她在文本上格外忠实于原文,创造性的翻译转换并不多见。总体来看,其译诗在语言风格上较为接近原诗,在外在形式尤其是节奏韵律上较好地还原了原诗之特点,但情感和诗意的传递似有欠缺。笔者在后文"个案研究五:柏桦诗歌英译译者风格评析"中有更进一步的分析。

二、译诗精选 10 首①

100. 海的夏天②

该是怎样一个充满老虎的夏天
火红的头发被目光唤醒
飞翔的匕首刺伤寂寞的沙滩
急速而老练的海湾怒吼着
举起深深的鲜花
迎接奔跑的阿拉伯少年

有毒的舌头和燃烧的荆棘
包围了广大的火焰
瘦小的结石般的心
溶化鲸鱼、嘴唇和浪潮

叛逆的动乱的儿子
空气淹死了你的喘气和梳子
你的笨拙的头发和感情

黄昏的情调,血的情调
精致的破坏,任意的破坏
蜜蜂和白鸟领着道路
去眩晕

---

① 因涉及版权问题,此处无法一一呈现这 10 首诗的英文译文,仅注明译文出处,以便读者查阅。部分中文原诗在前文中已出现,此处省略。
② 详见 Bai Hua, *Wind Says*, trans. by Fiona Sze-Lorrain, Zephyr Press and The Chinese University Press, 2012, pp. 5—7。

去孤独地埋葬浩瀚

黑暗的洞穴和指尖
将熄灭你的青春和梦想
将杀害你阴险的岁月和勇敢

是怎样的舌尖舔你
怎样的大炮轰你
一支小翅膀或万支箭羽

晶莹的泪花打开
钥匙、美人鱼、纤细的流浪儿
以及整个黎明的灿烂无比

愤慨的夏天
有着狷介的狂躁和敏感
愁绪若高山、若钟楼

历史和头颅熊熊崩坍
是谁在警告，在焚烧，在摧毁
海的短暂的夏天

1984年3月

101. 在清朝①

---

① 详见 Bai Hua. *Wind Says*. pp. 45—47。

102. 李后主①

遥远的清朗的男子
在 977 年一个细瘦的秋天
装满表达和酒
彻夜难眠、内疚
忠贞的泪水在湖面漂流

梦中的小船像一首旧曲
思念挥霍的岁月
负债的烟
失去的爱情的创伤
一个国家的沦落

哦,后主
林阴雨昏、落日楼头
你摸过的栏杆
已变成一首诗的细节或珍珠
你用刀割着酒、割着衣袖
还用小窗的灯火
吹燃竹林的风、书生的抱负
同时也吹燃了一个风流的女巫

1986 年暮春

103. 献给曼杰斯塔姆②

---

① 详见 Bai Hua. *Wind Says*. p. 41。
② 详见 Bai Hua. *Wind Says*. pp. 59—61。

104. 教育①

我传播着你的美名
一个偷吃了三个蛋糕的儿童
一个无法玩掉一个下午的儿童

旧时代的儿童啊
二十年前的蛋糕啊
那是决定我前途的下午
也是我无法玩掉的下午

家长不老,也不能歌唱
忙于说话和保健
并打击儿童的骨头

寂寞中养成挥金如土的儿子
这个注定要歌唱的儿子
但冬天的思想者拒受教育
冬天的思想者只剩下骨头

1989年冬

105. 以桦皮为衣的人②

这是纤细的下午四点
他老了

---

① 详见 Bai Hua. *Wind Says*. p. 93。
② 详见 Bai Hua. *Wind Says*. p. 111。

秋天的九月,天高气清
厨房安静
他流下伤心的鼻血

他决定去五台山
那意思是不要捉死蛇
那意思是作诗:

"雪中狮子骑来看"

1990 年 12 年 11 日

106. 山水手记①

一

像原始人面对一个奇迹
我面对你的翻译和声音

二

毛泽东说:不要鹅蛋看不起鸡蛋。
枕草子说:水中的鸭蛋是优雅的。

三

年轻姑娘继续谈着风景,

---

① 详见 Bai Hua. *Wind Says*. pp. 131—139。

一只燕子的飞翔会带来肉体的潮湿。

四

他有着黎明式的精神,但准时是他忧伤的表现。

五

鸟儿,
我心烦意乱
鸽子……
南京清晨的悸动

六

风景有些寂寞的洋气
在一株皂角树下
凉风……
藤椅,
一本五十年代的画册

七

他肠子里绞着算盘
他上演眼泪。

八

好听的地名是南京、汉城、名古屋。

九

年轻人烧指甲是会发疯的呀。

十

星期天,一个中年女教师
在无休止地打一条狗。

十一

我认为的好人是南京人吕祥,衢州人黄慰愿,合肥人胡全胜。

十二

爱流泪的胖子笑了,这一节值得留念。

十三

被焦虑损坏的脸是叶利钦的脸。

十四

这是春天的桌子,春天的椅子,春天的酒。

十五

一个深夜爱说话的体育教师今天专程去加拿大的月亮下哭泣。

十六

姓名叫杨伟的人不好,

应该改一个名字。

十七

一个美丽的男诗人发胖了,这是可悲的,他蓄上胡子就显得可爱了;另一个男诗人流着眼泪说谎,而且头发又稀疏,就显得可耻了。

十八

我曾写过一行"向笑开枪",
这很古怪。

十九

一个吃乌梢蛇时表情严肃的人是无趣的,一个在初夏头发多油的人是色情的;爱抒情的人注定了是坏人,而坏人的嘴都是长得不好看。

二十

最柔软的女人是贵州女人。

二十一

我认识一位中国诗人,走路
像子弹一样快。

二十二

金鱼,这个词适合这张脸。

二十三

在柏林
我生出了第一根白发
是为记。

二十四

更明亮的在泻下
更强硬的在泻下
我想到机械化的钢琴心

二十五

1997年,10月
从斯图加特到图宾根
买一张周末车票35马克
但一次可乘坐5人。

二十六

他用榔头砸蚂蚁。

二十七

那仆人捡起两节狗屎尾随而去
那老人搓着两个核桃若搓着两个睾丸

1995年—1997年

107. 风在说①

> 睡觉的愿望就像一场追寻。
> ——赫塔·米勒

一

风儿,已躺下,
黑暗里,风之絮语比风本身还沉:

她在瘦下去,仅仅三天,
脸就有了一缕放陈的梨子味

树叶开始发黄,不远处
一股怀旧的锈铁迎面吹度

这时,我会想,
她的呢喃为何如缎被上的金鱼呢?

冰凉欲滴……
最后的"变形记"终被打开:

她"越不想活,就越爱化妆"。
越爱在平静中飞旋起她酒后的烦闷。

二

睡下的风,继续讲着另一个故事:
它在轻叩我的不安:

---

① 详见 Bai Hua. *Wind Says*. pp.161—165。

35年过去了,那卧病多年的父亲
已在风景中死去;
乡间,在竹林中,
那丧父的儿子也垂垂老矣,
我从此痛失我的知青岁月

——深冬,绝对的午后
腊猪头在灶膛里已煨了一昼夜
那虚胖的儿子请我去吃
是的,吃!我记得:
这一天,天空比一只眼睛还要小
这一天,你的请吃声恍若大唐之音

三

风从深夜起身,开始哈气,
第三个故事由情(不自禁地)说出:

早年,61岁的花花公子何来悲伤,
脸上总溢满社会主义右派的笑容;
骑着妖娆的自行车,他常常
一溜烟就登上南京卫岗的陡坡

如今他已痴呆,整天裹一件睡衣,
裸着下体在室内晃荡,
他浪漫的妻子受不了他的臭味
以及他外表的苍老和内心的幼稚

终于,他最后的时刻到了,
睁眼睡入军区医院的病床;

戴上呼吸机,开始分秒必争的长跑
整整三个月,他似一个初学呼吸的人类

不停地跑呀,不能停下,停下就是死亡。
很快,岁月在他那曾经灿烂的屌上枯谢了
很快,岁月走过的地方,都轻轻撒一点
他独有的尿味、皮肤味、香水味

2011年1月27日

108. 人物速记①

一

端着那不自知的发奋之姿
他学习写作,
日日夜夜不苟言笑
一如南方来的冰冻之客。

垂暮之夜酒、沉默之水果
以及花生
通通被他吃掉
一如粮食喂养着一具未来的尸体。

二

她递给我一枚指甲,我将其擦亮
那指甲边缘有光

---

① 详见 Bai Hua. *Wind Says*. pp. 167—169。

我会消逝。
但鱼化石；
但"一些瞬间的我也许会在她的身上继续生存"。

三

那少年在一碧幽潭里见识了晚春的深夜
现在，他在四川省军区操场上
无限地、无限地……
拨弄着一辆自行车永恒的铃铛。

四

在柏林，Kumiko家的花园里
我见识了一地嫩绿的核桃
那天下午，凉气感人、室内安静
我们畅谈着生活……
从一册书里，我们甚至找到了
日语中的白居易

突然，她老年的眼光美极了
正迎向今后岁月的某个人；
突然，天色转暗、寒风叩窗
一位年轻的注定的画神呵
——他为我们带来了朗读
带来了更多的风景与前程……

五

深夜的沙发刚刚睡去，摸一摸
上面还有才离开的客人的余温

室内烟雾缭绕,残茶冷却,
他提走了一袋瘦词、一袋失眠的思想

在南方,春寒冻坏了我的食指
清晨,听春燕呢喃吗?
不。最初的燕子是阴郁的。
那就孤独地吃完早餐
孤独地坐在电脑前开始一天的工作

2010年12月19日——2011年1月6日

109. 西藏书:无常(二)①

阅读这本书时,
室内的光线已变暗。这一页翻过去——

我开始幻想尼泊尔寺院上空的秋云……
如此短暂;
我那微细的毛发呀,它在变。
那些卑贱的人或高贵的人终将死去……

记忆——

急流冲泄、一滑而过

一位身材高大的上师在那里讲经。

2010年11月22日

---

① 详见:Bai Hua. *Wind Says*. p.173。

第二部分
柏桦诗歌翻译研究举隅

个案研究一:《在清朝》的"西行漫记"
——以《在清朝》的英文文本分析为中心[①]

杨安文

20世纪80年代,在朦胧诗落潮、第三代诗歌迅猛崛起的时期,柏桦以其独特的气质和才赋成为彼时诗界耀眼的明星。北岛曾称他为"中国最优秀的抒情诗人",张枣说他是自己在"80年代所遇到的最有诗歌天赋的人"。在海外,柏桦同样受到很高的评价,哈佛大学东亚语言文明系教授王德威认为,"柏桦的诗歌是中国当代最好的诗歌之一,精妙并扣人心弦";著名德国汉学家顾彬则说,"作为日常生活的诗人,柏桦像宋朝的大诗人一样,到处可以找到诗歌",并认为他与里尔克一样,是"真实的""诚实写作的典范"。[②]柏桦早期(2000年以前)的诗歌产量并不高,不足百篇,但许多诗篇都备受关注,广受读者喜欢。这些诗歌中的绝大部分在80年代末就开始了"西游漫记"的序曲,被陆续译介到海外,现已被翻译成英语、法语、德语、荷兰语、日语等多国文字。[③]《在清朝》便是其中的一首。本文以《在清朝》及其四个英文译本为对象进行文本细读,从诗歌形式、语言风格、遣词用句等方面进行译本间的对比分析,探讨各译本在诗歌审美、诗意呈现、文化传递等方面翻译处理的得失,并提出针对性建议,以促进《在清朝》及柏桦诗歌在英语世界的传播与接受。

[①] 此文原发表于《现代中国文化与文学》2018年第3期,总第26期。
[②] Bai Hua. *Wind Says*. trans. by Fiona Sze-Lorrain. Zephyr Press and The Chinese University Press, 2012, back cover page.
[③] 据笔者统计,柏桦2000年以前正式出版的诗有98首,其中被译为英文的有82首,译为法文的有24首,译为德文的有16首,译为荷兰语的有6首,译为西班牙语和日语的各有1首。

一、诗篇简介

《在清朝》写于 1986 年秋,最早发表于柏桦的个人诗集《表达》(漓江出版社,1988 年),是诗人自评的早期诗歌代表作之一①,深受国内读者和诗歌研究者的喜爱。该诗同时也是柏桦诗歌在海外译介最多的诗之一,有四个英文译本发表于七个不同的刊物或英文诗集,另有一个法语译本在法国三个不同刊物发表,一个西班牙译本分别在阿根廷和墨西哥的刊物发表。诗人 2016 年在法国出版的法文诗集《在清朝》正是以此诗命名。以下是该诗各译本情况一览表:

表 1 《在清朝》各译本情况一览表

序号	译本类别	译 者	发表国家	发表刊物/诗集	发表时间
1	法语译本	Chantal Chen-Andro（尚德兰）	法国	*Noir surblanc / une anthologie*（《诗集:黑白之间》）,fourbis(福尔比斯出版社),第 24—25 页	1998 年
2	法语译本	Chantal Chen-Andro（尚德兰）	法国	*Leciel en fuite / Anthologie de la nouvelle poésie chinoise*（《消逝的天空:中国新诗选》）,Circé(西尔瑟出版社),第 114—115 页	2004 年
3	法语译本	Chantal Chen-Andro（尚德兰）	法国	*Sous les Qing*（《在清朝:柏桦法语诗集》）,Éditions Caractères（文字出版社）,第 39—41 页	2016 年
4	西班牙语译本	Francoise Roy（弗朗索瓦丝·罗伊）	墨西哥	*Unasoledad de cien años Nueva poesía China* 1916—2016（《中国新诗的百年孤独:1916—2016》）,Valparaíso(瓦尔帕莱索出版社),第 94—95 页	2016 年

---

① 柏桦:《柏桦代表作》,载《当代作家评论》,2010 年第 5 期。

（续表）

序号	译本类别	译　者	发表国家	发表刊物/诗集	发表时间
5	西班牙语译本	Francoise Roy（弗朗索瓦丝·罗伊）	阿根廷	*Poesía China Contemporánea/Abriendo alas hasta el infinito*（《无限伸展的翅膀：中国当代诗选》），leviatán（利维坦出版社），第37—39页	2016年
6	英译本A	李赋康	澳大利亚	*Scripsi*（《我所写》），1991年第7卷第1期，第289—290页	1991年
7	英译本B	Fiona Sze-Lorrain（菲奥娜·施-罗琳）	奥地利	*Poetry Salzburg Review*（《萨尔茨堡诗歌评论》），2011年第19期，第179—180页	2011年
8	英译本B	Fiona Sze-Lorrain（菲奥娜·施-罗琳）	中国	*Carrying and Crossing: Cultural Heritage and the Path of Contemporary Poetry*（《负载与穿越：文化传承与当代诗歌路径》），第85—86页	2011年
9	英译本B	Fiona Sze-Lorrain（菲奥娜·施-罗琳）	美国	*Wind Says*（《风在说》），Zephyr Press and The Chinese University Press（西风出版社和香港中文大学出版社联合出版），第44—47页	2012年
10	英译本C	Brian Holton, Lee Man-Kay and W. N. Herbert（霍布恩，李文姬，赫尔伯特）	英国	*Jade Ladder: Contemporary Chinese Poetry*（《玉梯：中国当代诗歌》），Bloodaxe Books Ltd（血斧出版社），第109—110页	2012年
11	英译本D	Eleanor Goodman, Ao Wang（顾爱玲，王敖）	美国	*New Cathay: Contemporary Chinese Poetry*（《新华夏集：当代中国诗选》），Tupelo Press（蓝果树出版社），第21—22页	2013年

(续表)

序号	译本类别	译 者	发表国家	发表刊物/诗集	发表时间
12	英译本 D	Eleanor Goodman（顾爱玲）	中国	Enclave（《飞地》），海天出版社，2014 年第 8 辑，第 130—131 页	2014 年

　　由于笔者外语能力所限，本文仅重点对比分析该诗的四个英文译本。译本 A 由国内译者李赋康所译。该译者于 1989 年在北京外国语大学读研究生时翻译了柏桦的 57 首诗，合成为一本柏桦英文诗集，取名"The Sky-watcher: Selected Poems of Bai Hua"（《望气的人：柏桦诗歌选集》），但因种种原因没有出版。其中的 9 首译诗经修改发表于澳大利亚文学杂志《我所写》（1991 年第 7 卷第 1 期），另有 4 首经香港翻译家孔慧怡修改后发表于香港《译丛》杂志（1992 年第 37 期）。李赋康是最早成规模译介柏桦诗歌的译者①，对于柏桦诗歌的"西行"起到了重要作用。译本 B 的译者是法籍新加坡裔诗人、翻译家菲奥娜·施-罗琳，她是柏桦汉英双语诗集《风在说》的译者，同时还翻译了宇向、蓝蓝、张枣、海子等诗人的个人诗集。菲奥娜译作产量丰富，自己还兼任樱桃出版社（Cerise Press）和蓬勃出版社（Vif éditions）编辑，在国外不少诗歌杂志和网络上发表了许多译诗，产生了较为广泛的影响。译本 C 是由英国著名汉学家、翻译家霍布恩所译，他是杨炼诗歌的主要英译者。此译诗刊于英国血斧出版社出版的中国当代新诗选《玉梯：中国当代诗歌》，该书在西方诗歌界和汉学界都产生了较大的影响。译本 D 则由美国诗人翻译家顾爱玲所译。顾爱玲是哈佛大学费正清中国研究中心研究员，翻译了王小妮、臧棣等中国当代诗人的诗集，同时还翻译了一本中国当代打工诗选。这位翻译家凭着对中国诗歌的热爱，努力使自己能成为中美之间诗歌交流与互动的桥梁。

　　如诗之标题所示，此诗所写为历史大题材。清朝延续近 300 年，是中国历史上最后一个大一统的封建王朝，此间中国从封建社会进入半封建半殖

---

① 在李赋康 1989 年翻译《望气的人》（The Sky-watcher）时，《中国文学》英文季刊（1989 年冬季刊）刊发了由张西蒙（Simon Johnstone）翻译的柏桦的成名诗作《表达》，但仅此一首，不成规模。

民地社会,由发展、鼎盛到衰落、终结,这一朝代是中国历史的重要转折点。如此大题材,诗人并没有采用宏大的历史叙事,或从某一重要历史人物或重大历史事件切入,而是独辟蹊径,采用了充满旧时代色彩的一连串平淡的语汇意象,拼缀成一个个场景片段,呈现出一个个清朝民间生活情境,进而绘制出一幅清朝农耕社会古朴、安闲、富足、文化繁荣的美丽画卷。细察其内容的选择与铺排,可发现看似随意撷取、信手拈来的语汇组合,竟涵盖了清朝社会的政治、经济、文化、教育、科技等诸多方面,为读者呈现了鲜活生动的清朝社会景观:

政治:选拔长指甲的官吏,用款税激励人民

经济(原始农耕经济):货币两地不同,用谷物兑换茶叶、丝、瓷器,财富似乎过分

军事:朝廷增设军机处

教育:科举大公无私,严于身教,办学校,编印书籍

科技:科学不能适应

文化:夜读太史公,整理地方志,哲学如雨

艺术:山水画臻于完美,纸张泛滥,灯笼得了要领,建筑弄得古香古色

宗教、民俗:一座座庙宇向南,办祠堂

生活方式:安闲,牛羊无事,百姓下棋,风筝遍地,诗人不事营生,饮酒落花

价值观念:孩子敬老,母亲屈从于儿子

品读原诗,读者可从三个层面进行诗意解读:第一是文本浅层,通过一系列名词意象堆叠组合,营造出一股清朝时期的古风、古韵,绘制出一幅中国传统民俗风情的美好画面,呈现出清朝社会一派闲适、祥和的生活景象。第二是文本深层,从整个中国历史的视角,看清朝尤其是晚清时期的政治社会风貌,呈现出晚清社会的动荡与风雨飘摇,传统农耕社会的落后,西方现代化的影响,对现代科学的不适应,国民的焦躁,欲学西方走上现代化之路的急切,欲革新自我、摆脱传统封建社会桎梏却难以实现的愤怒与无奈。第

三个层面则是言说自我,借古喻今。如诗人所言,诗中的"清朝"也指诗人居住的城市成都。成都的古典、闲适、悠懒、宜居,成都的丰富民俗文化,得以保留和延续的古典传统,都是诗人向往的理想家园的写照。诗的前三节呈现的农耕生活画面也是诗人浓郁乡村情结的映射,第三节中"诗人不事营生""饮酒落花"正是诗人渴求却难以实现的理想生活状态;最后一节"无端端的着急"似在说诗人自己,恰是诗人急性子的生动呈现,透露出了柏桦骨子里的"下午激情"和"加速度"的夏天情结。①

二、文本分析

1. 文本形式

原诗和四个译本的文本形式(诗行数、诗节数、句数、字数等)统计如下表:

表2 《在清朝》中英文本形式(诗行数、诗节数、句数、字数等)统计

文本	诗节数	诗行数	句数	总字数	行平均字数	行字数范围
原诗	7	41	7	272	6.6	3—10
译本A	7	41	7	207	5.0	3—9
译本B	7	41	7	206	5.0	4—10
译本C	7	41	7	260	6.3	3—12
译本D	7	41	7	224	5.5	3—9

如表2所示,原诗共有7个诗节,共41行,每节的行数不完全一致,分别为:7,6,6,5,6,5,6。全诗末行无标点,但每一诗节在介词短语"在清朝"的统领之下,为语义独立的一个片段,实为1句,故认定全篇共有7个句子。四个译本在形式上与原诗基本对应,诗节数、诗行数相同,但各译本每行首字母大写的情况及行末标点有所不同。译本A全篇每行首字母均为大写,

---

① 相关形象和细节参见柏桦所著《左边:毛泽东时代的抒情诗人》第一卷第一章"蛋糕"(柏桦:《左边:毛泽东时代的抒情诗人》,南京:江苏文艺出版社,2009年,第3—11页)和柏桦的诗《夏天,啊,夏天》《骑手》等。

行末无标点。译本 B 和译本 D 则是每个诗节首行首字母大写,其余诗行均为小写,可推测译者是利用诗行首字母大写的方式进行断句。译本 C 全篇每个诗行首字母均为小写,不太符合英语诗歌惯例。标点方面,除译本 D 最后一行行末有一个句号之外,各译本行末均无标点,与原诗一致。

在文本字数方面,各译本的英文词数均比原诗中文字数少,可见四个译者总体均依照原文的形式和内容,采用较为简洁、精练的语言进行对照翻译。统计数据显示,译本 C 单词数最多,译本 B 最少,四个译本的行平均字数均低于原诗,译本 A、B、D 均在原诗行字数范围(3—10 个字)内,唯译本 C 略有超出。比较四个译本可发现,译本 C 与原诗对应更为紧密,表达上更加追求准确和流畅,因而用词最多,总字数和行平均字数均超过其他译本。

2. 文本词类分析

为准确得出原诗中各词类使用所占比例,笔者除统计原诗字数(272 个字)以外,还将中文用词按词性一一划分,分类统计①,得出原诗共计用词 164 个。同时对四个英文译本也进行了词性分类统计,统计结果如下:

表3 《在清朝》中英文本词类统计表——实词

文本	作者/译者	总字/词数	名词		动词		形容词		量词		数词		代词	
			数量	比例	数量	比例	数量	比例	数量	比例	数量	比例	数量	比例
原诗	Bai Hua	272/164	70	42.7%	36	22.0%	15	9.1%	6	3.7%	5	3.0%	3	1.8%
译本 A	Li Fukang	207	75	36.2%	41	19.8%	22	10.6%		0.5%	1	0.5%	10	4.8%
译本 B	Fiona	206	87	42.2%	34	16.5%	19	9.2%		1.0%	2	1.0%	3	1.5%
译本 C	Brian Holton	260	96	36.9%	39	15.0%	24	9.2%		1.2%	3	1.2%	6	2.3%
译本 D	Eleanor Goodman	224	88	39.3%	39	17.4%	18	8.0%		1.3%	3	1.3%	6	2.7%

---

① 本研究依据中国社会科学院语言研究所词典编辑室编写的《现代汉语词典》第 7 版(商务印书馆,2017 年)中所列词条及词性标注,进行中文文本的词性分类划分。人名、地名等专有名词不作拆分,直接统计为 1 个名词。

表 4 《在清朝》中英文本词类统计表——虚词

版本	译者	总字/词数	介词		副词		助词		连词		冠词	
			数量	比例	数量	比例	数量	比例	数量	比例	数量	比例
原诗	Bai Hua	272/164	13	7.9%	9	5.5%	4	2.4%	3	1.8%		
译本 A	Li Fukang	207	29	14.0%	13	6.3%	2	1.0%	5	2.4%	9	4.3%
译本 B	Fiona	206	24	11.7%	8	3.9%	1	0.5%	8	3.9%	20	9.7%
译本 C	Brian Holton	260	32	12.3%	16	6.2%	8	3.1%	14	5.4%	22	8.5%
译本 D	Eleanor Goodman	224	33	14.7%	5	2.2%	7	3.1%	5	2.2%	20	8.9%

从表3、表4数据可知,原诗实词使用占比为82.3%,使用的词类由多到少分别为名词、动词、形容词、量词、数词、代词,虚词使用占比为17.7%,使用的词类由多到少分别为介词、副词、助词和连词。实词使用最多的是名词(42.7%)和动词(22%),占全诗用词的64.7%,是构成原诗意象和叙事的主体词类,固然是研究关注的重点。同时还值得注意的是,原诗中形容词和副词使用比例不高,仅占全诗用词的15.4%。名词和动词的使用比例高,形容词和副词的使用比例相对较低,这一定程度上反映了诗人写作的客观、冷静与节制,力求以朴实、无过多修饰的语言和看似不带任何感情色彩的描写,客观呈现清朝时期的历史画面。这其实是一种柏桦式的"冷抒情"方式,诗中大量带有清朝时期民俗、民风、社会文化特色的名词意象堆叠组合所呈现的美好画面已然表达了诗人对传统乡村生活的热爱,而精当运用的几个形容词则透露了诗人在更宏大的社会历史层面的反思和表达。

接下来看译文的词类使用情况。四个译本词类使用情况相似。总体而言,使用的词类由多到少是:名词、动词、介词、形容词、冠词、副词、连词、代词、助词和数词。其中,名词和动词使用最多(译本 A 为 56%,译本 B 为 58.7%,译本 C 为 51.9%,译本 D 为 56.7%),这与原诗的情况一致。与中文原诗不同的是,英文译诗使用介词较多,中文没有的冠词使用也较多。通过数据还发现,四个译本形容词和副词使用的数量差异较大:译本 A 为 35 个,译本 B 为 27 个,译本 C 为 40 个,译本 D 为 23 个。可见译本 B 与译本 D 修饰语使用较少,呈现的翻译文本更偏客观性,与原诗的特点较吻合,而译本 A 与译本 C 修饰语使用较多,相较而言文本会带有更多的感情色彩。尤其是译本 C 使用最多,这也印证了前文就该译本词数最多的分析:译者为追求译文的准确性而不吝使用更多的形容词和副词。

最后再回到中文原诗使用最多的名词。以下列出每个诗节所用名词:

第一节:清朝,理想,牛,羊,百姓,棋,科举,货币,谷物,茶叶,丝,瓷器
第二节:清朝,山水画,纸张,风筝,灯笼,要领,庙宇,南,财富
第三节:清朝,诗人,营生,面子,酒,落花,风,日,池塘,水,鸭子,马,牛
第四节:清朝,人,夜,太史公,清晨,地,朝廷,军机处,官吏
第五节:清朝,胡须,人,身教,言谈,农村,字,孩子,老,母亲,儿子
第六节:清朝,款税,人民,水利,学校,祠堂,书籍,地方志,建筑
第七节:清朝,哲学,雨,科学,人,事业,一八四二年

一眼尽可观之,绝大部分名词都有明显的清朝时代特征,尽显古风、古味。这些名词的"元素意象"自身所承载的语义形成了一个展现清朝社会景观的"语义场",即读者可感受的"审美感知场"。正是这样的"语义场"决定了原诗的古风基调。这也就要求译者在翻译时,需要有意识地选用一些体现古风、古韵的英文词汇,以还原原诗之基调和意境。

同时还可以发现,这样一个以"古"为主的"语义场",却"生硬地"穿插了几个明显带有现代气息的名词(理想,货币,要领,财富,哲学,科学,事业,大公无私),并且一半都集中在最后一节。此似诗人有意为之,零星现代词汇的渗入,似在隐喻晚清时期西方现代化的"入侵",社会动荡,"科学不能适应"。以"今"渗"古",形成一种"不和谐"的反差,带来一种艺术张力,这可视为此诗最后一节在主题上进行升华的秘密武器。

三、译本对比分析

1. 诗题翻译的背后

对本诗诗题《在清朝》的翻译,四个译本的差异在于是否在"Qing Dynasty"前加定冠词"the"。"清"指朝代,"公元1616—1911,女真族人爱新觉罗·努尔哈赤所建,初名后金,1636年改为清"①。"清朝"除了可指朝代,亦可指清朝这一段中国历史。就英语冠词的用法而论,名词前加定冠词,表特指,加零冠词(即不加冠词)泛指一般概念。此处若加上定冠词,则强调特指清朝在中国历史长河中近300年的这一段历史,强调过去这个特定的历史朝代;若加零冠词,则将清朝作为一个宽泛的、抽象的概念,强调"永恒的"清朝。结合前文对原诗主题的把握,可知诗人意在展现一个自己喜爱的"永恒的"清朝,一个可"酌古参今"的清朝,故对诗题的翻译采用零冠词更为妥当。

从原诗主题呈现这一角度,我们再来看四个译本的时态选择。译本A、B、D采用了过去时态,译本B则采用了现在时态。原诗描写的是已成为历史的清朝,用过去时态固然没有问题。然而,在文学文本中,选用历史现在时(historical present)或曰戏剧性现在时(dramatic present)也是十分常见的。当现在时和过去时都可作为选择对象时,过去时主要侧重对一时一地的个人体验的描述,而现在时则用于把受时空限制的一次体验变成普遍的、恒常的经验。② 选用过去时态强调呈现清朝过去的这一段历史,选用现在时态则让读者如临其境,诗歌叙事的代入感、现场感更强。所以,笔者认为选用现在时态更符合原诗之主题和意境。

2. 第一诗节翻译对比分析

(1) 安闲和理想越来越深

A:Leisure was leisured, ideal idealized

---

① 中国社会科学院语言研究所词典编辑室:《现代汉语词典》第7版,北京:商务印书馆,2017年,第1064页。

② 黄国文:《翻译研究的语言学探索》,上海:上海外语教育出版社,2006年,第158页。

B：ease and ideals flourish

C：idleness and the ideal went deeper and deeper

D：lightheartedness and idealism grew deeper

"安闲"一词,实为两词,指"安静清闲"①。该词呈现出清朝社会一派闲适祥和的生活景象,"牛羊无事,百姓下棋"正是对"安闲"的注解。四个译本选用了四个不同的单词翻译"安闲"。笔者运用语义场义素分析的方法,将四个词的语义特征(义素)呈现如下②：

	time away from work(空闲,闲暇)	freedom from pain or disturbance(无痛苦,无忧虑)	quiet, peace(安静,平静)	being unemployed(无工作)	being lazy(懒惰)	being unburdened or merry of heart(无负担,快乐)	being free from anxiety(无忧无虑)
leisure	+	−	−	−	−	−	−
ease	+	+	+	−	−	−	−
idleness	+	−	−	+	+	−	−
lightheartedness	−	−	−	−	−	+	+

通过以上语义分析图表可见,仅"ease"一词可准确表达"安闲"的"安静清闲"二意,其余用词均有所欠缺,尤其是译本 D 译为"lightheartedness"更是谬之千里了。

"理想",指"对未来事物的想象或希望(多指有根据的、合理的,跟空想、幻想不同)"③。译本 A、B、C 译为"ideal",译本 D 译为"idealism"。二词的释义如下：

> ideal：the highest conception of anything, or its embodiment(理想)；a standard of perfection(完美标准)；that which exists in the

---

① 《现代汉语词典》第 7 版,第 8 页。
② 此处英文单词释义来自《钱伯斯英语词典》第十三版(*The Chambers Dictionary 13th Edition*, 2014)："leisure",第 875 页；"ease",第 485 页；"idleness",第 756 页；"lightheartedness",第 885 页。
③ 《现代汉语词典》第 7 版,第 800 页。

imagination only(想象中的事物).①

idealism: a tendency towards the highest conceivable perfection(完美趋势); love for or the search after the best and highest(理想追求); impracticality(理想化,不切实际); the doctrine that all reality is in its nature psychical(唯心论).②

显然,"idealism"的词义于原诗中的"理想"而言有所偏离,甚至会带来误解和歧义(误以为是指哲学层面的唯心主义)。译为"ideal"当是正确选择。

此句中,"越来越深"用于修饰"安闲和理想",表达程度上的深入。译本A采取了意译。"leisure"在古体英语中可作动词,意为"(archaic)to make leisurely"③。"idealize"意为"to regard or represent as ideal"④。将译本A的此句回译则为"空闲被空闲了,理想被视为理想了",显然让人不知所云。译本B也采取了意译,将"越来越深"译为"flourish",该词意为"to grow luxuriantly; to be prosperous"(茁壮成长;繁荣)⑤,亦与原诗之意相左。译本B和译本D则直接将"深"译为"deep"。据"deep"作为副词的英文释义"at or to a great depth"⑥,该词通常指空间距离上的深入。英语中另有一词"further"(at or to a greater distance or degree)⑦,既可指距离之深,也可指程度之深,笔者认为该词更合原诗之意,故该诗行可改译为"ease and ideals go further"。

(2) 牛羊无事,百姓下棋

A: Cattle and sheep jobless, commons playing chess

---

① 据《钱伯斯英语词典》第十三版,第755页。
② 同上,第755页。
③ 同上,第875页。
④ 同上,第755页。
⑤ 同上,第589页。
⑥ 同上,第403页。
⑦ 同上,第617页。

B：cows and sheep do nothing, the folks play chess

C：cows and ships were at peace, the people played chess

D：cows and sheep were idle, people played chess

此句中，"牛羊"泛指牲畜，指可供人役使的家畜。在古代中国，饲养家畜的主要目的是获得农耕的劳动力或交通工具。"牛羊无事"当指非农忙季，农活不多，乡村生活清闲；"百姓下棋"与前文的"安闲"呼应。译本 B、C、D 均将"牛"译为"cows"，这便是文化差异使然，因为西方社会饲养的牛通常是产奶供人食用的奶牛，故译为"cows"并不妥当。此处既然泛指家畜，不妨选用"cattle"（domesticated mammals including oxen, etc and also horses, sheep, etc）[①]一词。

"百姓"指"军人和官员以外的人，平民百姓"[②]，在四个译本中有三种不同翻译。笔者对三个词的语义特征分析如下[③]：

	people, collectively or distributively（人，人们）	a body of persons held together by a common origin, speech, culture, political union, or by a common leadership（人民）	The common people（平民）	those of one's own family, relations（家属，亲属）
Folk(s)	+	+	+	+
People	+	+	−	−
(the) Common(s)	−	−	+	−

由上表可见，"folk"和"people"语义都太过宽泛。从语义准确性和单一性的角度看，"(the) Common(s)"可用。但考虑到与原诗的古风基调一致，笔者认为，"(the) commonalty"一词更为恰当。据《牛津英语词源词典》，"commonalty"是英国 16 世纪时使用的词汇，意即"the commons"[④]。故此句可改译为"Cattle are at leisure, the commonalty play chess"。

---

① 同上，第 247 页。

② 《现代汉语词典》第 7 版，第 29 页。

③ 此处英文单词释义来自《钱伯斯英语词典》第十三版："folk"，第 593 页；"people"，第 1146 页；"common"，第 317 页。

④ 据《牛津英语词源词典》(Oxford Dictionary of English Etymology, 1966)，第 195 页。

(3) 科举也大公无私

A：Imperial exams just and selfless

B：even imperial exams are fair and selfless

C：and imperial exams were just and fair

D：the imperial examination was impartial

此句中"科举"乃是具有"旧时代"色彩的词汇，指"从隋唐到清代朝廷通过分科考试选拔官吏的制度"①。"大公无私"则明显具有"新时代"气息，据《现代汉语词典》该词有两义：一指"完全为人民群众利益着想，毫无自身自利之心"，二指"处理公正，不偏袒任何一方"。② 显然此处取第二义。两词的组合立刻带来一种戏剧化的张力，诗人似要"以古讽今"：旧时之科举尚能公平公正，今时之"科举"（如高考）是否能做到"大公无私"？再看译文，四个译本将"科举"都译为"imperial exams"，非常贴切。然而"大公无私"的译法就各显神通了。译本A和译本B用了"selfless"，当是错取了该词的第一义进行翻译。译本C和译本D的译文均符合原诗之义。据《牛津英语词源词典》，"partial"一词源自古法语词汇"*parcial*"，始用于15世纪③，故"impartial"一词古风浓厚，用以形容清代之科举，当属最佳。

3. 第二诗节翻译对比分析

(1) 山水画臻于完美

A：Landscape painting reaching perfection

B：landscape art defines perfect

C：landscape painting had attained perfection

D：landscape painting neared perfection

据《现代汉语词典》，"臻"指"达到（完美的境地）"④，"臻于完美"指达到

---

① 《现代汉语词典》第7版，第735页。

② 同上，第240页。

③ 据《牛津英语词源词典》，第654页。partial：inclined to favour one party or individual（偏爱的，偏心的）.

④ 《现代汉语词典》第7版，第1664页。

完美的境地。译本 B 采取了意译,但在动词"define"后面接形容词"perfect"令人费解。译本 A、C、D 分别使用了三个不同动词"reach""attain""near"搭配"perfection"。显然"near perfection"(接近完美)与原句之义有出入。比较"reach"和"attain"二词的英文释义①,二词均有"达到"之义,但前者意思更为宽泛,后者则强调通过努力达到某种目标,取得某种成果。故此处取"attain"为上。

(2) 纸张泛滥,风筝遍地

A：Papers overproduced, kites seen everywhere

B：a flood of paper, kites everywhere

C：papers were overflowing, kites everywhere

D：paper was abundant, kites flew everywhere

"泛滥"为贬义词,通常"比喻坏的事物不受限制地流行"②。然而在此句中其并非为贬义,而是喻指清朝造纸业发达。译本 A 意译为"overproduced",带有些许贬义。译本 B 则将原句的主谓结构改为名词短语"a flood of paper",强调的中心不在"泛滥",而在"纸张",且"a flood of"乃指"大量",并无中文的"泛滥"之义。译本 C 采用直译"overflowing",与"papers"搭配似有不合,却也呈现了原诗突破语言常规的"诗性"语言特点。译本 D 译为"abundant",译出了该词的引申义,虽因意思过于直接而缺少诗意,但尚有助于英文读者理解原诗。

(3) 灯笼得了要领

A：Lanterns all inspired

B：lanterns lead the way

C：lanterns were well-proportioned

---

① 据《钱伯斯英语词典》第十三版：reach, to arrive at, to succeed in touching or getting; attain to (usd with for or after),第 1297 页；attain, to reach or gain by effort, to accomplish to reach, arrive at (archaic),第 94 页。

② 《现代汉语词典》第 7 版,第 365 页。

D：lanterns understood the essentials

"要领"即"要点"①,"灯笼得了要领"指灯笼制作掌握了要领,喻指灯笼制作工艺成熟,质量上乘。纵观四个译本,四者似乎都"不得要领"。译本 A 译为"all inspired",意即"灯笼被完全激发"。译本 B 译为"lead the way",指"灯笼领路导航"。译本 D 译为"understood the essentials",可回译为"灯笼明白了要领"。唯有译本 C 与原文之义较为接近,"well-proportioned"②指灯笼大小匀称,比例协调,反映出了灯笼质量上乘的一个方面。拙以为选用"well-made"(cleverly and competently made, produced, constructed)③一词,可表达出灯笼的样子精美、做工考究,更契合原句之义。

4. 第三诗节翻译对比分析

(1) 诗人不事营生、爱面子

A：Poets cared nothing but their faces

B：poets have no trade, save face

C：poets cared nothing for a living, only for reputation

D：poets didn't work for a living, concerned with reputation

"营生"指"职业,工作"④,"不事营生"指不工作,不以从事某一职业来谋生计。此句连同下一句形象地展现了许多中国旧时文人的生活状态和理想追求。"爱面子"是中国人自古以来的特点。译本 A 漏译了"不事营生",且"cared nothing but their faces"也无法准确表达出国文化中"爱面子"之义。译本 B 将"营生"译为"trade"(an occupation, way of livelihood, *esp* skilled but not learned)⑤,较为贴切,但"爱面子"译为"save face"却欠准确。据《钱伯斯英语词典》,"save one's face"⑥为"避免蒙羞,挽回面子"

---

① 《现代汉语词典》第 7 版,第 1526 页。
② 据《钱伯斯英语词典》第十三版,第 1778 页。
③ 同上。
④ 《现代汉语词典》第 7 版,第 1572 页。
⑤ 据《钱伯斯英语词典》第十三版,第 1653 页。
⑥ 同上,第 551 页。

(avoid humiliation or appearance of climbing down)之义。译本 C 和译本 D 都基本译出了原句之义，但尚有不足。"面子"不仅关乎"reputation"，还关乎"dignity"。故笔者将此句改译为"poets care nothing for a living, only for dignity and reputation"。

（2）风马牛不相及

A：Not knowing each other

B：at complete odds

C：–just so horses in heat do not couple with cattle①

D：everything was at odds

"风马牛不相及"为一成语，语出《左传·僖公四年》："君处北海，寡人处南海，唯是风马牛不相及也。""风"指"雌雄相引诱"，"比喻两者全不相干"②，此处戏指前文的两只鸭子各游各的，互不相干，一副怡然自得的样子，尽显诗人笔调的冷峻、幽默。译本 A、B、D 都回避了该成语的翻译，其解释性的翻译亦不合原句之义："Not knowing each other"讲两只鸭子彼此互不认识，"at complete odds"(at odds：at variance ［不一致］)③说两只鸭子完全不一样，"everything was at odds"更是令人不知所云。唯有译本 C 准确地译出该成语之义，并采用脚注的方式进行了解释说明。此法之优点在于可向英语读者传递更多的中国传统文化信息，展示汉语的魅力。

5. 第四诗节翻译对比分析

（1）夜读太史公，清晨扫地

A：Reading Shi Ji at night, sweeping floors in the morning

B：reads Sima Qian at night, sweeps the floor in the morning

---

① 此为译者在译文中所注：This line references *Zuo Zhuan*, 4th year of Duke Xi. See Legge's translation, *Tso Chuan*, *Duke Hsi* in *The Chinese Classics*. One metaphoric interpretation of this line is "Even if my herds wander far away, they'll never come into contact with yours", i.e. why do you make war on me when we are so far apart we can do no harm to each other.

② 《现代汉语词典》第 7 版，第 390 页。

③ 据《钱伯斯英语词典》第十三版，第 1067 页。

C: reading the Grand Historian① in the night, sweeping the floor at dawn

D: read The Grand History at night, swept at dawn

众所周知,中国的第一部纪传体通史是《史记》,又名《太史公书》②,作者为西汉司马迁。此句中的"太史公"正是指司马迁。"夜读太史公"实指夜读《史记》。从本诗节起,诗之氛围开始骤变,从前三节轻松、闲逸的民间生活描写,进入了严肃、紧张的政治社会描写。诗人为增强故事性和戏剧化效果,在此节中虚构了"一个人梦见一个人","夜读太史公"暗示了这是一个心怀天下、极具社会责任感的人。他勤奋刻苦,代表了敢于自我革新、追求上进的新生力量。对于"太史公"的翻译,译本 A 采用汉语拼音直接译为"Shi Ji",可能会让没有传统文化背景的英语读者不知所云。译本 B 直接译为"Sima Qian",符合原诗所指,但由于没有加注,英语读者同样可能面临文化信息空白。译本 D 译为"The Grand History",意指《史记》,带来的问题与译本 B 一样。译本 C 译为"the Grand Historian",并加注说明,当为上译。

(2) 而朝廷增设军机处

A: While the court opening the Bureau of Military Affairs

B: the court creates more military sites

C: and the Court established the Council of State

D: the court created a Military Office

"军机处"全称"办理军机事务处"或"办理军机处",清雍正八年设立,因参决军国大事,又称"枢垣,枢廷"。③ 其类似于皇帝的"私人秘书处",实际为清朝最高权力机构,总揽军、政大权,由皇帝直接掌控。译本 A 与译本 D 的翻译与该机构名较为接近。译本 B 的翻译可回译为"朝廷新建了更多的军事基地",显然与原文不符。译本 C 将"军机处"直接译为"the Council of

---

① 此为译者在译文中所注:The Grand Historian is Sima Qian (ca. 145 or 135 BC—86 BC), author of the *Historical Records*.

② 夏征农、陈至立:《辞海》第六版索引本,上海:上海辞书出版社,2009 年,第 1714 页。

③ 同上,第 994 页。

State",类似西方国家的国务院,又有过之。笔者赞同直译"军机处"其名,再行加注说明其实际为最高权力机构,故将此句改译为"and the court establishes the Bureau of Military Affairs①"。

6. 第五诗节翻译对比分析

(1) 严于身教,不苟言谈

A：Strict with themselves, hard to talk with others

B：behave strictly, converse little

C：were strict on teaching by example, solemn in speech and manners

D：taught by example instead of with words

"身教",即"用自己的行动做榜样"②,"不苟",指"不随便,不马虎"③。本句传递了中国传统文化重身教的教育观,形象地呈现了的严格要求自己、寡言少语的人物形象,很容易让我们联想到旧时的教书先生或父母长辈的严苛形象。译本 A 的"strict with themselves"只译出了"对自己严格要求",没有译出"身教"之义。译本 C"were strict on teaching by example"可回译为"对身教严格要求",与原句之义有出入;后一句"solemn in speech and manners"则过度翻译了,原句不涉及"manners"。译本 D"taught by example instead of with words"则漏译了"不苟言谈"。比较之下,译本 B"behave strictly, converse little"为最佳,以简练的语言较为准确地传递了原文的意思。

(2) 母亲屈从于儿子

A：Mothers looking to their sons

B：mothers listen to their sons

C：mothers ceded power to their sons

D：mothers submitted to their sons

---

① Under the emperor's direct control, it's just like his private secretariat. In fact, it's the top state organ in charge of military and political power.

② 《现代汉语词典》第 7 版,第 1158 页。

③ 同上,第 107 页。

"屈从"一词带有贬义,指"对外来压力不敢反抗,勉强服从"①。但在此诗句中,其并非指母亲迫于儿子的压力或权威而不得不选择让步。由于受儒家"百善孝为先"思想的影响,在传统中国社会子女对父母的孝顺是极为重要的传统美德,所以才有上一诗句"孩子们敬老"。既然"孝为先",儿子不应该对自己的母亲作威作福。此处的"屈服"当指母亲一切为了儿子,一切顺从儿子,因为她们的希望和依靠是儿子,她们的价值需要通过儿子才能得以体现。母亲对儿子毫无条件地投入与付出,期待他们长大以后能给以忠诚的报答。基于这样的理解,将"屈从"译为"cede to"或"submit to"均不恰当。译本 B 译为"listen to② their sons",可回译为"听从她们儿子(的意见)",也未能表达原句丰富的文化含义。译本 A 则采取了意译,"look to③ their sons"表达出了原句母亲指望儿子、依靠儿子的隐含之义,相较之下为最佳。

7. 第六诗节翻译对比分析

(1) 办水利、办学校、办祠堂

A: Setting up irrigation, schools, temples

B: build irrigation, schools and temples

C: irrigation works were built, schools managed, ancestral halls maintained

D: and built irrigation works, schools, temples

"祠堂"指"在封建宗法制度下,同族的人共同祭祀祖先的房屋"④,在英美文化中没有,属于文化空白。"temple"⑤指"寺庙,神殿",与"祠堂"完全不同。译本 C 译为"ancestral halls",是为可理解、可接受之翻译。更值得注意的是,原句中的三个并列动词都是"办",但其内在意义却不尽相同。译本 A、B、D 都使用了同一个动词,仅译本 C 注意到三个"办"的不同含义,分别译为"build""manage""maintain",与后面的三个宾语搭配得天衣无缝,

---

① 《现代汉语词典》第 7 版,第 1077 页。
② 据《钱伯斯英语词典》第十三版,第 892 页。listen to: to follow advice.
③ 同上,第 902 页。look to: to depend on (for); to take care of.
④ 《现代汉语词典》第 7 版,第 213 页。
⑤ 据《钱伯斯英语词典》第十三版,第 1605 页。temple: a building or place dedicated to, or regarded as the house of, a god; a place of worship.

十分准确地表达了原句之义,实属佳译。

(2) 编印书籍、整理地方志

A: Printing books, filing local documents

B: print books, classify annals

C: books were printed, local gazetteers assembled

D: books were printed, gazetteers collected

"地方志"即方志,是"记载某一地方的地理、历史、风俗、教育、物产、人物等情况的书,如县志、府志等"①,与"地方史"有区别。"地方史"以记叙某地有史以来的人类社会活动为主,重在记叙过去;"地方志"则是对自然和社会的记叙并重,以记叙现状为主,也兼及过去。如此可见,"地方志"在英美文化中也属文化空白。"document"意为"文件,文献,证据"②,"gazetteer"仅指"地名辞典"③,两词与"方志"大相径庭。据《钱伯斯英语辞典》,"annals"意为"records of events under the years in which they happened; historical records generally; yearbooks"④,与"方志"之内容有交叉,但仍偏重"史"。鉴于英语中无对应"方志"之词,笔者认为可译为"local annals",再以加注的方式说明其在中国传统文化中所涵盖的内容,故将此句改译为"books are printed, local annals⑤ edited"。

8. 第七诗节翻译对比分析

(1) 哲学如雨,科学不能适应

A: Philosophy raining, sciences embarrassed

B: philosophy is rain, science can't adapt

---

① 《现代汉语词典》第7版,第367页。
② 据《钱伯斯英语词典》第十三版,第454页。document: a paper, *esp* of an official character, affording information, proof or evidence of anything.
③ 同上,第632页。gazetteer: a geographical dictionary, a reference book containing alphabetical entries for places of the world, with maps, etc.
④ 同上,第52页。
⑤ Local annals refer to a book that records the geography, history, customs, education, property, people, *etc* of a certain place.

C：philosophy poured down like rain, science couldn't keep up

D：philosophy fell like rain, science couldn't adapt

"哲学如雨"隐喻在清朝人文学科发达，人人皆"哲学家"，深谙儒家哲学，人人皆"文学家"，善舞文弄墨、诗词歌赋。然而"科学不能适应"，清朝时期，思想封闭守旧，外来科学技术被视为"巧技"，不为这个以人文为重的社会所轻易接受。译本 A 用"embarrassed"（窘迫的，尴尬的）①译"不能适应"，稍有过之。译本 C 译为"couldn't keep up"（不能保持同步）②，同样与原文之义有出入。译本 B、D 所用的"adapt"③一词准确呈现了原句之义。

（2）有一个人朝三暮四

A：There being a man dangling, wandering

B：a fickle-minded man

C：someone was playing six and two threes④

D：one man changed his mind night and day

"朝三暮四"为一成语，语出《庄子·齐物论》，"原比喻聪明人善于使用手段，愚笨的人不善于辨别事情，后来形容反复无常"⑤。此句连同最后的三句乃本诗主题升华的点睛之笔。结合最后一句"他于一八四二年死去"可知，"有一个人"并非指具体的某个人，而是隐喻清朝时期的中国。那时的清朝社会，传统、落后、封闭、发展缓慢，与西方殖民者的"入侵"、对现代科学的"不适应"、社会变革的遇阻与阵痛相互交织、撕扯、对抗，变为一个浮躁的、愤怒的、风雨飘摇的中国。随着 1842 年鸦片战争结束，西方列强打开中国大门，中国开始沦为半殖民地半封建社会，那个传统的中国"死去"。故此句

---

① 据《钱伯斯英语词典》第十三版，第 500 页。embarrassed: self-conscious, ashamed or awkward; perplexed; constrained.

② 同上，第 836 页。keep up: to continue, to prevent from ceasing; to maintain in good condition; to keep pace (with).

③ 同上，第 16 页。adapt: to make fit or suitable; to modify; to adjust.

④ Literally "3 in the morning and 4 at night"—a quotation from the Zhuangzi story about the monkeys dissatisfied with their 3 nuts in the morning and 4 nuts at night, who were pacified with the offer of 4 in the morning and 3 at night.

⑤ 《现代汉语词典》第 7 版，第 1654 页。

的"朝三暮四"字面上指浮躁多变,实则比喻社会动荡,国家的改革与发展毫无头绪。欲革新而不成,则"无端端地着急",因浮躁而易怒,"愤怒成为他毕生的事业"。这一"急"一"怒",不正是中国国民从近代以来直到今天,在走向现代化的路上,所表现出来的典型的"国民特性"吗?

再来看四个译本对"朝三暮四"的翻译。译本 A 所用的"dangle"指"松散地悬挂着或垂着摆动"①,"wander"指"闲逛,游荡"②,无法表达该词字面意义或引申意义。译本 C 同前文翻译成语的处理方式一样,采用了加注的方式,在注释里译者对"朝三暮四"这个成语的典故进行了说明。"six and two threes"是一英语俗语,与"six and half a dozen"③意同,指"两个同样的选择或情形"。译者在英语中找到了一个与"朝三暮四"的成语典故描述相近的俗语表达,但其意思却与"朝三暮四"现今所指的"反复无常"完全不沾边,更谈不上在此诗句中的引申意义了。译本 D 译为"changed his mind night and day",译出了"易变"之义,但原句想表达的"浮躁"之义体现不足。译本 B 选用了"fickle-minded"一词,据《钱伯斯英语词典》,"fickle"意为"inconstant in affections, loyalties or intentions; changeable"④。该词呈现的"无常、易变"准确而丰富地刻画了心浮气躁的那个"他",与原诗本节之意境最为契合。

9. 韵律使用分析

柏桦诗歌的美,相当一部分体现在其特有的音乐性,在其隐藏于字里行间的节奏和旋律,一种诗人独特的融入其血脉的声音。诗人在论述自己早期的诗观时指出:"诗和生命的节律一样在呼吸里自然形成。一当它形成某种氛围,文字就变得模糊并溶入某种气息或声音。此时,诗歌企图去作一次

---

① 据《钱伯斯英语词典》第十三版,第 392 页。dangle: to hang loosely or with a swinging motion.
② 同上,第 1762 页。wander: to ramble or move with no definite object, or with no fixed course, or by around about way.
③ 同上,第 1458 页。six and half a dozen: having alternatives which are considered equivalent, equally acceptable.
④ 同上,第 570 页。

侥幸的超越,并借此接近自然的纯粹,但连最伟大的诗歌也很难抵达这种纯粹,所以它带给我们的欢乐是有限的、遗憾的。从这个意义上说诗是不能写的,只是我们在不得已的情况下动用了这种形式。"① 可见柏桦诗歌的"声音""音乐性"之重要性。《在清朝》以诗题贯于每节之首,犹如场景切换之提示,为读者呈现一幅幅展示清朝社会全貌的生动画卷。同时,此类"重章叠句""回环反复"之写作手法,自然带来一种节奏美。原诗各行长短不一,以短句为主,每行六至八个字居多,视觉上错落有致,乐感上抑扬顿挫、节奏感强。比较四个译本可发现,译本 A 显示了译者对原诗的节奏和韵律的敏锐感知,从译文中读者可以看到译者在译文句式结构和尾韵上努力再现原诗的尝试。以下是原诗前四节每节第三行:

牛羊无事,百姓下棋
纸张泛滥,风筝遍地
饮酒落花,风和日丽
夜读太史公,清晨扫地

每行两句对仗,且句尾押韵。再看译本 A 的对应译句:

Cattle and sheep jobless, commons playing chess
Papers overproduced, kites seen everywhere
Drinking over flowers falling, when breezy and sunny
Reading Shi Ji at night, sweeping floors in the morning

译诗与原诗的对仗形式一致,节奏感相似。在用韵方面,原诗通篇协韵,协尾韵"i",诗行中同时伴有多个协该韵的字。第一节:第 3 行"棋",第 7 行"器";第二节:第 3 行"地";第三节:第 3 行"丽",第 6 行"及";第四节:第 3 行"地",第 5 行"吏";第六节:第 1 行"励",第 2 行"利",第 3 行"籍"

---

① 黄梁:《地下的光脉》,台北:唐山出版社,1999 年,第 215—216 页。

"理";第七节:第4行"急",第5行"毕",第6行"去"。此外,全篇还协"-i"韵(因其作为整体认读音节的一部分放在"zh""ch""sh""z""c""s""r"之后,读音与"i"略有不同)。第一节:第2行"事",第3行"私",第4行"时";第二节:第1行"纸",第6行"似";第三节:第1行"诗""事""子",第2行"日",第3行"池",第4行"只""子";第五节:第3行"字",第4行"子",第5行"子";第六行:第5行"志";第七节:第3行"四",第6行"死"。译本A基本再现了原诗的协韵的特点,全篇也有两个尾韵的安排,一个是协辅音/s/或/z/,如第一节"chess""selfless""place",第二节"surplus",第三节"faces",第四节"Affairs",第五节"others""sons",第六节"taxes""temples""documents",第七节"embarrassed""business";另一个尾韵(也有少数行间韵)则协元音/ə/,如第一节"leisured""china",第二节"everywhere""inspired""southward""surplus",第三节"together""other",第四节"another""Affairs""year",第五节"non-bearded""others",第七节"embarrassed""wandering"。可见,中国译者李赋康翻译时在再现原诗的韵律和音乐美感方面所作的努力。另外的三个译本中则找不到明显的韵律安排。

四、结　　语

通过以上对柏桦名诗《在清朝》英文译本的对照分析,我们可以感受到,不同的译者对原文有着不同的理解和阐释,呈现出不同的译文风格和特点,其必然给《在清朝》这首诗在英语世界的"漫游"带来不同的影响。原诗在诗歌美学层面所具有的丰富的艺术内涵、所蕴含的诗人的独特而丰满的思想情感,能否得以在译文中得以有效传递,取决于译者能否"戴着音韵和节奏的镣铐在绳索上跳舞",既能跳得灵活自如又能富于艺术美感。这绝非易事,却并非不可追求。

《在清朝》的四个英语译本中,就外在形式、节奏韵律以及对原诗的理解而言,译本A体现了译者李赋康的母语优势,其对原诗的理解准确、深入,对原诗音乐性的感知到位,但出现的问题是英语语言表达的准确性尤其是用词的精确度不够。在句法结构上,译本A少数诗行用了完整的句子,大部分诗行都采用了名词加分词构成的独立主格结构,且无规律性,显得不够严谨。就译诗的准确性、语言的流畅度而言,译本 C 当属最佳,上文多处分析已有论及。同时,译本 C 亦尽力再现原诗中的中国传统文化要素,如两处成语的翻译都采取了直译加注的方式,为英语读者很好地呈现了成语背后丰富的文化内涵。但也正是由于译者霍布恩对于译诗内容准确性的追求,译诗用词最多,在形式上没能再现原诗语言简洁的风格。这实在难以苛求,内容与形式历来难以兼得。就体现原诗语言风格方面,译本 B 明显占优,用词最少,语言简练,且少用修饰语(形容词和副词使用比例低),呈现客观性,较好地再现了原诗的"冷抒情"风格。译本 D 亦类似,形容词和副词使用比例最低,但其翻译选词的准确性亦有所欠缺,部分地方显示对原诗的理解存在一定问题。笔者认为,对于译诗内容和形式的兼顾固然困难,但并非无对应之策。既然是翻译,忠实于原文,对原诗内容的准确再现,译诗用词的准确选择,当是首要考量。于此基础上,在语言风格、外在形式、节奏韵律上尽量呈现原诗之特点,当属可接受或能被认可的诗歌翻译。基于这样的认识,笔者参考四个英文译本,取众家之长,将此诗进行了改译,以期为该诗的英语读者提供另一个参考。译诗全文如下:

In Qing Dynasty

In Qing Dynasty
ease and ideals go further
cattle are at leisure, the commonalty play chess
the imperial exams are impartial
currencies vary from place to place
sometimes they barter grain
fortea leaves, silk, and porcelain

In Qing Dynasty
landscape paintinghas attained perfection
papersare overflowing, kites everywhere

lanterns are well-made

temple after temple face south

there seems an excess of wealth

In Qing Dynasty

poets care nothing for a living, only for dignity and reputation

drinking with petals falling, the wind gentle and the sun warm

the pond-water fertile

two ducks swim and greet the wind respectively

just as horses in heat do not couple with cattle①

In Qing Dynasty

a man dreams of a man

reading the Grand Historian② at night, sweeping the floor at dawn

and the court establishes the Bureau of Military Affairs③

selecting long-nailed officials each year

In Qing Dynasty

men both bearded and beardless

behave strictly, converse little

country folk are reluctant to learn to read

children look up to the old

mothers look to their sons

---

① This line references *Zuo Zhuan*, 4th year of Duke Xi. See Legge's translation, *Tso Chuan, Duke Hsi* in *The Chinese Classics*. One metaphoric interpretation of this line is "Even if my herds wander far away, they'll never come into contact with yours', i. e. why do you make war on me when we are so far apart we can do no harm to each other".

② the Grand Historian is Sima Qian (ca. 145 or 135 BC—86 BC), author of the *Historical Records*.

③ Under the emperor's direct control, it's just like his private secretariat. In fact, it's the top state organ in charge of military and political power.

In Qing Dynasty

with taxes people are motivated

irrigation worksare built, schools managed, ancestral halls maintained

books are printed, local annals① edited

Buildings are made antique

In Qing Dynasty

philosophy is like rain, science can't adapt

someone is fickle-minded②

anxious for no reason

rage becomes his life-long career

until he died in 1840

附：原诗及四个译本对照版

在清朝

A：In Qing Dynasty

B：In the Qing dynasty

C：in the Qing Dynasty

D：In the Qing Dynasty

安闲和理想越来越深

A：Leisure was leisured, ideal idealized

B：ease and ideals flourish

C：idleness and the ideal went deeper and deeper

D：lightheartedness and idealism grew deeper

---

① Local annals refer a book that records the geography, history, customs, education, property, people, *etc* of a certain place.

② "朝三暮四" is a Chinese idiom, a quotation from the Zhuangzi story about the monkeys dissatisfied with their 3 nuts in the morning and 4 nuts at night, who were pacified with the offer of 4 in the morning and 3 at night. In Modern Chinese, it's used to describe a person inconstant in affections, loyalties or intentions.

牛羊无事,百姓下棋

A: Cattle and sheep jobless, commons playing chess

B: cows and sheep do nothing, the folks play chess

C: cows and ships were at peace, the people played chess

D: cows and sheep were idle, people played chess

科举也大公无私

A: Imperial exams just and selfless

B: even imperial exams are fair and selfless

C: and imperial exams were just and fair

D: the imperial examination was impartial

货币两地不同

A: Moneys varied from place to place

B: different currencies in two places

C: currencies were different in different places

D: every place had its own currency

有时还用谷物兑换

A: Sometimes crop was used to exchange

B: sometimes they barter crops

C: sometimes even grain as exchanged for

D: grain could be used to barter

茶叶、丝、瓷器

A: Tea, china, silk

B: for tea, silk andchina

C: tea leaves, silk, porcelain

D: for tea leaves, silk, porcelain

在清朝

A: In Qing Dynasty

B: In the Qing dynasty

C：in the Qing Dynasty

D：In the Qing Dynasty

山水画臻于完美

A：Landscape painting reaching perfection

B：landscape art defines perfect

C：landscape painting had attained perfection

D：landscape painting neared perfection

纸张泛滥，风筝遍地

A：Papers overproduced, kites seen everywhere

B：a flood of paper, kites everywhere

C：papers were overflowing, kites everywhere

D：paper was abundant, kites flew everywhere

灯笼得了要领

A：Lanterns all inspired

B：lanterns lead the way

C：lanterns were well-proportioned

D：lanterns understood the essentials

一座座庙宇向南

A：Temples after temples looking southward

B：temples after temples turn southward

C：temple after temple faced south

D：temple after temple faced south

财富似乎过分

A：Seemingly riches being surplus

B：even wealth seems over the top

C：there seemed an excess of wealth and fortune

D：the wealth seemed excessive

在清朝

A：In Qing Dynasty

B：In the Qing dynasty

C：in the Qing Dynasty

D：In the Qing Dynasty

诗人不事营生、爱面子

A：Poets cared nothing but their faces

B：poets have no trade, save face

C：poets cared nothing for a living, only for reputation

D：poets didn't work for a living, concerned with reputation

饮酒落花,风和日丽

A：Drinking over flowers falling, when breezy and sunny

B：drinking over fallen leaves and fine weather

C：drank wine as petals fell, the wind gentle and the sun warm

D：drinking under falling petals, in warm sunny weather

池塘的水很肥

A：Water in ponds fertilizing

B：fat pond water

C：even the pond-water as fertile

D：the lakes brimmed with water

二只鸭子迎风游泳

A：Against the wind two ducks swimming together

B：two ducks swim and greet the wind

C：ducks swam in pairs before the wind

D：two ducks swam against the wind

风马牛不相及

A：Not knowing each other

B：at complete odds

C：-just so horses in heat do not couple with cattle

D：everything was at odds

在清朝

A：In Qing Dynasty

B：In the Qing dynasty

C：in the Qing Dynasty

D：In the Qing Dynasty

一个人梦见一个人

A：A man dreaming of another

B：a man dreams of a man

C：someone dreamed about someone

D：one man dreamt of another

夜读太史公,清晨扫地

A：Reading Shi Ji at night, sweeping floors in the morning

B：reads Sima Qian at night, sweeps the floor in the morning

C：reading the Grand Historian in the night, sweeping the floor at dawn

D：read The Grand History at night, swept at dawn

而朝廷增设军机处

A：While the court opening the Bureau of Military Affairs

B：the court creates more military sites

C：and the Court established the Council of State

D：the court created a Military Office

每年选拔长指甲的官吏

A：Appointing long-nailed officials each year

B：appoints officers with long nails each year

C：every year promoted long-nailed mandarins

D：each year selecting officials with long fingernails

在清朝

A：In Qing Dynasty

B：In the Qing dynasty

C：in the Qing Dynasty

D：In the Qing Dynasty

多胡须和无胡须的人

A：Both the bearded and the non-bearded

B：men with beards and men with no beards

C：men both bewhiskered and clean-shaven

D：men with and without beards

严于身教，不苟言谈

A：Strict with themselves，hard to talk with others

B：behave strictly，converse little

C：were strict on teaching by example，solemn in speech and manners

D：taught by example instead of with words

农村人不愿认字

A：Countryside people refusing to learn to read

B：country folks refuse to read

C：country folk were reluctant to learn their letters

D：farmers didn't want to learn to read

孩子们敬老

A：Children looking up to the aged

B：children respect the old

C：children respected their elders

D：the young respected the old

母亲屈从于儿子

A：Mothers looking to their sons

B：mothers listen to their sons

C：mothers ceded power to their sons

D：mothers submitted to their sons

在清朝

A：In Qing Dynasty

B：In the Qing dynasty

C：in the Qing Dynasty

D：In the Qing Dynasty

用款税激励人民

A：People encouraged with taxes

B：taxes motivate people

C：with taxes and with dues the people were heartened

D：taxes inspired the people

办水利、办学校、办祠堂

A：Setting up irrigation, schools, temples

B：build irrigation, schools and temples

C：irrigation works were built, schools managed, ancestral halls maintained

D：and built irrigation works, schools, temples

编印书籍、整理地方志

A：Printing books, filing local documents

B：print books, classify annals

C：books were printed, local gazetteers assembled

D：books were printed, gazetteers collected

建筑弄得古香古色

A：Buildings being all made antique

B：lend architecture a classical touch

C：habitations decked out in the antique style

D：the architecture was designed to look antique

在清朝

A：In Qing Dynasty

B：In the Qing dynasty

C：in the Qing Dynasty

D：In the Qing Dynasty

哲学如雨，科学不能适应

A：Philosophy raining, sciences embarrassed

B：philosophy is rain, science can't adapt

C：philosophy poured down like rain, science couldn't keep up

D：philosophy fell like rain, science couldn't adapt

有一个人朝三暮四

A：There being a man dangling, wandering

B：a fickle-minded man

C：someone was playing six and two threes

D：one man changed his mind night and day

无端端地着急

A：Anxious out of no reason

B：anxious for no reason

C：gratuitously anxious

D：always unreasonably anxious

愤怒成为他毕生的事业

A：Taking wrath for his life-long business

B：ends his lifelong career in rage

C：rage became his life-long career

D：resentment became his lifelong vocation

他于一八四二年死去

A：Who died in 1840

B：dies in 1842

C：until, in 1840, he died

D：until his death in 1842.

个案研究二：从比较文学变异学视角看霍布恩英译柏桦诗歌[①]

杨安文　牟厚宇

曹顺庆教授创立的比较文学变异学为译介学研究提供了坚实的理论基础，拓展了文学翻译研究的视野和方法。本文从比较文学变异学理论视角，以柏桦诗歌霍布恩英译为例，从文化过滤、文学误读与误译等方面，探究诗歌文本在翻译中的变异现象，并深入分析其产生的原因。本文认为，在诗歌翻译中因文化过滤和文学误读产生变异是一种常态，正是这种"创造性叛逆"使得看似不可译的诗歌得到有效的语言转换。在肯定译者主体性与创造性翻译的价值同时，本文亦指出，译者应避免因缺乏译入语文化知识而导致的误译，尽力将原文的文化信息准确有效地转化至译文中。

一、比较文学变异学

比较文学作为一门独立学科自19世纪末产生以来，其发展大体分为三个阶段：第一阶段是法国学派的实证性影响研究；第二阶段是美国学派的平行研究；第三阶段则是中国学派的变异研究。法国的影响研究本质上是实证性的国际文学关系史研究，注重可考察的"关系"，放弃各国文学的"比较"。法国学派的奠基人梵·第根提出："比较文学的对象是本质地研究各国文学作品的相互关系。"[②]但这种完全摆脱美学意义的实证研究也在相当

---

① 此文原发表于《中外文化与文论》第43辑，2019年。
② 梵·第根：《比较文学论》，戴望舒译，台北：台湾商务印书馆，1995年，第55页。

程度上限制了比较文学的学科发展,因而遭到了美国学派学者的强烈反对。由美国学派提出的"平行研究"强调审美性研究,主张恢复比较文学的"比较",比较文学应该把美学价值批评重新引进比较文学学科领域之中。① 随着 20 世纪 80 年代比较文学引入中国,中国学者开始对西方比较文学的学科体系进行反思。无论是法国学派还是美国学派,都是在西方文明体系内进行求同性的研究比较。随着东方国家的相继崛起,跨文化、跨文明研究已是大势所趋,而在中西方这两种异质文明的文学研究中,我们不难发现,"变异性"和"差异性"远远超过"关联性"和"同源性"。

曹顺庆教授于 2005 年在《比较文学学》一书中正式提出"比较文学变异学",首次将变异学纳入比较文学研究中的一个基本理论范畴,并在其著作《比较文学教程》中将变异学具体分为五大研究领域:语言变异研究、文化变异研究、文学文本变异研究、跨国与跨文明形象研究和文学的他国化研究。曹教授指出,可比性的基本立足点是"同源性"和"类同性",不过不是只有它们才有可比性,"变异性"和"差异性"同样可比,这是比较文学变异学的根本理论所在。② 从最初的"同源性"到变异学"异质性"的转变,为比较文学提供了全新的研究视角,是比较文学学科理论的重大突破。

值得注意的是,曹教授将译介学也纳入了比较文学变异学的研究领域,认为译介学是比较文学变异学中研究语言层面的变异的分支学科③。文学变异学下的语言变异研究主要指文学现象穿越语言的界限,通过翻译而在目的语环境中得到接受的过程,也就是比较文学中的翻译研究。④ 传统的译介学作为比较文学的一个分支,通常被划分为媒介学的研究范畴,但随着全球化语境下的翻译文化转向,以"忠实"和"作者中心"为基础的传统译学理论开始动摇,取而代之的是以译者和译文为主要研究对象的翻译研究;它关心的不是语言层面上出发语与目的语之间如何转换的问题,而是原文在这种外语和本族语转换过程中信息的失落、变形、增添、扩伸等问题。⑤ 曹教授提出的

---

① 曹顺庆、李卫涛:《比较文学学科中的文学变异学研究》,载《复旦学报》,2006 年第 1 期。
② 曹顺庆:《比较文学教程》,北京:高等教育出版社,2010 年,第 21 页。
③ 同上,第 112 页。
④ 曹顺庆:《比较文学学》,成都:四川大学出版社,2005 年,第 30 页。
⑤ 谢天振:《译介学》,上海:上海外语教育出版社,1999 年,第 1 页。

变异学正是着眼于跨异质文明下的文化/文学的交流与碰撞,从译本语言层面的变异现象分析其深层次的原因及内在规律。因此,在比较文学变异学的视阈下重新界定译介学,既符合翻译研究的文化走向,又进一步明确和深化了译介学的内涵,为翻译变异现象的研究提供了新的研究范式。本文力图用比较文学变异学理论,以著名诗人柏桦的代表诗作及译者霍布恩的英译本为例,分析诗歌翻译中的语言及文化变异,以及产生这些变异的原因。

二、柏桦诗歌及译者简介

柏桦是 20 世纪 80 年代"后朦胧"诗人的杰出代表,是中国当代最有影响力的诗人之一。柏桦为读者所熟知的是其早期创作的诗歌(1980 年代至 2000 年),虽总量不多,不足百篇,但许多诗歌堪称经典,备受海内外读者关注和喜爱。柏桦早期的大部分诗歌自 80 年代末被陆续译介到海外,翻译成英语、德语、法语、荷兰语、西班牙语、韩语、日语等多国文字①。在经过十年的诗歌创作停滞期②之后,柏桦于 2007 年开始恢复写诗,且风格有所转变,创作量惊人③。由于柏桦复笔后的诗歌大量化用典故,使用隐喻,互文性、跳跃性强,给读者的理解带来一定困难,对于国外译者或汉学家而言,翻译此类诗歌更是不易。在柏桦现已正式发表或出版的英译诗中,仅四分之一是其复笔后创作的诗歌。然而,正是这些看似难以翻译的诗歌,给了敢于挑战的译者创造性翻译的空间,将晦涩难懂的原诗有效转换为英语读者可以领会、感受的英语诗歌。霍布恩就是这样的译者。

霍布恩是蜚声中外的汉学家、翻译家。他出生于苏格兰边区城镇加拉希尔斯,中学时期接受传统苏格兰式教育,系统学习了拉丁语、希腊语、法语和

---

① 据笔者统计,柏桦 2000 年以前正式出版的诗有 98 首,其中被译为英文的有 82 首,译为法文的有 24 首,译为德文的有 16 首,译为荷兰语的有 6 首,译为西班牙语和日语的各有 1 首。
② 据柏桦多本诗集作品所标注的创作时间,诗人在 1997 年完成《山水手记》创作之后息笔,直到 2007 年创作长诗《水绘仙侣——1643—1651:冒辟疆与董小宛》,后者标志着诗人恢复诗歌创作。
③ 据统计,自 2007 年以来出版的柏桦诗集有 18 种,其中包括英文诗集和法文诗集各 1 种,其中诗人 2007 年以来创作的诗歌超过 1000 首。

英语,而后进入爱丁堡大学和杜伦大学进行汉学研究并取得硕士学位,毕业后曾在爱丁堡大学、杜伦大学和香港理工大学教授汉语及汉英翻译。霍布恩不仅在汉学研究领域颇有建树,更是一个出色的文学翻译家。他翻译了我国著名朦胧派诗人杨炼的诗集,并完成了中国古典名著《水浒传》的苏格兰语译本。霍布恩的诗歌翻译得到了汉学界及中国诗人们的高度认可。由霍布恩领衔翻译、杨炼编选的中国当代新诗选《玉梯:中国当代诗歌》,自2012年由英国著名的血斧出版社出版以来广受好评。柏桦就霍布恩对自己的诗歌翻译更是不吝赞美之辞,认为他创造性的翻译转换使得译诗甚至超过了原诗。

霍布恩翻译的柏桦诗歌共12首,其中7首是柏桦早期经典诗歌,载于《玉梯:中国当代诗歌》,另外5首全部为柏桦复笔后创作的诗歌,发表于《人民文学》在海外推出的英文版《路灯》2013年夏季号上。这12首诗均非霍布恩选出,是由编辑选出交其进行翻译。而霍布恩在整个翻译过程中,没有与原诗作者取得任何联系,全凭自己对诗歌文本的理解,独立完成翻译。在香港中文大学翻译研究中心第四届《译丛》文学翻译杰出讲座中,霍布恩指出"译者实际上同时扮演解读者(interpretive personas)、幽灵作家(ghost writers)和创作者(composers)多重角色,介于原作者与既定读者之间,译者往往会对原作品有所取舍及加工,文学翻译可理解为一种再创造的行为,这亦可归类为译者的自我选择——选择用何种方式在何种程度上以何种文字效果解读作品"。① 可见,霍布恩强调译者主体性,强调译者享有对翻译文本的"自主权"和"决策权"。这样的翻译观也就决定了在他的译本中,文学翻译的"创造性叛逆"或"变异"是必然的。

三、柏桦诗歌霍布恩英译中的变异现象

1. 文化过滤与文学翻译变异

在翻译研究文化转向的背景下,翻译已不仅仅是单纯的语言文字转换,

---

① 引自香港中文大学中国文化研究所网页:http://cloud.itsc.cuhk.edu.hk/enewsasp/app/article-details.aspx/C1E4F4D98C9C63CC3DC8E4B115B1A894/。

更重要的是不同文化之间的交流与沟通,是两种异质文化的比较,因而文化过滤和文学变异是不可避免的。接受者在不同的文化背景下,对异质文化和文学必然会产生有选择的接受和拒绝,从而导致文学变异。曹顺庆教授指出,引起文学变异的第一大要素是文化过滤。"任何接受者都生长于特定的时空里,在这个特定的文化时空里,接受者受其社会、历史、文化语境和民族心理等因素的制约,形成了独特的文化心理与欣赏习惯,这种独特的文化构成必然会影响接受者对外来文学与文化的接受……也就意味着承认在文化文学交流过程中,接受者对交流信息存在着选择、变形、伪装、渗透、叛逆和创新的可能性。"① 这种"叛逆"和"创新"就是我们熟知的创造性叛逆,是因文化过滤而产生的文学变异现象。霍布恩在柏桦诗歌翻译中出现的文化过滤现象主要分为两种:译入语文学传统引起的文化过滤和中西思维方式引起的文化过滤。

(1) 文学传统的文化过滤

每个民族都有自身的文学传统,在文学作品的题材选择、语篇组织、思想感情及审美情趣上都有诸多不同,译者在翻译过程中会根据自身的文学传统对原文本进行文化过滤。本文首先以《假儿歌》一诗为例,分析文学传统的文化过滤是如何影响翻译实践的。

《假儿歌》是柏桦20世纪后创作的新诗代表作之一。顾名思义,"儿歌"指的是为儿童创作的、适合儿童唱的歌谣。② 因为接受主体是儿童,儿歌大多音韵流畅,节奏轻快,内容也简单易懂。但诗题拟为"假儿歌"证明本诗与真正的儿歌有所不同。全诗共五节,每行诗都为五字,篇幅短小精巧,并采取了整齐的句式结构,读起来朗朗上口,具有儿歌的形式特点。但细看内容,诗人似乎把一堆毫无关联的事物与人名拼凑结合,让人摸不透其中的逻辑,是谓"假儿歌"。全诗节奏缓和,语调平淡,出现的各类事物人名也是诗人凭自己的喜好信手拈来,无论是诗词戏剧还是人名菜名都一一入诗,处处透露着闲逸之气,体现了柏桦所倡导的逸乐诗学。柏桦认为,逸乐作为一种

---

① 曹顺庆:《比较文学教程》,北京:高等教育出版社,2010年,第97—99页。
② 《现代汉语词典》第7版,第344页。

合情理的价值观或文学观长期遭受道德律令的压抑。生命应从轻逸开始,尽力纵乐,甚至颓废。生命并非只有痛苦,也有优雅与逸乐,也有对于时光流逝、良辰美景以及友谊和爱情的缠绵与轻叹。① 在这短短十行的小诗里,诗人用看似简单的名词堆砌,表现了轻逸优雅的诗学态度。以下为《假儿歌》的第二节:

> 红,是寂寞红
> 春,是玉堂春
> 秋,是汉宫秋
> 鱼,是黄花鱼②

霍布恩的译文如下:

red	is *Lady In Red*
spring	is *Might As Well Be Spring*
autumn	is *When Autumn Leaves Start to Fall*
fish	is *Like A Sturgeon Touched For The Very First Time*③

这四行诗中分别列出了四个意象:寂寞红、玉堂春、汉宫秋和黄花鱼。其中《玉堂春》和《汉宫秋》是我国家喻户晓的戏剧作品,前者讲的是明朝名妓苏三(玉堂春)与吏部尚书之子王景隆曲折的爱情故事,后者全名为《破幽梦孤雁汉宫秋》,取材于王昭君出塞的历史故事。"寂寞红"出自唐代诗人元稹的五言绝句《行宫》:"寥落古行宫,宫花寂寞红。白头宫女在,闲坐说玄宗。"抒发了从盛唐到中唐的盛衰之感。黄花鱼则是中国寻常百姓家餐桌上的一道美食,也是我国重要经济鱼之一,广泛分布于黄海、东海、渤海和南海地区。这四个意象与中华文化结合紧密,要译出其中的文学意蕴着实不易,

---

① 唐小林、柏桦:《关于柏桦诗学的对话》,载《当代作家评论》,2010年第5期。
② 柏桦:《革命要诗和学问》,台北:秀威资讯科技股份有限公司,2015年,第125页。
③ Bai Hua. "Mock Nursery Rhyme", Brian Holton, tran. *Pathlight*, 2013 (Summer):134.

只能通过译者加注使外国读者了解这几部诗词戏剧作品。但即便是有详尽的注释,假如读者不了解柏桦的逸乐诗观,也很难明白为何诗人将这四个毫无关联的意象并置。

霍布恩精通中西文化,深知此处直译很难为外国读者所接受,故省去了此节诗中的中国文化成分,将原诗的四个文化意象巧妙地对应了四句英文歌词:*Lady In Red* 是爱尔兰歌手克里斯·蒂伯(Chris De Burgh)的成名曲;"Might As Well Be Spring"出自 1945 年美国电影《爱州博览会》里的原声歌曲 *It Might As Well Be Spring*;"When Autumn Leaves Start to Fall"出自歌曲 *Autumn Leaves*,这原本是一首法文歌,后来被翻唱为英文版本。"Like A Sturgeon Touched For The Very First Time"出自麦当娜的单曲 *Like a Virgin*,为了与诗行开头的"fish"相呼应,译者还别具匠心地将原歌词"virgin"改为了"sturgeon"(鲟鱼)①。霍布恩的翻译着实令人咋舌,原诗的中国文学文化元素荡然无存,取而代之的是美国流行音乐文化。但原诗所用的四个意象本无任何逻辑理据,全凭诗人的喜好罗列入诗,霍布恩将西方流行音乐的歌词随意对应,与原诗的闲逸优雅倒有异曲同工之妙。

除此之外,原诗与译文确有一共同之处:两者所描写的都是中西方家喻户晓的事物。《玉堂春》和《汉宫秋》是中国流传已久的名剧,《行宫》也是唐诗经典之作,黄花鱼更是中国路人皆知的舌尖美味。*Lady In Red* 在世界范围内取得巨大成功,成为克里斯·蒂伯最著名最热销的歌曲;*It Might As Well Be Spring* 拿下了奥斯卡最佳原创歌曲奖;*Autumn Leaves* 是《廊桥遗梦》和《怨妇悲秋》两部著名电影的配乐;*Like a Virgin* 更是麦当娜风靡全球的代表作。用西方的名曲代替中国熟知的诗词戏剧,使译诗更加符合接受者的文化传统,更容易被外国读者所接受。霍布恩此译文正是文学翻译过程中文化过滤的一大范例,充分体现了跨异质文化接受者的主体性、选择性和创造性。

就诗歌的文体特征而言,诗必须有节奏韵律,这是诗歌艺术形式的重要

---

① 霍布恩在"译者注"中提到,他吃过黄花鱼,认为是一种与鲟鱼(sturgeon)同类的淡水鱼,故未根据词典译为"Yellow Croaker"。我们知道黄花鱼是一种海鱼,此处应该是译者搞错了。"译者注"来源:Brian Holton. "Translator's Note", *Pathlight*, 2013 (Summer):137.

特征,也是诗歌在各民族文学传统中的共通之处。现代汉语诗歌虽"不拘格律",主张"诗体的大解放",看似是对古典诗歌形式的背叛,实则并未与古典诗歌完全决裂,既有对古典诗歌的继承,也在其基础上开拓创新,探索了许多现代诗歌独特的"声音"。柏桦在《我的几种诗观》一文中就谈及了自己的诗歌声音观:"诗歌中的声音应从两方面来讲,一是诗歌的音韵、节奏、押韵、排列等形式功能,二是写诗者的语气、语调、态度、气质。当我们说他写诗有一种独特的声音,便是对写者的赞美,尤其赞美他写诗时的姿态和语气……声音在诗歌中至关重要……诗歌中的声音是最具魅力的部分,其中也具有情感、意义以及某种区别于他人的神秘禀性。"①诗歌的声音对诗歌创作如此重要,想要在译文中尽善尽美地呈现出原诗的形式之美更非易事。"众所周知,在诗歌翻译中,文字的意义和意象均可翻译,唯独声音无法译,因此才有弗罗斯特所说的一句名言,'诗是翻译所失掉的东西'。"②

以《踏青》一诗为例,我们便能看出柏桦诗歌中的独特"声音"。

红墙里的人儿想回家
青蛙躺在白杨树下
是哪一种花在坚持着柔情
迎春花,哦,不,一朵无名的花

我看到女孩用小手投掷皮球
我看到素食者手握一把细沙
老年即命令,断肠即天涯
处处花园开满大地
处处怜惜倾洒

而我惟一的俊友啊

---

① 柏桦:《我的几种诗观》,载《名作欣赏》,2012年第6期。
② 同上。

惟一的春天的舞蹈家
我想,我想
我想分享你明净的前额①

反抗、痛苦和暴力成分在柏桦早期的许多诗中都有体现,但闲适的抒情诗也是柏桦诗歌创作中不可或缺的一部分。原诗是诗人写给倾心的女孩儿以表爱慕之情的,整首诗节奏温和舒缓,是典型的柏桦慢节奏抒情诗。全诗各诗行错落有致,多数诗行行尾押"a"韵,诗中加粗部分便是协韵之处,整首诗朴素清新,却又带有浓浓的中国古典之风。诗句结尾处诗人将"我想"反复吟唱三遍,表现出诗人急于表达爱意却又无从说起的踌躇之感,刻意放缓的节奏加上诗句本身的不押韵使最后两行在整首诗中显得如此突兀而特别,成为全篇的点睛之笔。

我们再来看霍布恩的译文:

the character inside the red walls wants to go home
the frog lying prone under the poplar trees
is which flower, insisting on tendresse?
Jasmine? oh, no–a flower that is nameless

I see a girl throwing a leather ball from her little **hand**
I see a vegetarian holding a fistful of fine **sand**
old age is a command, heartbreak the ends of the **earth**
everywhere gardens of flowers cover the **land**
everywhere tender pity is pouring **forth**

yet, my one and only dear companion and **friend**
my one and only dancer at springtime's **end**

---

① 柏桦:《山水手记》,重庆:重庆大学出版社,2011年,第100页。

I want, I want

I want to share my joy in your brow, so cool, so radiant①

新诗提倡不拘格律、解放诗歌,在诗歌形式上舍弃了传统律诗严格的格律要求。原诗无平仄格式,韵律上虽然尾押"a"韵,但并不是句句有韵,押韵之处也不讲声律规则,因此许多翻译者倾向于将中国的新诗翻译成英语的自由诗。霍布恩的译文虽无传统英诗整齐的扬抑格式,但在翻译原诗韵脚上却是费了心思。霍布恩将原诗第二节的尾韵翻译为"aabab"的形式,是英诗五行体的常用韵脚。原诗最后两行本不押韵,译者却将其改为了英诗"aabb"的随韵,并将最后两个短语单独置后,加快了原诗刻意放缓的节奏。如此一来,原诗结尾的独特"声音"在译诗中也消失了。霍布恩此处的翻译体现了他一贯坚持的归化翻译策略,将原诗的自由韵脚处理成传统英诗的尾韵格式,使译诗在形式上更加符合译入语读者的审美,更容易为译入语读者所接受。

(2) 中西思维方式的文化过滤

人类的思维方式是定型化的思维形式和思维方法,是人类历史长期发展的产物。思维方式是沟通文化与语言的桥梁。一方面,思维方式体现于民族文化的所有领域,包括物质文化、制度文化、行为文化、精神文化和交际文化,尤其体现于哲学、科技、文学、美学、艺术以及宗教、政治、法律等生产和生活实践中;另一方面,思维方式又是语言生成和发展的深层机制,语言又促使思维方式得以形成和发展。② 各民族的思维方式有共通性,也有差异性。在翻译过程中,译者必须充分考虑中西思维方式的差异性,才能成功实现翻译中思维方式的转换。

《献给曼杰斯塔姆》③写于1987年晚秋,是柏桦知名度较高、在海外译介较多的诗作之一。曼杰斯塔姆是俄罗斯白银时代的代表诗人,也是阿克梅派的主要代表人物,其作品深受古典主义的影响,且带有浓重的悲剧色

---

① Bai Hua. "Spring Jaunt", Brian Holton, W. N. Herbert & Lee Man-Kay, tran. In W. N. Herbert & Yang Lian. *Jade Ladder: Contemporary Chinese Poetry*. Northumberland: Bloodaxe Books Ltd., 2012, pp. 113—114.

② 连淑能:《论中西思维方式》,载《外语与外语教学》,2002年第2期。

③ 柏桦:《惟有旧日子带给我们幸福》,南京:江苏凤凰文艺出版社,2017年,第27—28页。

彩,不仅对当时的苏联诗风产生了巨大影响,更是在全世界都饱受赞誉。然而,就是这样一位才华横溢的诗人,他的作品在1928—1973年的近半个世纪中,一本也没有在苏联出版过。① 他一生穷困潦倒,居无定所,在两次流放中耗尽心力,最终长眠于劳改营。全诗是柏桦献给曼杰斯塔姆的一首凄凉的颂歌,诗中塑造的曼杰斯塔姆性格单纯,勇于反抗黑暗的现实,是一个可歌可泣的伟大诗人形象。

《献给曼杰斯塔姆》共有三个英文译本,译者分别为李赋康、菲奥娜以及霍布恩。李赋康是柏桦诗歌译介最早的中国译者,在对原诗曼氏形象的理解和中文诗韵律的把握上比较到位,翻译中十分注意译诗与原诗的对等;菲奥娜作为华裔新加坡人,虽然能说中文,但她久居国外,诗歌创作多用英语;霍布恩出生于苏格兰,从小接受传统的西方文化教育。本文选取李赋康和霍布恩两个译本进行对比分析,从而体现出迥然不同的中西文化背景对译文造成的巨大影响。

请看以下两个诗行的翻译:

我梦想中的诗人
李译:You poet in my dream
霍译:the poet in my dream

穿过太重的北方
李译:Walking through the overloaded north②
霍译:passed through a north too heavy③

汉诗英译,时态的选择是一大难点。由于中文表达中没有动词词尾的变化,我们只能通过动词本身的含义和时间副词、动态助词来显示

---

① 马克·斯洛宁:《苏维埃俄罗斯文学》,上海:上海译文出版社,1983年,第257页。
② Bai Hua. "To Osip Mandelstam", Li Fukang tran. *Scripsi* 7 (1), 1991, pp. 283—284.
③ Bai Hua. "For Mandelstam", Brian Holton, W. N. Herbert & Lee Man-Kay, tran. In W. N. Herbert & Yang Lian. *Jade Ladder: Contemporary Chinese Poetry*. Northumberland: Bloodaxe Books Ltd., 2012, pp. 111—112.

时间关系。诗中"穿过"一词指"从一个地点或时间移动到另一个地点或时间"①,词语本身没有显示任何的时间关系。"中诗常常不拘泥于一时一地,具有一种超越时空观念的、普遍的、恒常的美感魅力。而英语译本却因其细分确指的特征,常常需要增加词语,运用时态和功能词语等语法手段来表达比较明确的时间与空间的观念。"②因此我们只能从诗歌内容判断时态。原诗是作者对曼杰斯塔姆形象的一次大胆想象,诗人与曼杰斯塔姆虽未曾谋面,但通过曼诗的译介作品和他人书写的传记,诗人了解曼杰斯塔姆一生的坎坷,并感同身受,所以在诗中幻想了曼杰斯塔姆从出生到死亡的过程。一方面,诗人描写的是已逝诗人曼杰斯塔姆,选择一般过去式无可厚非。但原诗不是对曼杰斯塔姆一生遭遇的纪实性描写,而是诗人的创造式想象,许多场景和意象为诗人虚构,所以选择历史现在时(historical present)或戏剧性现在时(dramatic present)也是合理的,即用一般现在时代替一般过去时。

两者有何区别呢?当现在时和过去时都可作为选择对象时,过去时主要侧重对一时一地的个人体验的描述,而现在时则用于把受时空限制的一次体验变成普遍的、恒常的经验。③这一节诗是对曼氏的童年进行幻想,讲述曼杰斯塔姆神经敏感的诞生。"北方"代指俄罗斯,因其纬度较高,气候寒冷的缘故。而曼杰斯塔姆出生于华沙,"穿过太重的北方"指的是他幼年从华沙来到彼得堡生活。在诗人的幻想中,我们似乎能看到年幼瘦弱的曼杰斯塔姆正穿过荒凉冷寂的俄罗斯向读者缓缓走来。

从整篇诗歌来看,《献给曼杰斯塔姆》不仅是诗人对曼杰斯塔姆形象的再塑造,也是诗人与曼杰斯塔姆一次深入灵魂的对话。诗歌以问句开篇("那个生活在神经里的人,害怕什么呢?"),有问便有答,下面的回答可以看作诗人的自问自答,也可能是诗中曼杰斯塔姆对诗人的回答("不!害怕声音,那甩掉了思想的声音")。随着诗行的推进,主体"我"与"你"不停地对话,甚至有了惺惺相惜的情感,二者融为一体,曼杰斯塔姆已经是诗人灵魂

---

① 《现代汉语词典》第 7 版,第 501 页。
② 朱徽:《汉诗英译的语法问题》,载《外国语》(上海外国语大学学报),1995 年第 6 期。
③ 黄国文:《翻译研究的语言学探索》,上海:上海外语教育出版社,2006 年,第 158 页。

的一部分,他的精神永远不会逝去。如此看来,霍译使用的一般过去时与原诗的情感基调确有不符之处,而中西思维方式的不同是导致两位译者选择不同时态的根本原因。中国自古以来都十分重视模糊性思维,对事物的本质只求神似而不求精确,"只可意会,不可言传"。而精确性是近代西方社会的重要特征,重视逻辑推理,强调二元对立,将科学理性放在第一位。拿绘画来说,中国画讲究"气韵生动",不拘泥于物体外表的形似,以写意为主;西方画则强调客观真实,善用透视法、解剖学,以写实为主。原诗就像一幅中国的写意画,用简练的笔法描绘出曼杰斯塔姆的童年景象,其中很多留白之处留给读者自行想象。诗中描绘曼杰斯塔姆童年的场景并非诗人亲眼所见所感,而是头脑中虚构的模糊画面,是充满诗意的想象之物,所以李译使用现在进行时以契合原诗的意境;霍布恩没有将此处当作诗人虚构的场景,而是力图记录曼杰斯塔姆幼年离家这一过去事件,所以他选择用一般过去时以明确时间关系,如同注重写实的西洋画。李霍两人的译文深刻反映了中西思维方式差异所带来的文化过滤现象。

2. 文学误读与误译

可以说,文学误读是伴随着文化过滤的产生而产生。"静态的文本提供的信息与读者解读时所获取的信息之间往往不尽相同"[①],这种"不尽相同"即为文化过滤,其产生的后果就是误读。在文学翻译中,译者的误读必然产生误译。误译即偏离原文本的错误的翻译,分为无意误译和有意误译。无意误译主要是由于译者对译入语的文化信息缺乏了解,而有意误译是指"为了迎合本民族的文化心态大幅度地改变原文的语言表达方式、文学形象、文学意境等等;要么为了强行引入异族文化模式,置本族的审美趣味的接受可能性于不顾,从而故意用不等值的语言手段进行翻译"[②]。在跨异质文化交流中,由于文化背景的不同,译者不免按照自身的文化传统和思维方式对文本进行解读和翻译,造成文学误读和误译现象,有意误译更是作为一种翻译

---

① 屠国元、朱献珑:《译者主体性:阐释学的阐释》,载《中国翻译》,2003年第6期。
② 谢天振:《翻译研究新视野》,福州:福建教育出版社,2015年,第111页。

策略广泛应用于翻译实践中。斯坦纳曾指出,"在翻译史上,幸运的误读,往往是新的生命的源泉"①。误译对文本提出了不同角度的阐释,赋予原文本全新的意义,为译者的创造性叛逆提供了空间。

以下为《假儿歌》的第四、五节:

附录一:
狠好,周瘦鹃
静好,胡兰成

附录二:
早行,齐韵叟
晚来,华铁眉

霍译如下:

APPENDIX 1
merciless good   is Air Rested Kailed
unmoving good   is Tray Tor Eggs Siled

APPENDIX 2
early off   is Old Master Rhymester
late back   is Wah! Iron Eyebrows

这两节诗中最吸引眼球的便是人名的翻译。人名翻译一直是文学翻译的一大难点,因为各民族的人名都具有深厚的文化内涵,与其社会环境、传统习俗、语言、宗教等都有密切联系,历史上的一些人名已具有大众社会文化认知所固有的联想内涵和明显的褒贬印记。原诗第四节出现的两个人名

---

① Steiner, George. *After Babel: Aspects of Language and Translation*. Oxford University Press, 1975, p. 295.

"周瘦鹃"和"胡兰成"便是如此。周瘦鹃是我国现代杰出的作家、文学翻译家和盆景艺术家,后因林彪、"四人帮"的残酷迫害而死,是一个正面的英雄人物。胡兰成因追随汪精卫、为汪精卫执笔发表卖国社论而被打上"大汉奸"的烙印,1945年日军战败后逃亡日本,又因一生八次婚娶及多次的露水情缘背负"浪荡子""负心汉"的骂名。

初读这两句译文,读者大多会一头雾水。"Air Rested Kailed"与"Tray Tor Eggs Siled"从语义上看毫无意义,就是几个毫无联系的单词随意拼凑而成,但经过仔细观察我们便能发现译者的良苦用心。"Air"和"Rested"两个单词连读时发音与"Arrested"十分接近,而"Kailed"发音与"Killed"也十分相似。同理,将"Tray"与"Tor"连读后单词发音接近"Traitor","Eggs"与"Siled"连读的读音接近单词"Exiled"。如此一来,"周瘦鹃"的翻译便是"Arrested Killed"(逮捕并被害死),"胡兰成"则是"Traitor Exiled"(流亡的叛徒),隐喻了两人的真实遭遇。霍布恩显然对两个人名背后的联想意义有所了解,所以选择用归化的翻译策略将其文化背景显性化,而他用连读谐音的文字游戏将真实的翻译隐藏起来,又为译诗增添了几分幽默诙谐之趣。

如上所述,英雄与汉奸是周瘦鹃和胡兰成两个人名在中国社会的固有内涵,但个体文化心理结构有时也会与这种固有内涵相左。事实上,诗人柏桦对两人的文学作品都是推崇备至,尤其是胡兰成。在文章《从胡兰成到杨键:汉语之美的两极》中,柏桦毫不吝啬对胡兰成的溢美之词:"胡兰成的《今生今世》……可谓字字皆是古典珍珠,中国乡村的诗意在他笔下几抵神仙世界,因此我更乐意称作者为诗人,他的文字当然亦是最上乘的诗歌。每每读罢他诗一般的文字,我都不禁掩卷长叹:在胡先生面前,我辈居然舞文弄墨,居然作诗。"可见诗人对胡兰成的文字有着何等的仰慕之情。于诗人而言,胡兰成的联想意义不是"大汉奸""负情汉",而是"最上乘"的文学家。"静好,胡兰成",乃是出自胡兰成的名句"岁月静好,现世安稳"。显然霍布恩的翻译有悖于原诗作者之意,此处的误译应是由于译者对诗人柏桦该诗创作意图的误读。但"胡兰成"一名的褒贬标记并不会因一人而改变,提及胡兰成,多数中国人想到的仍是叛国通敌之名而不是风花雪月之文,译入语读者更是如此。霍布恩的误译虽然有违原诗作者所表达的情感，却更符合译入语读者对"胡兰成"一名的联想意义，更容易为译入语读者接受。

"齐韵叟"和"华铁眉"的翻译更是误译之典范。两个人名均出自张爱玲的翻译小说《海上花》，齐韵叟是上海翻云覆雨的风流人物，府第豪华，有钱有势；华铁眉是官宦世家子弟，也是上海滩小有名气的才子，在书中两人的名字与其性格和命运没有明显的双关隐喻。霍布恩抑或是不清楚两个人名的出处，将名字按照字面意思拆分后直译："Old Master Rhymester"意为"年老的做诗大家"；"Wah! Iron Eyebrows"更是诗人无厘头的翻译，"Wah"是汉字"华"的粤语音译，发音与英文单词"Wow"相近，表示对一个人长了一双铁眉惊叹不已。事实上，此处霍布恩是希望通过对人名的创造性翻译，带来一种香港武术电影的感觉①，"Wow"像是功夫大师李小龙在打斗时发出的招牌式叫声。毫无疑问，此处两个人名的拆分直译是误译，然而，如果将两个英语读者并不熟悉的小说人物的名字直接译出，恐会让英语读者完全不知所云。正是霍布恩的有意误译，使译诗在原诗优雅逸乐的诗意中又增添了些许诙谐之感，实属霍译的创造性叛逆。

接下来再以《苏州记事一年》的英译为例，看看无意误译的现象。该诗是诗人基于一本苏州黄历的阅读感受而作，是一首运用民族方言书写苏州民俗的诗歌。诗中平实的语言，古典的韵味，类似骈文的节奏，令一种平淡而祥和、丰足而美好的苏州民间生活跃然于纸上。然而，诗中大量的中国传统文化习俗和表达却给翻译的语言转换带来了困难。因文化差异和理解障碍带来的误译也就在所难免。

以下为《苏州记事一年》第7节第1、2句：

清明，小麦拔节，踏青游春
深蓝、浅绿插入水中②
Qingming Festival: wheat straw cut, early Spring picnics

---

① 参见布莱恩所写的"译者注"：Brian Holton, "Translator's Note", in *Pathlight*, 2013 (Summer): 137.
② 柏桦：《惟有旧日子带给我们幸福》，南京：江苏凤凰文艺出版社，2017年，第51—54页。

shafts of deep blue and light green in the water[①]

清明是中国传统的二十四节气之一,一般在4月5日前后。清明时节,气温变暖,雨水增多,正是庄稼生长的好时节。"拔节",是"指水稻、小麦、高粱、玉米等作物生长到一定阶段时,茎的各节自下而上依次迅速生长"[②]。而祭祖和踏青是清明节的两大传统礼俗,"踏青游春"正是描写其中之一。恐因不知拔节一词之意,译者将"小麦拔节"译为"wheat straw cut"(割掉麦秆),误将小麦快速生长理解为"收割小麦"。同时,译者将"踏青游春"译为"early Spring picnics"(早春之际外出野炊),更是典型的误译。首先,"踏青"指的是"清明节前后到郊外散步游玩(青:青草)"[③],将其译为"野炊"显然有所偏离。其次,译者因不了解中国传统节气的初春、仲春、暮春之具体时期,错误地认为处于暮春时期的清明是在初春之际。

再如第11诗节第1、2行:

五月五,端午出自蒲剑
也出自夏至的替身
Fifth Month fifth day: Dragon Boat Festival comes with swords of rushes
comes out of the stand-in for Summer Solstice

以及最后1诗节第1、2行:

除夕之末,男孩怀旧
果子即压岁,即吉利

[①] Bai Hua, "The Suzhou Year", trans. by Brian Holton, W. N. Herbert and Lee Man-Kay, in *Jade Ladder: Contemporary Chinese Poetry*. Northumberland: Bloodaxe Books Ltd., 2012, p. 115.
[②] 《现代汉语词典》第7版,第19页。
[③] 同上,第1261页。

End of New Year's Eve: boys talk of absent friends
with melon seeds comes a new year and good luck

端午节是中国四大传统节日(春节、清明节、端午节、中秋节)之一,端午习俗有赛龙舟、吃粽子、挂菖蒲艾叶等。"端午出自蒲剑"便是说端午挂菖蒲的习俗。由于菖蒲叶片呈剑形,又称为蒲剑。端午节将其挂在门口,可避邪保平安。而此处译者可能由于缺乏对中国传统节日习俗的了解,不知蒲剑为何物,便将其按汉字拆分直译为"swords(剑) of rushes(蒲草)"。这样的误译,虽形象地呈现了该植物的形状,却让英语读者无法将其对应到"calamus"(菖蒲)这种实际所指的植物上。同样,最后一诗节中的"果子即压岁",译者误将"果子"按汉字拆开直译成了"melon seeds"(瓜果的种子)。事实上,此处诗人讲的是老苏州除夕人们给孩子送压岁果子的传统习俗。压岁果子通常选橘子和荔枝,因"橘""荔"和"吉利"同音,除夕将压岁果子放在枕边,正月初一早上醒来吃掉,祝福新的一年大吉大利。显然,"果子"的误译,让英语读者无法理解其为何能带来"吉利"。

上述几处无意误译均是由于文化差异、对原语文化信息了解的缺失而产生的误解和误释。尽管从比较文学变异学的视角看,在跨语际翻译实践中,文学误读不可避免,且是一种创新,具有其自身独特的价值,但译者仍应竭力避免,翻译时应做足功课,尽力将原文原汁原味的文化信息准确有效转化到译本中,令译入语读者了解并感受到异质文化、文学的美。

四、结　语

曹顺庆教授提出的比较文学变异学为译介学研究提供了坚实的理论基础,拓展了文学翻译研究的视野和方法。本文以比较文学变异学理论视角,从中外文学传统和中西思维方式差异导致的文化过滤与文学翻译变异方面,以及文学误读与误译方面,分析了柏桦诗歌霍布恩英译中的变异现象及其产生原因。霍布恩的译本看似脱离原文,与原诗无法一一对应,实际上是从译入语文学、文化接受的角度对原文进行了改写和再创作,通过创造性的翻译解决了柏桦诗歌中看似不可译的语言文化转换难题。在跨异质文明的文学交流过程中,在跨语际翻译实践中,由不同的文学传统、意识形态、思维方式等因素引起的翻译变异现象是不可避免的。正确认识到这一点有利于我们在翻译实践和翻译批评时,理性客观地看待变异现象。正是这种变异——翻译中的"创造性叛逆",造就了译入语读者能够接受的译文,让原作在异国文学中获得新生。也只有译入语读者、文化市场及社会能够接受的翻译文学作品,才能真正意义上促进中国文学在海外的交流与传播。

个案研究三：柏桦诗歌《夏天还很远》中英文本对照分析

杨安文

作为1980年代中国新诗热潮中的"后朦胧"诗人杰出代表,柏桦是中国当代最具影响力的诗人之一。中国当代著名诗人北岛曾称他为"中国最优秀的抒情诗人"。台湾诗人、批评家黄梁认为"柏桦诗歌以情韵深远、风格鲜明、气象从容的汉诗精神,开辟一代诗风"。德国汉学家顾彬说,"作为日常生活的诗人,柏桦像宋朝的大诗人一样,到处可以找到诗歌",并认为他与里尔克一样,是"真实的""诚实写作的典范"。[①] 哈佛大学王德威教授认为,"柏桦的诗歌是中国当代最好的诗歌之一,精妙并扣人心弦"[②]。柏桦诗歌在海内外广受读者欢迎,曾荣获安高(Anne Kao)诗歌奖、《上海文学》诗歌奖、柔刚诗歌奖、《红岩》随笔奖、"红岩文学奖"之诗歌奖等诸多奖项。柏桦迄今已出版诗集24本,其中英、法文诗集各1本,德文诗集(合著)2本,已正式发表的诗歌一千多首,其中数百首被译为外文发表在多个国外刊物上。

"夏天是柏桦诗歌的季节",如柏桦英文诗集《风在说》译者菲奥娜·施-罗琳所言,"四季更替,柏桦却偏爱夏天,在其诗歌特有的叙事中,他总在冥想的诗句里、精确聚焦的晕映画面中回到夏天"[③]。据统计,柏桦以夏天为主题或与之密切相关的诗歌有23首,在诗人的自传体回忆录《左边:毛泽东时代的抒情诗人》中,"夏天"这个词出现次数多达66次。柏桦与夏天的约

---

① Bai Hua. *Wind Says*. trans. by Fiona Sze-Lorrain. Zephyr Press and The Chinese University Press, 2012.
② 同上。
③ 同上。

定成为一种永恒,贯穿于诗人各个阶段的作品之中。本文拟以《夏天还很远》这首夏天主题诗歌为研究对象,通过对原文本和四个不同的英译文本的对照分析,探析各译本在词汇和语法层面,以及诗歌韵律呈现方面的处理方式及得失,并提出针对性建议,以促进《夏天还很远》及柏桦诗歌在英语世界的品读与赏析。

一、诗篇简介

《夏天还很远》写于 1984 年冬天,是诗人自己最喜欢的一首诗,[①]也是柏桦诗歌在海外译介最多的诗之一,共有 4 个英语译本,2 个德语译本,1 个法语译本。该诗虽仅是柏桦众多夏天主题诗歌的一首,但却独一无二:在其他夏天主题的诗中,母亲是绝对的主角,那个被诗人称作"下午少女"的母亲,在他儿时就将其"母亲激情"注入诗人的血液,造就了诗人早期这些夏天主题的诗歌是火热的、激情的、加速度的、"极左的"。而《夏天还很远》是唯一一首写到父亲的诗。与母亲不同,父亲"对人与事充满了习惯的文雅及亲切的专注","父亲形式"令这首诗"夜凉如水,舒缓婉约,气氛弥漫着一种过去的光辉"。[②] 反复吟咏此诗,我们可以感受到诗人所抒发的怀旧之情,对过去美好光景的回忆和怀念,对父亲的认同与思念,希望父亲不要老去、永远年轻的渴求,同时还能体会诗人对时间和生命的流逝的忧伤和不舍。该诗内容看似简单,实则蕴含丰富的韵味和浓浓的诗意,同时也是体现柏桦诗歌独特音乐性的代表作品。

二、译本情况

由于笔者外语能力所限,本文仅重点对比分析该诗的四个英文译本。译本 A 由李赋康和孔慧怡合译,于 1992 年发表在香港《译丛》杂志第 37 期[③],是

[①] 柏桦:《左边:毛泽东时代的抒情诗人》,南京:江苏文艺出版社,2009 年,第 218 页。
[②] 同上。
[③] Bai Hua. Summer is Still Far Away (J). trans. Li Fukang with Eva Hung. *Renditions* 37, 1992: 101—107.

该诗最早的英文译本。译本 B 出自 2011 年在华盛顿出版的英文诗集《推开窗：当代中国诗歌》①，由美国著名汉学家、翻译家陶忘机翻译。译本 C 来自柏桦的英文诗集《风在说》②，该诗集于 2012 年由西风出版社和香港中文大学出版社出版，译者为新加坡裔法籍诗人、翻译家菲奥娜·施-罗琳。译本 D 是由加拿大诗人、著名汉学家戴迈河翻译，该译本没有纸质出版，直接登载于莱顿大学的网页上。③ 笔者通过译者与诗人的通信及译本原稿资料推断，翻译的时间大致在 1995 年。

三、文本形式

该诗共有 4 个诗节，29 个诗行，每行字数为 5—12 字。全诗除第 4 节第 5 行有 1 个问号外，其余诗行句末均无标点符号。四个英文译本在形式上与原文完全对应，诗节、诗行及标点与原文完全一致。但各个译本每行首字母大写的情况有所不同。译本 A 和 B 每个诗行首字母全部大写，译本 D 每个诗节第一句和最后一句首字母大写。译本 C 则是有的诗行首字母大写，有的没有，看似凌乱无规律，实际是译者通过首字母大写的方式来帮助读者断句。译者认为只是作为上一句中一部分的诗行，其首字母就采用了小写。此外，形式上该诗运用了重章叠句的写作手法，每一诗节最后一句相同，并且与标题一致，这种回环反复的表达方式带来了音韵美和节奏美。标题《夏天还很远》看似与诗歌的怀旧、感伤主题没有关系，实则关系密切、暗藏玄机：标题中的"远"并非指物理距离的远，而指时间概念上的长远，于诗人而言，夏天是美好的时光，《夏天还很远》传达出诗人对美好日子的追求与向往。而另一方面，诗人运用重章叠句的手法便从音乐性上带来另一效果：

---

① Bai Hua. Summer Is Still Very Far Away (A). tran. John Balcom. In Qingping Wang (ed.). *Push Open the Window: Contemporary Poetry from China* (C). Washington: Copper Canyon Press，2011. pp. 57—61.

② Bai Hua. 2012. Summer Is Still Far (A). trans. Fiona Sze-Lorrain. *Wind Says*. Zephyr Press and The Chinese University Press，2012. pp. 19—23.

③ 诗歌翻译文本在莱顿大学网页的链接：http://leiden.dachs-archive.org/poetry/index.html。

反复吟咏则可感受到对美好时光流逝的忧虑。四个英文译本也都完全按照原文再现了每一诗节最后相同的这一诗句。

四、译本对比分析

1. 隐身的人物角色翻译处理：代词的使用

诗歌文本中的主体、主角——或可称为诗歌文本世界中的"角色"（persona）——的把握，是理解现代诗歌的关键。"角色"是文本世界的主角，诗歌情景中的发声者，思想的表达、剧情的铺陈都通过这个主体的视角呈现。然而诗歌里通过人称代词表明的人物角色"我"或"你"，并非一定指诗人自己或读者。文本世界中的"我"常常是戏剧情景中的角色的"我"，尽管这个"我"常常会带有诗人自己的视角、经历和体验；"你"有时看似指被称呼人或读者，实是指角色的"我"，站在一个中间的、显得客观的立场，通过"你"的视角言说"我"的思想或感受。然而我们常常见到的是，新诗文本中很少出现甚至并不出现人称代词，诗的"角色"在文本中隐身，而"角色"也常常在一首诗中频繁转换。这一特点毫无疑问带来了诗歌理解的困难，但同时也给诗歌文本的理解和阐释带来了广阔空间。正是这一模糊性、不确定性或开放性，才让诗歌的生命在不同的阅读、不同的翻译和阐释中延续着新的生命力。

《夏天还很远》是一首怀旧诗，全诗总体以诗人自身为叙述主体，描写了诗人的怀旧之情和对父亲的思念之情。诗人在2016年与法国诗歌爱好者、数学家阿兰（Alain）探讨该诗的翻译时，提到这首诗有很强的故事性，里面有两个人物，一是诗人自己，另一个是诗人的父亲；诗人在诗中与父亲对话，尽管文本世界的说话者就是诗人真实的自己，全诗并没有出现人称代词"我"。

在第一诗节，诗人描写时光流逝，自己担忧、害怕美好时光一去不复返，忧虑之情油然而生。第二行的"某种东西"便是指这种忧虑之情。值得注意的是，原诗表述的是"某种东西暗中接近你"，不是"我"。此处正是上文提到

的通过"你"的视角言说"我"的思想或感受,实是一种忧虑之情暗中接近"我",诗人自己。以下是这一诗行的四个译本翻译:

某种东西暗中接近你

A：Silently something approaches *you*

B：Secretly, something approaches *you*

C：something nears you in the dark

D：something approaches *me* in the dark

前三个译本均与原文一致,将人称代词"你"译为"you",从文本翻译上讲这固然是准确的。然而第四个译本却直接进行了人称转换,译为"I"。译者戴迈河应当是体会到了诗人的实际所指,或许是为了让读者更容易理解原诗,他选择了转换人称,使英语读者能够清晰地把握诗歌言说的主体。这在某种程度上也就降低了原诗的理解难度。

第二诗节与第一诗节相似,诗人同样在感叹时间无情地飞逝,同时怀念过去与父亲在一起的日子,表达对父亲的思念之情。第一行"真快呀,一出生就消失"并无特指动作的主体,泛指任何东西,想要达到的戏剧化效果是时光流逝太快,无法抓住。

真快呀,一出生就消失

A：So fast! Vanished at birth

B：It happened so fast, vanishing at birth

C：How fast, it vanishes at its birth

D：Really fast, vanishing as soon as it's born

从上文可见,四个译本都选择将"一出生就消失"的动作主体补译出来。后三个译本均选用代词"it"代指动作的发出者,给英语读者可能带来的困惑是"it"究竟指什么,容易带来的误导是:误以为"it"指前文提到的"某种东西"或指下一句的动作主体"所有的善"。而第一个译本选用分词的形式"Vanished at birth",则更容易让读者认为"消失"的主体是下一诗句的主语"所有的善"。事实上,本节第一句和第二句并非从属关系,是独立的两行诗句。"所有的善在十月的夜晚进来",是因为诗人的父亲是十月出生的,表达诗人对父亲的认可和思念。基于此,笔者认为,第一诗行可保持原文没有动作主体即没有主语的句法结构,与原文一样,给读者提供开放式的文本理解空间,这样会比误导读者好。上文提及的法国数学家阿兰对本句给出了他的翻译,即"So fast, once born then disappears",笔者认为是较好的翻译处理。

在第二诗节第四行"巨大的宁静如你干净的布鞋"中出现了代词"你"。不难理解,此处的"你"与第一诗节第二行的"你"(实指"我")不同,是指诗人的父亲,父亲喜欢穿清洁的白衬衫和干净的布鞋①。这正是诗人在诗中与父亲的对话。

在第三诗节中,诗人在继续描写回忆中当时的感觉,主体仍然是"我"。由于原诗没有出现任何人称代词,文本中的"人物"看似不明确,给译者确定每一个动作的主体带来了困难。

偶然遇见,可能想不起

A：A chance encounter, perhaps bringing no recognition

B：Meeting by chance, perhaps *you* can't recall

C：A chance encounter, *I* can't quite remember

D：A chance encounter, *you* probably don't remember

外面有一点冷

A：A little chilly outside

B：It was a little cold outside

C：A little cold outside

D：it was a little cold outside

左手也疲倦

A：The left hand is tired

---

① 柏桦:《左边:毛泽东时代的抒情诗人》,南京:江苏文艺出版社,2009 年,第 218 页。

B：*Your* left hand was tired, too

C：*my* left hand is tired

D：*my* left hand was tired

暗地里一直往左边

A：In the darkness heading left

B：Secretly *you* walked all the way to the left

C：It keeps sliding to the left in the dark

D：all the while it was secretly moving to the left

偏僻又深入

A：Where hidden deep within

B：Far away, deep in

C：far yet profound

D：remote and thoroughgoing

那唯一痴痴的挂念

A：Is that one incurable yearning

B：The sole infatuation of *your* heart

C：The one and only silly nostalgia

D：that single silly thought of *you*

四个版本的翻译呈现出了不同译者对动作主体的不同理解。译本 A 与原文一致，避开提及动作主体，留出了开放式的理解和阐释空间。译本 B 则认定动作的主体是"你"，在第一、四行加入了主语"you"，并在第三、六行通过加入物主代词"your"明确了情景中的人物。然而，第四行"暗地里一直往左边"的动作主体应该是第三行的"左手"，加入主语"you"应该是理解错误。① 与译本 B 不同，译本 C 认为动作的主体是"我"，在第一行加入了主语"I"，第三行加入物主代词"my"，将原文本中暗藏的动作主体明晰化了。译

---

① 笔者与诗人讨论此句的理解时，诗人提到"左手也疲倦"是当时在创作这首诗时的真实感受：左手乏力，不自主地往左边下垂。"暗地里一直往左边"正好展现了我们熟悉的柏桦式神秘忧愁。

本 D 则认为这一诗节中的"角色"在转换,第一行加入了主语"you",第四行"左手也疲倦"译为"*my* left hand was tired","角色"转换成了"我",感觉有些突兀,容易给理解造成困难。

在第四节前三行及倒数第二行,诗人描写了一种复杂的感受,想要改掉自己性格中的一些缺点(如性急、冲动、优柔寡断等)却总也改不了的后悔、忧伤。这四行的动作主体都是"我"。在第四、五行中,诗人再次与父亲对话:"小竹楼、白衬衫/你是不是正当年?"表达的是希望父亲不要老去、永远年轻的浓厚感情。在这一情景中的"人物"便转换成了"你",指诗人的父亲。

再不了,动辄发脾气,动辄热爱

A：No, no longer quick to anger, nor quick to love

B：Never again easy to anger, easy to love

C：No longer quick-tempered or impassioned

D：Never again, losing *my* temper or loving passionately at a touch

拾起从前的坏习惯

A：Picking up old bad habits

B：To take up those old bad habits of *yours*

C：*you* pick up bad habits from the past

D：gather up the bad old habits

灰心年复一年

A：Year after year *you* lose heart

B：Losing heart with each passing year

C：disheartened year after year

D：year after year depressed

小竹楼、白衬衫

A：*Your* bamboo hut, *your* white shirt

B：A small bamboo house, a white shirt

C：Little bamboo house, a white shirt

D：the small bamboo building, a white shirt

你是不是正当年？

A：But are you still the same?

B：Are you in the prime of life?

C：Are you in the prime of life?

D：are you in the prime of life?

难得下一次决心

A：Decisiveness is rare

B：Seldom can a decision be made

C：For once, a rare resolution

D：it's rare to reach a resolution

通过译文对比可见，前三个译本都通过添加代词"you"或"your"说明本节的"角色"主体是"你"。固然如前文所述，"你"也可理解为言说自我，但就容易与后面"你是不是正当年"中的"你"（指诗人的父亲）混淆，不利于英语读者对本节的理解。第四个译本在本节第一句中通过加入物主代词"my"明确了本节的"人物"主体是"我"，与原诗暗藏的动作主体一致，是较为贴切的翻译。

在现代诗歌翻译中，代词的选用是难点，涉及对原诗的深入理解，对暗藏于诗中的"角色"主体的准确把握。译者通常会按照自己的理解加入人称代词或物主代词表明动作主体。但如上文对四个译本代词使用的分析可见，使用不当容易误导读者。笔者倾向于选择与原诗基本保持一致，原诗中没有出现人称的地方，译诗中也尽量避免使用，给读者留下文本理解的开放空间。

2. 时间维度的把握：时态的选用

在英文句法中，除使用时间副词和介词短语以外，主要通过动词时态（现在时、过去时和将来时）和体（进行体和完成体），即动词词尾变化和增加助动词来显示话语说出的时间与话语中描述的事件发生的时间之关系。而在中文表达中没有动词词尾的变化,我们只能通过动词本身的含义和时间副词、动态助词来显示时间关系。由于中英文句法的这一差异,语言精练、内容常常晦涩难懂的现代诗歌在翻译过程中,如何选用时态(tense)和体(aspect)亦成为难点。

《夏天还很远》通过描写诗人创作时的即时感受,表达怀旧之情和对时间飞逝、挽留不住的感伤,主体选用一般现在时符合此诗创设的时间语境。四个译本中,译本 A 和 C 全诗使用了一般现在时,而译本 B 和 D 全诗主体采用一般现在时,部分诗行则使用了过去时。

真快呀,一出生就消失

A:So fast! Vanished at birth

B:It *happened* so fast, vanishing at birth

C:How fast, it vanishes at its birth

D:Really fast, vanishing as soon as it's born

所有的善在十月的夜晚进来

A:All goodness enters this October night

B:All that is good *entered* on an October night

C:All goodness arrives one October night

D:on an October night all that's good enters in

第二诗节第一行"真快呀,一出生就消失",此处可理解为是诗人当下的一种感受和体验,感叹时间飞逝,一闪而过。第二行"所有的善在十月的夜晚进来"是诗人想象的一种常态:每到十月父亲的生日,所有美好的东西都会到来,暗含了诗人对父亲浓浓的爱。四个译本中,仅译本 B 使用了过去时"happened""entered",与本节诗描写诗人当时感受的现在基调不相吻合。译本 A 使用一般现在时,并且译为"this October night",英语读者会理解为是当下的这个十月。译本 C 和 D 采用了一般现在时,没有特指是哪一个"十月",相较更为贴切。

在第三诗节,不同译本也采用的不同时态。译本 A 和 C 采用的一般现

在时,而译本 B 和 D 则采用了过去时:

偶然遇见,可能想不起

A：A chance encounter, perhaps bringing no recognition

B：Meeting by chance, perhaps you can't recall

C：A chance encounter, I can't quite remember

D：A chance encounter, you probably don't remember

外面有一点冷

A：A little chilly outside

B：It *was* a little cold outside

C：A little cold outside

D：it *was* a little cold outside

左手也疲倦

A：The left hand is tired

B：Your left hand *was* tired, too

C：my left hand is tired

D：my left hand *was* tired

暗地里一直往左边

A：In the darkness heading left

B：Secretly you *walked* all the way to the left

C：It keeps sliding to the left in the dark

D：all the while it *was* secretly moving to the left

如前文所述,本节仍然是诗人描写创作时那种即刻的感受,并非回忆过去发生的某个事件。"偶然遇见,可能想不起",是描写诗人的一种幻觉,偶然同父亲在街上擦肩而过,却一下没想起。这是诗歌中的惯用手法,即正话反说,为了加重情感,使情更深、意更切。"左手也疲倦/暗地里一直往左边",也是诗人将即时身体的感受带入了诗歌。诗人对此曾解释道:"我是一个对身体极为敏感的诗人,写这首诗时,我的左手感觉无力,这引起我警觉,我顺手把这种现场身体感觉写了进去。"这样的描写,自然地加重了诗人那熟悉而神秘的忧愁。基于上述理解,翻译时采用一般现在时才符合原诗创设之意境,能让读者更有现场感,更能感受到诗人在当下的那种淡淡的忧愁和思念。

此外,笔者注意到,在第一诗节的第三至六行,译本B与其他三个译本不同,将原文的谓语动词短语结构译为非谓语的现在分词形式:

坐一坐,走一走

A:Sit a while, walk a while

B:*Sitting , walking*

C:Sit a while, walk a little

D:sit for a while, walk a bit

看树叶落了

A:Look at the falling leaves

B:*Watching the leaves drop*

C:watch the leaves fall

D:see the leaves fall

看小雨下了

A:Look at the drizzling rain

B:*Watching the rain fall*

C:watch the light rain

D:see the sprinkling rain

看一个人沿街而过

A:Look at a man walking down the street

B:*Watching* as someone walks down the street

C:and a man crossing a street

D:see someone walk along the street, cross it

应该说,现在分词非谓语形式的运用,能让读者感受到动作正在进行,强调动作的同时发生,给读者带来的情景感更强。用动词短语则强调动作的全过程,每个动作的独立性。但由于原诗此处未明确提及动作主体,实际的主语"我"被省略了,翻译时若使用现在分词非谓语形式容易带来的误解是分词的逻辑主语是前一句的"something",故笔者认为此处使用动词短语比较合理。

3. 词汇使用对比分析

诗歌翻译中译者对词汇的选择受到诸多因素的影响,包括译者对原诗的理解,对目标语词汇的精确把握,同时还受到诗体美学和韵律安排的影响。试看《夏天还很远》第二诗节第二行的四个译本:

> 所有的善在十月的夜晚进来
> A:*All goodness* enters this October night
> B:*All that is good* entered on an October night
> C:*All goodness* arrives one October night
> D:on an October night *all that's good* enters in

此诗句中的"善"译本 A 和 C 译为"Goodness",译本 B 和 D 则译为"All that is good"。"Goodness"指"virtue, excellence, benevolence"(善良,美德)①,更多指具有伦理价值判断的、道德层面的善。而在原诗中,诗人所说的"所有的善"指的是"所有好的东西",是诗人的一种主观感受:父亲的方方面面都好,并非一定是指美德。故笔者认为此处译为"all that is good"更符合原诗之表达。

接下来看第三诗节第六行的四个译本:

> 那唯一痴痴的挂念
> A:Is that one incurable yearning

---

① 据《钱伯斯英语词典》第十三版,第 658 页。

B：The sole infatuation of your heart

C：The one and only silly nostalgia

D：that single silly thought of you

"挂念"一词指"因想念而放心不下"①，思念中还有一丝担心。译本 A 翻译为"yearning"，该词主要指"渴望，渴求（得到某物）"（yearn：to desire strongly or feel longing for）②。译本 B 选用了"infatuation"这个词，从其动词"infatuate"的英文意思"to inspire with a foolish or unreasoning passion"③可知其意为"迷恋，痴念"，更多指男女之爱，也没有包含挂念的全部含义。译本 C 使用了"nostalgia"一词，该词意为"怀旧，念旧"（the desire to return to some earlier time in one's life, or a fond remembrance of that time）④，常指对过去美好日子的怀念。译本 D 则选用了"thought"一词，呈现出的是"关心，体贴"（care, considerateness）⑤之意，仍不能完整表达原文之意。译本 A 译者李赋康先生最近对本诗进行了重译，将"痴痴的挂念"译为"loving concern"，笔者认为较为贴切。

此外，本诗有的译本还出现了明显的用词错误。如第一诗节第六行：

看一个人沿街而过

A：Look at a man walking *down the street*

B：Watching as someone walks *down the street*

C：and a man *crossing a street*

D：see someone walk *along the street*, *cross it*

"沿街而过"似乎给外国译者带来了理解上的歧义，从下面摘录的法国数学家阿兰与诗人的邮件内容可以体会产生歧义的原因：

---

① 《现代汉语词典》第 7 版，第 475 页。
② 据《钱伯斯英语词典》第十三版，第 1819 页。
③ 据《钱伯斯英语词典》第十三版，第 779 页。
④ 据《钱伯斯英语词典》第十三版，第 1051 页。
⑤ 据《钱伯斯英语词典》第十三版，第 1623 页。

阿兰邮件的相关内容：

"看一个人沿街而过"，菲奥娜翻译的是"and a man crossing a street"：只有"过"的意思，没有"沿"的意思。其他两个翻译都一样："Watching as someone walks down the street""voirquelqu'un passer le long de la rue"①只有"沿"的意思，没有"过"的意思！

柏桦回信的相关内容：

"看一个人沿街而过"的意思是指：我看见一个街对面的人（我的父亲）沿着街道走了过去……

由此可见，外国译者容易将"沿"和"过"分开，认为"沿"是指沿着街走，"过"是指过街。因此译本 C 译为"crossing a street"，而译本 D 干脆把两层意思都在译文中体现出来。

再如，本诗第四节第三行：

灰心年复一年
A：Year after year you *lose heart*
B：*Losing heart* with each passing year
C：*disheartened* year after year
D：year after year *depressed*

译本 D 选用了"depressed"一词指"灰心"，这显然是不准确的。"depressed"指"沮丧的，情绪低落的，压抑的"。译本 B 选用"disheartened"当是最为准确的翻译。

---

① 此处 Alain 所指的法语译本是法国翻译家尚德兰（Chantal Chen-Andro）的译本，选自 2016 年法国文字出版社（Caractères Press）出版的柏桦法语诗集《在清朝》。

4. 韵律呈现对比分析

柏桦诗歌的美,相当一部分体现在其特有的音乐性,在其隐藏于字里行间的节奏和旋律,一种诗人独特的融入其血脉的声音。诗人在论述自己早期的诗观时指出:"诗和生命的节律一样在呼吸里自然形成。一当它形成某种氛围,文字就变得模糊并溶入某种气息或声音。此时,诗歌企图去作一次侥幸的超越,并借此接近自然的纯粹,但连最伟大的诗歌也很难抵达这种纯粹,所以它带给我们的欢乐是有限的、遗憾的。从这个意义上说诗是不能写的,只是我们在不得已的情况下动用了这种形式。"①可见柏桦诗歌的"声音""音乐性"之重要性。这种音乐性一方面体现为平仄有规律交替的变换之美。《夏天还很远》四个诗节行尾平仄暗含规律,第一诗节全部为仄声,第二诗节以平声为主,第三诗节以仄声为主,第四诗节平仄交替,声音起伏变幻,情随声婉转而来。

音乐性的另一方面则在于诗行中的韵,虽无固定规律,但吟咏之时总能感受到柏桦特有的诗歌旋律,总会发现诗人或精心安排或随"生命的节律"自然形成的行内韵和脚韵。《夏天还很远》除了前文所述采用了重章叠句手法,带来了音韵美和节奏美效果以外,诗人在全诗的用韵上有精心安排。首先全诗通篇协韵,协"an"韵,在行内韵和脚韵均有体现,同时全篇多处亦有含"an"韵的字:第一节第 2 行"暗",第 6 行"沿",7 行"天"(行内韵)、"远"(尾韵);第二节第 2 行"善""晚",第 3 行"全",第 5 行"边"(行内韵)、"婉"(尾韵),第 6 行"签"(尾韵),第七行"天"(行内韵)、"远"(尾韵);第三节第 1 行"然""见",第 2 行"面",第 3 行"倦"(尾韵),第 4 行"边"(尾韵),第 6 行"念"(尾韵),第 7 行"天"(行内韵)、"远"(尾韵);第四节第 2 行"前"(行内韵)、"惯"(尾韵),第 3 行"年"(尾韵),第 4 行"衫"(尾韵),第 5 行"年"(尾韵),第 6 行"难",第 7 行"天"(行内韵)、"远"(尾韵)。其次,在部分诗节也有内部的押韵,如第一诗节内协"uo"韵,第 3 行"坐",第 4 行"落",第 6 行"过"(尾韵)。再如第四诗节内协"ai"韵,亦可看作全篇协韵"an"韵的转韵,

---

① 黄梁:《地下的光脉》,台北:唐山出版社,1999 年,第 215—216 页。

第 1 行"再""爱"(尾韵),第 2 行"坏",第 4 行"白"。这些声音在诗中构成了和谐的旋律,令全诗充满了音乐美感。

然而诗中的音乐性却很难在翻译中得以转换和呈现,如诗人在《我的几种诗观》一文中所述:"众所周知,在诗歌翻译中,文字的意义和意象均可翻译,唯独声音无法译,因此才有弗罗斯特所说的一句名言,'诗是翻译所失掉的东西'。"①尽管如此,译者仍应当竭尽全力,通过英文的语言形式和诗歌韵律呈现方式,还原原诗的音乐美感。传统英语诗歌是通过音步(foot)来形成诗歌的节奏(rhythm),音步根据重读与非重读音节的不同组合可分为不同类型,如抑扬格(由一个非重读音节加上一个重读音节构成),扬抑格(由一个重读音节加上一个非重读音节构成)等。一行诗中音步的数量和类型的组合便形成了该诗行的格律(metre)。英诗由轻、重读音节交替形成的格律,类似于古诗由汉字的平仄四声形成的音调起伏、抑扬顿挫,在现代诗中已经很少采用。而英语诗歌中的押韵(rhyme)在现代诗中仍比较普遍,其与汉语诗歌有相似之处,也有尾韵和行内韵之分。但由于汉语诗歌仅押韵母,且一个字仅一个音节,押韵相对单纯。英语诗歌由于既可押元音也可押辅音,同时押韵的音节可以在单词的开头、中间或结尾,因此要复杂很多,可分为押全韵(Full Rhyme)或半韵(Half Rhyme),半韵又包括头韵(Alliteration)、谐元韵(Assonance)和谐辅韵(Consonance)。现代诗中较常见的是尾韵、头韵和谐元韵。尽管英、汉诗歌押韵有一定相通之处,但由于两种语言完全不同的语言形式,汉诗中的韵也很难转换到英诗中。

仔细对比原诗和四个英文译本,我们可以看到四个译者都完全保留了原诗形式,但都或多或少丢失了原诗的音乐美感。相较之下,译本 C 较好地呈现原诗的节奏和韵律感。原诗从标题开始,通篇协"an"韵,译本 C 押韵虽没有原诗那么多,但也做到了从标题起通篇押了尾韵/a:/:标题中的"far";第一诗节第 2 行"dark",第 7 行"far";第二诗节第 7 行"bookmark",第 8 行"far";第三诗节第 4 行"dark",第 6 行"nostalgia",第 7 行"far";第四诗节第 2 行"past",第 7 行"far"。值得注意的是,译者菲奥娜在翻译标题

---

① 柏桦:《我的几种诗观》,载《名作欣赏》,2012 年第 6 期。

《夏天还很远》时,与其他译者不同:

A:Summer is Still Far Away

B:Summer is Still very Far Away

C:Summer Is Still Far

D:Summer's Still Far Away

通过上文的押韵分析,可以感受到译者强烈的传递原文韵律的意识。全篇除了押/aː/韵以外,译者还在通篇行间或行尾安排了谐元韵/ai/:第一诗节第 2 行"while",第 5 行"light";第二诗节第 2 行"arrives""night"(同时也是行内韵),第 5 行"mild",第 6 行"like";第三诗节第 2 行"outside",第 3 行"tired",第 4 行"sliding";第四诗节第 4 行"white",第 5 行"prime"。这一用韵营造了另一旋律,进一步加强了译诗的韵律感。再者,译诗中还有明显体现原诗的节奏美感的句子:"Sit a while, walk a little / watch the leave fall / watch the light rain;A chance encounter, I can't quite remember"(同时也是行内韵)。第三诗节中的"A little cold outside / my left hand is tired"不仅押韵,还具有英语诗歌的格律美,很好地展现了原诗的音乐性。

五、结　　语

以上是笔者结合《夏天还很远》中文原诗的赏析,从对隐身的人物角色翻译处理,时态和时间维度把握——代词的使用,词汇使用准确性,以及诗歌韵律呈现等四个方面,对四个英译本进行了对比分析。正所谓"诗无达诂",诗歌文本语言精练、简洁,高度浓缩,思想内容艰深隐晦,本身就具有理解和阐释的开放性,这也正是诗歌的魅力所在。如伽达默尔所言,"翻译就是解释",翻译本身首先便是译者作为读者对原文本的阐释过程。也正是翻译以及不同译者的不同翻译,给诗歌文本的阐释带来了宽阔的延展空间,延续了原文本在目的语世界的生命。然而,我们并不能因此而否认文本确定性的存在,赫施区分了文本的"含义"和"意义"两个概念,指出"含义"是固有的文本符号所规定的,是确定的并可以复现的。诗歌文本的翻译同样如此,尽管具有意义的开放性,但原诗语言符号所固化的"含义",译者应当竭力通过语言转换使之准确呈现。

四个英译者在处理诗歌文本的人物角色翻译时,都倾向于按照自己的理解,以添加代词的方式使原文中隐身的人物主体显示出来。这样有助于英语读者对诗歌的理解,却同时带来误导读者、产生偏离原文"含义"的理解的风险。笔者的建议是在进行翻译转换时,尽量保留原文本的开放结构,避免主观上加入人称代词或物主代词而限制读者的理解。从时态和时间维度把握来看,译本 A 和译本 C 展现了译者对原诗意境准确而深入的理解。而无论从词汇使用层面还是韵律呈现层面,译本 C 都显示了优于其他三个译本的翻译处理,在外在形式,语言风格,尤其是节奏韵律上较好地呈现出了原诗之特点及魅力。笔者在菲奥娜译本的基础之上,结合其他三个译本的优点,对笔者认为需要改进的地方进行了修改,同时对部分选词和句式结构进行了调整,以期能更好地传递原诗的节奏和韵律,让读者尽可能地体会到原诗带有浓浓中国风韵的音乐美。

修改译本如下:

Summer Is Still Far

A day goes, a day comes
Something nears you in the dark
Sit a while, walk a bit
Watch the leaves drop
Watch the rain fall
And a man walking down the street
Summer is still far

So fast, once born then disappears
All that's good arrives one October night
So beautiful, entirely unnoticed

A huge calm like your clean cloth shoes

By the bed, the past is dim and mild

Like an old box

Like a faded bookmark

Summer is still far

A chance encounter, you probably don't remember

A little cold outside

The left hand is tired

It keeps sliding to the left in the dark

Far yet profound

The one and only loving concern

Summer is still far

Never again, easy to anger, easy to love

Take up the bad habits from the past

Year after year losing heart

The small bamboo house, a white shirt

Are you in the prime of life?

Seldom can a decision be made

Summer is still far

Winter 1984

附:原诗及四个译本对照版

夏天还很远

A: Summer is Still Far Away

B: Summer is Still very Far Away

C：Summer Is Still Far

D：Summer's Still Far Away

一日逝去又一日

A：A day goes, a day comes

B：One day passes after another

C：Days come and go

D：Day after day passes away

某种东西暗中接近你

A：Silently something approaches you

B：Secretly, something approaches you

C：something nears you in the dark

D：something approaches me in the dark

坐一坐,走一走

A：Sit a while, walk a while

B：Sitting, walking

C：Sit a while, walk a little

D：sit for a while, walk a bit

看树叶落了

A：Look at the falling leaves

B：Watching the leaves drop

C：watch the leaves fall

D：see the leaves fall

看小雨下了

A：Look at the drizzling rain

B：Watching the rain fall

C：watch the light rain

D：see the sprinkling rain

看一个人沿街而过

A：Look at a man walking down the street

B：Watching as someone walks down the street

C：and a man crossing a street

D：see someone walk along the street, cross it

夏天还很远

A：Summer is still far away

B：Summer is still very far away

C：Summer is still far

D：Summer's still far away

真快呀，一出生就消失

A：So far! Vanished at birth

B：It happened so fast, vanishing at birth

C：How fast, it vanishes at its birth

D：Really fast, vanishing as soon as it's born

所有的善在十月的夜晚进来

A：All goodness enters this October night

B：All that is good entered on an October night

C：All goodness arrives one October night

D：on an October night all that's good enters in

太美，全不察觉

A：Too beautiful, quite unnoticed

B：So beautiful, entirely unnoticed

C：Too beautiful, beyond notice

D：too beautiful, entirely unseen

巨大的宁静如你干净的布鞋

A：A gigantic quietude like your clean cloth shoes

B：A great serenity like your clean cloth shoes

C：Vast serenity like your clean cotton shoes

D: a huge calm, like your clean cloth-shoes

在床边,往事依稀、温婉

A: Beside the bed, vague memories of the past, warm

B: The past, vague and gentle, lingers by the bedside

C: By the bed, the past feels hazy and mild

D: by the bed, the past is dim, warm and gentle

如一只旧盒子

A: Like an old box

B: Like an old box

C: like an old box

D: like an old box

一个褪色的书签

A: A faded bookmark

B: A faded bookmark

C: a faded bookmark

D: a faded letter

夏天还很远

A: Summer is still far away

B: Summer is still very far away

C: Summer is still far

D: Summer's still far away

偶然遇见,可能想不起

A: A chance encounter, perhaps bringing no recognition

B: Meeting by chance, perhaps you can't recall

C: A chance encounter, I can't quite remember

D: A chance encounter, you probably don't remember

外面有一点冷

A: A little chilly outside

B：It was a little cold outside

C：A little cold outside

D：it was a little cold outside

左手也疲倦

A：The left hand is tired

B：Your left hand was tired，too

C：my left hand is tired

D：my left hand was tired

暗地里一直往左边

A：In the darkness heading left

B：Secretly you walked all the way to the left

C：It keeps sliding to the left in the dark

D：all the while it was secretly moving to the left

偏僻又深入

A：Where hidden deep within

B：Far away, deep in

C：far yet profound

D：remote and thoroughgoing

那唯一痴痴的挂念

A：Is that one incurable yearning

B：The sole infatuation of your heart

C：The one and only silly nostalgia

D：that single silly thought of you

夏天还很远

A：Summer is still far away

B：Summer is still very far away

C：Summer is still far

D：Summer's still far away

再不了,动辄发脾气,动辄热爱

A：No, no longer quick to anger, nor quick to love

B：Never again easy to anger, easy to love

C：No longer quick-tempered or impassioned

D：Never again, losing my temper or loving passionately at a touch

拾起从前的坏习惯

A：Picking up old bad habits

B：To take up those old bad habits of yours

C：you pick up bad habits from the past

D：gather up the bad old habits

灰心年复一年

A：Year after year you lose heart

B：Losing heart with each passing year

C：disheartened year after year

D：year after year depressed

小竹楼、白衬衫

A：Your bamboo hut, your white shirt

B：A small bamboo house, a white shirt

C：Little bamboo house, a white shirt

D：the small bamboo building, a white shirt

你是不是正当年?

A：But are you still the same?

B：Are you in the prime of life?

C：Are you in the prime of life?

D：are you in the prime of life?

难得下一次决心

A：Decisiveness is rare

B：Seldom can a decision be made

C：For once, a rare resolution

D: it's rare to reach a resolution

夏天还很远

A: Summer is still far away

B: Summer is still very far away

C: Summer is still far

D: Summer's still far away

个案研究四：英语世界里的望气者
——柏桦诗歌《望气的人》中英文本对照分析

杨安文

作为20世纪80年代中国新诗热潮中的"后朦胧"诗人杰出代表，柏桦是中国当代最具影响力的诗人之一。中国当代著名诗人北岛曾称他为"中国最优秀的抒情诗人"。台湾诗人、批评家黄梁认为，"柏桦诗歌以情韵深远、风格鲜明、气象从容的汉诗精神，开辟一代诗风"[1]。德国汉学家顾彬说，"作为日常生活的诗人，柏桦像宋朝的大诗人一样，到处可以找到诗歌"，并认为他与里尔克一样，是"真实的""诚实写作的典范"。[2] 哈佛大学王德威教授认为，"柏桦的诗歌是中国当代最好的诗歌之一，精妙并扣人心弦"[3]。柏桦诗歌在海内外广受读者喜爱，曾荣获安高诗歌奖、《上海文学》诗歌奖、柔刚诗歌奖、《红岩》随笔奖、"红岩文学奖"之诗歌奖等诸多奖项。柏桦迄今已出版诗集24本，其中英文、法文诗集各1本，德文诗集（合著）2本，已正式发表的诗歌一千多首，其中数百首被译为英文、法文、德文、荷兰文等外文，发表在国内外多个刊物及网络上。柏桦许多早期创作的诗歌（1980年代至2000年）广受海内外读者的推崇和喜爱，《望气的人》便是其中一首。本文以该诗为研究对象，通过对原文本和四个英文译本的对照分析，探析各译本在词汇、语法、诗意以及诗歌韵律呈现等方面的翻译处理及

---

[1] 黄梁：《大块抒情，坦荡吟诗——漫步在柏桦诗歌的温润境界里》，载柏桦：《望气的人》，台北：唐山出版社，1999年，序言第XX页。

[2] Bai Hua. *Wind Says*. trans. by Fiona Sze-Lorrain. Zephyr Press and The Chinese University Press，2012，back cover page.

[3] Bai Hua. *Wind Says*. trans. by Fiona Sze-Lorrain. Zephyr Press and The Chinese University Press，2012，back cover page.

得失，并基于分析提出修改建议，以促进《望气的人》及柏桦诗歌在英语世界的品读与赏析。

一、诗篇简介

《望气的人》写于1986年暮春，是柏桦自评的早期代表作之一①，诗人于1999年在台湾出版的个人诗集正是以此诗命名②。该诗是柏桦诗歌在海外译介最多的诗之一，这也许是因为该诗的主题与中国古老的传统文化有关，对西方读者而言充满了新奇性和神秘性。据任继愈在《中国佛教史》中记载，望气是"依据云气的色彩、形状和变化来占验人事吉凶的一种方术"，"望气方术的理论根据是天人感应的神学目的论"。③ 诗中"望气的人"即指观运气之人，通过登高望云预卜凶吉，类似于占卜家。柏桦在《左边：毛泽东时代的抒情诗人》里提到了创作该诗的起由：在阅读中被历史故事里望气者神奇的预言能力所吸引，如范增在鸿门宴前登高望刘邦之气，发现其帝王气盛，告知刘邦，刘邦却因充耳不闻而酿成大祸。④ 正是这一好奇之心启发了诗人的创作灵感。诗人自言，此诗的新意在于以诗的形式呈现了一个神秘的"望气的人"的形象，揭开了传统中国文化中望气术、望气士的神秘面纱。

该诗第一诗节是人物的出场，是对望气士形象的总体呈现：行色匆匆，总在行走之中，登高望远，观云望气。云气在望气者眼里变幻莫测，呈现出不同的颜色（金色、赤色、黑色等）和不同的图案（几何图案、兽形图案等）。接下来的第二、三、四节，通过三个具体的故事情景，描写了望气者从云气里看到了什么。从"宫殿"到"穷巷""山谷""乡间"，从"英雄"到"儿童""导师"，望气者似乎能洞穿一切，预知一切，这正是诗人想要烘托的神秘感，将古老的传统文化中的望气之术生动、形象地呈现在读者眼前。最后一节与第一节呼应，望气士开始了下一段工作旅途，"已走上了另一座山巅"。五个诗节

---

① 柏桦：《柏桦代表作》，载《当代作家评论》，2010年第5期。
② 柏桦：《望气的人》，台北：唐山出版社，1999年。
③ 任继愈：《中国佛教史》，北京：中国社会科学出版社，1981年，第40页。
④ 柏桦：《左边：毛泽东时代的抒情诗人》，南京：江苏文艺出版社，2009年，第124页。

呈现五个空间、五个情境,却又情景交融、浑然一体。"全诗各部以同质的音色自然交叠","诗意空间深阔、音色协和","其空间质性特征是长久以来被认知断层所遗忘的意境诗学,它的阅读界面的渗透性均衡优美,想象空间大,经得起历时性的品味、吟咏"。①

二、译本情况

该诗共有 5 个英语译本,其中 3 个译本发表于国外期刊,1 个译本发表于国内期刊,另有 1 个译本未在刊物发表,仅载于荷兰鹿特丹国际诗歌网②。此外,该诗还有 1 个法语译本,由法国汉学家、诗人尚德兰翻译,发表于 4 个不同的法国刊物或诗集,1 个荷兰语译本,由荷兰汉学家柯雷翻译,发表于 2 个不同的荷兰刊物。由于笔者外语能力所限,同时考虑学术严谨性,本文仅考察 4 个正式发表于刊物的英文译本。译本 A 由柏桦诗歌最早的译介者、诗歌翻译家李赋康于 1989 年所译,经著名汉学家闵福德修改润色后,于 1991 年发表于澳大利亚《我所写》杂志第 7 卷第 1 期,是该诗最早的英文译本。③ 译本 B 选自 2011 年在美国华盛顿出版的英文诗集《推开窗:当代中国诗歌》,由美国著名汉学家、翻译家陶忘机翻译。④ 译本 C 选自柏桦的英文诗集《风在说》,该诗集于 2012 年由西风出版社和香港中文大学出版社出版,译者为新加坡裔法籍诗人、翻译家菲奥娜·施-罗琳。⑤该译本同时于 2011 年发表于美国的一份当代国际诗歌和短篇小说杂志《苦桃》(*The Bitter Oleander*)第 17 卷第 2 期。⑥ 译本 D 由美国当代诗人、翻译

---

① 黄梁:《新诗评论集:想像的对话》,台北:唐山出版社,1997 年,第 213 页。
② 该译本由澳大利亚翻译家西敏(Simon Patton)所译,载于荷兰鹿特丹国际诗歌网,网址为 https://www.poetryinternationalweb.net/pi/site/poem/item/11553/auto/0/CLOUD-DIVINER。
③ Bai Hua. The Skywatcher. Li Fukang (trans.). *Scripsi* 7 (1), 1991: 289—290.
④ Bai Hua. The Seer. John Balcom (trans.). In Qingping Wang (ed.). *Push Open the Window: Contemporary Poetry from China*. Washington: Copper Canyon Press, 2011, pp. 58—61.
⑤ Bai Hua. *Wind Says*. trans. by Fiona Sze-Lorrain. Zephyr Press and The Chinese University Press, 2012, pp. 38—39.
⑥ Bai Hua. Cloud Diviner. Fiona SZE-Lorrain (tran.). *The Bitter Oleander* 17 (2), 2011: 112—113.

家、哈佛大学费正清中国研究中心研究员顾爱玲翻译,于 2014 年发表在《飞地》杂志第 8 期上。①

从文本形式来看,原诗有 5 个诗节,每节 4 行,行尾均无标点符号。全诗共 172 个字,127 个词。② 4 个英文译本在形式上与原文基本对应,诗节、诗行与原文完全一致,仅译本 A 部分诗行行尾增加了标点符号。笔者对比了译者李赋康的原译文和闵福德的修改译文,发现行末标点均为后者所加。4 处行末增加了逗号,据推测是为了体现前后两个诗行归属一个句子,2 处增加了句号,意在强调断句。此外,各译本各诗行首字母大写的情况也有所不同。译本 A 和译本 B 全篇所有诗行首字母均为大写。译本 C 和译本 D 则不同,均利用诗行首字母大写的方式进行断句,但两个译本断句的处理也不尽相同。在译本单词数方面,译本 A 为 128 个词,译本 B 为 144 个词,译本 C 为 122 个词,译本 D 为 119 个词。各译本的用词数与原诗较为接近,可见四位译者总体上均依照原诗内容,采用简洁、精练的语言进行对照翻译。相较而言,陶忘机的译本在语言转换上更为追求准确、流畅,因而用词最多。

三、译本对比分析

1. 意旨的把握:诗题翻译的背后

《望气的人》是一首与中国传统文化相关且充满神秘色彩的诗,古风、古韵浓厚,如同《在清朝》《苏州记事一年》《李后主》等诗一样,该诗被认为是体现柏桦汉诗风格的力作,诗中流淌着古典之美和汉风之美。对于以西方读者为主的英语读者而言,对诗题的理解是把握本诗意旨关键。如前文所述,"望气"是指通过观云气预卜人事吉凶,"望气的人"指的是望气士或望气者,古代一种带有神秘主义色彩并与宗教神学有一定联系的"高级职业"。诗题

---

① Bai Hua. The Aura-Seer. Eleanor Goodman (trans.). *Enclave* (8),2014:133—134.
② 本研究是以中国社会科学院语言研究所词典编辑室编写的《现代汉语词典》第 7 版(商务印书馆,2017 年)中所列词条及词性标注为依据,进行中文文本的词数统计。

"望气的人"本身即透出古风色彩,并以其古典神秘性引人阅读、赏析。以下是四个译本对题目的翻译:

> 望气的人
> A:The Sky-watcher
> B:The Seer
> C:Cloud Diviner
> D:The Aura-Seer

译本 A 将"望气的人"译为"The Sky-watcher"。"watcher"指"守望者,观察者"(someone who watches)①,"The Sky-watcher"可回译为"天空观察者",台湾有一家世界著名的天文望远镜制造商 Sky Watcher,中文名为"天空守望者"。可见,"The Sky-watcher"所指宽泛,让读者产生的联想更多是观察天体。而本诗中的"望气"是看天观云气,西方读者由于没有相近的文化背景,并不能将"天空观察者"与预卜吉凶联系起来,因而难以领会本诗之意旨。译本 B 则译为"The Seer"。"seer"指"预言家,先知"(a person who sees into the future),虽道出了"望气的人"的本质属性,却没有反映出其预卜吉凶的方式。译本 D 则更进一步,译为"The Aura-Seer"。但"Aura"指的是"氛围,气氛",而非"云气"。译本 C 则译为"Cloud Diviner"。"divine"指"预卜,占卜"(to foresee or foretell as if divinely inspired),"diviner"可指"预言者,占卜者"。"Cloud Diviner"准确地表达出是通过观察"cloud"(云气)来预卜吉凶,最为接近原文之意。同时还值得注意的是,A、B、D 三个译本都加了定冠词"The",仅译本 C 未加。考虑到本诗是通过虚构描写一个特定的望气者的形象和工作情形,展现古代望气士这一神秘职业,标题宜加上定冠词,特指诗人具体描写的这位望气士。综上所述,笔者认为,采用显化的方法将诗题译为"The Cloud Diviner"能够比较准确地呈现诗人塑造的"望气士"形象,有助于读者把握该诗意旨。

---

① 本文所引用的英文释义全部出自《钱伯斯英语词典》第十三版。

2. 时间维度的转换:时态处理

原诗是利用虚构创设的故事情景,通过对"望气的人"的外在形象、气质和工作情形的描写,给读者呈现出中国古代望气士这一神秘形象及其神奇的超自然的预见能力。因此,原诗叙事的时间基调宜选择现在时,或称"戏剧性现在时"(Dramatic present)。四个译本中,B、C、D译本选择的基本时态是一般现在时,部分句子使用了现在完成时或现在进行时。译本 A 的时态使用稍显混乱,第一节使用了一般现在时,第二节至第五节却使用了一般过去时。原诗第二节至第五节恰恰是描写望气士的工作情形以及他从云气中看到了什么,使用现在时态尤其是现在进行时能让读者身临其境,画面感、现场感更强。

由于中文表达中没有动词词尾的变化,我们只能通过动词本身的含义和时间副词、动态助词等来显示动作的时间维度。这就使得译者在翻译时如何选择动词的"体"(aspect)成为难点。请看以下三个诗行的翻译:

一个英雄正动身去千里之外
A:A hero, *starting* for beyond the horizon
B:A hero sets off on a journey beyond a thousand miles
C:A hero embarks on a thousand-mile journey
D:a hero sets off on a thousand li journey

两个儿童打扫着亭台
A:Two boys *were sweeping* the balcony—
B:Two boys sweep the pavilion
C:Two children *are sweeping* the pavilions
D:Two children sweep the pavilion terraces

独自在吐火、炼丹
A:Spat out fire, made the philosopher's stone—
B:Alone *amid shooting flames, alchemizing*
C:spits fire, brews elixir on his own

D：sits alone, *spitting fire, performing alchemy*

中文里的动态助词"正""着""在"常常表示动作正在进行，或处于某种状态之中，对应到英语翻译里常常用动词的进行体。在本诗中诗人展现的是望气者透过云气看到的正在发生的场景，在上述这三行诗中用进行体当是合理选择。强调动作正在进行，除了采用谓语动词的进行时态以外，还可以通过动词非谓语形式，如现在分词作伴随状语（sits alone, spitting fire, performing alchemy），强调动作同时发生，或用动名词短语搭配特定的介词（Alone amid shooting flames, alchemizing），同样可表达正在进行的时间概念。以上例举的第一行诗，译本 B、C、D 均使用了一般现在时，没有传递出动作正在进行的意思，缺乏情景感、现场感。译本 A 使用了非谓语形式的现在分词结构，虽能体现正在进行之意，但句法结构上却不够严谨。以上例举的第二行诗，译本 A 和 C 恰当地使用了进行时态。对第三行诗，译本 B 和 D 选择使用了动词非谓语结构，同样体现出了动作正在进行之中。

再请看下面三个诗行的翻译：

望气的人**看到**了

A：The skywatcher *saw* with his inner eye

B：The *seer* sees

C：The cloud diviner can *see*

D：The aura-seer *watches*

望气的人**看穿**了石头里的图案

A：The skywatcher *saw* through the design

B：The seer *sees* through the pattern in a stone

C：The cloud diviner *sees* patterns in the stones

D：The aura-seer *sees* patterns in the stones

望气的人**已**走上了另一座山巅

A：The skywatcher *was already* on another high

B：The seer *is already* at the top of another peak

C：The cloud diviner *has left* for the next summit

D：The aura-seer *has already left* for another summit

中文表达里的"了"或"已经……了"通常表示动作已经完成，一般可对应为英语动词的完成体。但也不能一概而论，具体问题需具体分析。以上例举的第一、二诗行，动词后面虽有"了"，但原文描写的是望气士看到的即时的情景，翻译时不宜使用完成时态。除了译本 A 使用了过去时以外（上文已论及使用过去时的不合理性），另外三个译本都采用了一般现在时。而第三行诗的情况却有所不同："已走上了另一座山巅"既可理解为已经在山巅之上了，也可理解为正在去山巅的路上。译本 B 使用了一般现在时，强调已经站在山巅之上的状态，译本 C 和 D 则使用了现在完成时，强调已经出发去往另一座山巅的路上。两种阐释及随之而来的两种选择均可接受。笔者认为采用完成时态更佳，强调望气者又开始了新的征程，与开篇望气士"行色匆匆"走在出发路上相呼应，呈现出望气士的工作状态是在周而复始的匆匆行进之中。

3. 词汇使用对比分析

诗歌语言精练，用词考究，这给诗歌翻译的词汇选择提出了很高要求。要想准确把握中英文词汇的准确含义从而做好翻译转换，必须要了解语言背后丰富的历史、文化，了解特定词汇在特定文化语境中的习惯用法和特别涵义。诗歌翻译中译者对词汇的选择受到诸多因素的影响，包括译者对原诗准确深入的理解，对目标语词汇的精准把握，同时还受到诗歌美学因素的影响，如节奏、韵律等方面的考量。下面从本诗中抽出部分诗行，对词汇层面的翻译进行对比分析。

首先请看第一节的第三、四行：

眼中沉沉的暮霭

A：Out of his misty, heavy eye

B：The heavy evening mist in his eyes

C: In his eyes, the dense dusky mist

D: The dense evening mist in his eye

长出黄金、几何与宫殿

A: *Gold, geometry and palaces keep growing*

B: *Out of which grow gold, geometry, and palaces*

C: grows gold, geometry and palaces

D: grows gold, geometry, and palaces

  这两句诗描写望气者透过双眼,看到了"黄金、几何与宫殿"从沉沉暮霭中"长出"。"黄金"比喻指云气呈现金色,或五彩绚丽,这是"天子之气"。"几何与宫殿"指云层呈现的不同图案,代表不同的预兆,"如果两军对垒而战,看到云底部大而前面呈细长形,那么双方'当战'"①,如果云层呈现龙虎等兽的形状,则是天子气的象征。"宫殿"正是象征通过观云气看到的天子之气,居此方之人物必成帝王。理解两句诗后再来对比各译本的翻译。四个译本都将"长出"译为"grow",但译本 A 和 B 是将"gold, geometry, and palaces"作为"grow"主语,而译本 C 和 D 则是作为其宾语。我们知道,中文表达中说某个地方长出某个东西,在英文中应该表述为某个东西从某个地方长出来(something grows from someplace)。因此,译本 C 和 D 错将主语用作宾语,使得译文令人费解。

  接下来看第二诗节。在本节中,望气者看到了一个布衣出身的人,一个未来的英雄正"动身去千里之外"。"穷巷""草鞋""布衫"表明了他的出身,"西风"的意象常指秋天的萧瑟、凄凉,带有一定的悲情色彩。"西风突变"隐喻了他在逆境中奋发,"寒门出贵子,逆境出人才",英雄就要在这里诞生。"他激动的草鞋和布衫",除了指望气者看到"英雄"意气风发,激动上路,同时亦可反观望气者"激动的"看着这一切,"以我之眼观万物,万物皆着我之色彩"。由此可见,上述几个关键意象的翻译直接影响本诗的意境。

---

① 任继愈:《中国佛教史》,北京:中国社会科学出版社,1981 年,第 40 页。

穷巷西风突变

A：*The ghetto* stormed of a sudden,

B：In *a slum lane* the west wind suddenly turns

C：In *a poor quarter*, the west wind turns abruptly

D：In *the poor quarter*, the west wind suddenly changes

译本 B 将"穷巷"直译为"a slum lane","slum"(an overcrowded, squalid neighborhood)已有"贫民窟"之意,再把"巷"刻意用"lane"译出,显得画蛇添足。原诗此处意在强调这位"英雄"出身贫寒,用"the poor quarter"便能朴实、准确地表达其意。同时要注意的是,译本 A 通过意译的方式将重要的意象"西风"淹没了,这显然不妥,要知该词的消失也直接将"英雄"的身世背景抹掉了一半。

一个英雄正动身去千里之外

A：A hero, starting for *beyond the horizon*

B：A hero sets off on *a journey beyond a thousand miles*

C：A hero embarks on *a thousand-mile journey*

D：a hero sets off on *a thousand li journey*

"千年之外",泛指遥远的地方,而非在数字层面指准确的距离。译本 D 译为"a thousand li journey",刻意将"里"译为"li",而非英语中表示距离的"mile"(英里)。看似准确的翻译,实则可能会给西方读者带来理解障碍。既然是泛指遥远,用"a thousand-mile journey"可达到同样的意义效果,又不会带来理解障碍,何乐而不为?

他激动的草鞋和布衫

A：In his linen coat and *straw shoe-excited*

B：His *agitated straw sandals* and cotton clothes

C：his *agitated grass sandals* and toga

D: his *hastening grass sandals* and tunic

如上文所述,此句中的"草鞋"和"布衫"是中国古代平民的典型装束,表明"英雄"的布衣身份。草鞋一般以干草(稻草、麦秸或玉米秸等)为材料编织,是类似于拖鞋或带子鞋一类的凉鞋。译本 A 译为"straw shoe"显然不准确,"shoe"一般指完全包住脚趾的封闭式鞋。其他译本选用的"sandal"(凉鞋)一词比较符合草鞋的形状特点。但译本 C 和 D 译为"grass sandals",给人的感觉是草鞋是用鲜草而不是干草做的,亦欠妥。译本 B 的"straw sandals"相对准确。另外,本句中"激动"一词,三个译本都译为"agitated",笔者认为有待商榷。"agitated"通常指某人"心烦意乱或焦虑不安",原诗中的"激动"当指"英雄"要出发干一番大事业的兴奋与激动。故笔者认为选用"excited"(兴奋的,激动的)一词,拟人化使用,更符合原诗的意境。

第三节各译本对部分词语的翻译也值得讨论。译本 A 将"亭台"译为"Balcony"(阳台,露台)显然不准确。"坐对空寂的夜晚"中的"坐对",译本 A 译为"sit against",意为坐靠着 "the evening sky"(傍晚的天空);译本 C 仅译出了"对"(faces an empty twilight)却漏了"坐";译本 D 则只译出了"坐"(sits in the empty still twilight)。只有译本 B 通过现在分词做伴随状语,准确地译出"坐对"(sits facing the desolate evening)。"空寂"一词可作两种理解,一是空虚寂寞,二是空旷寂静。原诗本节描写望气者看到的是山谷依然,钟声依旧,儿童打扫亭台,一派自然祥和的景象。望气者冷静地看着这一切,其超凡脱俗、隐逸世间的高人形象跃然纸上。由此可见,"坐对空寂的夜晚"并不意在表达望气者深感孤独寂寞的感情色彩。"desolate"(lonely; forlorn; totally lacking in inhabitants)一词强调凄凉、孤单,用在此处并不合适,用中性色彩的"empty"(having nothing inside)更为贴切。

最后看第四节。在本节中,望气者看到了一个道士在独自吐火炼丹。原诗中的"导师"取谐音,实指道士。道士乃传道之士,作为布道传教者,在现代话语中称其为导师倒也说得过去。然而由于中国历史文化的缘故,神仙崇拜成了道士的宗教信仰,"道"被具化为了"仙",得道成仙成了他们的根本追求,故以炼制金丹、服食丹药为根本的修炼方术,以求长生不老。望气者不仅看到了这一切,还看到作为炼丹原材料的金属矿石——"石头"里的奥秘。望气者比如"神仙"一般的道士还高出一等,此处无疑烘托出了望气者神秘的超能力,预卜先知,洞穿一切。"干枯的导师",把炼丹道士为炼丹不惜以身试药,从而身体受损、体型干瘪的形象生动地呈现出来。"导师"这一现代词汇的谐音换用,某种程度也是对道士痴迷炼丹、追求长生不老的一种讽刺。同时,"干枯的导师"也与"吉祥之云宽大"这个出场的背景形成一种悖论的张力。

基于以上理解,我们再来对比四个译本对此诗节部分词汇的翻译:

一个干枯的**导师**沉默

A: A dry-boned, silent *master*

B: In silence, a withered *old master*

C: A quiet shriveled *master*

D: the silent wizened *master*

如上文所述,"导师"一词实际指道士。四个译本都将其译为"master",该词意思非常丰富,既可指师傅、工匠,也可指教师、教练,甚至大师、行家,与"导师"之意接近,但却无法令英语读者联想到"道士"。笔者认为此处可直接译为"Daoist"(道士),有助于英语读者对本节的理解,尤其是帮助理解下一句——导师为何要吐火、炼丹。

独自在吐火、炼丹

A: Spat out fire, *made the philosopher's stone* –

B: Alone amid shooting flames, *alchemizing*

C: spits fire, *brews elixir* on his own

D: sits alone, spitting fire, *performing alchemy*

英语中"alchemy"指"炼金术","炼丹"译为"alchemizing"或"performing alchemy"均可接受。但译本 A 译为"made the philosopher's stone",意思令人费解。译本 C 译为 "brews elixir","elixir"指"炼金药、长生不老药",这是对"丹"的准确理解和翻译,但所用动词"brew"指"酿造(茶、酒等),调制(饮料等)",与"炼丹"(丹炉中烧炼矿物以制造"仙丹")的含义是不相吻合的。前者酿的是液体,后者炼的是固体。

> 望气的人看穿了石头里的图案
> A：The skywatcher saw through *the design*
> B：The seer sees through *the pattern* in a stone
> C：The cloud diviner sees *patterns* in the stones
> D：The aura-seer sees *patterns* in the stones

本节中最后一行中的"图案",译本 A 的翻译同样欠佳。"design"通常指"设计或装饰图案"。"pattern"指某物自身呈现出的某种形状或式样的图案。此处望气者看到的"图案",是石头本身呈现的图案,实际是一种象征意义(前文已述),故译为"pattern"符合原意。

可见,诗歌翻译中的词汇选择体现了译者对源语和目标语词汇的精准理解能力,以及对词汇背后所蕴含的文化和意象的感知能力。同时,不同的词汇选择也体现了译者对原诗不同的理解和阐释,对原诗意旨不同程度的感受和领会。译诗中选词用词是否得当,很大程度决定了译诗能否有效转换原诗之内容。

4. 句法结构转换分析

现代诗在写作手法上较为自由,根据诗歌的不同类型、风格和诗人各自的语言习惯有不同的选择。在句法单元上的并置结构(juxtaposition)是现代诗的重要句式特征。比如,在超现实主义诗歌中,诗人往往会使用意象并置或叠加(superposition),故意不点明意象词之间的相互关系,生成一种模糊的、不确定的、多义甚至难以理解的意象组合,从而带来一种出人意料的、奇特的艺术效果。但在叙事诗或故事性较强的抒情诗中,诗人常常采用散文式的诗歌语言,诗句在句法上较为完整,通常一至两个诗行构成一个完整的句子。在诗歌翻译中,我们发现,部分原诗里本是完整句子的诗行,被转换为短语结构,以意象并置的方式呈现在译诗中。比较《望气的人》的四个译本可见,译本 A 多处将原诗中的完整句子以独立主格结构(通常为名词加现在分词、过去分词或介词短语)呈现,另外三个译本则较为忠实于原文,除个别诗行外,基本都采用与原文对应的完整的句子。试比较下面两行诗的翻译:

更远的山谷浑然

A: *The farther valley in harmony*

B: Farther beyond is the valley in its wholeness

C: Farther valleys merge into one

D: Farther valleys smudge together

零落的钟声依稀可闻

A: *A broken bell dimly heard nearby*

B: Sporadically, the tolling of a bell is still faintly heard

C: *the chimes of bells, faint and few*

D: *the faint scattered sound of bells*

　　两行诗的中文原文均为完整的句子。"更远的山谷浑然",指远处绵延的一座座山谷连成一片,融合一体。第一行中的"浑然"是形容词充当句子谓语,指"浑然天成、浑然一体",呈现的是一种静态、悠远的美。译本 C 将"浑然"译为动词短语"merge into one",意为"融合为一体",译本 D 译为"smudge together",可理解为"模糊成为一片";两个译本虽基本达意,但强调的却都是动作而非状态。译本 A 则转换了句法结构,以独立主格结构的形式呈现,介词短语"in harmony"呈现出一种和谐自然的状态,但意思与原句稍有出入。译本 B 用介词短语"in its wholeness"作表语,较好地呈现了远处的山谷浑然一体的静态美。第二行诗"零落的钟声依稀可闻"为完整句子,但除译本 B 以外的三个译本都将其转换为短语结构,尤其是译本 A 将其与上一行诗形成短语并置,结构对应,带来了较好的诗意效果。虽然译本 C 和 D 同为名词短语结构,但译本 D 将形容词"faint""scattered"放在名词前,重心落到了名词上;译本 C 则将形容词"faint and few"后置,重心落到了形容词上,能更好地呈现钟声的"零落"与"依稀可闻"。

再看最后一节前两行的翻译:

乡间的日子风调雨顺

A:Time passed in the tranquil countryside,

B:*Rural days of good weather*

C:Wind and rain agree in village days

D:In the village, the wind and rain are mild

菜田一畦,流水一涧

A:*A bed of vegetables, a brook of water.*

B:*Ridged rectangular fields, a stream of running water*

C:*A vegetable field, a flowing stream*

D:*a vegetable patch, a flowing brook*－

原诗第一行是完整的句子,第二行则是典型的并置结构,与第一行诗共同呈现出闲适、美好的乡村生活画面。三个译本对于第一行都选择了完整句子翻译;译本 A 采取了一定程度的意译,可回译为"宁静的乡村岁月逝去",意思有些走样;译本 C 将"风调雨顺"译为"Wind and rain agree",意思令人费解;译本 D 译为"the wind and rain are mild",意为"风雨柔和不剧烈",不能传达出原句所蕴含的风雨均匀适度、适合庄稼生长之意。译本 B 采用了转换句法结构的方式,将原句译为名词短语,一方面比较准确地表达了原诗的意思,另一方面又与下一行的两个短语并置在结构上相呼应,且实现了两个诗行的押韵("whether""water"),音美形美,诗意浓厚。

根据英国翻译理论家卡特福德的翻译转换理论[①],上述句法结构方面

---

① 参见谭载喜:《西方翻译简史》(增订版),北京:商务印书馆,2010 年,第 210 页。

的转换属于范畴转换（Category Shift）下的单位转换（Unit Shift），这是将源文本变为目标文本时偏离形式对应（Formal Correspondence）的常见表现，在翻译实践中是常用的翻译转换手段。在汉英诗歌翻译中，译者或为了使译诗如原诗一样简洁精练，或为了以短语形式的并置达到意象叠加的效果，或为了还原原诗的节奏韵律，时有将原诗语法结构完整的句子以短语结构形式译出。值得注意的是，译者应把握好此类单位转换的度，否则译诗将显得句法混乱，语意不清。

5. 韵律使用分析

《望气的人》语言质朴、流畅，看似没有古典诗歌的节奏和韵律，但通过吟诵可立刻感受到其跳动的节奏和优美的韵律，散文式的语言在一张一弛的节奏中呈现出一种古风古韵、悠远绵长的怀旧情调。在节奏方面，虽然诗行长短不一，但这种融入诗人呼吸的节律能随处可察："穷巷西风突变/一个英雄正动身去千里之外"，"乡间的日子风调雨顺/菜田一畦，流水一涧/这边青翠未改/望气的人已走上了另一座山巅"。在用韵上，全篇有贯穿首尾的协韵"an"，不仅体现在尾韵上，诗行中也有多处协韵，在下面列出的诗行中黑体加粗的字或词便是通篇协韵之处。在本诗中还可发现第二个用韵安排，每个诗节中均有一行（在第一、三、四、五诗节中是第三行，在第二诗节中是第二行）协"ai"韵，基本是尾韵，下面诗行中斜体加粗的字是协韵之处。同一诗篇中有两条协韵的旋律（"an""ai"也可视为转韵关系），形成了全篇充满音乐美感的复调韵律。

望气的人

望气的人行色匆匆
登高眺**远**
眼中沉沉的暮霭
长出黄金、几何与宫**殿**

穷巷西风突**变**
一个英雄正动身去千里之**外**
望气的人**看**到了
他激动的草鞋和布**衫**

更远的山谷浑**然**
零落的钟声依稀可闻
两个儿童打扫着亭**台**
望气的人坐对空寂的傍**晚**

吉祥之云**宽**大
一个干枯的导师沉默
独自**在**吐火、炼**丹**
望气的人**看穿**了石头里的图**案**

乡**间**的日子风调雨顺
菜**田**一畦,流水一**涧**
这**边**青翠未改
望气的人已走上了另一座山**巅**

1986 暮春

通过分析该诗的四个英语译本可见,在三位外国译者的译本中基本找不到体现原诗节奏韵律的刻意安排,唯有在中国译者李赋康的译本里能明显感受到用韵的别有用心。犹如在原诗中全篇协"*an*"韵,译本 A 全文有尾韵的安排,并且是谐元韵/ai/。同时可发现在部分诗行行间也有使用带/ai/韵的词汇,以尽力呈现原诗通篇协韵的特点。请见下面译文中斜体加粗的部分:

The *Skywatcher*

tran. by Li Fukang

The *skywatcher* is in a hurry, walking
Up a mountain near the *sky*
Gold, geometry and palaces keep growing
Out of his misty, heavy *eye*

The ghetto stormed of a sudden,
A hero, starting for beyond the *horizon*
In his linen coat and straw shoe—*excited*
The *skywatcher* saw with his inner *eye*

The farther valley in harmony,
A broken bell dimly heard *nearby*
Two boys were sweeping the balcony—
The *skywatcher* sat against the evening *sky*

The clouds were vast and auspicious.
A *dry*-boned, *silent* master
spat out *fire*, made the philosopher's stone—
The *skywatcher* saw through the *design*

Time passed in the tranquil *countryside*,
A bed of vegetables, a brook of water.
While the green remained on this *side*,
The *skywatcher* was already on another *high*

除了尽力体现原诗的押韵特点之外,译本 A 还力求在译诗中呈现形式美和节奏美。特别在第一诗节中,译者将原诗第三行和第四行顺序进行调整,以实现第一、三行和第二、四行分别在形式、节奏和韵律上形成呼应。在形式及用韵上,第一行与第三行、第二行与第四行句子长度相近,且行尾协韵:"walking"对"growing",协辅韵/ɪŋ/;"sky"对"eye",协尾韵/ai/。可见译者有意模仿英诗 abab 的韵式。在节奏上,形成相同的以重读音节为中心的"弹跳节奏"(Sprung Rhythm)①,尤其是第二、四行:

    Up a mountain near the *sky*
    Out of his misty, heavy *eye*

  着重号对应的音节为重读音节,两行均为四个,形成相同的节奏。可见译者翻译时用心良苦。然而,同时我们也发现,内容和形式难以兼得,译者为了模拟原诗的韵律与乐感,一定程度牺牲了诗歌翻译的准确性,有因韵害意之嫌。而另外三个译本未能体现原诗的韵律特点,可能因为其外国译者未能很好感知原诗的节奏与用韵,也可能是译者虽有感知,却在内容与形式的取舍上,选择将忠实于原文、准确传递原文之意放在首位,因而无法很好呈现原诗韵律之美。

四、结　　语

  以上是笔者结合柏桦名诗《望气的人》中文原诗的赏析,从诗歌意旨的领会,时间维度的把握、词汇的恰切使用、句法结构的转换以及诗歌韵律的呈现等五个方面,对四个英译本进行了对比分析。正所谓"诗无达诂",诗歌文本语言精练、简洁,高度浓缩,思想内容也时常艰深隐晦,本身就具有理解和阐释的开放性,这也正是诗歌及诗歌翻译的魅力所在。如

---

  ① "弹跳节奏"由英国诗人霍普金斯(Gerald Manley Hokins,1844—1889)提出,指不按照传统英诗的音步结构,只以重音节为中心,前后可依附数量不等的轻音节,形成诗歌节奏。参见赵毅衡:《诗神远游:中国诗如何改变了美国现代诗》,成都:四川文艺出版社,2013 年,第 210 页。

德国哲学解释学大家伽达默尔所言,"一切翻译就已经是解释","所有翻译者都是解释者",①翻译过程本身首先是译者作为读者对原文本的阐释过程。也正是翻译以及不同译者的不同翻译,给诗歌文本的阐释带来了宽广阔的延展空间,延续了原文本在目的语世界多姿多彩的生命。然而,我们并不能因此而否认文本确定性的存在,美国解释学理论代表人物赫施区分了文本的"含义"(Significance)和"意义"(Meaning)两个概念,指出"含义"是固有的文本符号所规定的,是确定的并可以复现的。② 诗歌文本的翻译同样如此,尽管具有意义的开放性,但原诗语言符号所固化的"含义",译者应当竭力通过有效语言转换使之得以呈现。

不论是在词汇层面,还是在时态、句法结构等语法层面,上述的四个译本的翻译处理都各有特点,各有优势。总体来看,就内容的有效转换以及语言的准确性而言,当是陶忘机的译本最佳;从诗歌"形美"的角度尤其是就呈现原诗的韵律与音乐美感而言,当属李赋康的译本最好。笔者认为,一首好的译诗,首先应该是内容忠于原诗,语言转换的准确性至关重要。但诗之所以为诗,是其语言和形式具有"诗的特质",如果翻译之后完全丧失了原文"诗之美感",仅是两种语言所谓的"对等"转换,也称不上好的译诗。而原诗"美感"和"诗意"的成功转换和呈现,除了需要译者具有源语和目的语深厚的语言功底和语言转换能力,更需要译者对中文和英文诗歌敏锐的理解和感知力,对中国古今历史、文化和诗歌传统的学习和了解。基于以上讨论,笔者结合四个译本之优点,对该诗译文修改如下,供大家批评:

The Cloud Diviner

The cloud diviner is in a hurry, walking

Up a mountain near the sky

Gold, geometry and places keep growing

---

① 伽达默尔:《真理与方法》(下卷),洪汉鼎译,上海:上海译文出版社,1999年,第490、494页。
② 相关内容参见王岳川:《现象学与解释学文论》,济南:山东教育出版社,1999年,第16—17页。

Out of the heavy evening mist in his eye

In a poor quarter, the west wind turns suddenly
A hero is embarking on a thousand-mile journey
The cloud diviner sees
His straw sandals and line clothes, excited

Farther valleys merging into one
The chimes of bells, sporadic and faint
Two children are sweeping the pavilions
The cloud diviner sits facing the empty twilight

Auspicious cloudsare vast
A silent withered Taoist
Sits alone shooting flames, alchemizing
The cloud diviner sees patterns in the stones

Rural days of good weather
A vegetable field, abrook of water
It's still jade green on this side
The cloud diviner has left for anotherhigh

Late Spring, 1986

附：原诗及四个译本对照版
望气的人
A：The Sky-watcher
B：The Seer
C：Cloud Diviner

D: The Aura-Seer

望气的人行色匆匆

A: The skywatcher is in a hurry, walking

B: The seer is in a hurry to be off

C: The cloud diviner scurries by

D: The aura-seer hurries

登高眺远

A: Up a mountain near the sky

B: To ascend and gaze into the beyond

C: scanning from heights

D: surveying from great heights

眼中沉沉的暮霭

A: Out of his misty, heavy eye

B: The heavy evening mist in his eyes

C: In his eyes, the dense dusky mist

D: The dense evening mist in his eye

长出黄金、几何与宫殿

A: Gold, geometry and palaces keep growing

B: Out of which grow gold, geometry, and palaces

C: grows gold, geometry and palaces

D: grows gold, geometry, and palaces

穷巷西风突变

A: The ghetto stormed of a sudden,

B: In a slum lane the west wind suddenly turns

C：In a poor quarter, the west wind turns abruptly

D：In the poor quarter, the west wind suddenly changes

一个英雄正动身去千里之外

A：A hero, starting for beyond the horizon

B：A hero sets off on a journey beyond a thousand miles

C：A hero embarks on a thousand-mile journey

D：a hero sets off on a thousand li journey

望气的人看到了

A：The skywatcher saw with his inner eye

B：The seer sees

C：The cloud diviner can see

D：The aura-seer watches

他激动的草鞋和布衫

A：In his linen coat and straw shoe—excited

B：His agitated straw sandals and cotton clothes

C：his agitated grass sandals and toga

D：his hastening grass sandals and tunic

更远的山谷浑然

A：The farther valley in harmony

B：Farther beyond the valley in its wholeness

C：Farther valleys merge into one

D：Farther valleys smudge together

零落的钟声依稀可闻

A：A broken bell dimly heard nearby

B：Sporadically, the tolling of a bell is still faintly heard

C: the chimes of bells, faint and few

D: the faint scattered sound of bells

两个儿童打扫着亭台

A: Two boys were sweeping the balcony—

B: Two boys sweep the pavilion

C: Two children are sweeping the pavilions

D: Two children sweep the pavilion terraces

望气的人坐对空寂的傍晚

A: The skywatcher sat against the evening sky

B: The seer sits facing the desolate evening

C: The cloud diviner faces an empty twilight

D: The aura-seer sits in the empty still twilight

吉祥之云宽大

A: The clouds were vast and auspicious.

B: Auspicious clouds expand

C: Auspicious clouds unfold

D: Auspicious clouds spread

一个干枯的导师沉默

A: A dry-boned, silent master

B: In silence, a withered old master

C: A quiet shriveled master

D: the silent wizened master

独自在吐火、炼丹

A: Spat out fire, made the philosopher's stone—

B: Alone amid shooting flames, alchemizing

C：spits fire, brews elixir on his own

D：sits alone, spitting fire, performing alchemy

望气的人看穿了石头里的图案

A：The skywatcher saw through the design

B：The seer sees through the pattern in a stone

C：The cloud diviner sees patterns in the stones

D：The aura-seer sees patterns in the stones

乡间的日子风调雨顺

A：Time passed in the tranquil countryside,

B：Rural days of good weather

C：Wind and rain agree in village days

D：In the village, the wind and rain are mild

菜田一畦，流水一涧

A：A bed of vegetables, a brook of water.

B：Ridged rectangular fields, a stream of running water

C：A vegetable field, a flowing stream

D：a vegetable patch, a flowing brook—

这边青翠未改

A：While the green remained on this side,

B：It's still jade green on this side

C：the crispy green stays unchanged here

D：here the bright green hasn't changed

望气的人已走上了另一座山巅

A：The skywatcher was already on another high

B：The seer is already at the top of another peak

C: The cloud diviner has left for the next summit
D: The aura-seer has already left for another summit

个案研究五：柏桦诗歌英译译者风格评析

杨安文

以上四个有关柏桦诗歌英译的个案研究从中英文本形式、诗歌意旨的把握、时间维度的转换、隐身的人物角色的显现、词汇层面的"对等"使用、句法结构的转换以及诗歌音韵节律的呈现等方面，对《在清朝》《夏天还很远》《望气的人》《献给曼杰斯塔姆》等诗的多个译本进行了文本比较分析。尽管每一首诗涉及的几位译者并不完全相同，但通过一首诗多个译本的平行比较，以及译者在多首诗中呈现出的共同的翻译特点，我们可以十分清楚地看到几位译者的译本特点和翻译风格。

就保留原诗的外在形式、节奏韵律以及对原诗文本的准确理解而言，中国译者李赋康明显占据上风，这得益于他的母语优势，同时也因其对文学及诗歌的热爱，他对原诗文本的理解准确而深入，对原诗音乐性的感知十分到位。这些优势使得他的译本能够准确地传递原诗的文本意义，特别是能够较好地还原原诗的"形美"，呈现原诗的韵律与音乐美感。毫无疑问，在这一点上李赋康是几位译者中做得最好的。然而，也正是因为他极力模拟原诗的韵律与乐感，译文意义的准确性受到了一定影响，有时甚至牺牲了译文语言的基本规范（当然从某种角度讲，在诗歌语言中打破常规似乎是诗人惯常的做法）。此外，李赋康早期译诗的英语语言表达的准确性尤其是用词的精确度不够，语法规范意识不够强，在句法结构上，译诗中语法意义上完整的句子用得少，许多诗行都采用了名词加分词构成的独立主格结构，且无规律，显得有些凌乱、不够严谨。这可能是因为译者追求还原原诗精练、简洁的语言风格，从而牺牲了句法规范。自2018年以来，李赋康开始再译柏桦诗歌,译诗在语言层面、原诗结构的有效转换以及原诗"声音"(尤其是节奏)的再现等方面,都有质的飞跃。李赋康认为,译诗应当文体先行,文体是魂,对原文本的文体把握错了,方向就错了,就不能处理好语调(tone)、结构(structure)、文本肌理(texture)、词语颗粒度(granularity)四个要素。他总结柏桦诗歌的翻译应当先"声",后"象",再"意",所以必须强化节奏;译诗时,译者不可面面俱到,应该首取原文本独特优异之秉性,或声音,或意象,或意义,然后在译文中突出呈现;好的诗歌翻译不是词的对应,而是诗意有效转换,要突破原文,有所创造。可见,李赋康延续了早期注重传递原诗节奏、韵律和意境的翻译风格,同时进一步强调译诗的有效性,即译诗语言在英语语境中是否具有诗意,在英语读者读来是否是诗。

  译者菲奥娜的译本显得中规中矩。在外在形式上,其译本与原诗几乎完全对应,在语言风格上总体接近原诗。通过4首诗多个译本的比较,可以发现菲奥娜的译本用词数几乎都是最少的,其译本语言精练,且修饰语(形容词和副词)使用比例低,客观性强,较好地再现了原诗的"冷抒情"风格。在内容上,她注重忠实于原文,较好地实现了文本字面的对应转换。然而,她在翻译的创造性上却显得不足,对原诗意境、节奏、诗人独特的气息韵味等方面的有效转换还不够,使译诗显得较为平淡。不突破原诗结构和字面的对应也许是菲奥娜作为译者的翻译准则。当然,正如其在《风在说》序言里谈到的,作为译者她能有多大的自由度,这本身就是一道难题。但无论如何,以译语有效传递原诗之诗意当是最为重要的。尽管如此,我们从以上的译本对比可以看到,菲奥娜是具有还原原诗节奏和韵律的意识的,在这一点上,她是几位外国译者中做得最好的。她在接受新加坡诗人德斯蒙德·官志诚明德访谈时,将自己作为译者的使命形容为"在另一种文化实体里置放和聆听柏桦的声音——通过拍打、驯服的方式,让它用英语歌唱"。对比《夏天还很远》这首诗的4个译本,无论从时态和时间维度的把握来看,还是从词汇使用和韵律呈现层面,菲奥娜译本都显示了优于其他3个译本的翻译策略,在外在形式、语言风格尤其是节奏韵律上较好地呈现出了原诗之特点与魅力。也许,正是因为菲奥娜追求与原诗相近的简洁的语言风格,其部分翻译呈现出简化原文的特点,有时影响了诗中意象的传递,有时又丢失了部

分诗意。正如艾米·罗素(Amy Russell)在《风在说》书评中所说的:

> 但有人一定会问,对于非中文读者而言翻译丢失了多少。诗的精华不可避免地会损失一部分。这可能意味着,在保留原诗形式的尝试中,翻译的简化会导致深度的丢失。有人可能会问:《风在说》译文的简化是在试图模仿原诗风格,还是遗漏的结果?①

译者霍布恩的译本显得最有特色,最有诗意,最能打动人。尤其是《献给曼杰斯塔姆》一诗的翻译,译本很好地传递了原诗的情感、节奏和意境,且多有创造性,部分诗句的译文在读感上甚至超过了原句,十分具有冲击力。对此后文会专门讨论。就《在清朝》一诗的翻译而言,霍布恩译文的准确性、语言的流畅度都是4个译本中最好的。同时,该译本亦尽力再现原诗中的中国传统文化要素,如两处成语的翻译都采取了直译加注的方式,为英语读者很好地呈现了成语背后丰富的文化内涵(尽管加注方式仍值得讨论)。但也正是由于霍布恩对于译诗内容准确性的追求,译诗用词最多,在形式上没能再现原诗语言简洁的风格。这实属苛求,内容与形式历来难以兼得。在还原原诗音乐性方面,霍布恩自然也是舍弃了相应的追求(仅就这两首诗而言)。译者李赋康十分推崇霍布恩的翻译,认为其创造性的翻译实现了原诗诗意的有效转换。"译诗译诗,但译出来先得是诗",李赋康如是说。看来,若李赋康同霍布恩能合作翻译诗歌,吸收利用对方所长,弥补自身不足,当能创造出更多诗歌翻译精品。

从以上译本对比情况来看,译者西敏和陶忘机的翻译风格与霍布恩大致相似。4首诗中,西敏只翻译了《望气的人》一首诗,他采取了更胜于霍布恩的充分翻译方式,用词最多,在内容的有效转换以及语言的准确性方面是5个译本中最好的,当然在诗歌形式上也是偏离原诗最远的。他在翻译创造性方面不及霍布恩。其次是译者陶忘机,其译文在内容的完整性和语言

---

① Russell A. Book Review: *Wind Says*, by Bai Hua. *South China Morning Post*, 2013—2—17. http://www.scmp.com/lifestyle/books/article/1150896/book-review-wind-says-bai-hua.

的准确方面要略逊于西敏。少数地方对原诗文本的理解存在问题,比如在《夏天还很远》的译文中,其对诗中隐身人物的角色把握不到位,导致添加出来的人物主角显得有些混乱。但在文本语言风格和外在形式方面,陶忘机译本比霍布恩和西敏更接近原诗,比如《望气的人》一诗,陶忘机译本的词数明显比西敏少,部分呈现出原诗语言精练、节奏明快的特点。从顾爱玲所译的《在清朝》和《望气的人》来看,其风格与菲奥娜有些接近,译本在语言风格上偏于简洁,用词数偏少,在形式上较为接近原诗。但其翻译选词的准确性有所欠缺,部分地方也显示出对原诗的理解存在一定问题。译文从语言到内容显得较为平淡,亮点不足。

综上所述可见,由于不同的译者有各自的翻译风格,对原诗文本有着不同的理解和阐释,所以不同的译本也呈现出不同的风格和特点,也各有优点和不足。原诗在诗歌美学层面所具有的丰富的艺术内涵,所蕴含的诗人独特而丰满的思想情感,能否得以在译文中有效传递,则取决于译者能否"戴着音韵和节奏的镣铐在绳索上跳舞",既能跳得灵活自如又能富于艺术美感。这绝非易事,却并非不可追求。正所谓"诗无达诂",诗歌文本语言精练、简洁,高度浓缩,思想内容也时常艰深隐晦,本身就具有理解和阐释的开放性,这也正是诗歌及诗歌翻译的魅力所在。如德国哲学解释学大家伽达默尔所言,"一切翻译就已经是解释","所有翻译者都是解释者",[①]翻译过程本身首先是译者作为读者对原文本的阐释过程。也正是翻译以及不同译者的不同翻译,给诗歌文本阐释带来了广阔的拓展空间,延续了原文本在目标语世界多姿多彩的生命。需要特别说明的是,笔者对上述各译本和译者的评论仅是基于笔者个人对原诗文本的理解和阐释,具有一定主观性。然而,在另一方面,我们也不能否认文本确定性的存在。美国解释学理论代表人物赫施区分了文本的"含义"和"意义"两个概念,指出"含义"是固有的文本符号所规定的,是确定的并可以复现的。[②] 诗歌文本的翻译同样如此,尽管具有意义的开放性,但原诗语言符号所固化的"含义",译者应当竭力通过

---

① 伽达默尔:《真理与方法》(下卷),洪汉鼎译,上海:上海译文出版社,1999 年,第 490、494 页。

② 参见王岳川:《现象学与解释学文论》,济南:山东教育出版社,1999 年,第 16—17 页。

有效的语言转换使之得以再现。

　　笔者认为，诗歌翻译既然是翻译而非创作，首要考量当是对原诗内容的准确再现，译诗用词的准确选择、结构的有效转换。一首好的译诗，首先应该在内容上忠于原诗，语言转换的准确性至关重要。但诗之所以为诗，是其语言和形式具有"诗的特质"，如果翻译之后丢失了原文"诗之美感"，在目标语读者看来完全没有"诗意"，仅是两种语言所谓的"对等"转换，也称不上好的译诗，甚至根本称不上是"诗"。而原诗"美感"和"诗意"的成功转换和再现，除需要译者具有深厚的源语和目标语功底和语言转换能力以外，更需要译者对中英文诗歌敏锐的理解力、感知力以及诗意转换的创造力，需要译者对中国古今历史、文化和诗歌传统的深入学习和了解。

个案研究六：柏桦诗歌中外译者
合作翻译案例述评

杨安文

在当前中国诗歌外译活动中，中外译者合作翻译被普遍认为是一种可取的翻译模式。无论古诗还是现代诗翻译，都有许多中外译者联手翻译出优质译本的成功案例，如英国汉学家理雅各(James Legge)与王韬合作翻译《诗经》，美国诗人宾纳(Witter Bynner)与江亢虎合作翻译《玉山》，美国诗人王红公(Kenneth Rexroth)与钟玲合作翻译《兰舟：中国女诗人》等。旅美诗人译者明迪可谓是推动中外诗人译者合作翻译的典范，她主编的英文诗集《新华夏集：当代中国诗选》中有相当多诗歌都是她与美国诗人译者合作完成。她同时还力推中外诗人互译项目，推动中国当代诗人与国外诗人加强交流与翻译合作。诗人海岸也特别推崇中西译者合作翻译，他主编的两本汉英双语诗集《中国当代诗歌前浪》《归巢与启程：中澳当代诗选（中国卷，汉英对照）》中的许多诗歌都是他与英美诗人合作翻译而成。柏桦诗歌翻译中，涉及中外译者合作翻译的正是收入明迪和海岸主编的2部诗集中的译诗。合作翻译通常是中国译者初译，再由外国诗人译者（其母语是翻译目的语）予以润色、修改、完善。

然而，并非所有译者都赞同合作翻译的模式。前文已有统计，柏桦诗歌的28位译者中，有21位都是独立完成翻译。其中，译者菲奥娜对合作翻译持极为否定的态度。如此多的译者不愿意选择合作翻译模式，说明理想的合作并不容易，涉及中外译者之间是否能真诚有效地交流，是否能够彼此信任、包容和理解。文化背景的差异常常导致中外译者理解和表达的差异，双方需要细致、耐心地沟通才能合力推出精品译作。

以下以译者李赋康与澳大利亚诗人阿米莉娅·戴尔合作翻译的两首诗

为例,通过对两位译者前后译文的对比分析,探讨中外译者合作翻译模式下译本质量提升的实际效果。

一、《望气的人》译文对比

2018年,李赋康应诗人、诗歌翻译家海岸的邀稿翻译两首柏桦诗歌,他选择了《望气的人》(1986)和《一切黑》(2018)两首诗,意在体现不同时期柏桦诗歌风格的变化。李赋康初译之后,澳大利亚诗人阿米莉娅·戴尔再润色修改,最终形成译文终稿,发表于包慧怡和海岸主编的诗集《归巢与启程:中澳当代诗选(中国卷,汉英对照)》(2018)。该诗集由复旦大学和澳大利亚科廷大学共同创立的中澳创意写作中心(China-Australia Writing Centre)推出,其澳洲卷也即将出版。事实上,李赋康早在1989年就对《望气的人》进行了首译,该译诗于1991年经英国汉学家闵福德修改后发表于澳大利亚文学杂志《我所写》。前文比较分析的《望气的人》四个译本之一就是1991年译本。此次复译,李赋康对该译本做了较大幅度修改,译文全文如下:

The Air Alchemist

The air alchemist's in a hurry walking
Up the high, looking afar
Out of the evening mist in his eyes
Growing gold, geometry and palaces

A sudden west wind took the ghetto
A hero's starting for thousand miles beyond
The air alchemist saw
His agitated straw sandals and cloth shirt

Farther, the valley in harmony
Shattered tolls vaguely heard

Two boys were sweeping the terrace
The air alchemist sat in the solitary evening

Auspicious clouds, vast
A dry-boned master, silent
Alone he was blowing fire to the alchemy furnace
The air alchemist saw the patterns inside the stone

The countryside life went on, fair and fine
A field of vegetables, a brook of water
While it's still green on this side
The air alchemist was on another mountain top①

对比前一译本可见,李赋康首先将诗题"望气的人"由上一版的"The Sky-watcher"改为"The Air Alchemist"。"alchemist"指"炼金(丹)术士",而"望气的人"指通过观云气预卜人事吉凶的占卜之士,显然还是有偏差。笔者认为"diviner"一词更准确,且用"air"一词也不能表达"云气"之意,故认为译作"Cloud Diviner"更为贴切。其次,李赋康对上一版中的部分用词欠准确的地方进行了修改,如将"balcony"改为"terrace",将"design"改为"patterns",还对漏译的地方进行了补充,如上一版将"坐对空寂的傍晚"译为"sat against the evening sky"("空寂"未译出),新版改为"sat in the solitary evening"。此外,李赋康还在句式结构上作了改进,如第四节的前两句,将原译文"The clouds were vast and auspicious. / A dry-boned, silent master"改为"Auspicious clouds, vast / A dry-boned master, silent",在形式、节奏、韵律上都有明显提升。总体来看,李赋康修改后的译文在语言上更为精练,用词更为准确,节奏感更强。再来看阿米莉娅在李赋康译文基础上的修改版:

---

① 该译文引自李赋康提供给笔者的阿米莉娅修改后的对照稿。该译本经李赋康作个别修改后发表在其新浪微博上,网页地址为 http://blog.sina.com.cn/s/blog_6afcfcfa0102xqgk.html,读取时间:2020 年 1 月 15 日。

The Air Alchemist

The air alchemist's in a hurry walking
High, looks far out
Of evening mist his eyes
Grow gold geometry and palaces

West wind abruptly took
Thousands of miles beyond a hero
The air alchemist saw
His straw sandals and shirt agitate

Further: valley in harmony
Shattered tolls vaguely heard
Two boys sweep the terrace
The air alchemist sat in lonely lateness

Auspicious clouds, vast
Dry-boned master, silent
Solitary work on alchemical fire
The air alchemist saw patterns inside stone

Country life goes on just fine
A field of vegetables, a stream of water
While this side is still green
The air alchemist is atop another mountain[①]

---

① 选自《归巢与启程：中澳当代诗选（中国卷，汉英对照）》，西宁：青海人民出版社，2018 年，第 205—206 页。

对照两版译文可见,阿米莉娅对李赋康的译本作了细致的、大幅度的修改。首先,从外在形式来看,原译文有132个单词,修改后译文仅有109个单词,后者明显更为简洁。阿米莉娅删去了原译文中的10处冠词,8处为定冠词"the",2处为不定冠词"a"。译者用零冠词替代定冠词,将原译文中过度的名词"特指"改为一般意义上的"泛指",如"evening mist""valley""patterns""country life",使译文呈现的意境更为开阔,也更为精练。然而,删去不定冠词的两处却值得商榷。"wind"一词指风的种类或方向等时,需要与不定冠词连用或使用复数形式①,故"west wind"前删掉"a"欠妥。另一处是删去"dry-boned master"前的"a",只能理解为将其看作专有名词,这与原诗中"一个干枯的导师"之意不相吻合。其次,阿米莉娅还力求以词的简化和结构的转换来淬炼译文。例如,她将原译文第五诗节第一行"The countryside life went on, fair and fine"修改为"Country life goes on just fine";原文第四节第三行为"独自在吐火、炼丹",李赋康按原诗句结构将其译为一个完整句子"Alone he was blowing fire to the alchemy furnace",阿米莉娅则将其转换为名词短语结构"Solitary work on alchemical fire",在避免将"吐火"硬译为"blowing fire"的同时,亦使译文语言更为简洁、地道。再次,阿米莉娅在译文中倾向于运用拟人化的手法。例如,原诗第二节第三、四句为"望气的人看到了/他激动的草鞋和布衫",李赋康完全按原文的结构译为"The air alchemist saw / His agitated straw sandals and cloth shirt",阿米莉娅则将其修改为"The air alchemist saw / His straw sandals and shirt agitate"。可见,她在翻译技巧上采用了卡特福德翻译转换理论所指的"结构转换"(structure shift)和"词类转换"(class shift),将原句中修饰"草鞋和布衫"的形容词"激动的"(agitated)转换为动词"激动"(agitate)充当宾语补足语。这样一来,就将"望气的人"看到的重心由原句的"草鞋和布衫"转换为"草鞋和布衫在激动",结构的转换带来了拟人化的效果,使诗句呈现的意境更具动感,画面感更强。

但另一方面,阿米莉娅对译文的修改也有不少问题,首先是时态使用的

---

① 霍恩比:《牛津高阶英汉双解词典(第9版)》,北京:商务印书馆,2018年,第2467页。

混乱。笔者在前文已有论述,该诗采用"戏剧性现在时"(Dramatic present)当是最佳选择。李赋康将译文的时态统一为过去时态,虽非最佳,但也无过。阿米莉娅在译文中则是现在时态和过去时态混用,第一诗节为现在时,第二诗节为过去时,第三诗节两者皆有,第四诗节为过去时,第五诗节为现在时,着实令人费解。仔细分析,译者似乎对原诗有这样的理解:首尾两个诗节是对现时情景的描写,中间三节是对过去情景的回溯。笔者注意到,原诗中出现了助词"了"的地方,如"看到了""看穿了",译者都使用了过去时,原诗中出现了助词"着"的地方,如"打扫着",译者使用了现在时态,这便出现了第三诗节里同时用了现在时态和过去时态的情况。这似乎反映出阿米莉娅对中文助词功能的机械理解,可以猜测,在进行时态选择时,正是这种机械理解才导致了时态使用的混乱。其次,部分诗句的翻译处理也反映出阿米莉娅对译文精练、简洁的追求损害了原诗意旨的准确传译。例如,原诗第二诗节第一行为"穷巷西风突变",修改后的译文为"West wind abruptly took","穷巷"不见了,英雄出身贫寒的意思丢了。此外,笔者认为,"abruptly took"也无法表达"突然刮起"大风之意。① 另一处例子是第三诗节第四句"望气的人坐对空寂的傍晚",阿米莉娅的译文是"The air alchemist sat in lonely lateness"。"lateness"一词无法表达出"傍晚"之意,而将"空寂"理解为寂寞,译为"lonely"则与原诗句空旷寂静的意境有所出入。

二、《一切黑》译文对比

再来对比另一首诗《一切黑》的译文修改情况。这首诗创作于2018年,代表了柏桦复笔后诗歌中比较典型的一种风格:追求诗歌的音乐性而忽略其逻辑意义。柏桦在2007年1月与诗人王敖通邮件时就曾谈道:"我就一贯坚持声音是绝对的,意义是附带的,或次要的,有时甚至可以忽略。"这其实也是其"逸乐"诗观的一种体现:追求声音的"玩味",词汇的"游戏",在"音

---

① 据《钱伯斯英语词典》第十三版,第1587页,"take"一词有"to have the intended effect; to work"(具有预期效果;起作用或有效)之意,译者将其用作"突出刮起"大风之意有不妥。

乐"中游戏诗歌。且看这首诗的中文原文：

一切黑

飞奔的黑空气里
我听到它的喘气
敛翅伪装的黑瓢虫
打完麻药，准备
做一个开颅手术。

藏而不露黑中黑
黑夜黑发黑衣裤
哪种人？所有人！
常常他们想要的
并非他们所需的。

卷上珠帘总不如
嘴唇黑，喉咙黑
口水浪波非眼波
闪电风暴在滚动！

2018年4月27日①

整首诗围绕着"黑"字展开，形式工整，节奏明快，音乐感强。虽如诗人所说，意义是附带的、次要的，但诗人通过"黑"的事物和感受的"随机"堆砌，营造出神秘的"黑色"氛围和意境，其开放的意义空间似在召唤读者以自己的方式去打开。显然，翻译这样的诗极具挑战。译者翻译的重点应该是尽

---

① 选自《归巢与启程：中澳当代诗选（中国卷，汉英对照）》，西宁：青海人民出版社，2018年，第207页。

力还原原诗的音乐性,对译文形式的追求应该超过意义的追求。接下来我们先看译者李赋康的英语译文:

All Darkness

In the dark air galloping
I hear it's gasping
A dark ladybird, wing folded
Just etherized, and ready for
A craniotomy

Darkest of all is the hooded
Dark night, dark hair and dark pants
Which kind of people? All people!
They often ask for
What they do not want.

The pearl curtain is rolled up, unveiling
Dark lips and dark throat, alluring with
The wave of mouth water but not that of eyes
Rolling lightning, rolling storm!①

李赋康的译文总体贴近原文的字面意思。可以看出,对于部分晦涩难懂的诗句,他作出了与原文同样简洁且比较有效的转换,如将"藏而不露黑中黑"译为"Darkest of all is the hooded",彰显出翻译的灵活性和创造性,将"闪电风暴在滚动!"译为"Rolling lightning, rolling storm!",既译出了字面意思,也译出了节奏和气势。在传递原诗的节奏和韵律上,译文也显示

---

① 该译文引自李赋康提供给笔者的阿米莉娅修改后的对照稿。该译本经李赋康作个别修改后发表在其新浪微博上,网页地址为 http://blog.sina.com.cn/s/blog_6afcfcfa0102xpy8.html,读取时间:2020年1月15日。

出他作出的努力,如第一诗节第一、二行的"galloping""gasping",第三行的"A dark ladybird, wing folded"。但与原诗相比,译诗形式感和节奏感仍显逊色,对诗人玩味"音乐"的特点彰显不够。再来看阿米莉娅·戴尔的修改译文:

Dark Matter

Galloping black air flying
Gasping air hear
A dark ladybird, wing-folded
Etherized, prepared
For its craniotomy

Hide hoods darkly visible:
Black night on black hair on brief's black
What of them? All of them!
What they do are not is want
They ask for or wish for often

Pare pearl curtain unroll, unveil
Dark lips larynx dark throat through
Alluring waves of saliva desire but eyes
Rolling storm flash rolling break!①

可以发现,阿米莉娅·戴尔对李赋康的译文同样作了大幅度修改。首先,从外部形式上来看,修改后的译文更简洁(原译文79词,修改后译文73词),阿米莉娅删除了原译文中出现的所有定冠词"the"(4处)和连接词

---

① 选自《归巢与启程:中澳当代诗选(中国卷,汉英对照)》,西宁:青海人民出版社,2018年,第207页。

"and"（3 处），以模仿原文的紧凑感。其次，阿米莉娅应该是体会到了原诗重形式轻意义的特点，着力在译文中还原原诗的形式、节奏、韵律美感。比如，她将原译文第一诗节第 4 行中的"and ready for"改为"prepared"，使该诗行"Etherized, prepared"形式上既简洁对整，又押上半韵（谐辅韵）；将第二节第三行"Which kind of people? All people!"改为"What of them? All of them!"，更好地还原了原文的形式美和短促的节奏感（原文为"哪种人？所有人！"）。这两处修改既增进了形式美，又准确传递了原文字面意思。但我们也注意到，阿米莉娅在更多地方牺牲了原文的字面意义，以实现其对"音乐性"的追求。比如在第一诗节中，为了与第一句译文"Galloping black air…"在音韵上对应，阿米莉娅将原文第二句的主语"我"去掉，改为"Gasping air hear"；在第三诗节的第一句中，为强化声音和视觉效果，增加了动词"pare"，形成了"pare""Pearl"和"unroll""unveil"两组对应词；同样地，在第二句中增加了名词"larynx"，形成了"lips""larynx"和"throat""through"两组对应词。译文虽很好地模仿了原文的对称形式和节奏，但在意思上却无法与原文对应，且令人费解。但有一处修改可谓两全其美：原诗第二诗节第二句为三个名词并置结构"黑夜黑发黑衣裤"，原译文是标准的对照翻译"Dark night, dark hair and dark pants"，阿米莉娅则通过加上两个副词"on"将并置关系改为修饰关系，使译诗的意象更丰满奇幻："戴着黑发、穿着黑裤的黑夜"。同时，她将原译文的"pants"改为"briefs"，与"black"协辅韵，并构成三个相似音对"black night""black hair""briefs black"，使该句节奏感、音乐感极大提升。可见，就该诗而言，阿米莉娅对原译文的修改润色效果非常明显，很好地提升了原译文的形式感和音乐感，一定程度还原了原诗玩味声音的特点，但译文基于逻辑意义的可读性却受到影响，可能使读者对部分诗句有不知所云的感觉。

综上所述，阿米莉娅对李赋康译文的修改可谓有功有过。在语言风格、特点方面，她的修改译文更为精练、简洁，符合原诗的风格特点；在音韵节律方面，第二首诗的修改译文很好地还原了原诗的形式感和音乐感，凸显了原诗的音乐性。此外，作为以译入语为母语的译者，阿米莉娅的用词更为准确,语言表述更为地道。然而,也许正是阿米莉娅对译文精练紧凑和音乐感的追求,导致部分译文的意义甚至意境与原诗有所背离,可谓"因韵害义",重视形式,丢了内容。阿米莉娅的修改译文在某些地方意思含混不清,也可能是因为其对原诗的理解本来就有一定障碍。即使是中文母语译者,对现代诗的理解都会遇到诸多困难,这一点可以理解。但在中外译者合作翻译的模式下,这种问题应该可以避免。据笔者了解,两位译者并未有过沟通和讨论,李赋康尽管并不赞同阿米莉娅许多地方的修改,但鉴于她是以英语为母语的诗人译者,又是诗集出版方指定的外方合作者,便无条件接受了她的修改意见。这恰恰说明,缺乏有效沟通的合作翻译,其效果也会大打折扣。英国汉学家霍布恩曾说:"要想提高汉英文学翻译的质量,唯有依靠英汉本族语译者之间的小范围合作。汉语不是我的母语,我永远无法彻底理解汉语文本的微妙与深奥;反之,非英语本族语的译者,要想将此类内涵丰富的文本翻译成富有文学价值的英语,且达到惟妙惟肖的程度,绝非一件容易的事。可一旦同心协力,何患而不成?"①所以,中外译者需要发挥各自优势,相互配合,乐于沟通,只有真诚地合作,才能共同翻译出上乘的诗歌译文。

---

① 霍布恩:《驶向天堂的码头——杨炼长诗〈同心圆〉译后记》,载《中西诗歌翻译百年论集》,上海:上海外语教学出版社,2007年,第633页。

后　记

　　诗歌翻译历来是文学翻译的重中之重，而中国当代诗歌的外译无论在理论研究层面还是在翻译实践层面，一直都是一大难题和痛点。中国当代诗歌巨大的诗学价值，文化、社会和历史价值都不容置疑，而海外对其了解还远远不够，在中国文化走出去的大背景下，中国当代诗歌的翻译研究与实践十分必要和迫切。

　　柏桦是中国当代优秀诗人，被普遍认为是"后朦胧"诗人的杰出代表，是自20世纪80年代以来国内最早被译介到海外并得到较多关注的当代诗人之一。柏桦迄今已创作诗歌近万首，已发表或出版诗歌约1500首。早期创作的百余首诗歌绝大部分都被译介到海外，且不少诗歌有不同语种的多个译本，可以说已经在一定程度上经典化。截至目前，柏桦诗歌被28位中外译者翻译成英语、法语、德语、西班牙语、俄语、荷兰语、韩语、日语8种外文，译介至美国、英国、法国、德国等15个国家以及中国香港、澳门和台湾；在总共320首外译诗歌中，英译诗歌占236首。

　　本书基于笔者长期搜集整理的柏桦诗歌英译的第一手文献资料，结合笔者有关中国当代诗歌在海外的译介研究成果编著而成。本书以柏桦不同时期的经典诗歌为语料，精选国内外14位知名译者的109个翻译文本，以汉英对照方式呈现，并对每一位译者的背景情况、翻译成就、翻译策略、翻译风格等进行概要介绍。在本书第二部分，笔者列入了6篇柏桦诗歌英译研究论文，从诗歌翻译实践层面，探析不同中外译者诗歌翻译的策略与风格、优势与不足；同时以部分多译本柏桦诗歌英译文本为研究对象，开展诗歌翻译对比研究,通过对诗作原文与译文的对比,以及中国译者与西方译者不同译本的对比,从诗歌英译的"形""音""义""情"四个方面进行文本细读与分析,探索国内外诗歌译者在文本解读和翻译策略选择上的差异,阐释诗歌翻译变异的情况及原因,并对诗歌译介模式、翻译策略和方法提出建议。可以说,本书内容具有前沿性、系统性、时新性,诗歌文本及翻译文本具有代表性和经典性,对中国当代诗歌的翻译实践和译介研究均有一定的学习和参考价值。

另外,本书第三章收录了翻译家西敏的 8 首译诗,但因客观条件限制,笔者至今未能与译者及出版方取得联系。若两方得知后慨允,笔者将不胜感激。

本书承蒙西南交通大学研究生院"十四五"规划教材建设项目立项资助,谨此致谢。

杨安文

2025 年 2 月

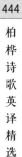

图书在版编目(CIP)数据

柏桦诗歌英译精选/杨安文编著.—上海:华东师范大学
出版社,2025.—ISBN 978-7-5760-5840-6

Ⅰ.I227

中国国家版本馆CIP数据核字第2025FF1192号

华东师范大学出版社六点分社

本书著作权、版式和装帧设计受世界版权公约和中华人民共和国著作权法保护

柏桦诗歌英译精选

著　　者　杨安文
责任编辑　卢　荻
责任校对　古　冈
封面设计　卢晓红

出版发行　华东师范大学出版社
社　　址　上海市中山北路3663号　邮编　200062
网　　址　www.ecnupress.com.cn
电　　话　021-60821666　行政传真　021-62572105
客服电话　021-62865537
门市(邮购)电话　021-62869887
地　　址　上海市中山北路3663号华东师范大学校内先锋路口
网　　店　http://hdsdcbs.tmall.com/

印 刷 者　上海景条印刷有限公司
开　　本　787×1092　1/16
印　　张　28.75
字　　数　230千字
版　　次　2025年5月第1版
印　　次　2025年5月第1次
书　　号　ISBN 978-7-5760-5840-6
定　　价　78.00元

出 版 人　王　焰

(如发现本版图书有印订质量问题,请寄回本社客服中心调换或电话021-62865537联系)